VISION IN SILVER

BOOKS BY ANNE BISHOP

THE OTHERS SERIES

Written in Red

Murder of Crows

Vision in Silver

THE BLACK JEWELS SERIES

Daughter of the Blood

Heir to the Shadows

Queen of the Darkness

The Invisible Ring

Dreams Made Flesh

Tangled Webs

The Shadow Queen

Shalador's Lady

Twilight's Dawn

THE EPHEMERA SERIES

Sebastian

Belladonna

Bridge of Dreams

THE TIR ALAINN TRILOGY

The Pillars of the World

Shadows and Light

The House of Gaian

VISION IN SILVER

A NOVEL OF THE OTHERS

ANNE BISHOP

A ROC BOOK

ROC
Published by the Penguin Group
Penguin Group (USA) LLC, 375 Hudson Street,
New York, New York 10014

USA | Canada | UK | Ireland | Australia | New Zealand | India | South Africa | China
penguin.com
A Penguin Random House Company

First published by Roc, an imprint of New American Library,
a division of Penguin Group (USA) LLC

First Printing, March 2015

 REGISTERED TRADEMARK—MARCA REGISTRADA

LIBRARY OF CONGRESS CATALOGING-IN-PUBLICATION DATA:
Bishop, Anne.
Vision in silver / Anne Bishop.
pages cm.— (A novel of the others; 3)
ISBN 978-0-451-46527-6 (hardcover)
1. Women prophets—Fiction. 2. Shapeshifting—Fiction. I. Title.
PS3552.I7594V57 2015
813'.54—dc23   2014034235

Printed in the United States of America
1   3   5   7   9   10   8   6   4   2

Set in Albertina MT   •   Designed by Elke Sigal

*For
Jennifer Crow*

ACKNOWLEDGMENTS

My thanks to Blair Boone for continuing to be my first reader and for all the information about animals and other things that I absorbed and transformed to suit the Others' world; to Debra Dixon for being second reader and providing insights about police procedures; to Doranna Durgin for maintaining the Web site; to Adrienne Roehrich for running the official fan page on Facebook; to Nadine Fallacaro for information about things medical; to Anne Sowards and Jennifer Jackson for the feedback that helps me write a better story; to Jennifer Crow for the monthly gatherings and the gleeful exchange of information about many, many subjects; and to Pat Feidner for always being supportive and encouraging.

A special thanks to the following people who loaned their names to characters, knowing that the name would be the only connection between reality and fiction: Bobbie Barber, Elizabeth Bennefeld, Blair Boone, Douglas Burke, Starr Corcoran, Jennifer Crow, Lorna MacDonald Czarnota, Julie Czerneda, Roger Czerneda, Merri Lee Debany, Michael Debany, Mary Claire Eamer, Sarah Jane Elliott, Chris Fallacaro, Dan Fallacaro, Mike Fallacaro, Nadine Fallacaro, James Alan Gardner, Mantovani "Monty" Gay, Julie Green, Lois Gresh, Ann Hergott, Lara Herrera, Robert Herrera, Danielle Hilborn, Heather Houghton, Pamela Ireland, Lorne Kates, Allison King, Jana Paniccia, Jennifer Margaret Seely, Denby "Skip" Stowe, Ruth Stuart, and John Wulf.

GEOGRAPHY

NAMID—THE WORLD

CONTINENTS/LANDMASSES

Afrikah

Australis

Brittania/Wild Brittania

Cel-Romano/Cel-Romano Alliance of Nations

Felidae

Fingerbone Islands

Storm Islands

Thaisia

Tokhar-Chin

Zelande

Great Lakes—Superior, Tala, Honon, Etu, and Tahki

Other lakes—Feather Lakes/Finger Lakes

River—Talulah/Talulah Falls

Mountains—Addirondak, Rocky

Cities and villages—Ferryman's Landing, Hubb NE (aka Hubbney), Jerzy, Lakeside, Podunk, Shikago, Sparkletown, Sweetwater, Talulah Falls, Toland, Walnut Grove, Wheatfield

DAYS OF THE WEEK

Earthday

Moonsday

Sunsday

Windsday

Thaisday

Firesday

Watersday

© 2012 Anne Bishop

This map was created by a geographically challenged author who put in only the bits she needed for the story.

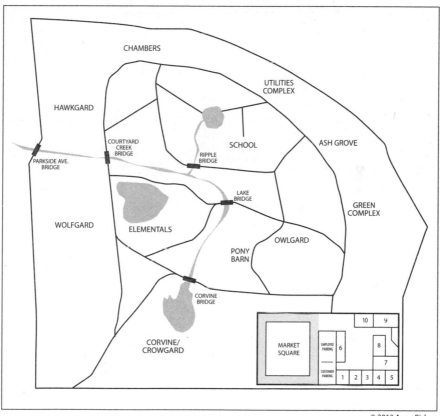

© 2012 Anne Bishop

1. Seamstress/Tailor & efficiency apartments
2. A Little Bite
3. Howling Good Reads
4. Run & Thump
5. Social Center
6. Garages
7. Earth Native & Henry's Studio
8. Liaison's Office
9. Consulate
10. Three Ps

VISION IN SILVER

A Brief History of the World

Long ago, Namid gave birth to all kinds of life, including the beings known as humans. She gave the humans fertile pieces of herself, and she gave them good water. Understanding their nature and the nature of her other offspring, she also gave them enough isolation that they would have a chance to survive and grow. And they did.

They learned to build fires and shelters. They learned to farm and build cities. They built boats and fished in the Mediterran and Black seas. They bred and spread throughout their pieces of the world until they pushed into the wild places. That's when they discovered that Namid's other offspring already claimed the rest of the world.

The Others looked at humans and did not see conquerors. They saw a new kind of meat.

Wars were fought to possess the wild places. Sometimes the humans won and spread their seed a little farther. More often, pieces of civilization disappeared, and fearful survivors tried not to shiver when a howl went up in the night or a man, wandering too far from the safety of stout doors and light, was found the next morning drained of blood.

Centuries passed, and the humans built larger ships and sailed across the Atlantik Ocean. When they found virgin land, they built a settlement near the shore. Then they discovered that this land was also claimed by the *terra indigene*, the earth natives. The Others.

The *terra indigene* who ruled the continent called Thaisia became angry when the humans cut down trees and put a plow to land that was not theirs. So the Others ate the settlers and learned the shape of this particular meat, just as they had done many times in the past.

The second wave of explorers and settlers found the abandoned settlement and, once more, tried to claim the land as their own.

The Others ate them too.

The third wave of settlers had a leader who was smarter than his predecessors. He offered the Others warm blankets and lengths of cloth for clothes and interesting bits of shiny in exchange for being allowed to live in the settlement and have enough land to grow crops. The Others thought this was a fair exchange and walked off the boundaries of the land that the humans could use. More gifts were exchanged for hunting and fishing privileges. This arrangement satisfied both sides, even if one side regarded its new neighbors with snarling tolerance and the other side swallowed fear and made sure its people were safely inside the settlement's walls before nightfall.

Years passed and more settlers arrived. Many died, but enough humans prospered. Settlements grew into villages, which grew into towns, which grew into cities. Little by little, humans moved across Thaisia, spreading out as much as they could on the land they were allowed to use.

Centuries passed. Humans were smart. So were the Others. Humans invented electricity and plumbing. The Others controlled all the rivers that could power the generators and all the lakes that supplied fresh drinking water. Humans invented steam engines and central heating. The Others controlled all the fuel needed to run the engines and heat the buildings. Humans invented and manufactured products. The Others controlled all the natural resources, thereby deciding what would and wouldn't be made in their part of the world.

There were collisions, of course, and some places became dark memorials for the dead. Those memorials finally made it clear to human government that the *terra indigene* ruled Thaisia, and nothing short of the end of the world would change that.

So it comes to this current age. Small human villages exist within vast tracts of land that belong to the Others. And in larger human cities, there are fenced parks called Courtyards that are inhabited by the Others who have the task of keeping watch over the city's residents and enforcing the agreements the humans made with the *terra indigene*.

There is still sharp-toothed tolerance on one side and fear of what walks in the dark on the other. But if they are careful, the humans survive.

Most of the time, they survive.

CHAPTER 1

Thaisday, Maius 10

Meg Corbyn entered the bathroom in the Human Liaison's Office and laid out the items she'd labeled the tools of prophecy: antiseptic ointment, bandages, and the silver folding razor decorated with pretty leaves and flowers on one side of the handle. On the other side of the handle, engraved in plain lettering, was the designation *cs759*. For twenty-four years, that designation had been the closest thing she'd had to a name.

She had a name now and a real apartment instead of a sterile cell. In the compound where she had been raised and trained ... and used ... she'd had one friend: Jean, the girl who wouldn't allow anyone to forget that she'd once had a home and a family outside the compound—the girl who had helped Meg escape.

Now Meg had many friends, and it didn't matter to her that most of them weren't human. The *terra indigene* had given her a chance to have a life, were helping her find ways to live with the addiction that would eventually kill her. But Simon Wolfgard, leader of the Lakeside Courtyard, insisted he'd seen someone like her who had survived long enough to become an old woman.

She wanted to believe that was possible. She hoped this morning's experiment might provide a clue to how it was possible.

After checking to make sure she hadn't forgotten anything they would need, Meg sat on the closed toilet seat and waited for Merri Lee, the human friend who was learning to work as her listener and interpreter.

The *cassandra sangue* saw prophecies when their skin was cut. They were trained to describe the visions and images. But the girls weren't taught how to interpret what they saw. That would have been pointless. The moment a girl began to speak, a euphoria filled her, veiling her mind and protecting her from what those images revealed. In fact, the only way a blood prophet *could* remember what she saw was to keep silent. If she didn't say the words out loud, she remembered what she saw.

It took a particular kind of determination—or desperation—to endure the agony that filled a girl when she didn't speak after her skin was cut. And experiencing the euphoria that was almost orgasmic was the whole reason *cassandra sangue* became addicted to the cutting in the first place.

It took a particular kind of courage to acknowledge that she couldn't completely escape the addiction after so many years of being cut on a regular schedule for someone else's profit. The prophecies inside her would not be denied. Whether she wanted to or not, Meg *needed* to cut.

That was the reason today's appointment with the razor was so important. She wasn't experiencing the pins-and-needles feeling that indicated something was going to happen. Nothing pushed at her, and that made this morning the perfect time to discover what happened when she made a controlled cut.

The back door of the office opened. A moment later, Merri Lee stood in the bathroom doorway holding a small pad of paper and a pen.

They were both petite women around the same age, and both had fair skin. But Merri Lee had dark eyes and dark, layered hair that fell below her shoulders, while Meg had clear gray eyes and short black hair that was still mostly a weird orangey red from her efforts to disguise herself when she'd run away from the man known as the Controller.

"Are you sure about this?" Merri Lee asked. "Maybe we should wait until Simon and Henry get back from Great Island."

Meg shook her head. "We should do this now, before the office opens and there's additional . . . input . . . that might change what I see. Vlad is working at Howling Good Reads today. We can tell him about the prophecy—and he's close enough if we need help."

"All right." Merri Lee pulled over a chair from the little dining area, set it just outside the bathroom doorway, and sat down. "What should I ask you?"

Meg had thought about this. When clients had come to the Controller's compound, they had a specific question. She wasn't looking for anything that defined, but she needed *some* kind of boundary. "This is what you should ask: What should the residents of the Lakeside Courtyard watch for during the next fortnight?"

"That's pretty vague," Merri Lee said. "And . . . fortnight?"

"If I ask about a specific thing in the Courtyard, something else might be overlooked—and *that* might be the important thing the Others should know about," Meg replied. "Two weeks is enough time. As for 'fortnight,' I just learned that word and like the sound of it. I think it fits in with prophecies better than saying 'two weeks.'"

"But if this doesn't work, if we don't get anything useful, then you've made the cut for nothing," Merri Lee argued.

"Not for nothing," Meg said. The euphoria was reason enough to cut. That wasn't something she would say to her friend, so she offered a different truth. "If I can stretch out the time between cuts because one cut will supply the warnings we need for two weeks and quiet the pins-and-needles feeling that pushes me to cut, I'll have more years to live. And I do want to live—especially now that I have a real life."

A beat of silence. Then Merri Lee said, "Ready?"

"Yes." Opening the silver razor, Meg laid the blade flat against her skin, its one-quarter-inch width providing the perfect distance between cuts—the distance that kept prophecies separated without wasting valuable skin. She lined up the back of the blade with the last scar on her left forearm. Then she turned her hand and cut just deeply enough for blood to flow freely and, equally important, for the cut to leave a scar.

Agony filled her, the prelude to prophecy. Hearing someone crying—someone no one else could hear—Meg gritted her teeth, set the razor aside, and positioned her arm to rest in the bathroom sink. Then she gave Merri Lee a sharp nod.

"What should the residents of the Lakeside Courtyard watch for during the next fortnight?" Merri Lee said. "Speak, prophet, and I will listen."

She spoke, revealing everything she saw. The images faded with the sound of the words as waves of euphoria produced a delicious tingle in her breasts and a rhythmic tug between her legs, replacing the pain.

She didn't know how long she floated on the pleasure produced by the euphoria. Sometimes it seemed to fade within moments of identifying the last image, while at other times she drifted for a while in a haze of physical pleasure. When she became aware of her surroundings again, Meg realized enough time had passed that Merri Lee had bandaged the cut, cleaned the razor, and washed the sink.

The blood of the *cassandra sangue* was dangerous to humans and Others alike. It had been used to make gone over wolf and feel-good, two drugs that had caused so much trouble throughout Thaisia in the past few months. That was the reason why, when they made plans for this cut, she and Merri Lee agreed that all the blood would be washed away, and the bandages would be collected later and taken to the Courtyard's Utilities Complex for incineration.

"Did it work?" Meg asked. "Did I speak prophecy? Did I see anything useful?" Her voice sounded rough, and her throat hurt. She wanted to ask Merri Lee for a glass of water or maybe some juice, but she couldn't rouse herself enough to say anything more.

"Meg, do you trust me?"

That sounded like an ominous way to answer her own questions. "Yes, I trust you."

Merri Lee nodded, as if coming to a decision. "Yes, it worked. Better than we could have hoped. I need a little time to sort the images into some kind of order."

Not a lie, exactly, but not the truth either.

Meg studied her friend. "You don't want to tell me what I said, what I saw."

"No, I don't. I really don't."

"But—"

"*Meg.*" Merri Lee closed her eyes for a moment. "No one in the Courtyard is in immediate danger, but you said a couple of things that were . . . disturbing, things I'm not sure how to interpret. I want to do a preliminary shuffling of images, like we did the last time when we drew the images on index cards and kept arranging them until they told us a story. Then I'll go to Howling Good Reads and talk to Vlad."

"I didn't see anything bad happening to Sam? Or Simon? Or . . . anyone here?" In human form, Sam Wolfgard looked to be around eight or nine years old now, but he was still a puppy. And Simon was her friend. Just the thought of something happening to either of them made her chest hurt.

Merri Lee shook her head. "You didn't say anything that would indicate someone here was going to be in trouble." She touched Meg's hand. "We're both learning how to do this, and I want someone else's feedback before you and I talk about what you saw. Okay?"

No immediate danger. None of her friends at risk. "Okay."

"It's almost nine o'clock. You should eat something before you open the office."

Meg followed Merri Lee out of the bathroom, feeling a little light-headed. Yes, she needed to eat, needed a little quiet time. Needed to figure out what to say to whichever Wolf had guard duty today. Even if she tried to avoid him, the Wolf would smell the blood and ointment. She was pretty sure she could talk John into not sounding an alarm, and if it was Skippy's turn as watch Wolf, a couple of cookies would distract him. On the other hand, if Blair, the Courtyard's primary enforcer, showed up with Skippy, as he usually did . . .

Maybe Merri Lee was right about telling Vlad before someone started howling about the cut and brought *everyone* running to demand answers.

"Merri?" Meg said as Merri Lee opened the office's back door. "I didn't see anything else about the Others?"

Merri Lee shook her head. Then she frowned. "Well, you did see paws digging."

"Digging?" Now Meg frowned. "Why would that be important enough to see in a vision?"

"Don't know. Maybe Vlad or the Wolves will be able to figure it out." Merri Lee hesitated. "Will you be all right? You're not dizzy or anything?"

"No, I'm fine."

"Remember to eat."

"I will."

As soon as Merri Lee closed the back door, Meg looked in the under-the-counter fridge. In the compound, the Walking Names who looked after the girls never gave them a choice about what to eat after a cut. They were fed well, but they were never given a choice. About anything.

Unable to decide, Meg warmed a small piece of quiche and half a beef sandwich in the wave-cooker. She poured a glass of orange juice, then took her meal into the sorting room.

She could select one of the CDs she'd borrowed from Music and Movies and listen to music while she ate. Or she could look at one of the magazines she was using to provide herself with images for the prophecies.

But she didn't want new sounds or new images right now. She wanted to know what she had seen. She wanted to help figure out what the images meant.

And even though her friend had tried to be reassuring, Meg wanted to know what she'd seen that Merri Lee didn't want to talk about.

Vladimir Sanguinati, comanager of Howling Good Reads, settled behind the desk in the bookstore's office. Turning on the computer, he ignored the scant stack of paperwork and wrote a quick e-mail to Stavros Sanguinati, who lived in Toland, the big East Coast city where the largest book publishers were located.

Human book publishers, that is. Since the shakeup in the Midwest Region a couple of weeks ago, shipments of all kinds of material had slowed down, whether those materials came from the Midwest or not. So it *was* possible that the human publishers really were out of so many of the books he'd ordered for the store and were waiting for the next shipment of paper in order to print copies of backlist books and new titles. Or they could foolishly be out of stock only for orders sent in by the *terra indigene*.

Stavros would find out. Like Grandfather Erebus, he enjoyed old movies and often played at being a caricature of his own kind, the country vampire wearing blue jeans, a plaid shirt, and work boots who said things like, "Ve vant a six-pack of blood." But when he was on official business for the Toland Courtyard, Stavros followed the Sanguinati tradition of wearing black, and there was nothing countrified about him when he arrived in a limousine, dressed in a suit of the finest material.

Stavros was euphemistically called the Toland Courtyard's problem solver. Knowing how the other vampire solved problems, Vlad could almost pity any human who received an official visit. So Stavros would encourage businesses to put stores like Howling Good Reads first when they were filling back orders, and Vlad would be able to fill the requests coming in from the *terra indigene* settlements that received goods from the Lakeside Courtyard. The goods manufactured by humans were the only reason the *terra indigene* on the continent of Thaisia tolerated the continued existence of those invasive monkeys. If goods were no longer supplied, humans had value as only one thing: meat.

As Vlad sent the e-mail, he heard someone coming up the stairs. Hesitant footsteps but not furtive ones. Could be someone in the human pack wanting to use the computer in the Business Association's room, which took up the other half of HGR's second floor. They were supposed to ask permission before going into that room, and the newer employees were still getting used to working for, and dealing directly with, the Others. That could explain the hesitation.

When Merri Lee stopped in the doorway and he saw the look on her face, Vlad understood that the hesitation he'd heard was because she knew he wasn't going to like whatever she had come to tell him. He closed the e-mail program and waited to see what the exploding fluffball wanted.

When Howling Good Reads had been open to human customers, he'd heard human females refer to him as "eye candy," which meant his dark hair and eyes, his olive skin, and his handsome face easily attracted his prey. For him, feeding was often combined with foreplay.

But Merri Lee had never shown any sexual interest in him, which proved she was more sensible than other human females, and since she was dating a police officer, he didn't think she was about to throw herself at him now.

Which meant he *really* wasn't going to like her reason for coming up here to find him.

"Is there something I can do for you, Ms. Lee?" he finally asked when she continued to hover in the doorway.

She rushed in and sat in the visitor's chair.

She's shaking, he thought, suddenly wary. "What's wrong?"

"Nothing. Yet," Merri Lee replied. "You need to tell the watch Wolf not to get upset and stir everyone up."

It occurred to him that he didn't know who was supposed to be on duty today. Nathan Wolfgard, one of the Courtyard's best enforcers, was usually the Wolf on guard when Meg was working in the Human Liaison's Office. But Nathan was on leave for a couple more weeks, running with the Wolves in the Addirondak Mountains, free to shed his responsibilities along with the human skin. The Sanguinati were more at home in human cities since smoke, their other form, made them ideal predators in an urban environment. But shifters like the Wolves, Bears, and various feline gards found life in a Courtyard a constant strain.

Working in a Courtyard was a sacrifice some *terra indigene* made for the benefit of the rest of their kind. They kept watch over the two-legged predators who had come to Thaisia from other parts of the world. They made it possible for humans to exist on this continent. Vlad wondered if any humans realized that—or realized what happened to the places granted to humans when a "civilized" place like a Courtyard disappeared.

But those thoughts weren't important right now, not with this female staring at him from the other side of the desk.

"What will upset the Wolf?" he asked, having an uneasy feeling that he already knew the answer.

"Meg made a cut."

Vlad's hands closed into fists, but he stayed seated.

"We planned it for this morning," Merri Lee said hurriedly. "A kind of experiment."

Let her talk. "Something upset Meg?"

"No. See, that was the whole point. Making a controlled cut when nothing was pushing her."

A thousand cuts. Supposedly that's all a *cassandra sangue* could make before the cut that would kill her or drive her insane. And it wasn't just the cuts made with a razor. Any injury that broke skin counted as part of that number. Most of those girls wouldn't see their thirty-fifth birthday, and here was Meg cutting without a reason.

Addiction was its own reason. That would explain why Meg had chosen a time when Simon Wolfgard and Henry Beargard were away from the Courtyard. But that didn't explain Merri Lee coming to see him.

He needed to sound calm, reasonable. Merri Lee was a member of Meg's human pack, and the two girls had shown an ability to work together to interpret prophecy. "Was the experiment successful?"

Merri Lee nodded. "It was different from the last time I assisted. After the initial . . . discomfort . . . Meg began speaking. Lots of images. I think she heard some things too, but the sounds were part of the images. I wrote them down." She handed him a sheet of paper.

Vlad studied the long list. "What does that mean?" He pointed to a *P* in parentheses after some of the words.

"It's a pause," Merri Lee said. "That was different from the last time. This time Meg paused, like a rest in music, so I thought each group of words made up a picture." She handed him index cards.

He took them reluctantly. "What was the question you asked?"

"We asked what the residents of the Lakeside Courtyard should watch for during the next fortnight."

"Residents? Not just the *terra indigene*?"

She hesitated. "No. We said *residents*, not just the Others. So what Meg saw applies to everyone who lives in the Courtyard."

Which meant *everyone* included Meg and Merri Lee.

Vlad looked at the "stories" on the index cards and felt chilled.

Help Wanted: NWLNA

Trail Fire (blaze/inferno?). Path Compass/Compass Path?

Pregnant girl on dirt road. Silver razor. Blood. "Don't! It's not
    too late!"

Girl crying. Silver razor. Broken deer beside highway
    (roadkill).

Brown bear eating jewels.

Vegetable garden. Paws digging, hands planting.

For Sale signs.

Some of the "stories" meant nothing to him. But if he was interpreting others correctly, all of the *terra indigene* would need to act swiftly.

Vlad studied Merri Lee. Some of the "stories" meant nothing to him, but they *did* mean something to her.

"Which ones do you understand?" He placed the index cards on the edge of the desk where she could reach them.

She hesitated, then pointed to "Help Wanted: NWLNA." "Above the door of the Liaison's Office are the letters *HLDNA*, which stand for 'Human Law Does Not Apply.' *NWLNA* stands for 'No Wolf Lover Need Apply.'" She swallowed hard and wouldn't meet his eyes. "In the past week, quite a few employment ads in the *Lakeside News* have those letters at the end, and I've seen a couple of those signs in shop windows."

"I see." And he did see. Label anyone who wanted to keep peace between humans and the *terra indigene* as a Wolf lover, especially if that person directly interacted with the Others in any capacity, and force those people to choose between having a job and feeding their families, and opposing the fools who would provoke a fight that would end with many, many humans dead or driven out of the city.

Thinking about the humans who worked in the Courtyard and two basic things everyone needed—food and shelter—he asked, "Are these letters applied only to jobs or also to housing?"

Merri Lee didn't answer him, and that was answer enough.

"What else?" Vlad asked.

"It . . . It's not for me to say."

He leaned forward. She flinched.

"Say it anyway," he suggested.

"Ruth Stuart and Karl Kowalski. Everyone is being encouraged to make some kind of garden this summer and grow a few vegetables to supplement what you can find in the market. Well, Ruth and Karl bought the material and built the raised vegetable bed for their apartment building with the understanding that they would be able to use half the bed and the other tenants in the building, including the landlord, would share the other half. But once the work was done, the landlord gave them notice, said they're unacceptable tenants. He wants them out by the end of Maius because he's already got *acceptable* people moving in on the first of Juin. That gives Ruth and Karl three weeks to find another place and move. They signed a lease for a year, and they've barely had time to get settled in their new place. That *man* says he isn't going to reimburse them for the materials *they* bought or return their security deposit or the last month's rent, which they paid when they signed the lease. If they were acceptable *before* they did all the work, why are they unacceptable now? And if this guy gets away with it, what's to stop the next landlord from pulling the same thing?"

What was to stop *this* landlord from pulling the same trick on the next tenant? Sounded like it could be a human-versus-human problem. Humans cheated one another all the time.

But Karl Kowalski was one of the police officers who worked directly with the leaders of the Courtyard to keep any minor collisions between humans and Others from escalating into a major fight. If Kowalski was being branded a Wolf lover and was being driven out of his home because of it, the Others needed to pay more attention to things that on the surface seemed strictly the business of humans.

On the other hand, if Ruthie was the unacceptable tenant because she actually worked for the Lakeside Courtyard now, then the trouble with this particular landlord was no longer strictly human business, was it?

Something to discuss with Grandfather Erebus.

At least Merri Lee, all fired up now in defense of her friends, was acting more like her usual self rather than a flinching bunny. She was telling him about

Ruthie and Kowalski, but she was also revealing what she and Michael Debany were facing. Debany was another police officer who dealt with the Others, and Merri Lee worked for the Courtyard. Right now, she lived in one of the efficiency apartments above the seamstress/tailor's shop, but sooner or later, she and Debany would want to live together as a mated pair and would face the same hostility.

"Anything else?" he asked. She'd already given him plenty to think about, but he sensed the girl wasn't finished.

Merri Lee pointed to the warning about something not being too late. "I don't think that was part of the vision. I think Meg shouted that in an attempt to warn the girl she saw in the vision." She blew out a breath. "Both 'stories' about girls included a silver razor. The blood prophets are in trouble, aren't they?"

"Trouble" might be a small word for what could be happening to those girls.

"Thank you, Ms. Lee," Vlad said, ignoring her question. "You and Meg have given me a lot to consider. But now it's time we all started the workday. You're filling out orders in the bookstore today, aren't you?"

"Yes. What orders I can fill, anyway." Merri Lee stood up, but she didn't make a move toward the door. "Ruth wasn't going to tell you about the vegetable bed or the other part."

"Then I'm glad you told me."

Vlad listened to Merri Lee go down the stairs before pushing away from the desk and walking over to the windows that overlooked Crowfield Avenue.

Damn monkeys kept chattering about the Humans First and Last movement on the radio and in the newspaper. Humans were an upstart species compared to the *terra indigene*, who, in one form or another, had been walking in the world long before the dinosaurs. But humans thought *they* should control the world, and the speeches made by members of the HFL movement encouraged that kind of thinking.

Didn't humans realize the *terra indigene* had heard such words before? Didn't humans understand that such words were a warning that a fight for territory was building under the surface?

Didn't they wonder what had happened to cities, and civilizations, the previous times humans had made such claims?

Fine, Vlad thought. *Let it come. You monkeys have no idea what's out there in the wild country. But you'll find out. If you start a fight with the Others in Thaisia, you will find out.*

As he idly watched the traffic moving along Crowfield Avenue, he saw a car pull up across the street. Two men got out, gathered some material from the trunk, and began pounding a sign into the yard of one of the large stone apartment buildings across the street from the Courtyard. Then they went across the yard of a two-story wood house and pounded another sign into the lawn of the other large stone apartment building.

Vlad looked over his shoulder at the index cards sitting on the desk. He studied the FOR SALE signs that had just been put up across the street.

Can't wait to discuss this with Simon, he thought as he returned to the desk and sent a quick e-mail to all the Sanguinati living in Thaisia. *What Meg saw is already in motion, which means the blood prophets, the sweet blood, are already in danger.*

He closed the e-mail program and left Howling Good Reads, not even stopping long enough to tell Merri Lee he was leaving. Shifting to his smoke form, Vlad raced to the Chambers to report to Grandfather Erebus.

To: All Sanguinati in Thaisia
Subject: NWLNA

Read the want ads in human newspapers. Look for the letters *NWLNA*.
They stand for 'No Wolf Lover Need Apply' and are a strike against humans who are not enemies of the *terra indigene*. Make a list of the businesses that placed those ads. Also, check for those letters in rental ads for
apartments or houses. Gather information but do nothing else. The real
prey are two-legged predators from a pack called Humans First and Last.
They hide among the rest of the humans, and seeing NWLNA is a sign of
their presence in your territory.

The Sanguinati will call these humans Venom Speakers because they
poison other humans with their words.

Keep watch and report. Let the Venom Speakers come out into the
open. Then they will be easier to kill.

—Vladimir Sanguinati on behalf of Erebus Sanguinati

CHAPTER 2

Thaisday, Maius 10

Simon Wolfgard parked the minivan in the lot designated for passengers taking the ferry to Great Island. He started to open his door, then turned to his companion, Henry Beargard. "What did Vlad want when he called?"

"He wants the Business Association to meet as soon as we get back to the Courtyard," Henry replied. "He says we should set up meetings with Lieutenant Montgomery and Dr. Lorenzo as soon as possible. Maybe Captain Burke as well."

"What happened?" Simon growled, feeling his canines lengthen to Wolf size.

"Nothing of immediate concern, but many things have to be talked about and dealt with. Meg is fine," Henry added. "Vlad went over to the Liaison's Office and checked before he called."

He knew how to interpret *those* words. "She cut herself and saw prophecy."

Henry nodded. "Meg is concerned because Merri Lee didn't want to tell her what was seen, but Vlad says both girls are fine. The cut was carefully made and well tended. In fact, despite being concerned about the prophecy, Meg sounded cheerful and relaxed and said something about a symbol for a new beginning but waved off Vlad's attempt to find out what that meant by saying it was a girl thing."

Simon didn't want to poke his nose into a "girl thing." Potentially dangerous territory, that. But the words did indicate the cut physically wasn't a cause for concern.

If there was something wrong with Meg, Vlad wouldn't be dismissive, espe-cially when Grandfather Erebus, the leader of the Sanguinati in Lakeside—and perhaps the leader of the Sanguinati throughout the Northeast Region, or even the whole of Thaisia—took a personal interest in the girl he called the sweet blood.

Not technically a girl, Simon thought as he and Henry locked the minivan and walked to the booth that sold tickets for the ferry. Meg was twenty-four years old. An adult female. But *cassandra sangue* retained the sweetness of a child's heart, which was one reason they were considered not prey.

The other reason was that blood prophets were Namid's creation, both won-drous and terrible, and far more dangerous than anyone had realized. That had been the reason the Others had demanded what humans called full disclosure—reveal anyplace that housed blood prophets or face extermination of the entire town that conspired to keep the girls a secret.

The whole continent had been shaken by the *terra indigene* hunting down a man known as the Controller. The Others in the Midwest Region, where the compound was located, had not only destroyed the man and those who worked for him; they had shown human authorities what the laws allowing "benevolent ownership" meant to the *cassandra sangue* who were kept in compounds like that.

Meg had come from that Midwest compound. Simon had found her cell while looking for her friend Jean, and just the memory of Meg's scent in that place filled him with rage.

The man in the ticket booth waved them away. "No charge for you today. Best get down to the water. They're holding the ferry for you."

<Not a usual occurrence,> Henry said, switching to the *terra indigene*'s form of communication as they walked to the ferry.

<No. But when Steve Ferryman called and asked for this meeting, he sounded scared.>

Simon wasn't sure how the Intuits saw themselves—as a race separate from other humans or as a group of people who had been persecuted because of their particular ability to sense what was around them in ways other humans couldn't. Whatever that ability was called—intuition or second sight—the Intu-its didn't see visions, but they would get a feeling about something, good or bad. Driven out of human settlements generations ago, they had made their own bargains with the *terra indigene* and now had their own villages hidden in the wild country, out of reach of their persecutors.

But they hadn't always been out of reach. When they had lived among other humans, sometimes they had sired girl children who were more sensitive than the rest of the Intuits, girls who *could* see visions. Out of the Intuits had come the first *cassandra sangue*, the girls who saw warnings of things to come whenever their skin was cut.

In a way, they were all coming full circle. The Intuits, who had given up those offspring, thinking they were saving the girls as well as their other children, were now volunteering to be the caretakers of the girls who wanted to leave the compounds where they had been considered, and treated as, property.

Meg was not property. Not anymore. She was his friend—and she should have waited for him to return before using the silver razor.

As soon as he got home, he'd growl at Meg for being sneaky about this cutting. And he'd growl at Merri Lee too. That might make more of an impression.

Or not.

When Howling Good Reads had been open to human customers, the females who came sniffing around were there to see a *terra indigene* wearing fur or feathers or they were looking to take a walk on the wild side, viewing sex with a male who wasn't human as some kind of trophy. That behavior was easy to understand and ignore. But the Courtyard's human pack! Nothing simple about *those* females.

<Stop growling,> Henry said. <You're scaring the humans.>

He hadn't realized he'd been growling. A quick check of tongue over teeth warned him that he needed to shift his canines back to something closer to human before he smiled at the twitchy humans who were watching him.

"Good morning," the human male said as Simon and Henry stepped onto the ferry. "I'm Will Ferryman, Steve's brother. And this is our aunt, Lucinda Fish. We'll take you over to the island. Steve has a room reserved at the government building. You know where that is?"

"We do," Henry said.

"Do you mind if we stay outside?" Simon asked. The ferry wasn't a big craft, and he really didn't want to spend the time closed up in the cabin with a bunch of nervous passengers.

Nervous humans smelled more like prey, making it easier to react as a Wolf on the hunt—and making it much harder to back away once the scent of blood filled the air.

"Not a problem. Just don't lean over the rail too far," Will said. "Even a good swimmer can get in serious trouble in this current."

<Does he think we're that stupid?> Simon asked Henry as they made their way to the bow.

<No, but I think he's dealt with humans who were that stupid,> Henry replied.

Will and his aunt cast off the lines, and the ferry began its journey across the Talulah River.

Ferryman's Landing was an Intuit village divided by the river. Half the village was on the mainland, while the other half was on Great Island. Unlike Lakeside, which was a human-controlled city built on land leased from the Others, Ferryman's Landing had always been a human settlement controlled by the *terra indigene*. That meant the earth natives had the final say in everything humans did, whether it was putting up a new building or allowing someone to become a village resident, and they had no qualms about eliminating humans who tried to cause trouble.

That was a hard truth the residents of Talulah Falls were still learning, now that the town was no longer under human control.

"Looks like Steve Ferryman didn't want to wait for us to go up to the government building," Henry said when they were in sight of the ferry's dock and saw the two males who were watching them. "Or else Ming Beargard also has a reason to meet us."

The Black Bear claimed he was just a part-time peacekeeper on the island. But Ming was one of the few *terra indigene* on the island who actually ventured into the village itself, so saying Ming was just a peacekeeper was like saying Henry was just a sculptor. Lakeside's Grizzly was a member of the Business Association as well as the Courtyard's spirit guide. As such, Henry's opinion carried weight.

So did the paw that could, and would, wallop sense into a person.

<Steve asks that you remain on the ferry,> Ming told them. <The meeting place has been changed.>

A mantle of fur sprang up around Simon's shoulders. As a human, he was an adequate swimmer. As a Wolf, he was excellent. But he wouldn't want to test his strength and stamina against the Talulah River. He didn't like feeling suspicious that Steve Ferryman would bring them to the island and then not want them there, but he had no reason to distrust the village's mayor. Yet.

As soon as the ferry docked, Steve and Ming boarded. While Steve went up to the wheelhouse to talk to Will, Ming and Lucinda Fish encouraged the human passengers to disembark with alacrity.

The passengers looked at Henry and Simon and didn't need to be asked twice.

Still standing at the bow, Simon watched Roger Czerneda, the village's official police officer, and Flash Foxgard, another part-time peacekeeper, set up sawhorses, closing off access to the ferry. "Something's happening," he said quietly to Henry.

<Steve wants us to sit in the cabin and talk,> Ming said when the last passenger hurried up the dock and eased between the sawhorses.

<Is there a reason he doesn't want us on the island?> Simon asked.

<Too many humans want to talk instead of letting Steve be their voice,> Ming replied. <Many gathered in front of the government building in anticipation of your arrival. Steve slipped out the back door of the building in order to meet you here.>

<Do the Intuits have a feeling about this meeting?>

<Too many emotions, I think, but no feelings that guide.>

<That's not good,> Henry said. He walked into the cabin, leaving Simon to follow.

Steve Ferryman was a vigorous, healthy human male, lean muscled like a Wolf rather than bulky like a Bear. His dark hair was clean, and his brown eyes usually held a bright intelligence.

Today the man looked a bit . . . chewed. No, humans wouldn't say "chewed." Frazzled. Was that the human equivalent?

"Thanks for meeting me," Steve said. "Sorry to change the venue without warning, but it was the only way we could talk quietly. And if it becomes necessary, Will is ready to cast off and keep us in the middle of the river in order to avoid uninvited participation." He blew out a breath. "We have some baked goods from Eamer's Bakery, and Aunt Lu says the urn has fresh coffee, if you'd like some."

"What we'd like is the reason you called us here," Simon said.

Steve rubbed his hands over his face. "The whole village is scared. We are piss-in-the-pants scared, and we need help."

Simon stopped himself from ducking under the table and taking a sniff, but the aborted motion made Steve smile.

"It's an expression," Steve said. "It means we're very scared."

Humans had invented some useful swearwords and expressions, but *that* expression wasn't something Simon would be using anytime soon.

"This fear is because of the *terra indigene* now ruling Talulah Falls?" Henry asked.

"That's part of it," Steve agreed. He glanced at Ming.

"The Others in control of Talulah Falls feel a deep anger and distrust of all humans," Ming said. "And many earth natives around the Great Lakes think that the anger and distrust is deserved, that the human population in Talulah Falls needs to be winnowed down to only those who are necessary to run the machines and businesses humans previously claimed were vital. They look for excuses to kill humans and respond violently to any kind of trouble. Even humans making requested deliveries are at risk."

"That kind of anger comes from experience," Henry rumbled.

"I know. But that kind of anger is like fire—it will either burn out or spread."

"The Talulah Falls and Great Island Crowgard had a gathering, which is how we learned some of what is going on," Steve said. "The Falls Crows said the *terra indigene* brought in an enforcer who makes them uneasy. He's been given free rein in dealing with humans who cause any kind of trouble. They said his hair is long and fixed in many little braids with small bones woven into the ends— bones that sometimes clatter together and sound like angry snakes even when he is standing still. And the hair changes color. They saw some humans arguing with *terra indigene* like they were going to fight. The Crows looked away from the enforcer when the bones rattled and his hair started to change to black—but they saw the humans fall down dead."

"Do you know this form of *terra indigene*?" Ming asked.

Silence. Then Henry said, "The braids and bones are not familiar, but we know of this form. It is dangerous even to speak of it. If you must go to Talulah Falls, be very careful—and do not look at the enforcer if his hair starts to turn black."

A *Harvester,* Simon thought. The *terra indigene* had brought in a Harvester to deal with troublesome humans. Did Tess know there was another of her kind in the area? Was there any safe way to ask her? Probably not.

Simon focused his attention on Steve again. "What else is making you uneasy?"

"What's really shaking up our whole community is the five *cassandra sangue* girls you brought out of the Midwest," Steve said. "We thought they were adjusting to living here. At least, they seemed to be doing all right during the first few days. But now one or more of them is having some kind of emotional breakdown every day or falls into a catatonic state that lasts anywhere from a few minutes to a few hours. We don't know why this is happening. We don't know how to help them. We do know we need to move them out of the bed-and-breakfast and make other living arrangements for them, but what kind? And where? We tried to take them to our medical center for a basic checkup. Three of them messed themselves, and the other two ran away in a blind panic and came close to being hit by vehicles. Remember I told you about Jerry Sledgeman's family, how his niece had started cutting herself, then jumped into the river and drowned? You can imagine what seeing five young girls breaking down like this is doing to his whole family."

"You want us to take the girls away?" Henry asked.

Steve shook his head, a vehement movement. "The Intuits gave someone else the care of girls like these once before, and it's a shameful part of our history. We won't willingly do that again. But it's not just our community. *Every* Intuit village who took in some of the girls from that compound is having problems. I'm getting e-mails every day from village leaders begging for any information that might help. We don't want these girls to die, and we're all afraid they're going to."

"What about Jean?" Simon asked. "What does she say?"

Steve sighed. "Jean is . . . haunted . . . and barely able to function. She keeps saying Meg knows, Meg can help."

When Simon had rescued Jean, she had told him Meg was the Pathfinder, the Trailblazer. At the time, he'd liked the sound of those words. Now they sounded like big stones someone wanted to tie around Meg's neck before throwing her in the river to see if she could survive. But the girls he, along with Lieutenant Montgomery and Dr. Lorenzo, had brought out of the Controller's compound were between eight and eleven years old. Still puppies who depended on the adults in the pack for their survival. And Jean, who was an adult and very damaged from what had been done to her, was Meg's friend.

"I'll talk to Meg," Simon said, not happy about making that choice but pretty sure Meg would be more unhappy if some of the other blood prophets got hurt.

"Something that will help now," Henry said. "Your bodywalkers—doctors— should not wear the white coats around the girls. Their captors wore white uniforms and white coats. Meg is disturbed by those things. It is likely the other girls are disturbed by them too."

"That's something," Steve said. "I'll give everyone that information. Thanks."

"The *terra indigene* are willing to extend the village's land to build a new den for these girls," Ming said. "But first we need to know what to build."

Quite a concession, Simon thought. But it brought something else to mind. "That abandoned industrial complex and cluster of houses just off River Road. I know the land lease wasn't renewed because the businesses put too much badness in the land and water, but I wondered if there are any humans still living in those houses and which group of *terra indigene* controls the land now."

"The girls would be vulnerable there," Steve said immediately. "Access to the island is controlled; that's why they're here."

"Not for the girls," Simon agreed. "But I don't want any humans who manage to escape from Talulah Falls denning in those houses. I don't want a potential pack of enemies staking a claim on land between Lakeside and Great Island."

Steve looked at Ming before he said, "There were people still living in a couple of the houses a few months ago, but this past winter convinced them that they didn't want to be living out there alone when the weather closes in."

"The Hawkgard reported that the last humans packed up and left as soon as the road was passable," Ming said. "I have not heard of any *terra indigene* reclaiming that land as wild country. Do you want to claim it?"

"Not on our own," Simon replied.

"In that case, we would be willing to share responsibility for that land with the Lakeside Courtyard." Ming looked at Steve, who nodded.

"You have people who can check the buildings?" Simon asked Steve.

"Sure," Steve replied. "We have plumbers, carpenters, and all the rest. I'll put a team together to inspect each building and make a list of what each would need to be habitable again. And we'll check out the availability of water and electricity in the buildings." He hesitated. "I take it you're thinking of this as an invitation-only community?"

Simon nodded. He wasn't sure *who* should live in that community, but he was certain the land and buildings needed to remain under the Others' control.

Then he stood, feeling crowded in body and mind. "Enough."

Steve stood too, then tapped the box from Eamer's Bakery. "Take those with you for your coffee shop." He walked out of the cabin with Ming.

Outside, the sawhorses were moved and passengers boarded for the trip to the mainland side of the village. But no one entered the cabin.

Henry opened the bakery box, made a sound of approval, and took a fruit-filled pastry. "Good," he said after swallowing the first bite. "So. Are you wishing you'd gone to the Addirondak Mountains with Nathan?"

"No. But I do want to check with Vlad. If everything is still quiet in the Courtyard, I want to take a look at those houses since they're on our way home."

Right now he really wanted to shift out of this skin and be Wolf instead of having to think about human problems, but he didn't regret passing up the opportunity to spend time away from the Courtyard. He didn't regret staying in order to be with Meg. His human friend.

He just wished he knew why Meg, the Pathfinder, had decided to make a cut while he was away.

CHAPTER 3

Thaisday, Maius 10

Simon and Henry found a handful of young Sanguinati squatting in one of the abandoned houses in what Simon decided to call the River Road Community. They had come to Talulah Falls from *terra indigene* settlements around the Great Lakes, drawn by stories of a glut of easy human prey. But the *terra indigene* sent to deal with those surviving humans weren't interested in teaching youngsters how to live in a human town, and the Sanguinati had been scared off by the Falls' primary enforcer, with his braids and clattering bones.

After getting the youngsters' promise not to hunt in Ferryman's Landing, and promising in turn to tell Erebus about their current situation, Simon and Henry left, satisfied that they had a minimal guard on their new land acquisition.

As they turned into the Lakeside Courtyard's Main Street entrance and drove up the access way, they heard Skippy Wolfgard's mournful *arroooo*.

Putting the minivan in park, Simon studied the juvenile Wolf sitting at the back door of the Human Liaison's Office.

"*Arroooo! Arroooo! Arooeeooeeoo!*" <Meg won't let me in!>

Glancing at the clock on the dashboard, Simon huffed out a breath and rolled down his window. "Skippy. *Skippy!*"

"*Arroooo!*" <Meg won't let me in!>

Skippy had a brain that didn't always work right and often skipped over bits of information. In the wild country, that typically ended with the youngster making a fatal mistake. It was inconvenient in a Courtyard, but any youngster who survived to maturity usually grew out of the skippiness.

Skippy had been sent to Lakeside a few weeks ago. Most days he spent at least some time in the office with Meg, with enough Wolves working in the nearby buildings to prevent him from doing something too stupid—not to mention Nathan's usually being present as the official watch Wolf.

But understanding that the office wasn't always open was a bit of information Skippy's brain had trouble holding on to. Since Meg was probably still on her midday break, the youngster would howl himself hoarse and never realize she wasn't letting him in because she wasn't there.

Or else she was there and preferred having some barrier between her ears and that yodeling *arroo*—a sound Simon sincerely hoped Skippy would outgrow.

<Simon!>

Simon looked in the side mirror and saw Elliot Wolfgard, the Courtyard's consul and Simon's sire, standing outside the consulate. <Do something about that idiot Wolf. I'm on a call with Mayor Rogers and can barely hear the man.>

Seeing Vlad step out of the back entrance of Howling Good Reads, Simon got out of the minivan and told Elliot, <I'll deal with it.>

<Why won't Meg let him in?> Vlad asked as he strode toward the Liaison's Office, using the *terra indigene* form of communication instead of trying to shout over the howling.

<It's not time for her to open for the afternoon hours,> Henry said, joining Simon and Vlad.

Skippy, still howling at the closed door, didn't notice them.

<But she did come back to the office,> Vlad said, sounding grim. <I was coming over to check on her because Crystal Crowgard just called me to ask if Meg was still upset.>

<Upset about what?>

<Don't know.>

Simon stepped up to the door, startling Skippy, who leaped away with a yelp of surprise and banged his head on Vlad's knee. The vampire swore and grabbed for the Wolf, who proved he wasn't ready to join a hunt for anything that had hooves or horns when he tried to escape by running between Vlad's legs.

Henry caught Skippy, gently dumped the struggling Wolf in the enclosed yard next to the Liaison's Office, then shut the wooden gate. Since Skippy couldn't shift to another form and couldn't keep his brain focused long enough to learn how to open doors, he'd stay where Henry put him.

And hopefully he'd quickly forget where he'd been a minute ago and why he'd been howling.

Of course, Skippy tended to remember things at the most inconvenient times. Like now, when, sitting behind the gate, he resumed his howl about Meg not letting him in.

Shaking his head, Simon tried to open the office's back door.

Locked.

That door wasn't supposed to be locked when Meg was in the office, in case she needed help in a hurry. Like when she used the razor.

Growling, he fished his keys out of his jeans pocket, opened the back door, and hurried inside.

"Meg!" Simon turned toward a sound coming from the bathroom. "Meg, what . . ." He stopped. Stared.

That was new.

He took a cautious step toward her. Then, intrigued, he took another step. "Meg?"

<Simon?> Vlad asked. <What is it?>

<Stay outside,> he replied.

Even after Meg came to the Courtyard, he hadn't paid much attention to the physical appearance of the humans who worked for them. They did their work, and he didn't eat them. That was sufficient. But they'd never had a blood prophet living in the Courtyard before, so maybe this was a normal seasonal change?

No, not normal. Meg looked upset, so this must be a new thing for her too.

"You shed your old hair," he said. Well, she'd done something with it. He had a feeling this was one of those times when a male should express positive enthusiasm regardless of what he really thought—especially when he didn't really know what was going on.

Fortunately, he did feel positive—and curious.

Meg's weird orange hair was gone, and her head was covered by a coat that was glossy black and thick and so short it stuck straight up. He reached out, wanting to see if the hair felt as soft as it looked. "This looks like puppy fuzz."

Before he could give her a scritch behind the ear, she jerked away from his hand and wailed, "I don't wanna look like puppy fuzz!"

"Why not? Puppies are cute."

Her breathing started to hitch, and her eyes had a panicked, glassy look that reminded him of a young bison he'd seen once when he was a juvenile Wolf living in the Northwest Region. The youngster had challenged an older bull and took a blow to the skull that had hurt its brain. He and the other Wolves had watched it stagger around and around, unable to change direction or even stop. It eventually recovered and followed the rest of the herd.

If the pack hadn't already made a kill earlier in the day, that young bull would have been easy prey.

If you forced blood prophet puppies to see too many new images, their brains froze as if they'd taken a hard hit, just like the young bison. The girls he'd brought back from the compound had done that several times during the train ride back to Lakeside.

But this was the first time he'd seen that panicked look in Meg's eyes.

"Meg!" he said fiercely. What could he do? How could he help her?

Same way he'd helped the girls during the train ride. Hide the strange. New things frightened.

Simon rushed into the sorting room and yanked open the drawers under the counter, growling as he pawed through the contents and thought of the nastiest human swearwords he knew. He found the floppy fleece hat stuffed in the back of a drawer. Grabbing it, he ran into the back room, plopped the hat on Meg's head, then dragged her into the bathroom and positioned her in front of the mirror above the sink.

"Look!" he demanded, closing his hands around her upper arms and giving her a little shake. "This is Meg, wearing the floppy hat we bought to keep her head warm after she came home from the hospital. This is Meg, the Human Liaison for the Lakeside Courtyard. This is Meg, who is my friend, Sam's friend, Vlad's friend, Tess's friend, Henry's friend, Jenni's friend. *Look!*"

He watched the panic in her eyes fade, watched her absorb the image of their reflections in the mirror. With the hair hidden, she looked the same as she had yesterday, except for the bandage on her left forearm.

Now confusion, and a touch of fear, filled her gray eyes. "Simon . . ."

Upset with her and for her, but gentler now that she sounded like Meg again, he led her into the sorting room.

<Simon?> Henry called.

<I want Merri Lee here *now*,> Simon said. <Once I find out what's going on with Meg, the Business Association will meet.>

<Elliot too,> Henry said. <He has things to tell us about his talk with the mayor.>

<I'm going to deal with Meg first.>

<Is she all right?>

<She's not *hurt*, but . . . I don't know. I think this is a girl thing.> Wasn't that what Meg had told Vlad? That she was going to do a girl thing as a symbol for a new beginning?

Simon studied Meg as she leaned against the sorting table, looking exhausted. He hoped he hadn't bruised her arms when he dragged her into the bathroom, but if he had, he wouldn't be surprised when Henry swatted him—hopefully with a human hand and not a clawed Grizzly paw.

Merri Lee rushed into the sorting room. "Meg . . . ?" She jerked to a stop. "Mr. Wolfgard?"

"Take off the hat, Meg," Simon said. Merri Lee would look at Meg's new coat, make a casual remark, and then . . .

"*Wow!* That's radical."

Meg's breathing hitched. Simon turned on Merri Lee and snarled, "You are not being helpful!"

"Well, I'm sorry, but it *is* radical," Merri Lee stammered. "I can understand why Meg needs time to adjust to how she looks with hair that short."

"*Not helpful*," he warned, showing his teeth.

But Merri Lee wasn't paying attention to him. She was studying Meg. "You weren't prepared for how it would look, were you?"

Meg shook her head.

"Your hair was short when you first arrived at the Courtyard. Not *this* short, but short, so it must have been trimmed on a regular basis." Merri Lee continued to study Meg. "But not at a salon?"

"I don't remember my hair being cut," Meg said. "But sometimes I had odd dreams of things being done. The Walking Names took each of us to a room for a maintenance sleep. When I'd wake up, nothing seemed different."

Simon watched the two girls and shifted his weight. Merri Lee looked like she wanted to bite someone, so he wasn't sure if he needed to leap forward to protect Meg or leap away to protect himself.

"Did you watch the stylist cut your hair this time?"

"No. I could *feel* her using the comb and scissors, but I couldn't *see* her."

"Ah." Merri Lee nodded. "The stylist had the chair turned away so that when she was done she could spin the chair to face the mirror and surprise you with the new you?"

Meg nodded. "I think she knew something was wrong, but I couldn't stay, couldn't talk. . . . It wasn't *me* anymore."

Merri Lee sighed. "When I was eleven, my mother decided she didn't like my long hair and took me to her stylist to get it cut. I loved having long hair, and I didn't want my hair cut, but I wasn't given a choice. They had already decided between them that it was going to be *short* because that's what my mother wanted. So the stylist kept the chair turned away from the mirror while she cut my hair. Then she spun the chair around and told me it was such a cute haircut, and my mother smiled. . . ." She paused, then shook her head. "The point is, I didn't recognize the girl in the mirror. I saw a stranger and felt . . . disconnected."

"Yes," Meg whispered.

Simon stared at them. "Yes? *Yes?* You look the same, you smell the same. How can you not know you're you? Meg, *you turned your hair orange* and you didn't get upset. Not like this!" He growled as a thought occurred to him. "Did you get upset like this but kept it hidden from us?"

When she hesitated, his growl deepened. He couldn't have her staggering around and around like a brain-damaged bison. Not now. Not ever. Not his friend.

"You." He pointed at Merri Lee. "Starting today, you're working two hours less at the bookstore and coffee shop."

Merri Lee paled. "But I need those hours."

"That's not fair," Meg said, making an effort to stand on her own instead of leaning on the table. "Just because you don't like what she said—"

"I didn't say she'll be working less hours," Simon snapped. "But she'll be working here with you because you two are going to figure out *exactly* why this happened, *exactly* why Meg panicked, and what to do so it doesn't happen again."

"Simon, I'll be fine," Meg began.

"This isn't just about you," he said. "The girls we brought back from the compound are breaking down like you did just now, only it's happening to one or more of them every day. The Intuits don't know how to help them. The humans who know the most about blood prophets aren't going to help us give their *property* a way to live outside the safe cages. You know they won't. Jean called you the Pathfinder, the Trailblazer."

Merri Lee jolted. "What did you say?"

Simon eyed her. "Pathfinder. Trailblazer."

Merri Lee swallowed hard and looked at Meg. "Those were two of the things you said during the prophecy. Path and compass. Trail and fire. Those were things the *terra indigene* were supposed to watch for."

"You two are going to figure out what the *cassandra sangue* need—and what humans and Others need to do to help them stay alive," Simon said.

"What do you expect us to do?" Meg shouted. "Write *The Dimwit's Guide to Blood Prophets?*"

"Yes! That's exactly what I want you to do." Looking at their stunned expressions, he wondered if he'd been a little *too* honest. "Figure it out and write it up so we can pass on the information to everyone who is trying to help these girls."

"I'm not a writer," Merri Lee protested. "I can make notes, sure, but I can't write up something like that!"

"Ruthie will help you write it." There. Problem solved. Ruthie was a teacher. She wrote sentences all the time.

"Have . . . have you talked to Vlad?" Merri Lee asked. "Has he told you about this morning's prophecy?"

"Not yet." He looked at the girls and softened his voice. "Figure this out, Meg. Jean said you're the one who can do it."

Simon walked out of the office, closed the back door, and stopped. Just stopped. He couldn't call the other Wolves in the Courtyard to help him drive away this danger to his friend. This danger lived inside her, was part of her—like the blood swimming with visions and prophecies, like her fragile skin.

How was he supposed to protect Meg from Meg?

Tess stepped out of the back door of A Little Bite. It would have been easier for her to use the inside doorway between the two stores to reach the upstairs meeting room, so she must have come outside to check on him.

<You going to the meeting?> she asked, pointing to HGR's second floor.

<Yes.> He crossed the paved area behind the buildings, and they went up to the meeting together.

He didn't regret staying in the Courtyard in order to stay with Meg, but right now he wished he could shed all the human problems along with the human skin.

Meg and Merri Lee stared at each other.

"Before we deal with the other stuff . . ." Merri Lee waved a hand to indicate Meg's hair. "Why so short?"

"I got tired of the way deliverymen looked at my hair. I got tired of the way the Others looked at my hair. It wasn't supposed to be *orange!*" Meg huffed. "I went to the haircutters in the Market Square. I hadn't met the Crow who was working there. She *said* she could cut my hair to remove the orange part. But I thought there would be more left!"

Merri touched her dark, layered hair. "It took me years to find a stylist that I trust, so I never went to the salon in the Market Square. But I think the two women who worked there part-time were being paid to teach some of the Others to cut hair as well as provide haircuts. I wonder if the Crow had been learning to cut hair before the women quit, or if she simply volunteered to provide the service and doesn't know what she's doing."

"So now there's a semitrained Crow cutting everyone's hair?" Meg's voice rose. She pictured a cartoon drawing of a Crow cutting someone's hair, wildly waving the scissors while snips of hair flew everywhere. The image looked ridiculous enough to make her feel calmer.

"It wasn't careless," she said. "I couldn't see what was happening, but the movements felt deliberate, even thoughtful." The slight tug of hair being lifted, the sound of the scissors. Had the Crow become so absorbed in the movement, in the way the shiny scissors opened and closed, that she hadn't wanted the experience to end?

"Well," Merri Lee said after a moment. "Your hair is a solid black now. Not even a stray orange tip anywhere. And on the bright side, your hair will be easy to care for this summer."

Meg hesitantly brushed a hand over her head. Different. Everything would feel different; all her routines would need to be adjusted.

"What?" Merri Lee asked. "You've got a look on your face like you just realized something."

"I'm not sure. I need to use the bathroom."

"Do you have a spare pad of paper? I'll pick up a notebook at the Three Ps later that we'll keep in here for our notes."

"That drawer." Meg pointed. "I have an extra pad that fits the clipboard I use for deliveries."

She went into the bathroom, keeping her eyes focused below the level of the mirror. She studied her hands, the familiar shape. The familiar scars. Then she rested her fingers against her face and looked in the mirror. Fair skin with a hint of rose in the cheeks. Gray eyes. Black hair, eyebrows, eyelashes.

Today this is my face. This is the face Simon recognizes as Meg.

She lowered her hands. No panic this time.

She couldn't recall any training images of a person being surprised by having a haircut. Now she had the image of her own face in the mirror, shocked and unprepared for the physical alteration. And she had Merri Lee's story of a similar action that had shaken a person's sense of herself.

As Meg left the bathroom, she glanced at the under-the-counter fridge and realized she hadn't had lunch yet. If Merri Lee hadn't eaten either, maybe they could call Hot Crust and have a pizza delivered. Pizza was comfort food, wasn't it?

She crossed the threshold, glanced around, and froze. "No." She rushed to the CD player on the counter, knocking Merri Lee aside, and moved the stack of CDs from the left side of the player to the right.

Merri Lee took a step back. "Gods above and below, Meg! What's wrong with you?"

Meg pressed her hands on the stack of CDs. "You can't move these."

"I was just making a little room on the counter!"

"*You can't change the constant things!*" Meg screamed.

Merri Lee stared for a long moment. Then she stepped forward and placed her hand over Meg's. "Calm down. The CDs are back where they belong. Breathe, Meg. Just breathe."

Breathe. She could breathe. Simple. Routine.

"Will you be okay if I go into the back room and get us some water?" Merri Lee asked.

Meg nodded.

Merri Lee hurried out of the room, then hurried back in carrying a bottle of water and two glasses. After pouring the water, she handed a glass to Meg. They drank, avoiding eye contact, staying silent.

"Okay," Merri Lee said. "I guess it's time to ask some questions. You've been here four and a half months. Things change in this office every day, and you haven't freaked out until now. Was the haircut the trigger? The one thing too many? If you can't tolerate things changing, how have you survived? How *do* you survive? We need to figure this out."

"It's just a bad day," Meg protested weakly.

"Yeah, a bad day and the shock of the haircut. Emotional overload. I understand that, Meg. I do. Just like I understand experiencing information overload, when you just can't take in anything else. I even understand being a bit obsessive-compulsive about your things. But you pushed me aside and screamed at me. Which I guess is better than breaking down, because at least you're still interacting with me. And that's the point. You've done so much, and so much has happened to you in the past few months, and today—*today*—you reached your limit. But Simon said those other girls are breaking down every day, and they've been out of the compound less than a month. What about other girls who want to leave, who want to live outside and are faced with trying to cope?"

"I don't know how to help them." Tears stung Meg's eyes.

"Yes, you do, but what you did to help yourself you did instinctively. Now Meg, the Trailblazer, has to figure out what she did so that we can tell the other girls."

Brushing away the tears, Meg took another sip of water.

"The constant things can't change," Merri Lee prompted. "What makes something a constant thing?" She studied the stack of CDs. "Always five? But not the same five? And always to the right side of the player?"

"Yes." Meg looked around the room. "I expect things to change in the sorting room because that's what happens here. That is the function of the room. *Things* go in and out, but the *room* stays the same. The table is always in the same place. So is the telephone and the CD player. The pigeonholes in the back wall don't move."

"What about when you're at home?"

"I have a routine. I follow the routine, just like I follow the roads in the Courtyard when I'm making deliveries."

"And when the routine is disrupted? Like the times when our Quiet Mind class was canceled?"

"I feel . . . uneasy . . . until I decide what to do instead."

"Constant versus change. A limited tolerance for change within the constants. And feeling stressed when routines are disrupted."

Meg recalled images of expressions and decided *fear* was closest to what she saw on Merri's face. "You know something."

"I don't *know* anything yet. We need to get Mr. Wolfgard's permission to do a few experiments before I'll feel easy about telling someone else what I'm thinking. But if I'm right about why the blood prophets on Great Island are having breakdowns, all the *cassandra sangue* who left captivity are in serious trouble."

CHAPTER 4

Thaisday, Maius 10

Taking a seat at the low table in the Business Association's room, Simon studied the index cards Merri Lee had created from the visions Meg had seen, then handed them to Elliot, the only other person in the meeting who hadn't already seen them.

Girls and silver razors and roadkill. Why were the girls on the roads alone?

All right, Meg had traveled alone from the Midwest all the way to Lakeside, but she'd traveled by train and bus. She hadn't been walking beside a road where she might get hit by a car and be left to die like a raccoon or deer.

But she had walked the streets in Lakeside part of the time. At night. In a snowstorm. By herself.

Even puppies weren't that dumb or that foolishly brave.

Meg wasn't usually dumb or foolish. But she had been desperate when she ran away from the Controller, and other girls could be as desperate to get away. And yet . . .

"This feels wrong," Simon said. "Even if the humans are angry with us for making them say where the blood prophets are being kept, why would they let girls they considered valuable just wander off? That feels wrong."

"You think Meg made a mistake?" Henry asked.

"No." *But maybe we did. We don't think like humans, so maybe we made the mistake.* "Meg saw this as something we need to deal with, but the only *cassandra sangue* within reach of Lakeside are Meg and the girls living on Great Island. None of *them* are in danger of being roadkill."

"Meg and those girls aren't in danger," Vlad agreed. "But we received the warning, so we're the ones who can send the warning to the rest of the *terra indigene*. I sent out an alarm to the Sanguinati. They're already searching for any girls who appear lost or abandoned. And they're looking for any females lying next to a road or in a ditch. I also talked to Jenni Crowgard. She's asking all the Crowgard to search for blood prophets—and Starr and Crystal flew out to tell the regular crows. They'll spread the word among their own kind and will tell the Crowgard if they notice anything new in their territories."

"While you were dealing with Meg and Merri Lee, I called Joe and Jackson Wolfgard, telling them about these two visions," Henry said. "I also contacted some of the Beargard and Panthergard. Wolves, Bears, and Panthers will spread the alarm to the rest of the *terra indigene* in their regions and start searching. For now, that's all we can do."

None of them mentioned the one other thing they could do, didn't mention the one pack who hadn't been told about the warning yet.

"What else?" Simon said, nodding at the index cards Elliot set on the table.

"Within minutes of this controlled cut, we had answers to three of the things the *terra indigene* should watch for," Vlad said. "Meg herself is the Pathfinder and Trailblazer. Just after Merri Lee brought me those index cards, I watched humans pound FOR SALE signs in the lawns of two houses across the street from the Courtyard."

"Doesn't mean those are the correct signs," Elliot said.

"But it's likely they are," Vlad countered.

"Yes, it's likely, considering the accuracy of the prophecies Meg has shared with us," Elliot conceded. "Just like NWLNA is most likely an attempt to discriminate against any human who is willing to work for us or with us. When I met with Mayor Rogers yesterday, I saw a proposal for adding a symbol to the identity cards—a symbol that would tell other humans if a person was a 'Wolf lover.' Rogers *acted* flustered that I had seen the proposal and gave me all kinds of reasons why this would benefit the city and help smother unrest." Elliot gave them all a toothy smile. "I asked him if the identity cards of all the humans who have had sex with one of the *terra indigene* would carry that symbol since *they* had certainly earned the designation. Judging by the way his face changed color, I'm guessing at least one member of his family has taken a walk on the wild side. Not something a politically ambitious human would want known."

Henry frowned. "Instead of trying to justify stamping the identity cards, he should have said it was government business. We don't get involved with how humans govern themselves."

"We don't get involved until their squabbling becomes a threat to us," Simon said. "But we have provided assistance to humans who were persecuted because they didn't fit in with the rest. That's why the Intuits and Simple Life folk mostly live on land we control instead of living in human-controlled towns."

"I think Rogers left that proposal in plain sight to gauge my reaction," Elliot said. "But I also noticed a logo on a letter that hadn't been hidden well enough under the other papers on his desk—a letter I *don't* think he wanted me to see." He removed a piece of paper from his jacket pocket and set it on the table. "That's a rough sketch of the logo."

It looked like a jumble of lines in a circle until Simon realized it was an attempt to turn letters into a symbol. "Humans First and Last movement," he growled.

Elliot nodded. "I've heard whispers about secret handshakes, and this symbol is being displayed in all kinds of stores and businesses. There's a human in Toland going around speaking about what humans deserve, stirring up the rest of the monkeys and trying to convince them that they can exterminate the *terra indigene* and take control of the world."

"They might be able to kill the shifters living in the Courtyards, or even some of the shifters living in the land that borders a human town or city," Henry said. "But they'll never take control of the wild country. They'll never take control of Namid. The rest of the *terra indigene* will see to it."

"But the seed has been planted," Elliot argued. "The humans in Lakeside's government have already forgotten the consequences of attacking us, despite Mayor Rogers's predecessor being among those who were killed in retaliation. They look at Talulah Falls and refuse to believe that they and their city could end up the same way."

"What did you tell the mayor about the proposal?" Tess asked.

"I told him the *terra indigene* would not object to being able to identify human allies as long as we can also identify our enemies. If Lakeside's government decides to brand some humans as Wolf lovers, then the *terra indigene* will demand that every person supporting the Humans First and Last movement will have a similar stamp on their identity cards, because we do not wish to support businesses owned by such humans or supply those businesses with raw materials to make their products. Not that the humans who owned or worked in those businesses would want raw materials from us."

"Secret handshakes and symbols." Vlad shook his head. "I received an e-mail from Stavros just before this meeting. Some companies in Toland now require their employees to join the HFL movement in order to keep their jobs—and they won't hire anyone who refuses to join."

"This HFL is like a sickness spreading among the humans," Henry said.

Tess's hair began to coil. "When one kind of sickness spreads through a population, other kinds of sickness tend to follow."

A shiver of fear went through Simon as he remembered the other name for Tess's form of *terra indigene*: Plague Rider. He almost yelped when his mobile phone rang. "What?" he snapped.

"Simon? It's Meg. Merri Lee and I need your permission to take some pictures. Ruth has a camera with one of those memory cards that holds pictures, and Lorne says he can print out the pictures from the computer in Three Ps."

He frowned. "Pictures of what?" She sounded . . . odd. Excited and scared. Like a young Wolf the first time he joined the pack to hunt bison.

"Things in the sorting room, mostly. And maybe the area behind the office. It will help us do what you asked us to do."

"All right, but those pictures don't leave the Courtyard."

"Okay." Meg hung up.

"Meg, Merri Lee, Ruthie, and Lorne are going to take pictures," he said in response to all the questioning looks.

"Why?" Henry asked.

"Part of understanding the *cassandra sangue*." He continued before anyone had a chance to ask him what that meant. "The *terra indigene* need to find out if 'Wolf lover' is a term only used in Lakeside, or did the HFL movement create that brand to cause trouble throughout Thaisia?"

"I told Grandfather Erebus about Meg's prophecy," Vlad said. "An order has already gone out to all the Sanguinati to report any ad for employment or rental property that includes NWLNA in the description. That should tell us if the term is local, regional, or has infected the entire continent. It should also give us an idea of which businesses are owned by members of the HFL movement."

"Not many Sanguinati in the Midwest and Northwest regions," Henry said.

"Not that many in the Southwest either," Vlad replied. "We're better suited to the coasts and the larger human cities." He looked at Simon. "I'll give you a copy of the e-mail I sent to the Sanguinati. You can adjust the wording and send it on to the gards who keep watch over the other human places."

Simon nodded. He'd contact Joe and Jackson. They would spread the word among the Wolfgard.

"By the way," Vlad said. "Per Grandfather's instructions, the Sanguinati will refer to humans who belong to the HFL movement as Venom Speakers."

"And who is supposed to explain to the Snakegard that it wasn't meant as an insult to *them*?" Elliot grumbled.

"I don't think they'll be offended, because the name is a warning to all *terra indigene* that the words these humans speak are dangerous and shouldn't be dismissed."

"All right," Simon said. "This is a start to identifying our enemies among the humans in every city. Any thoughts about the vegetable garden Meg saw in the visions?"

Vlad told them about Kowalski and Ruthie being forced out of their new den and not being allowed to plant their share of the garden for food.

"Then we'll take care of our human pack, the true Wolf lovers," Simon said. "We'll offer them some of the bounty that can be found in the Courtyard. If they share the work, they can share the food."

"Food grows everywhere on this land," Henry said. "Sharing the work would mean giving the human pack access to most of the Courtyard and its residents. Risky for us, and risky for them."

"Sharing the work doesn't necessarily mean gathering the food or catching the meat," Simon countered. "Humans preserve foods in jars and make things out of fruit that can be stored and eaten during the winter. The Intuits and the Simple Life folk have been doing that kind of trading for generations, and all of us benefited. Maybe the Wolf lovers are the next group of humans who should be helped, for our sake as well as for theirs."

He waited while the rest of the Others in the room thought about it.

"We can expand the Green Complex garden to feed a couple of humans," Henry said as Tess, Vlad, and Elliot nodded their agreement.

"A dozen humans," Simon said. "We'll expand enough to feed a dozen humans. If they don't like what we can offer, they can fend for themselves."

"Which dozen people did you have in mind?" Tess asked.

He shrugged, but they could guess he was thinking of the other police offi-cers who were making an effort to know the *terra indigene*.

Ruthie and Kowalski were being driven out of their den because they were smart enough to work with the Others. What could the Courtyard do about that?

"Captain Burke's friends." Simon spoke slowly as he thought through the plan. "The ones the *terra indigene* rescued and brought to Lakeside. The humans selling the houses across the street wouldn't know them. They could look and report."

"You want us to buy those houses?" Tess asked.

"Yes," Simon replied. "A place for Wolf lovers to live."

"Those houses aren't part of the Courtyard," Elliot pointed out. "We'll have to pay taxes on them, as well as the rest of the expenses, just like humans do."

He nodded. "And we will control who lives in those dens, just as we will de-cide who will live in the houses in the River Road Community and who will re-ceive the raw materials needed to make things useful to us as well as humans."

No one had anything more to say about gardens or houses. After giving Henry a questioning look, no one had any ideas about a brown bear eating jewels.

"Are we done?" Simon waited for everyone to nod. "In that case, I think I should go to the Chestnut Street station and talk to Captain Burke and Lieu-tenant Montgomery." And while he waited for Blair to bring over a vehicle from the Utilities Complex, he could find out what Meg and her pack were doing with the camera.

No one lingered to talk except Elliot.

"If we buy those houses, it will cause trouble here," Elliot said, handing the index cards to Simon.

"There's already trouble here," Simon replied. "The mayor aligning himself with the HFL movement is proof of that. We just need to do whatever we can to protect ourselves so that if the Lakeside humans turn on us, the *terra indigene* and our humans in the Courtyard will have a way to survive."

Pater,

The trial runs for the pharmaceutical enhancements showed great potential, and I think the enhancements could be of significant value to the
last stage of HFL's plans. Unfortunately, the manufacturer went out of
business unexpectedly, and it is unlikely in this current climate that other
possible manufacturers will be willing to take the risk of providing the
product, despite significant monetary rewards. However, from what I understand, the final product is easy to produce if one has quality materials.
Therefore, I will discreetly send a sample of the raw material on the next
ship traveling to Cel-Romano. I also recommend exploring some of the
country villages in our homeland, since they would be the most likely
places to have what we seek. And having a local source, even if the material is of inferior quality, will reduce the amount we would need to export
from Thaisia.

—NS

CHAPTER 5

Thaisday, Maius 10

The girl stumbled along the side of the road, looking for something, *anything*, she recognized from the binders filled with training images.

Highway. Two lanes, a wide strip of grass called a median, and two more lanes with cars going in the opposite direction.

Here, the keepers had said. *This medicine will make you feel good.*

It *had* made her feel good; almost as good as the euphoria. She and the other girls had floated while being packed into a horse trailer. They'd stopped and started many times during the night, and each time they stopped, a girl was left by the side of the road.

The farm is closed, the keepers said when some of the girls cried and begged to go back. *Can't afford to keep you anymore.*

She'd seen something or heard something when they made the last cut, something she needed to remember. So important to remember. But she was so big and so tired and so alone out here. She'd never been alone except in her cell, and that didn't feel like being alone because she knew there were girls in the other cells all around her and the keepers were always present and always checking on her.

No one here now.

Too many images, too many sounds. They beat at her—fists made of images and sounds. Belly too big, too awkward. Hurting. She tried to tell them about the hurting when they led her from the trailer, but the keepers didn't listen.

The farm is closed. You have to go. Then the keepers said the last, and most frightening, thing. *If the Others find you, they'll kill you and the baby. They'll tear open your belly and eat the baby right out of you.*

Needed to find people, find the farm, find . . . something.

Police? No. Police wouldn't help the girls at the farm. That's why the place was a secret. When girls were taken away by the police, they were beaten so they would lose the babies. The keepers said so.

She stumbled on the gravel that made up the shoulder on this side of the highway. Taking awkward steps to avoid falling, she ended up in the right-hand lane. She saw the big truck approaching and took a step toward the shoulder.

Images of people and highways crowded her mind. Images of animals and highways crowded her mind. A word under the images of dead animals: road-kill.

She would stand on the shoulder of the highway and wave. Maybe the people in the truck would stop. Maybe they would give her a ride and take her back to the farm. Her belly hurt more and more. Rhythmic hurting. She needed to get back to the farm because rhythmic hurting meant something.

A blast from the truck's horn scared her. Had to move out of the way, had to . . .

She heard howling. Terrible howling.

The Others were coming! They would find her and . . .

She ran straight into the path of the truck. As it hit her, she remembered that *something* from the last prophecy—the woman's voice saying, "Don't! It's not too late!"

And then it was too late.

CHAPTER 6

Thaisday, Maius 10

Lieutenant Crispin James Montgomery extended his hand to the man who rose from the visitor's chair as Captain Burke made the introductions.

"I'm pleased to meet you, Mr. Denby," Monty said, shaking Pete's hand. "I'm glad you and your family made it to Lakeside all right."

"So am I. I don't think we would have made it without the *terra indigene*'s help," Pete said.

Pete Denby had assisted in the search for the Controller. When that assistance made him a target, he packed up his wife and two children and headed for Lakeside—a long drive from the Midwest Region of Thaisia. Their car was run off the road, a deliberate attempt to injure or kill Pete, but the Others intervened and provided an escort for the rest of the trip.

"Are you planning to go back to the Midwest?" Monty asked.

Pete's eyes held a bleak look before he gave Monty a too-hearty smile. "Don't think I have much future there." The too-hearty smile slipped. "Not sure I have much of a future here either."

"I already told you," Burke said. "I don't have a current tenant for the other side of the duplex, and you're welcome to use it."

"I appreciate that," Pete said. "But a roof over our heads is only half the problem."

"Problem?" Monty looked from one man to the other.

"We'll work it out," Burke said.

"Even you can't continue feeding four extra people on a single ration book," Pete said tightly.

"If you're going to relocate—," Monty began.

"In order to receive a ration book that can be used in Lakeside, one or more adults in the family need to be employed—and show proof of that employment," Pete said. "Apparently there is some fear that a glut of people coming in from other towns will try to get ration books without being part of the working population, which will create food shortages. If there are shortages, prices will go up and more people will end up with less."

"You went to two interviews since you decided to look for work here," Burke pointed out. "You turned down both offers."

"I'm not signing some damn 'loyalty pledge,'" Pete snapped. "Especially when the senior partners in the law firm turned evasive when I asked to whom or what I was supposed to pledge my loyalty."

Monty's stomach did a queasy roll. "Humans First and Last?"

"I think so. Have you heard the motivational speaker Nicholas Scratch?"

Monty caught the glance Burke directed at him. Yes, he'd heard, and heard of, Nicholas Scratch. The man came from the Cel-Romano Alliance of Nations, but Scratch was currently living in Toland with Monty's ex-lover and young daughter.

"I heard a couple of his recent speeches, and he's a persuasive bastard," Pete continued. "If I wasn't almost one hundred percent certain that the HFL were behind the threats to my family, I'd be more than halfway to believing they had the answer to anything and everything. Want your children to have more milk? Kill a Wolf."

"Pete," Burke began, looking toward the doorway of his office.

"It's not our fault that, as a species, you're pretty stupid."

Monty winced, then turned to face Simon Wolfgard as the Wolf stepped into Burke's office.

"I think we've shown we can be dangerous," Pete said.

"Being dangerous doesn't make you less stupid," Simon replied. "And being clever about inventing and making things isn't the same as being smart about the world. Sometimes there isn't enough food. Sometimes pups don't survive the starving time. When that happens, we don't like it either. We work hard to bring down meat for our packs and to feed our young, and we don't like it when another predator tries to take our kills."

"I don't think we understand your point, Mr. Wolfgard," Burke said.

Monty heard the emphasis on Simon's name and saw Pete turn pale as he realized he'd been overheard by a Wolf.

Simon stared at Pete, anger creating flickers of red in the amber Wolf eyes. "We will fight for what is ours. In the end, your young will have enough to eat because there will be fewer humans wanting a share. And our young will grow strong on all the meat harvested from the fight."

A tense silence filled the room. Then Pete said, "You're big on destruction."

"We adapt to the world, and we learn from other predators. That includes humans."

Monty caught Burke's eye and understood the message. "Mr. Wolfgard, perhaps you and I can continue this conversation elsewhere."

Simon scrubbed his dark hair with both hands. If he'd been in Wolf form, he'd probably give his whole body a good shake. What Monty found intriguing was how that action seemed to shake off the anger as well. A moment ago, Simon couldn't have passed for human. Now he looked like a handsome, active man in his mid-thirties who was dressed in the casual attire suitable for a bookstore owner. Now the amber eyes were the only clue that you were looking at a *terra indigene* Wolf.

"No. If he's the male the *terra indigene* helped to reach Lakeside, then it's him I came to see." Simon tipped his head toward Pete. Then he looked at Burke and Monty.

"And I came to see you about something else."

Pete stared at the Wolf. "You came to see me? Why?"

"To ask if you are willing to do a small job for the Courtyard."

Monty held his breath. He'd spent the past four and a half months building some trust between himself and Simon Wolfgard. His team interacted with Courtyard residents almost daily in an unofficial capacity, learning more about the Others than most humans were ever allowed to see—and providing examples of humans who peacefully interact with what lived in the Courtyard. All that work might be damaged by a man who had some reason to be resentful since his life had spun out of control because of assisting the *terra indigene*, even if it was indirectly.

But Pete Denby surprised him by saying, "What kind of job? Do you need a lawyer?"

"Not yet," Simon replied thoughtfully. "Two buildings across the street from the Courtyard are for sale. We want someone to look at them and tell us if they are suitable dens. If we buy them, we will need to hire a human who can settle the legal papers."

"Some of the *terra indigene* are going to live outside the Courtyard?" Monty asked. Simon Wolfgard was a progressive leader. He'd opened some stores to the general public and had more human employees than any other Courtyard on the continent. But he wondered if the Wolf wasn't being a bit *too* progressive right now.

"No," Simon said. "We'll offer them to humans who are being driven out of their dens because they choose to work with us or for us. Like Kowalski and Ruthie."

Douglas Burke was a big man whose blue eyes usually held a fierce kind of friendliness. But the look in those eyes as he rose from his chair behind the desk was fierce enough to make Simon growl in response.

"Excuse me?" Burke said.

Simon stopped growling and looked at all of them. "Kowalski didn't tell you?"

"I haven't heard about this," Burke said with enough anger that Monty felt the heat of it. "What about you, Lieutenant?"

"No," Monty replied. "I knew something was bothering him. I figured he would talk to me when he was ready."

"Why not ask Kowalski to take a look if he's the one who might be living there?" Pete asked.

"The humans who live there now would know his face," Simon said. "We want someone to look before the humans realize the Courtyard wants to buy the buildings."

"I'll charge my usual hourly rate," Pete said. "You'll get a written report about each building. All right if I bring my wife? She's the handyman in our family."

Simon cocked his head. "Your wife is male?"

Pete blinked. "No. I just meant she's the one who likes working with tools and doing repairs."

"Do you have someone to watch the children?" Burke asked.

"We can watch the puppies," Simon said.

Leap of faith, Monty thought, watching Pete struggle with the thought of handing his children over to Wolves . . . and whatever else might become curious about small humans.

"All right. Thanks," Pete said. "Is tomorrow soon enough?"

Simon nodded as he pulled a folded piece of paper out of his jeans pocket. "This is the phone number for Howling Good Reads. Call there when you're ready to look at the houses. Here are the addresses on Crowfield Avenue and the phone number on the For Sale signs."

"I'll set up an appointment with the property agent, and Eve and I will see you tomorrow."

Monty wondered if Simon was waiting for Pete to leave before telling them about the other thing that had brought a Wolf to a police station. There were aspects of the Courtyard the Others didn't share lightly. On the other hand, if Pete was going to do some house hunting for them, he was bound to meet the Courtyard's carefully guarded and special employee.

Simon studied Pete for a moment, then turned to Burke. "Have the police been told to search for girls left on the side of the road?"

"Any particular kind of girl?" Burke asked quietly.

"Girls with silver razors. Girls who are gestating." Simon growled. "Road-kill."

Burke's eyes looked like blue ice. "Here in Lakeside?"

Simon shook his head. "Beyond Lakeside and Great Island."

"How . . . accurate . . . is your information?"

"We sent out a warning to all the *terra indigene* in Thaisia because of what we were told. They're already searching. You're the last pack to hear the warning."

"We'll get the word out. Lieutenant?"

Monty looked at Simon and motioned toward the door. "I'll walk you out."

"My scent here is fresh. I can find the door to outside." Simon cocked his head. "This walking. It's like a female in a story saying she's going to powder her nose when she's really going to pee?"

Pete choked.

"Something like that," Monty said in a strangled voice. He walked out of Burke's office. Simon followed him.

Monty waited until they were outside. "Is Ms. Corbyn all right? That's how you know the information is accurate, because she made a cut?"

"Meg is fine—but she doesn't know about the girls yet." Simon shifted his weight from one foot to the other, a small sign of anxiety in someone who was usually bold and direct. "Humans paid a lot of money for prophecies. That makes the *cassandra sangue* valuable to the humans who run the compounds. Why would they leave girls on the side of the road?"

"The girls could have left on their own. Meg did."

"Meg *escaped*. These girls can tell police, can tell *us* they want to leave. They didn't have to run away and be alone." Simon's eyes were full of sadness and acceptance in equal parts. "We won't find some of them until they're dead."

"The police will be out there searching too, and we'll save as many as we can." Monty waited a beat. "Anything else?"

"Nothing that can't wait." Simon walked away.

While Monty watched Simon and Blair drive off, Louis Gresh, commander of the bomb squad, approached.

"You look like you've just found a ticking briefcase," Louis said.

"Close enough. But thank the gods, the bomb isn't in Lakeside this time."

"Anything I can do to help?"

"Plenty." Together, they went back inside to help Burke send the warning to police stations throughout Thaisia.

CHAPTER 7

Thaisday, Maius 10

*H*e looks sad, Meg thought as Simon walked into the sorting room and stopped when he realized Merri Lee and Ruth were with her. *He looks angry and sad.*

She rushed toward him. "What happened?" When he didn't answer, she looked at her friends, then back at him. "Simon? What happened?"

What were you supposed to do when a friend looked angry *and* sad but you didn't know why?

"You're the Trailblazer," Simon said. "You have answers, and we need answers."

"He's right," Merri Lee said.

Meg compared Merri Lee's face to training images. Pale. Sick. Upset.

She knows why Simon is upset. It's because of the prophecy, because of the thing she didn't want to tell me about.

Ruth, on the other hand, looked concerned, but she didn't look *knowing.*

"This is what we figured out." Merri Lee set a series of photographs on the sorting table. "Meg has created a framework of tangible things that acts as an anchor and keeps her from being overwhelmed by visual and auditory stimuli. The framework is a combination of big things like the sorting table and smaller things like where the CD player and the stack of CDs are placed on the counter. These are the constant things that can't change because Meg needs to count on them being exactly where they are."

"It's like the furnishings in Meg's room at the compound—," Ruth began.

"Cells," Meg said tightly. "They were called cells. They locked from the outside, and we only had what the Walking Names allowed us to have."

Ruth nodded to indicate understanding. "The cells' contents didn't change for as long as the girl lived in the compound. We think that lack of change balanced all the new images and videos the girls were shown as part of their training to describe the visions."

Meg didn't add her personal bit of speculation: that the sterility of the cells made the girls want to study the images—and made them more willing to cut in order to experience *some* stimulus. The addiction was still there, the craving for the razor and how the euphoria made her feel. It still veiled her mind to protect her from the visions, but the euphoria didn't feel as intense as the sensations she'd felt a few months ago. Or maybe she wanted to believe that because there were so many other kinds of pleasant stimulation now.

Something she needed to think about a while longer.

"We can't say if it's because of the training or simply how their brains work, but we think that, because they absorb *everything* around them, blood prophets suffer from information overload much faster than other people, and they zone out in order to give their minds a rest," Merri Lee said.

Meg could tell by the way Simon's ears had gotten a little furry and more Wolf shaped that he was listening hard to everything they were saying, but she wasn't sure if he understood what they were saying.

"When pups are young, they have to absorb everything too in order to learn about the world," he said. "Their constant things are the den and the pack."

"What happens when their little brains get tired?" Merri Lee asked.

Simon narrowed his eyes at Meg. "They curl up and take a nap."

Meg narrowed her eyes right back at him. He didn't look impressed. "Well, humans aren't built to take these quick little snoozes throughout the day."

His only comment was a huffed *tch* sound that told all of them what he thought of *that* human failing.

"The point," Ruth said, "is we tried to determine what makes up a constant and what makes something acceptable even when it changes."

Merri Lee pointed to the photos again. "For example, a vase could have flowers or not have flowers. A vase with flowers was *different*, but it didn't cause anxiety. The gate to Henry's yard could be open or closed. There could be food in the fridge here or not. But Meg *chose* where she put the CDs, and if someone changes the placement, that *does* cause Meg to feel upset."

"From what she told us, most days that would equal feeling a *little* upset," Ruth continued. "But a little distress on top of a little distress on top of a barrage of new images might push a blood prophet to cut herself in order to relieve the emotional pressure of feeling overwhelmed."

Simon stared at Meg and growled. "Things are *always* changing in the Courtyard."

"Yes," she said, hoping she could make him understand. Hoping he would keep his promise to let her have a life—even if having one killed her. "Every day when I make my deliveries, the Courtyard looks different. But it's a *good* different, a natural different."

"And Meg sees it as an active image," Merri Lee said. "We think that's part of it. By driving through the Courtyard—or walking or riding as a passenger—Meg is an active participant in a moving, changeable image. The land changes with the seasons. . . ."

"But my apartment doesn't change," Meg finished. "The furniture stays in the same place unless I move something."

Simon started to scratch behind one ear. Then his face colored as he realized his ears were Wolfy. Not meeting their eyes, he shifted his ears back to human shape.

"There's not a lot of stuff in your apartment," he said. "Not much furniture. We don't need much. . . ." He trailed off.

"Neither do I," Meg said. "Neither do the other girls."

"So . . . more Simple Life than Crow's hoard?"

She hadn't seen either of those things, but only one sounded soothing. "If Simple Life is more like our apartments, then, yes, like that."

"The immediate problem is the girls living on Great Island, right?" Merri Lee asked.

Simon hesitated, then nodded, leaving Meg to wonder who else needed help.

"Whoever is looking after the girls should clear their rooms of extraneous visuals—pictures on the walls, figurines on the tables, things like that," Ruth said. "They can take photos of all those things and make up a binder of images. Maybe allow each girl to look at the images and select a handful of items she would want in her room, then allow her to position them. But once she has 'set' her room, the girl's room *cannot change* unless *she* is the one making the change."

"Also, take a photo of each room as reference for the adults so they don't inadvertently change something," Merri Lee said. "Even a small difference of putting a book on a different shelf can be disorienting for these girls. Which we all learned when I moved the stack of CDs earlier today."

"Routine," Ruth said. "Flexibility wasn't part of the care or training in the compound. Everything that is different is a stressor for the girls."

"Someone could make a binder called 'Our Village' or 'Ferryman's Landing,'" Merri Lee added. "The girls can study images ahead of time, and their teacher or caretaker can discuss what else they might see, like cars moving on the street or people riding bicycles. Static images combined with a moving image. Then they can go out as an adventure, to see those things for themselves."

Simon focused on Meg. "You didn't have those things."

"But I have the routine that shapes the days. And I don't need a binder for the Courtyard because I'm familiar with most of the roads and buildings now." She wouldn't remind him that she hadn't expected to survive more than a few weeks, so she had gorged on images and experiences, determined to live while she could.

And she wouldn't tell him it was often her fear of what the scent of blood might do to predatory instincts that kept her from cutting more often than she did.

"Does that help?" she asked.

"It helps."

"Will you tell me why you're angry and sad?"

He glanced at Merri Lee, then looked at Meg and whined softly. "Some of the blood prophets have left the compounds. You saw them walking by themselves near roads. And some of them . . ."

Meg understood then why Merri Lee wouldn't tell her what she'd seen that morning. "I saw images that indicated some of them would die."

"Yes. But the *terra indigene* are searching for the girls now. So are the police. We'll find them, Meg. We will find them and get them to a safe place."

How many girls had she seen? "Where will you take them?"

"To Intuit villages or *terra indigene* settlements," Simon said. "Whatever is closest to the spot where we find them." He paused. "What should we do when we find them?"

What would have helped me if I had been alone and frightened, if I had been found by strangers?

"Images," Meg said. Merri Lee and Ruth nodded vigorously. "Tell the girls what is happening. Tell them how they will get from where they are to where they're being taken. We all have general images about traveling. Tell them the sequence so they can recall the training images that match. Then, if you can, *show* them a picture of the room that will be the safe place."

Her arms suddenly prickled so badly they burned, but she didn't dare rub her skin. Simon would recognize the warning of prophecy. So would Ruth and Merri Lee. They knew she shouldn't cut again today, having cut herself this morning, and Simon was already upset. She didn't want to think about how he would howl and growl if she pulled out the razor a second time in one day.

"I have to go," Simon said. "The rest of the *terra indigene* need to know these things."

"So do the police officers involved in rescuing the girls," Ruth said. "You should call them too."

He bared his teeth to show he didn't like someone giving *him* an order, but the teeth stayed human size, so he must have thought Ruth was right. That was probably the real reason he growled at them and said, "You write this down for the *Guide*."

Before they could protest, he walked out of the sorting room and slammed the back door as he left the office.

"Well . . . ," Merri Lee sputtered.

"I guess we should start writing *The Dimwit's Guide to Blood Prophets*," Meg said.

After a moment, Ruth nodded. "Yes, we should. And I think we should find someone who can draw so we can add a cartoon Meg pointing out important items."

"What?" Meg yelped.

"The cartoon Meg could be named Meg Pathfinder," Merri Lee said. "And she could provide Trailblazer Tips that other girls would find useful."

"I don't think we should call it *Dimwit's*," Ruth said. "Maybe just *The Blood Prophets Guide*."

"Yes," Meg whispered. The painful buzz under her skin faded to a light prickling in her fingertips. Then that, too, was gone. "A guide for the girls as well as the people trying to help them."

"All right." Merri Lee clapped her hands. "Let's see if we can use the computer in the Business Association's room to write up these first notes. Who should we ask for permission? Vlad or Tess?"

"Whichever one we find first?" Ruth said.

"The office needs to stay open a while longer," Meg said. "You go ahead and get started."

"You'll be okay here on your own?"

"*Arooeeooeeoo! Arooeeooeeoo!*"

Meg sighed as Skippy's yodeling *arroo* sounded just outside the sorting room's delivery doors. "I'll be fine. I'll walk out with you."

"Aren't you going to let him in?" Merri Lee asked.

"Not until I'm sure he's not trying to sneak a mouse into the office," Meg replied. "Especially since Nathan isn't here to sniff them out."

Her human friends hurried to the back door of A Little Bite. The juvenile Wolf, sans any furry toys, came into the office.

As Meg carefully filed the photos Ruth had taken for their experiment, she thought about the tone of the other girls' voices when they talked about the *Guide*. Not a dismissal of whatever bad thing was happening to the other *cassandra sangue*, but a distraction, an effort to help.

And that was a different kind of reference. A Life Reference.

Meg labeled that audio memory "cheering up a friend."

Standing at the upstairs window that gave him a view of the paved area behind the stores, Simon watched Merri Lee and Ruthie hurry toward A Little Bite while Steve Ferryman yapped at him over the phone.

"They didn't say you had to remove the wallpaper from the rooms, just the extra things that make the room look too busy," he said when Steve stopped for a moment. And why did humans put paper on walls anyway?

"Are the girls sure removing everything but essentials from the rooms won't cause more trauma?" Steve asked.

"No, they're not sure. But *telling* the blood prophet pups what to expect should help. I have to go. More calls to make."

"Thanks for this. Really."

Simon ended the call, then walked to the desk in HGR's office. Pointless to write e-mail. The packs would be out searching. Probably pointless to call and leave messages on the phones. But some Wolves did put on a collar that had a leather pouch attached in order to carry a mobile phone or some other human item. A howl carried for miles and didn't depend on poles and lines or metal towers to carry messages. A howl would travel from Wolf to Wolf, providing information to everyone within range. But police wouldn't recognize an "I found something!" howl; they would need a phone call.

He called Jackson first and condensed everything Meg's pack had told him into one sentence: treat the blood prophets like puppies who don't know anything and are afraid of everything.

Wasn't likely any of the girls would be found near Sweetwater, an area in the Northwest that contained an Intuit village and the *terra indigene* settlement where Jackson lived. A few weeks ago, a simple roadblock had been set up across the road leading to that area after a human village had been contaminated with gone over wolf, a drug made from the blood of *cassandra sangue*. No one could have left girls along that road without the Others knowing about it.

The phone rang under his hand, startling him enough to snap at the person on the other end. "What?"

"Simon?"

"Joe?" Something wrong. Terribly wrong. Kicked by a bison, ribs caved in wrong.

"We found . . . We didn't know . . ." Joe's howl of grief had Simon leaping to his feet.

"You found some of the girls?" Roadkill. Not all of those girls would have Meg's strength and desire to survive. Was that why Joe was grieving?

"A few. They're heavy with pups. *All of them* are ready to whelp."

When the *terra indigene* attacked the compound run by the Controller, they hadn't seen any gestating females. Pups old enough for schooling, yes, but no females bearing those pups.

Had the breeding females been kept in a different place from the girls who were cut? "What else?"

"We found the dead puppies," Joe whimpered. "Simon, they killed the puppies."

A horrible pain ripped through Simon. Memories of reaching his sister Daphne after she'd been shot. Memories of finding Sam cowering, his little paws covered in his mother's blood. Memories of Meg the first time he'd seen her, stumbling into Howling Good Reads half-frozen and looking for a job.

"What puppies?" He could barely shape the human words.

"Many of the *terra indigene* who were searching for the girls only recognize humans from the Others who can shift to that form. The Eaglegard and Hawkgard saw humans throwing noisy sacks into a lake many times before today, but they didn't understand. They just thought the stupid humans were fouling their own water supply. By the time some of the Crowgard flew by the lake and recognized the sounds coming from the last of the sacks as *crying baby* . . . Too late to save any of them."

Would they have done this to Meg? Would they have bred her on some kind of farm like livestock? Would they have thrown her pup in the lake if it had been male and useless for prophecies?

Cleaning house. Isn't that what humans called it when they wanted to avoid being punished for some wrongdoing? Cleaning house. Destroying the evidence that would show everyone they were bad, even for humans.

Maybe we should do a little housecleaning too.

He wasn't sure what else he said to Joe, or what Joe said to him, before he ended the call with a promise to send information about how to keep the rescued girls alive.

Humans. He had tried to watch them, work with them, even help some of them.

Right now, all he wanted to do was get rid of them before they hurt Sam. Before they hurt Meg.

He could, and would, rid the Courtyard of the sickness called *human* before it contaminated the *terra indigene*, before it changed them. He was, after all, the dominant Wolf, the leader.

He went downstairs. John Wolfgard took one look at him and cowered.

Simon took the keys from his pocket and calmly locked HGR's front door.

No escape from that direction.

"Simon?" Vlad's voice. Sharp. Almost challenging.

"All humans are banished from the Courtyard. I don't want to see them, hear them, smell them."

"What happened?" Tess's voice now. Just as sharp.

Simon turned and felt the fury explode in him when he spotted Merri Lee and Ruthie standing next to Tess, whose coiled red hair rapidly gained streaks of black.

Ignoring Tess's visual warning, Simon rushed at the girls, his hands shifting to accommodate Wolf claws.

"Filthy monkeys!" he howled at them. Spittle flew from his mouth. He swiped at Vlad when the vampire stepped between him and the girls. "Filthy, greedy monkeys! Meg's puppies aren't something you drown like a bag of kittens! But that's what you do, isn't it? You destroy anything to get what you want, anything that isn't exactly like you!"

He almost dodged Vlad when he leaped to attack Merri and Ruthie. He might have survived Tess. But Henry's big, furry arms caught him, lifting him off his feet so that all he could do was struggle and rage.

"Get out," Vlad said, pushing the girls toward the back door. "Get out of the Courtyard and stay away until I call you."

"But I live in the efficiency—," Merri Lee began.

"Find another place tonight," Vlad snapped.

"Give her ten minutes to pack a few clothes," Tess said. "Ruthie can run over to the Three Ps and tell Lorne to close up, then go to the medical office and tell Theral."

Simon howled. The prey was getting away!

"Go!" Tess said.

The girls ran toward the back of the store. But Merri Lee turned back. "What about Meg?"

<Our Meg!> Simon screamed.

"We'll look after Meg and keep her safe," Vlad said, watching Simon. "Go."

Simon panted. Hard to breathe. The prey was gone. No point fighting with the Grizzly now that the prey was gone.

"Simon."

Fucking vampire was right in his face again. Bite him!

"Who did you talk to?" Vlad asked quietly. "Simon? Who told you about Meg's puppies?"

Not Meg's puppies, but they might have been.

His mouth couldn't shape human speech. <Joe found . . .> Without the fury, he felt sick and too tired to fight with Vlad *and* Henry.

Henry hauled him up to the Business Association's room. Unable to stand being in that filthy human skin a moment longer, Simon tore off his clothes and shifted fully to Wolf. The relief was almost painful.

He curled up and studied Henry, who stood guard at the door.

<Meg?> he asked.

<We'll take care of Meg,> Henry replied. <You can see her when you're calmer.>

Henry wouldn't lie. With the humans out of the Courtyard, Meg would be safe.

Simon closed his eyes. Drifting in an uneasy sleep, he dreamed of Meg falling through the ice on Courtyard Creek, weighed down by bags that wailed and screamed.

Vlad hung up the phone with exaggerated care . . . and wondered how long Tess had been standing in the doorway.

"It's bad?" she asked.

He understood killing to eat, to survive. He understood killing an enemy. He understood killing to protect family and home.

But he didn't understand this. He wasn't sure there was any kind of *terra indigene* who could understand this.

One chance, he thought as he picked up the phone and dialed. *One chance to show us you're not all monsters.* "Come in so you can listen. I'd rather not repeat this more often than required."

Monty stepped into Burke's office to ask if the man wanted a cup of coffee, but the captain was on the phone, and his face was set and pale.

Retreating, Monty bumped into Kowalski, who grabbed his arm and pulled him toward his own desk, where Officers Debany and MacDonald waited for them, along with Louis Gresh and Pete Denby.

"Ruthie just called me," Kowalski said, speaking so low the other men had to lean in to hear him. "Something has happened, something bad, but the girls don't know what it is. Simon Wolfgard just banished *all* humans from the Courtyard. He's so pissing mad, he tried to attack Merri Lee and Ruthie."

Monty's heart banged against his chest. *Mikhos, guardian spirit, please spare us from having to fill out a Deceased, Location Unknown form for any of these girls.* "Are they all right?"

"Yeah. Tess, Vlad, and Henry intervened. Right now, the other two girls are with Ruthie at our apartment. Merri Lee is staying with us tonight. Lawrence can pick up Theral after his shift."

"Thanks," MacDonald said.

Pete looked at the rest of them. "Is this because of the girls everyone is searching for?"

"Ruthie doesn't think so," Kowalski replied.

"The Others knew about those girls before we did," Monty said. "Wolfgard wouldn't have lost control hours later, so it has to be—"

"Gentlemen," Burke said from his office doorway. "In here. Last one in, close the door."

Monty went in first. Pete Denby came in last, closing the door.

"I've just had two phone calls. The first was from a contact in a police department in the Northwest." Burke gave them all a chilling smile. "The girls the police and the Others are searching for? They're all pregnant. Every single girl who has been found so far is pregnant, and some of them were in labor when they were found."

"Gods, they must be terrified," Monty said.

"Scared to death. Literally, in some cases. It appears the girls have been brainwashed to believe that the police will beat them until they lose their babies. And that the Others will eat them. They're running away from help—and some girls have died as a result."

Monty studied Burke's face. "That's not the worst of it. That's not what pushed Simon Wolfgard over the edge a short while ago."

"The second phone call was from Vladimir Sanguinati." Burke's hands curled into fists. "Most people prefer not knowing about the laws allowing benevolent ownership. And even people who don't think humans should be able to 'own' another human will justify keeping troubled girls in special compounds for their own sake. How many of those people will try to justify not only breeding those troubled girls but also disposing of the unwanted offspring? Yes, gentlemen, apparently some of those compounds also have their own breeding farms. Can't have *that* little secret coming out, can we?"

"The *cassandra sangue* are all girls," Monty said. "Is there an orphanage for the boy babies?"

"Disposal, Lieutenant, not adoption. And *that* is what the *terra indigene* discovered while searching for the girls." Slowly, with effort, he forced his hands to open. "The people responsible for breeding these girls like livestock need to be found and prosecuted to the fullest extent of our law. The girls, and any surviving babies, need to be found and saved. The breeding farms need to be found and shut down. Lieutenant, I'm splitting up your team for the rest of the day. Each man will pair up with another officer from the station. That way there will be one man in each car who has had dealings with the Others. You go out to the farms around Lakeside. You check the barns, the outbuildings. You make a note of any building that could house these girls. If you run into trouble or run into anyone who doesn't want you looking around, you call for backup—or fire a couple of shots in the air. I was told that will bring a different kind of help."

"Captain?" Kowalski asked. "Do you think we'll find anything?"

"No, I don't. But we're going to search anyway in order to reassure *all* the citizens of Lakeside."

Pete Denby cleared his throat. "These girls. The ones who live around here. Do they need an advocate?"

"Not at the moment," Burke replied. "But it's good to know you're willing to stand for them in that capacity." He walked toward the door. "Let's do this, gentlemen."

"You're going out to search?" Monty said. Shouldn't the captain remain at the station to coordinate with other precincts, other captains? With the commissioner and the mayor?

"Oh, yes. I'm going out to search. I'll keep my mobile phone turned on so you can reach me in the field." Burke opened his office door and walked out.

Monty and the other men hurried to catch up to him.

Meg. The puppies.

Simon jerked awake and sprang to his feet.

Henry's warning growl convinced him to stay put.

He studied the Grizzly, whose hands were furry and clawed. Henry could do a lot of damage with those claws.

Right now, he hated the human form. Right now, he thought his heart would tear if he had to wear that skin. But he didn't think Henry would let him out of the Business Association's room while he was in Wolf form, so he shifted. He pulled on the jeans, then pondered the rips in the knit shirt he'd been wearing. Had Grizzly claws or sharp Wolf nails done that?

"I didn't bite any of them." His voice sounded rough, as if his body was resisting the shift to human.

"You would have."

Shame was an odd feeling. Despite their being human, he liked Ruthie and Merri Lee. More important, *Meg* liked them. He'd just been so angry at *all* of the monkeys for hurting girls like Meg. And he'd felt terrified that by wearing the human form as much as he did, by trying to understand them and have so much contact with them, he might absorb that terrible aspect of being human.

"Does Meg know about . . ." He swallowed. Couldn't say the words.

"Not yet." Henry shifted his hands back to human shape. "Meg is in no danger. We thought it was better to spread the word to the *terra indigene* who are searching for the girls so they know what to look for if they spot humans near water."

"Has anyone contacted Jackson Wolfgard or Roy Panthergard?"

"You were asleep only for a few minutes—just long enough for Vlad to find out why you were so angry and tell us and a few others in the Courtyard before he started contacting the Sanguinati to give them this new information."

"I'll call Jackson and Roy."

Henry dipped a hand in his pocket and held out a mobile phone. "Don't know where your mobile phone is. Vlad's using the phone in HGR's office, so you can stay in here and use my phone. I'll go down and use the phone in the store. Make some calls to the Beargard."

Staying in this room would keep him out of sight—and keep him away from any humans.

Simon took the mobile phone. "I would never bite Meg."

"I know that. But as long as you're up here, you won't have words with Tess. Right now, that's better for all of us."

He waited until Henry left the room. He didn't call Jackson or Roy. The first call he made was to the Liaison's Office to talk to Meg. But the line was busy, so he didn't have the comfort of hearing her voice.

Sighing, he called Jackson to tell him what else humans did to each other.

Meg gripped the phone's receiver so hard her hand hurt. "I don't know what happened. Was this part of the visions I saw?" She'd made the cut that morning. It felt like days had passed since then.

"No," Merri Lee said. "That's why we don't understand what happened. One minute Simon is telling the three of us to work together on the *Guide*, and the next minute he's kicking all the humans except you out of the Courtyard. Ruth and I have gone over it again and again, but we can't figure out what we did to upset him."

"I'll try to find out."

"Be careful." A pause. "That drug. The gone over wolf stuff. Could he have taken some of that accidentally?"

"No." Since the drug was made from *cassandra sangue* blood, he would have had to bite *her* or bite someone who had taken the drug. If he *had* bitten someone who had taken the drug, there would be a human acting violent and crazy too, and if that were the case, there would be Wolves and Sanguinati filling up the office to guard her, or they'd be hustling her back to her apartment.

"Are you sure you'll be all right staying there?" Merri Lee asked.

"I'm sure."

Meg set the receiver in the cradle. Someone knew why Simon had gone all "bite the human," but who would tell her? Not Vlad or Tess or Henry. They would—what was the word?—stonewall. Yes. They would stonewall because even if they had intervened to save Ruth and Merri Lee, Simon was still the leader of the Courtyard, and they would protect the leader and give him a chance to speak for himself. Jester Coyotegard might know and would tell her just to cause a bit of mischief, but she was pretty sure he wouldn't tell her over the phone, and she would have to close the office too long to drive over to the Pony Barn.

But there were other residents who usually knew what was going on in the Courtyard, and *they* would be at their shop in the Market Square.

Meg tore off a page from the pad of paper Merri Lee had left on the counter. She hunted through a couple of drawers before she found a thick-line marker and a roll of clear adhesive tape. Then she paused to consider what she was about to do.

She hadn't gone into Sparkles and Junk yet. Too many other things happening in the Courtyard over the past few months. Too many other things to see just in her daily routine. She'd yelled at Merri Lee for moving the stack of CDs, a clear indication that she needed some quiet time before she tried to deal with anything else. And with so many of the Others already stirred up about something, having an "episode" now could cause a lot of trouble.

Well, she just wouldn't have an "episode." At least, not until she got home and could hide from everyone.

She wrote *Back in ten minutes* on the paper, taped it to the office's front door, and hurried out the back door and over to the Market Square.

There were usually a few of the *terra indigene* picking up a bit of food from the butcher's shop or the grocery store. There was usually some activity at Music and Movies and at the library. Today the square was empty, felt deserted.

Hurrying to Sparkles and Junk, Meg felt relieved to find the shop open—until she stepped inside. The shop run by the Crows was a visual explosion of colors and shapes crammed together and piled high.

This was a mistake, Meg thought, holding the doorframe for support. Then she focused on Crystal, who stood behind a glass counter at the back of the store.

"It's our Meg." Feathers sprang up all over Crystal's head, a sure sign of distress.

She doesn't want to see me today, doesn't want to be the one who lets slip whatever they're all keeping from me. Just my being here is upsetting her. Can't ask and can't retreat without causing a different kind of trouble.

Keeping her eyes focused on Crystal so that she wouldn't be overloaded by the rest of the store, Meg walked up to the counter and forced herself to smile.

Crystal looked toward a curtained doorway behind her. "Jenni and Starr are making phone calls. Does our Meg need something?" More feathers replaced hair.

"I'm learning how to be in a place that has a lot of things. To help the other *cassandra sangue* so that they can go into shops too." Not a lie, just not the whole truth.

"Oh." Crystal looked around. "We have lots of treasures. Not so many as we did, but we still have lots. Do you want to look?"

Meg glanced down at the shelf she could see through the glass and felt dizzy. There must be an entire binder of images on that shelf alone! "No. I can't look at too many things at one time."

The feathers on Crystal's head smoothed into a more relaxed position. She picked up a green glass bowl and set it down in front of Meg. "Maybe this?" She dipped her hand into the bowl and came up with a handful of shiny coins. "I like to hold them, watch them shine as they fall back into the bowl. You can try it."

To please her friend, Meg dipped her hand in the bowl. Shiny coins. Crystal must have spent hours polishing so many coins. Or did she just keep the coins that were already shiny?

"This was good. Thank you," Meg said when the last coin fell back into the bowl. She started to turn away, bracing herself for the ordeal of walking to the door.

"Wait." Crystal dashed to one of the tables and rummaged through a basket. She hurried back to Meg and held out her offering. "I don't have the right kind of string. Blair might. You could ask. He wouldn't growl at *you*."

Sure he would.

Meg took the faceted oval piece of glass, not sure what to do with it.

"You hang it by a window, and rainbows will dance in your room!"

"This is wonderful. But I didn't bring any money."

"This is your first treasure hunt. You keep it. As a gift."

"A crystal from Crystal. Thank you."

"Is our Meg going back to the office now?"

"Yes. But I might sit in the Market Square for a minute before I do."

As she chose a bench in the square, Meg wondered how many of the Others would know exactly where she was by the time Crystal finished relaying the news about her first treasure hunt.

Vlad watched Meg hurry toward the Market Square. Unusual for her to break routine. Of course, this entire day had broken a lot of things that had been carefully established over months, even years. He wouldn't have been surprised if any of the other Wolves had lost control and turned on the girls today, but Simon? The leader who, just this morning, had talked about buying buildings to provide homes for these same girls?

He turned toward the desk, steeling himself to read the e-mail messages that had started pouring in as blood prophets were found in other parts of Thaisia, alive or dead. Then he heard a car pull into the area behind the store and looked out the window to see who was foolish enough to come here today.

Police car.

"Blessed Thaisia," he muttered as he raced out of the office, down the stairs, and out HGR's back door.

Three police officers worked with Lieutenant Montgomery to keep the peace between the humans living in Lakeside and the Courtyard. Karl Kowalski, Montgomery's partner and Ruthie's mate, had dark hair and brown eyes. The other two, Debany and MacDonald, had dark blond or light brown hair and blue eyes and were about the same height and build.

A matched pair, Vlad thought as he walked toward the car and the man who stepped out of it. Until recently Debany and MacDonald hadn't been around the Courtyard as much as Kowalski and Montgomery, so it wasn't always easy to tell them apart—unless you were a Wolf, who not only recognized the scent of each male but knew which female scent should also be present on their skin and clothes.

It took him a moment to decide it was Lawrence MacDonald who was wait-ing for him to approach. The officer still in the car, looking sweaty and pale, wasn't Debany.

"Mr. Sanguinati." MacDonald removed his hat and held it, making a notice-able effort not to fidget.

"You shouldn't be here," Vlad said. "You know that."

"Yes, sir, I do. But I have to ask. Is the Courtyard closed to humans for good or just today? Can Theral come to work tomorrow?"

Interesting question, especially when it was so obvious by MacDonald's control that the answer was very important.

"Can't she stay home for a day?" Vlad asked.

"Not alone." MacDonald looked uncomfortable. "She lived with someone for a while. He . . . hurt her, and she left. But he's caused trouble for her. That's why she moved to Lakeside, why she's living at my parents' house, trying to start over. Over the past few days, there have been phone calls to the house. Per-son hangs up as soon as someone answers. We think Jack Fillmore—that's his name, Jack Fillmore—we think he's looking for her. If he came to the house when no one else was home . . ."

Another girl at risk. Was the threat to Theral that much different from the men who had come after Meg? Vlad had a pretty good idea what Meg would say.

Would she forgive him, or Simon, if Theral was harmed by a bad human when being in the Courtyard, being *protected* by those who lived in the Court-yard, would have kept the girl safe?

"I'll talk to the other members of the Business Association," Vlad said, feel-ing reluctant but not seeing what else he could do. "I'll call you tonight with our decision."

MacDonald pulled a folded piece of paper out of his pocket. "All of my phone numbers, so you don't have to look them up. Thank you."

Vlad watched them back up and drive down the access way.

<Our Meg is returning to her office,> Jake Crowgard reported as he flew
back to his usual place on the wall that separated the delivery area from Henry's
yard.

Vlad hurried back to Howling Good Reads, slipping inside just as Meg came
into sight. A cowardly act? Perhaps. But, he thought, an understandable response.

What the Others had discovered about the other blood prophets and the babies would hurt her, and Vlad didn't want to be the one who hurt Meg.

Exhausted and heartsick, Simon returned to the Human Liaison's Office a few
minutes before Meg closed for the day. Every *terra indigene* who knew how to use
a telephone or send an e-mail had been put to work calling other Courtyards in
the Northeast Region and then beyond. He and Henry had made calls to the
Wolfgard, Panthergard, and Beargard in the Midwest and Northwest. Jenni and
Starr had sent word to the Crowgard in the Northeast and High Northeast. And
a little while ago, Jester Coyotegard showed up at HGR on behalf of the Elementals, who wanted to know why so many *terra indigene* were upset—and why *Meg*
was upset.

When they were returning from the Midwest last month, he'd told Lieutenant Montgomery and Dr. Lorenzo that until someone no longer needed to
breathe, a human couldn't hide from Air. The Elementals rarely took notice of
individuals unless provoked or, in Meg's case, intrigued. But Jester's appearance
had made him realize there had been one group of *terra indigene* who could have
found the abandoned *cassandra sangue* faster than the rest of them. It just hadn't
occurred to him to ask for their help.

After explaining why it was so urgent to find the blood prophets who were
alone and frightened, Simon told the Coyote about the sacks being thrown into
lakes and ponds. He didn't know what, if anything, the Elementals who lived in
the Lakeside Courtyard would do with the information, but if they told the rest
of their kin, there was a chance of finding more of the girls and babies alive.

Lieutenant Montgomery had called to let the Business Association know
that police officers throughout Thaisia were out there searching. Montgomery
also said that many government officials were sounding outraged and fierce
when television reporters asked questions about the abandoned girls.

Simon didn't ask how many of those outraged humans had bought a cut on any of those girls. But Vlad, who had listened to the news reports, took note of who denied the existence of blood prophets.

The *terra indigene* in Lakeside had done as much as they could today. Just one more thing for him to do.

He opened the back door of the Liaison's Office and looked around. How little was the little thing that was too much for Meg to absorb?

But she had learned how to do a job, and she did it so well she had changed how the Others saw the people who worked for them. She had learned how to take care of herself, was learning how to cook simple meals. She had even learned how to drive, more or less. Not that anyone in the Courtyard would let her go out on the city streets, but she chugged along just fine in her Box on Wheels as she made deliveries to the various complexes where the Others lived.

Meg, the Trailblazer. The one who could show the other girls how to live and survive and enjoy the world they'd seen only in pictures.

He walked into the sorting room. Meg stopped tidying the stacks of magazines and waited.

"They killed the babies," he said, not knowing how else to tell her. "Humans like the ones who caged you put babies in sacks and threw them into water to drown. The girls who were left beside roads weren't from the compounds; they came from dens where females had their pups."

Her hands trembled. "Is that one of the things I saw in the prophecy? Was that one of the things Merri Lee didn't want to tell me?"

"No. You saw the girls who were in trouble, not the babies."

She said nothing. He waited. A Wolf knew how to be patient.

"Dragging the lake," Meg said. "Are the police going to drag the lakes?" She smiled bitterly. "I know that phrase because I read it in a couple of thrillers recently. But I don't recall any training images that would match those words."

"Wouldn't that be an important image if someone wanted to find a missing human?" Simon asked. Humans did drown by accident.

"It should have been a training image. But I don't think the people who owned blood prophets wanted girls to have an image of what happened to the boy babies when they were taken away." Meg shuddered. "After Sam began shifting to human form, I wondered if I'd ever had a younger brother. In the compounds, there were no boys being trained to see visions. Just girls. How many old sacks do you think they'll find in the lakes?"

"I don't know." He hurt because she was hurting. He wanted to lick her face and find a meaty bone for her to gnaw on. He wanted to entice her into a game so she would think about something else. But he knew from experience that nothing could provide enough distraction to eliminate that kind of hurt.

"Simon? Could we go to the Wolfgard Complex and play with the puppies?"

Maybe there was a distraction that would help. "Sure we can. It would be good to do that." Tomorrow he would think about human things again. Now he would spend some time with his own kind—and with his friend.

As he and Meg locked the back door of the Liaison's Office, Vlad approached them from HGR.

"I closed for the day," Vlad said. "We're not open for human customers, and any *terra indigene* who want a book can borrow one from the Market Square Library. And I've had enough of—" His mobile phone rang.

"Aren't you going to answer it?" Meg asked.

"No." When it stopped ringing Vlad took the phone out of his pocket and shut it off.

"We're going up to the Wolfgard Complex," Simon said.

"I have to report to Grandfather Erebus. Why don't we ride together?" Vlad looked at Meg. "Simon can shift and ride in the back of the BOW. I'll drive over to the Chambers and then pick you up when you're ready to go home."

"I can drive," Simon said.

"Not tonight," Vlad said quietly. <Neither of you should drive tonight,> he added. <You don't look like you can hold the human form much longer, and Meg doesn't need the mental effort right now.>

Simon nodded. Vlad was right about him not being able to hold the human form much longer. He couldn't get a measure of Meg's fatigue, but she crossed the short distance between the office and the garages as if she'd run a long way through deep snow and every step now was an effort to survive.

Since they'd already locked up the office and bookstore, Simon went into the garage that housed one of the BOWs to strip off his clothes and shift. Vlad obligingly stood where he would block Meg's view. Not that Simon had any inhibitions about a human seeing him naked or shifting, but he was still careful to avoid Meg seeing him naked. He'd made the shift from Wolf to human once without thinking, and her confusion about seeing him as a naked human had almost broken their friendship.

He shook out his fur and waited for Vlad to set his clothes in the back of the BOW. When he jumped in, he made sure his tail was out of the way before the back door closed. Then Vlad and Meg got in the front seats. After Vlad backed out of the garage and stopped long enough to close the garage door, they headed for the Wolfgard Complex.

The BOWs were electric-powered vehicles that were used in the Courtyard. They had two seats and a cargo area that was just big enough for a grown Wolf if he kept his tail tucked. It wasn't his fault that Meg's head—and that newly cropped hair—was so close to his muzzle that he couldn't help but sniff it.

No stinky smells anymore from whatever she had used to dye her hair. Now the hair smelled of the shampoo made by the *terra indigene*, and it smelled like Meg.

He gave the side of her head a quick lick before she squealed and ducked away from him.

Tasted like Meg. Felt like puppy fuzz.

Too bad he couldn't hold her down and give her a proper grooming like he used to do with Sam. Could *still* do with Sam.

When they arrived at the Wolfgard Complex, the pups were outside playing some kind of game with the juvenile Wolves.

Vlad barely had time to stop the BOW before Meg scrambled out of the vehicle.

<Meg!> Sam's happy *arroo* was followed by those of other pups as they all crowded around her.

<It's the Meg!> <Does the Meg have cookies?> <Tug game?> <Chase you!>

<Let me out,> Simon growled at Vlad. Excited pups could easily forget to be careful with Meg.

He almost smacked his head, too impatient to wait for Vlad to lift the back door fully before he leaped out of the BOW.

Then he stopped and watched Meg and Sam. Strong bond between them. Trust and love.

Was Meg's little brother at the bottom of a lake? Did she really want to know that kind of truth about the humans who had kept her? Did he?

The rest of the Wolfgard who lived in Lakeside came over to where Meg was hugging all the pups, but especially Sam.

<Uncle Simon?> Sam said. <Meg's eyes are leaking. Is she sick?>

<No, she's not sick. She's . . .>

Couldn't tell the pups what had happened today, especially not Sam, who had seen his mother shot, had been with her as she bled to death. The pup didn't need to hear about humans killing their young. Instead, Simon howled the Song of Sorrow.

The adult Wolves took up the song. Most of them knew at least some of what had happened. He heard Blair's voice, and Elliot's. Then Jane and John and the rest. Then the juveniles and pups. And something else. A voice he'd never heard before.

Meg, kneeling in the grass, one arm around Sam. Meg, howling, adding her voice to the grieving.

When the howling ended, all the pups were pressed around Meg. The pack offering comfort.

Simon watched her as Sam left for a minute and returned with one of the soft ropes, offering the distraction of play. He watched her as she ran around making squeaky noises, pretending to be prey while the pups chased her and the adult Wolves made sure the game didn't get too rough. He watched as she played tug with Sam.

She had spent most of her life isolated, even when she was surrounded by other humans. Now she was learning as much from the Wolves as she was from the humans about what it meant to have family.

She wasn't a Wolf. She wasn't *terra indigene*. Despite that, Meg was becoming one of them.

CHAPTER 8

Thaisday, Maius 10

"*You've reached the Borden residence. Leave your name, number, and the purpose of your call.*"

Monty hung up without leaving a message. He'd been trying to reach Elayne—or, more to the point, his daughter, Lizzy—since hearing about the abandoned girls and the disposal of *cassandra sangue* babies. Feeling heartsick, he wanted some assurance, *any* kind of assurance, that his own little girl was all right. But there had been no answer.

He turned on the news, half listening as he made a sandwich he had no interest in eating and poured another glass of wine.

"*In a day full of bewildering tragedies, the terra indigene and police departments all across Thaisia worked together to locate at-risk teenage girls who were wandering alone beside country roads and highways. The girls, left homeless by the sudden closing of several institutions that had cared for troubled teens, were suffering from dehydration and, in some cases, exhibited psychotic behavior when approached by rescue personnel.*

"*Motivational speaker Nicholas Scratch had this to say about today's tragic events.*"

Monty studied the man now filling the television screen—the man who was currently living with Elayne and Lizzy. Classically handsome with skin that might have been described as swarthy if it didn't have the gleam of a pampered life. Wavy dark hair that was long enough that it should have looked unkempt if it hadn't been perfectly styled to defy anything that might leave it mussed. Dark eyes that were filled with fiery sincerity.

Considering what had happened today, it wasn't surprising that Nicholas Scratch was much in demand. But even if Elayne was attending the news conferences with Scratch, someone should have been home with Lizzy once school let out for the day. Someone should have been answering the phone, especially this late in the evening.

"While humans everywhere applaud the efforts the Others have made today to assist in the search for these troubled children, we also recognize that it is the actions of the terra indigene *that set these tragic events in motion in the first place,"* Scratch said. *"The destruction of an institution in the Midwest, whose personnel allegedly engaged in questionable practices or forms of abuse, and the subsequent threats against any and all places that care for troubled girls, especially those with an addiction to self-harm, is at the core of today's tragedies. Would the personnel running these establishments have closed them so precipitously if they hadn't feared reprisals by creatures that cannot understand the pressure humans live with when under constant threat? Would they have left these girls to fend for themselves if they hadn't feared that the communities where they lived and worked would be destroyed? Clearly the number of suicide victims found by rescuers should be a sufficient message that these establishments are needed and should be left alone.*

"When humans asked what would be done with the rescued girls, the Others said the girls would be taken to safe, undisclosed locations," Scratch continued. *"Many of us are wondering tonight if these mentally fragile teenagers will ever be seen again."*

"They won't be seen again by humans like you," Monty muttered as he turned off the TV.

He had to admit that Scratch pushed all the right buttons, especially when earlier news reports were about the number of girls, many heavily pregnant, who ran out into the road and were struck by fast-moving vehicles.

It was easy enough to grab the spotlight by reminding everyone that the Others had started this by pressuring humans to reveal the locations of every place holding *cassandra sangue*. But the general population didn't know that the Others had forced the issue because the girls' blood was the main ingredient in the street drugs that had sparked violence in many towns across the continent. It was easy to point the finger and express fear for the girls the Others had taken out of reach, but what, if anything, would be said about the babies who had been disposed of by humans? Go ahead and bang the "we're all humans" drum but don't even whisper the words "benevolent ownership," which might make a few people wonder why these girls with their evenly spaced scars had been shut away in the first place.

The phone rang. Monty almost spilled the wine as he grabbed the receiver. "Hello?"

"Lieutenant? It's MacDonald."

Had something else happened? Was he being called back to work? *Please, gods, don't ask me to face anything more tonight.* "What can I do for you, Lawrence?"

"I got a call from Vladimir Sanguinati. He says the Business Association discussed matters, and they agreed that the girls should return to work tomorrow, and the Denbys should come by as planned. Just wanted to let you know."

"I appreciate the call. Good night, Lawrence. See you tomorrow."

"Good night, sir."

Monty ended the call, drank the wine, and almost dumped the uneaten sandwich in the trash can. Then he remembered seeing a new sign on the bus: WASTE TODAY, GO HUNGRY TOMORROW.

He wrapped the sandwich and put it in the fridge. The bread might be stale tomorrow, but he could warm it in the wave-cooker and have the sandwich for breakfast.

After washing the few dishes sitting in the sink, he headed for bed. But he stopped and stared at the phone. Then he picked up the receiver and called Elayne's number.

Someone picked up before the answering machine kicked in. Monty waited, but no one spoke.

"Elayne?" he said.

Nothing but heavy breathing on the other end of the line.

"Elayne?" Monty said again.

The person in Elayne's apartment hung up.

Monty set the receiver back in its cradle and continued to stare at the phone. There was no one he could call in Toland, no fellow officer who would do him the favor of swinging by Elayne's apartment. He'd been transferred from the Toland police force because he had killed a human to save a Wolf child who had been in human form. He'd been seen as a traitor to his own kind.

It could have been Elayne who answered the phone and decided to screw with him. Wasn't her typical way of dealing with him, but he wouldn't put it past her. She had blamed him for her sudden drop in social status and used Lizzy as a way to punish him, refusing to let him talk to his little girl. During one phone call a few weeks ago, she'd informed him that she and Lizzy were going to Cel-Romano with Scratch for the summer—and might not be coming back to Thaisia at all.

She and Monty hadn't married. He had no visitation rights beyond what she might allow. In fact, the only thing Elayne did for him when it came to Lizzy was cash the support checks promptly.

"Lizzy," Monty whispered as he picked up the receiver and dialed Elayne's number again.

"You've reached the Borden residence. Leave your name, number, and the purpose of your call."

Nothing this time. Not even heavy breathing.

Monty went to bed but didn't sleep. Captain Burke knew a lot of people. Someone in Toland might be able to tell him something. And Vladimir Sanguinati knew some of the vampires who ruled the Toland Courtyard. He'd rather owe Burke a favor than deal with Vlad, but he'd take whatever help he could get to confirm his little girl was all right.

CHAPTER 9

Firesday, Maius 11

The girl dreamed of rain and woke to the sound of something dripping. Where . . . ?

Not the compound where the white-coated keepers . . . That older girl, Jean, had called them Walking Names. And there was that other girl, the one who didn't come to lessons anymore. Well, a lot of girls stopped coming to lessons. A lot of girls stopped being allowed to walk outside in the fenced yard. Then one day their places at the table were empty.

But *that* girl. Her disappearance had been different. And, somehow, she was connected with the fight that destroyed the compound and . . .

They had covered the girls' heads. They had carried the younger girls, but girls her age were led through the corridors, stumbling over things that squished underfoot. And from the ceiling came the *drip-plop* of something falling. Something thick and wet.

Even with her head covered, she saw things. Or maybe she remembered some things she'd seen in visions. Bad things. Wet, red things that terrified her. And people who weren't people, who had teeth and claws and red eyes.

Then she and the other girls were put into vans or cars and taken away from the compound.

This is a village in the Northwest. You're going to stay here with us now, they had said. *They* were humans called Intuits.

What's your name? they had asked her.

Cs821, she'd replied. Her answer made them sad. So sad.

Eight girls had come to this place from the compound. The four unscarred girls were taken to another part of the village. The four girls her age—the ones who had their first set of scars but not too many beyond that—were put together in this single room. A barracks. That was the word for the training image that matched the room.

She wondered who usually lived there and what had happened to them. There were clothes in the lockers and books on the shelves that made up the bottom of the bedside tables.

You're free now, the new keepers had told her and the other girls. But the girls had no images of "free," no reference, no understanding of what was required of them in this place made of wood and glass, this place filled with images and sounds that didn't belong to the compound that, she'd been told her whole life, was the only safe place for girls like her.

She found the toilets out of desperation a few hours after they had arrived. She found that if she stood at the door of the room and asked loudly for food and water, someone would bring food for her and the other girls.

Would you like to eat in the dining room? Would you like to go outside? Would you like . . . ?

The food tasted different, even when it looked like something she remembered eating. The water tasted different. The air *smelled* different, a wild scent under the smell of unwashed girls.

Too much, too much. All too much. So much too much the other three girls spent most of their time curled up on their beds, and the more their new keepers tried to help, the more things overwhelmed them until they didn't want to find *anything* in this terrifying place.

The new keepers had locked up the silver razors, but there were several objects in the barracks that were sharp enough to make a cut.

The Walking Names would not have been so careless.

A shiver of pain followed by relief. No one to listen, but they whispered in the dark, craving the euphoria that would get them through the next barrage of images.

Don't you want a name? Don't you want to live?

How was she supposed to know if she wanted those things?

Every night they cut themselves and whispered in the dark. Then, one night, before she began to whisper, the girl saw a glimpse of herself in a vision. So she gritted her teeth and endured the agony of an unspoken prophecy. The pain ate her up inside and she wanted to scream and scream and never stop screaming. But she said nothing—and saw herself with sheets of paper and many colored pencils.

When she was young and learning to make letters and write words, she would draw the images from the day's lessons. So much joy from such a simple thing.

The Walking Names said she was diluting her ability to see prophecy, and she needed to be broken of this bad habit. They had special gloves made that kept her fingers laced together so she couldn't hold the pencil. But drawing gave her a different kind of euphoria, and it was so hard to resist making a little sketch whenever she had a pencil.

So the Walking Names withheld the paper and the pencils. They fed her pap that had no flavor, depriving her of the variety of taste and texture in food. When they had stripped her life of every possible bit of pleasure that was available in the compound, they cut her for the first time to show her the only pleasure that girls like her were allowed to have.

They made her afraid to touch a pencil or paper. But that night when she swallowed the words of prophecy, she saw herself drawing. She saw the look on her own face: joy.

She'd almost worked up the courage to ask for a pencil and paper when the other girls arrived. The mommy girls who looked sick and wild, abandoned by their old keepers and found by creatures to be feared above all else.

You're safe here, the new keepers, the Intuits, said as they settled the mommy girls in the other four beds.

They meant well, but they weren't experienced keepers.

The girl sat up, shivering.

The sound of something dripping.

Maybe one of the sinks in the room with the toilets? If she turned the faucet, would the dripping stop?

She got out of bed. Her bed was closest to the door; the toilets were at the other end of the room, past the rest of the beds.

Drip, drip, drip.

All the whispering had stopped.

Drip, drip, drip.

As she passed the next bed, her foot slipped.

A smell in the air. She remembered it from the compound, when her head had been covered as they took her away from the bad thing that had happened there.

She turned and rushed toward the door, patting the wall to find the light switch. The other girls would be angry when she turned on the overhead lights, but she didn't care. She needed to see.

She squinted as light filled the room. Then she looked at the floor. She looked at the girls in the beds who were past being overwhelmed by images and expectations.

They didn't want to live, she thought as she stared. *They chose this instead of trying to live.*

Easier to choose this. How much longer could she keep struggling to understand this place, these people? How could she learn what they wanted her to learn? She knew where to find the sharp objects. She could do what the other girls had done and . . .

She remembered the image of herself with the sheets of paper and colored pencils.

The girl pounded on the door and screamed. It wasn't until she heard people shouting and running toward her that she tried to open the door.

Not locked in. A test? Or a choice?

She flung the door open and fell into the arms of one of the men who had come running in response to her screams.

"I want to live!" she cried. "*I want to live!*"

"*You've reached the Borden residence. Leave your name, number, and the purpose of your call.*"

"Elayne, it's Monty. You're not going to see another support check unless I talk to Lizzy and have some confirmation that my daughter is all right."

Monty waited a moment, half expecting Elayne to pick up and start shouting at him for implying that she wasn't a good mother. Right now, he wasn't sure she *was* a good mother.

He hung up, then finished getting ready for work.

Radio and TV news reports were full of sound bites from Nicholas Scratch's speeches about the teenage girls, already troubled by an unhealthy addiction to cutting, being taken out of human control.

Scratch was careful not to make any mention of the girls being *cassandra sangue* or that most of the cuts on those girls had been made by men selling prophecies for profit. He didn't have any trouble pointing out that the *terra indigene's* imprudent actions were the reason behind the fifty percent suicide rate of the girls who had been released from the sheltered, structured life that had been designed for them by caring professionals. But he made no mention of the babies who had been killed to hide the evidence of breeding farms.

It was equally telling that most of the girls who had committed suicide had used a folding razor with a silver handle—the same kind of razor Meg Corbyn used, because each blood prophet had a sharp, shiny razor that was used exclusively on her.

If Elayne wanted to wave the banner for Scratch, that was her choice, but Monty wasn't going to stand back anymore and let Lizzy be pulled into that mess. Simon Wolfgard had said the *terra indigene* didn't harm children. While it was probably true that a Wolf wouldn't harm a child without provocation, Monty didn't think the Elementals or other kinds of *terra indigene* were always as concerned about who might suffer from their wrath.

Sooner or later, the *terra indigene* would realize that words could be as much of a danger to them as a physical weapon. Sooner or later, Nicholas Scratch, or someone else in the HFL movement, was going to say too much.

He stopped at his apartment door and looked back at the phone. This early in the morning, Elayne should have been home.

"Damn you," he said softly.

He had intended to go to court to gain some kind of custody that would prevent Elayne from taking Lizzy to another continent. He'd had to put personal needs aside when the pressure of finding the Controller and preventing an assault on all human settlements in the Midwest Region had consumed all his time and energy. A justifiable decision, since the threat to the Midwest had been immediate and the trip to Cel-Romano had been slated for summer, presumably after Scratch had finished his speaking engagements in Thaisia and was returning home.

But now summer was less than a month away. Now Monty needed to do something for himself and his little girl. And by a quirk of fate—or the gods' benevolence—he'd met Pete Denby, an attorney he could trust to represent him.

Returning to his bedroom, Monty opened the closet and removed the lock-box from the top shelf. Opening the box, he took out a copy of Lizzy's birth certificate, which listed him as her father, and a copy of the support agreement Elayne had insisted on when he'd been transferred to Lakeside and she'd refused to go with him.

After tucking the papers in the inside pocket of his suit coat, Monty replaced the lockbox and closed the closet door. Then he locked up his apartment and walked to the bus stop, arriving just in time to catch the Whitetail Road bus to work.

Simon,

Seven blood prophets killed themselves early this morning. The Intuits are in shock. They say they had conflicting feelings about bringing the girls to their village, but they ignored the bad feelings because they wanted to help. Now they say they will keep the young girls but not the girl who was in the room with the dead ones. She has scars and fresh cuts. I think they expect her to kill herself, and they're afraid of the impact another death will have on all of the children, not just the ones they're fostering.

The Intuit doctor says the surviving scarred girl is fifteen or sixteen years old. He gave her medicine to make her sleep so that we could move her. We brought her to the earth native settlement at Sweetwater, which is a mile from the Intuit village.

She said she wants to live. We don't know if she is strong like your Meg, but we were told she came from the same place. How do we keep her alive? *Should* we keep her alive? Does Meg have answers?

—Jackson

P.S. The Intuits told us the scarred girl is called *cs821*.

CHAPTER 10

At the Addirondak station, Nathan Wolfgard boarded the westbound train. He walked through two cars that were too full for comfort. The third had a few humans clustered near the front of the car but was otherwise empty.

Nathan sighed with relief. He'd hoped taking the earliest available train would reduce the number of humans on board. He'd spent almost two weeks in the Addirondak Mountains, running with one of the packs who guarded that piece of wild country, and he wasn't ready to interact with humans anymore than necessary.

He stopped at a seat and discovered this part of the car wasn't quite empty. Across the aisle was a human female scrunched in the seat next to the window.

He thought about moving a few rows farther down, but he had to get used to being around humans again. One small female was a good way to start.

Stowing his carryall in the rack above the seats, he pulled a book out of the side pocket and took the aisle seat. Too easy for a lone Wolf to get trapped if he was in the seat by the window.

He wasn't due back at the Lakeside Courtyard for another two weeks, but he missed being there. That was a surprise to him as well as the host pack. Even a Courtyard as large as Lakeside's could feel too small when it was inhabited by *terra indigene* whose forms were adversaries in the animal world. Earth natives didn't absorb everything from the forms they had chosen over the long years the sun had risen and set over Namid. They were first and always *terra indigene*.

But they learned from the predators they became, and certain traits were passed down to the young of each form.

Yes, there had been danger, threats, even attacks in the Lakeside Courtyard during the past few months, but there had also been a new kind of fun. Meg Corbyn, Human Liaison and squeaky toy, provided a different kind of interaction with humans. And her presence changed how some other humans approached the Others.

During the day, the Addirondak pack had hunted and played as they usually did. But after dark, after they sang to the world, the Wolves had asked about the Courtyard, about things they'd heard but didn't quite believe. Sure, the Intuits who lived in the human settlements tucked in the Addirondaks traded fairly with the Others. But none of those humans *played* with the Wolves. This Meg really played with him?

So at night he told them stories about Meg's first encounter with him after he'd been assigned to guard the office; about how she had coaxed Sam, Simon Wolfgard's nephew, out of a cage and how well the pup was doing now; about Skippy, the juvenile Wolf they had sent to Lakeside, catching a mouse and chasing Meg; about how she had met the leader of the Sanguinati—and had befriended Winter and the Elementals' ponies.

He told them about her sweet blood and the cuts she'd made in her own skin to see the warnings that had saved the ponies . . . and Sam. He told them about cookies that were being made now especially for Wolves. Well, for other *terra indigene* too, but mostly for the Wolves.

He'd learned more about humans in the past few months than he'd learned in all the time he'd trained to work in a Courtyard and cope with the close proximity of so many humans. He spent as much time in Wolf form as in human form. He ran and played and hunted in the Courtyard just like he could in the wild country. But then he could shift to watch a movie or read a book . . . or play an active, physical game better suited to the human form.

When the pack leaders asked him to talk to Simon about allowing a few Wolves to visit Lakeside to learn these extra human things, Nathan worried that he might have told a few stories too many. But Simon *had* talked about closing the stores to most humans so that *terra indigene* could learn about different kinds of stores and merchandise, and safely interact with humans who could be trusted.

Another reason he was heading home earlier than expected.

He had tried to call Simon, and then Blair, yesterday to tell them he was re-turning, but all the phone lines were busy, busy, busy. This morning he'd fielded so many last-minute requests from the pack that he'd barely gotten to the sta-tion in time to show his travel pass and receive a free ticket before the train pulled out. Now he realized no one yet knew he needed a ride home when the train reached the Lakeside station.

He'd call Blair when the train made its next stop. There were a lot of miles between the Addirondak Mountains and a city on the shores of Lake Etu.

After the conductor came through and checked his ticket, Nathan opened his book, a thriller by a human author. He'd read it when it came out a couple of years ago, but most of the Addirondak Wolves found it difficult to visit the hu-man settlements and go into stores to purchase things, so he'd traded the two new books he'd brought with him for this one to read on the way home—and made a mental note to ask Meg's human pack for ideas about how the *terra indi-gene* could get more stories.

He didn't know how much time had passed when a human male walked by his seat. Nathan raised his head and bared his teeth.

Intruder!

No, he thought, fighting for control. Not an intruder, as such. It was the pun-gent scent of the man's cologne that had triggered Nathan's response to a strange male trying to mark territory where he didn't belong. But the man might not have been trying to claim anything. The man could have come from the dining car and needed to pass through this car to return to his seat.

The *terra indigene* didn't like the smells humans used to disguise their own scent, but for the first time, Nathan wondered if males drenching themselves in a nose-pricking smell was equivalent to Wolves rolling on a dead fish to leave behind a stronger scent marker.

Now that he thought about it, that particular scent had been in the car when he sat down. It had been diluted by the fresh air that entered with the people going in and out, but it had been there.

Troubled by that but not sure why, Nathan took stock of his surroundings. Except for the stinky man, no other humans had entered this car since it left the Addirondak station.

Why was that wrong?

He looked down at the book but moved his head enough to study the passenger on the other side of the aisle.

Girl. Young enough that he would still consider her a puppy. Skin the color of milk chocolate. Big dark eyes. Braided black hair that was tied just under her ears and stuck out like two finger-long tails.

She was cheek to jaw with a fuzzy brown bear, and both of them were looking in his direction.

Why did humans give their offspring fake versions of predators that would happily eat those offspring?

Those two faces side by side did look cute, though.

Then he noticed the small dark hands clamped around the bear's hips, and those thin fingers squeezing and squeezing. He looked away because that was just creepy.

He caught the pungent cologne scent as the same human male entered the car again, walked through, then out the other door. But this time, Nathan caught something new in the scent that made him watch the human until the man left the car.

Then he gave the girl a quick look and realized what was wrong.

Humans and Wolves had one thing in common: they didn't leave their young alone for long. So where were the adults who should be around the girl? She'd been alone when he'd taken his seat. Had the adults gotten off the train and left her behind? There were stories about lost children. Wolves didn't like those stories. Maybe the girl should have gotten off at the Addirondak station?

He looked at the two strips of heavy white paper tucked above the seats. LAK on both, meaning there was someone else sitting with the girl who was also going to Lakeside. The conductor had tucked the same kind of strip above his seat after checking his ticket.

Okay, she hadn't missed her stop, which brought him back to the question of the adult. If the person left the girl alone in order to use the toilet, how long did it take to pee or poop? Or, on the other end, even if the adult was buying food and there was a line in the dining car, the other human should have returned by now.

The door at the far end opened, and the same man entered the car for the third time. As soon as the man passed the seats containing human passengers, his eyes focused on the girl in the same way Wolves would focus on an unprotected calf when they were hunting.

Nathan stepped into the aisle and snarled loudly. His fangs lengthened to Wolf size, and his amber eyes flickered with red, the sign of anger. Fur sprang up on his chest and shoulders. Fur covered his hands. His fingers shortened, and his fingernails changed to the sharp Wolf nails that would be more useful in a fight.

A woman sitting near the front of the car looked back at Nathan, sprang out of her seat, and ran from the car. A moment later, a conductor and security guard rushed in.

"What's going on?" the conductor asked.

The security guard's hand hovered over the gun still in its holster.

"Keep this male away from the child," Nathan snarled.

"There's just been a misunderstanding," the man said.

"*He stinks of lust.*" *That* had been the scent the man had been trying to hide beneath the stinky cologne. "If you won't keep him away from her, I will."

No doubt in anyone's mind how *he* would keep the man away.

The conductor stepped forward. "Honey, do you know this man?"

The girl shook her head and held the fake bear in front of her like a shield.

"Sir, come with us," the security guard said tightly. Ignoring the man's protests, the guard led him away.

Nathan didn't know, or care, where they took the man, but the conductor and security guard knew enough about the *terra indigene* not to try to walk the man past *him*.

He stood for a minute, struggling to shift back to looking human enough so the rest of the passengers in the car wouldn't panic. Then, instead of resuming his own seat, he sat down next to the child.

"I'm Nathan Wolfgard." He waited a beat while she stared at him. "Who are you?"

"I'm not supposed to talk to strangers."

That sounded like as good a rule as "Don't tease a skunk," but it wasn't helpful now. "I'm not a stranger; I'm like the Wolf police." He was pleased he'd thought of that as a way to explain being an enforcer for a Courtyard.

Of course, human police didn't tend to eat wrongdoers.

"Oh." She thought for a moment. "I'm Lizzy. And this is Boo Bear. He's my bestest friend." She thrust the fake bear close to Nathan's face.

He jerked his head back and took shallow breaths through his mouth.

Boo Bear needed a bath.

But . . .

Nathan leaned forward and sniffed the bear. Smears of old food around the nose. Peanut butter? Something human smelling that had dried crusty around the ears, as if she'd used the bear to wipe her nose. And then, on the bear's haunch . . .

Blood. Dried now, but the matted fur smelled of blood. If it hadn't been for the man's stinky cologne masking other smells, he would have caught the scent of blood before now.

Nathan took another delicate sniff. Not the girl's blood. The crusty around Boo Bear's ears smelled like her, but the blood didn't.

Nathan eased back, watching her as intensely as she watched him.

"Where's your . . . mother?" Took him a moment to remember the human word.

Lizzy lifted her shoulders in an exaggerated shrug and pulled Boo Bear close again.

"Did she come on the train with you?"

Head shake.

He didn't like that answer. He didn't like it at all. A pup shouldn't be traveling alone. But she had a ticket. In fact, she must have had *two* tickets. Otherwise, the conductor wouldn't have put two LAK strips over the seats.

So. No mother on the train. "Where's your father?" Nathan asked.

Now she perked up. "My daddy is a policeman. He lives in Lakeside."

Nathan studied her. "What is your daddy's name?"

"Crispin James Montgomery. If you're Wolf police, do you know my daddy?"

Nathan watched the conductor enter the car and slowly walk its length. The man didn't stop when he reached their seats, didn't ask any questions, but Nathan had a feeling the conductor and security guard would be walking through the cars a lot during this trip. He'd flushed out one human predator for them, but there could be more, and the guard's presence would keep the young protected.

Boo Bear's nose poked Nathan in the arm.

"Do you know my daddy?" Lizzy asked.

"Yeah. I do." *And I have a feeling he's not expecting you.*

CHAPTER 11

Firesday, Maius 11

Simon stared at the two stinky children who stood between Pete and Eve Denby. Not an unclean kind of stinky; more that there were so many smells covering them he couldn't identify *them*. Not without a closer, and more thorough, sniff that would have the parents snarling at him.

Not that he would blame Pete and Eve for snarling. All the humans who had returned to work this morning were pretending he hadn't been "bite all humans" angry yesterday, but they were as wary of him as they'd been before Meg started working in the Courtyard.

He wondered if there was a way human males said they were sorry about something without *saying* they were sorry. Because he wasn't sorry about being angry. *All* the *terra indigene* were angry about the blood prophet pups being killed. But he was sorry that he'd tried to bite Ruthie and Merri Lee, who weren't the kind of humans who would drown puppies or kittens . . . or babies.

Neither were Pete and Eve Denby, who had shown courage by coming here—and a confidence that their pups would be safe with the Others.

Which brought him back to the children, who looked as if they were waiting for him to sprout fur and grow fangs.

Irritating whelps. As soon as Pete and Eve were gone, he'd chuck them outside. *Caw, caw.*

And having them outside would make it easier for curious *terra indigene* to observe them.

"This is our son, Robert, and our daughter, Sarah," Pete said. "Children, this is Mr. Wolfgard. He runs the bookstore."

"Can you really turn into a wolf?" Robert asked.

"I'm always a Wolf," Simon replied. "Sometimes I shift to look human."

"Can you, like, get furry and stuff?"

Before he could decide if he wanted to answer that—and what did a young human mean by "stuff"?—there was a thump and a yelp at the back of the store. Then Ruthie hurried toward him, looking mussed and agitated, which was odd because she was usually a well-groomed female.

"Mr. Wolfgard?" she said.

First things first. Get the stinky children outside without upsetting the parents since he wanted them to look at the buildings that were for sale across the street. Then he'd deal with the thump and yelp.

"This is Ruthie Stuart, Officer Kowalski's mate. She will show your pups around the Market Square," Simon said.

Sarah giggled. Robert said, "We're not pups; we're kids."

Simon looked at Robert and Sarah, then at Ruthie.

Kids. He'd heard Merri Lee say something about when she was a kid. But the word didn't apply to her now because she was an adult, so it had never occurred to him that, maybe, humans had a little shifter ability that they outgrew as they matured. When she had said kid, maybe she had meant *kid*?

He eyed Robert and Sarah with more interest. "Little humans can shift into young goats?" Kids were tasty. Would human-turned-goat taste different from goat-goat?

"No," Ruthie said firmly. "Humans can't shift into any other form, and while human children are sometimes called kids, they are *never* goats." She took a breath and looked at Robert and Sarah. "It would be better not to use the word 'kid' in the Courtyard because goats are edible and children are not."

Simon watched all the color drain out of Eve Denby's face.

"What time are you supposed to look at the buildings?" he asked.

Pete hesitated, then looked at his wristwatch. "We should go now." He pulled a five-dollar bill from his pocket and held it up as he looked at his boy. "Share that with your sister and get a treat."

Robert took the money.

Another thump from the back room followed by a loud snarled curse. Then

Skippy Wolfgard bolted into the front of the store and spotted the money in Robert's hand.

<Cookie!>

Before Simon could grab him, the juvenile Wolf with the skippy brain snatched the money out of Robert's fingers, took a couple of quick chews, and swallowed.

Shit, fuck, damn, Simon thought. Grabbing Skippy's tail, he hauled the Wolf toward him before glancing at the boy. *No blood, no screaming, no missing fingers.*

As Simon changed his grip to hold Skippy by the scruff, the juvenile's eyes widened in surprise just before he barfed up the money and half a mouse.

Sarah squealed and jumped away from the mess. Robert leaned forward to get a better look.

<Blech cookie,> Skippy said.

"Sorry, sorry." John Wolfgard rushed to the front of the store. "He got away from me."

"He ate a mouse," Robert said, sounding intrigued.

"You ate a worm once and barfed up the worm *and* a penny you must have swallowed along with it." Eve sighed and looked at Simon. "Do you have any rags or something to clean that up?"

"I'll take care of it," Tess said, coming through the archway from A Little Bite.

Simon didn't bother to swear. Tess's hair was solid green and curling, a sign she was agitated about something.

The Denbys stared. Ruthie stood still. Skippy tried to squirm out of Simon's grip and eat the regurgitated mouse.

"You. Go with her." Tess pointed at the children, then at Ruthie. "You two go look at the apartment buildings." She pointed at Pete and Eve, then turned to John. "You take Skippy outside. And *do not tell Meg* he ate a mouse or she won't let him stay with her in the Liaison's Office."

Everyone rushed to obey, leaving him facing Tess over a puddle of barf.

"Find something to do," she said.

This wasn't the time to remind her that he was the leader. He edged around her and headed for the stairs. But he looked back and saw Tess watching him. She did not look happy.

Of course, he wouldn't be happy either if he had to clean up the barf. It smelled worse than the Denby children.

Leaving Jake Crowgard perched on the front counter in the Liaison's Office, Meg dashed over to the Three Ps, the Courtyard shop for paper, postage, and printing. When she'd opened the back door of her office a few minutes ago, she'd seen the lights go on in the shop, so she knew Lorne was getting ready for his workday.

Just need a couple of minutes to check on Lorne and make sure he's okay with being here today, Meg thought as she stepped into the shop. *Just need a few minutes to . . .*

She hadn't been inside the Three Ps. Everything she'd needed to do her work at the Liaison's Office had been provided, from the pens and pencils to the clipboard and pads of paper she used for it. Now she stood frozen just inside the doorway.

No prickling. No pins-and-needles feeling. No sense of prophecy. But as she looked at the sheer number of items on display, she knew entering the shop had been a mistake.

Then Lorne walked out of the back room and saw her. "Meg?"

He started to hurry toward her, then stopped, and she wondered what he saw in her face that made him look so worried.

"Is something wrong?" he asked.

There's no danger here, no threat, Meg thought, feeling panic start to bubble inside her.

"I'll call Simon." Lorne turned toward the counter and the phone.

"No!" Her vehemence surprised both of them. "No," she said again, struggling for control. "Don't call Simon. Not yet. I just need a minute."

She didn't talk to Lorne the way she talked to Merri and Ruth about images and how she and the other *cassandra sangue* had been trained in the compound. If she tried to explain, would he understand?

Only one way to find out.

"I've seen images of office supply stores," she said. "If this was a lesson, I would be shown an overall picture of the inside of the store. Then there would be images of the merchandise—one image to represent a particular kind of thing."

"So you would be shown the outside of an appointment book and maybe an inside page that would show a date?" Lorne asked.

Meg nodded. "We only had the images that the Walking Names wanted us to have, instead of *everything*." She gestured to indicate the shelves of merchandise that filled the walls and the two chest-high units that provided more display space.

Running out of time. She couldn't leave Jake on his own for too long, especially when it was her job to take deliveries.

Lorne looked around. "So without someone setting boundaries, you would try to catalog everything in the shop as different images?"

"Yes. When I lived in the compound, I could have absorbed a whole binder of images during the course of a day. But there are so many things to see in the Courtyard, doing that now would be overwhelming." Information overload. Blanking out because her mind had shut down for a few minutes. Had shut out the images.

Her reaction to being inside the Three Ps was another confirmation that the *cassandra sangue* could absorb only so much before they shut down—or looked for a way to relieve the pressure building inside them.

"Why did you come in?" Lorne asked.

After going inside Sparkles and Junk, she thought she could handle going into the Three Ps, but she couldn't get beyond the doorway. Not today. "I wrote a letter to my friend Jean. She lives on Great Island now. But it was on plain paper and sealed in an envelope."

Had she said anything worth saying in that letter? The act of writing it had absorbed her so much she couldn't remember what she'd said. Had she even said anything anyone else could understand, or had she rambled, caught by the fascination of watching the pen form letters?

Not the same as writing down information about the deliveries. That was simple. And it wasn't the same as keeping lists of books she'd read or music she liked, or even writing a few thoughts about her day. None of those things had the same compulsion to continue just for the sake of continuing.

Suddenly Meg understood why the Crow had cut her hair so short. Like Meg and writing a letter, she had been ensnared by a new experience and hadn't wanted it to end.

"You want some pretty stationary?" Lorne asked. "I have a few selections."

How much time would be lost filling page after page?

"Too much." Meg reached behind her for the door. Had to go back to the office, to the familiar.

"Wait right there." Lorne hurried over to a spin rack near the counter. He quickly selected a handful of items, then returned, holding them out to her. "Postcards. A picture on the front." He turned one over. "And blank on the other side. You put a stamp in this corner, and the person's address here." He pointed to the two places. "The other half is where you write a message. Confined space."

Confined space. The words should have conjured up an image of something she should hate. Instead, she felt relief.

Meg took the postcards. "I owe you money."

"Just take the cards today." Lorne opened the door for her, a gesture she understood meant she was supposed to leave. "We'll settle up later. Besides, it sounds like you've got a delivery," he added as they both heard the sound of a van's side door sliding open, then closing a moment later.

Meg hurried back to the office and reached the Private doorway in time to watch Jake pick up a pen with his beak and offer it to the deliveryman. The man nodded to Meg, took the pen from Jake, and made a notation on the paper attached to her clipboard.

A deliveryman dropping off packages. Familiar. Jake playing the pen game. Familiar.

She looked at the postcards in her hands, fascinated by the photographs of Talulah Falls. All that water pouring over the edge of the world, creating mist and rainbows.

Something new. A confined experience.

Meg dashed to the table in the sorting room and laid out the five postcards, picture side up. Three of them were of Talulah Falls. One was a deer half shrouded by a mist rising from the ground. And the last one . . . Big red rocks rising out of the ground, their tops flat.

Platcaus.

A fizz of excitement filled her. Plateau. Resting place. Stable place where things could stay the same for a while, giving the mind a chance to catch up.

Was that why, after doing so much and absorbing so much, she was struggling now? Living in the Courtyard, she absorbed more images and information in a day than she would have seen in a week at the compound. And even in the compound, although no one would have told the girls why it was done that way, there would be one week of new images, and then the next week they would look at things they had seen before.

Plateau. Resting place. She had done some of that instinctively, reaching for a magazine she'd perused before instead of looking at the new issue. But she hadn't done enough of it because she hadn't considered how important it was to stop *before* she reached overload. From now on, she would give herself more resting places.

And if *she* needed those resting places, so did the other girls—especially the girls who hadn't chosen to live in the outside world.

Meg picked up the phone in the sorting room and called Merri Lee. "Merri? I figured out another bit we need to put in the *Guide*."

CHAPTER 12

Firesday, Maius 11

S teve Ferryman drove out to the Gardner farm. The Simple Life folk didn't have telephones in their houses, and they sure didn't own digital cameras. Or any kind of camera, for that matter.

Would a drawing work as a reference for a blood prophet? Something he needed to ask.

After talking with Simon Wolfgard yesterday, he had taken his personal camera to the B and B where the five young *cassandra sangue* were staying and took pictures of each of the bedrooms—after he and several other men helped Margaret and Lara, the B and B's owners, clear the rooms of everything that wasn't considered essential or part of the room itself. He even took pictures of rooms the girls wouldn't normally see, like the laundry room. Then he took pictures of the outside of the building and the surrounding land—parking lot, grass, gardens, anything he could think of. While he did that, Roger Czerneda, armed with the village's new digital crime scene camera, took pictures of the village shops and public buildings, including the medical center, inside and out.

No one in Ferryman's Landing understood why looking at images instead of the real thing made such a difference to the girls, but it did. And understanding that no change was a small change for these girls helped the adults cope with helping the girls.

"Seeing life secondhand so it doesn't interfere with some damn prophecy," he muttered. Of course, anyone who hadn't seen Meg Corbyn not only functioning but thriving in the tsunami of sensory input that came with being the Human Liaison for the Lakeside Courtyard could understandably conclude that these girls needed a restricted, almost sterile environment in order to stay sane.

But they didn't need sterile. They just needed help adjusting to a world full of sensation. And they needed that help because they'd been *trained* to see the world as images.

Gods, he hoped that was true.

The B and B was a stopgap solution to housing the *cassandra sangue*. He had people working as hard and fast as possible to design and build a home for these girls that would give them a chance to thrive.

And the urgency wasn't just to save the five girls who were here. The girls who were *cassandra sangue* originally came from his own people, the Intuits—people who had such a finely honed sense of the world around them that they knew when something around them might turn good or bad. Some of them could sense a change in the weather before there was any discernible indication. Other Intuits had a sense for animals, knowing when to buy an animal over-looked by everyone else and when to walk away from a deal. Discriminated against and persecuted by humans who didn't want to deal with people who had such a sharp internal gauge, the Intuits had fled into the wild country and made their own bargains with the Others.

Now some Intuits worked as consultants for the *terra indigene*, listening as humans made a proposal to acquire more land, more minerals, more water, more of whatever they wanted that day. Some proposals were honest and sound and would benefit at least some of the *terra indigene* as well as humans. But other proposals offered nothing that the *terra indigene* would want.

Even with that sharp internal gauge, his people had made some bad mistakes in their dealings with other kinds of humans. Generations ago, they had handed over daughters who saw visions and made prophecies when their skin was cut in any way—girls who were driven insane by the things they saw and cut themselves for the euphoria that clouded their minds and made them feel good.

Having discovered what had been done to those girls during all the years since then, Intuit settlements throughout Thaisia were offering to take in the *cassandra sangue* and care for them as best they could.

They needed to learn because the gift, or curse, of prophecy was starting to reappear in Intuit families. Last year, the Sledgeman family here on Great Island had lost a teenage girl who had begun cutting—and threw herself in the Talulah River to escape from visions no one had understood until it was too late.

Yesterday he had typed up the things Simon had told him and e-mailed the information to the network of Intuit settlements in the Northeast Region. Some of them must have been connected to settlements in other parts of Thaisia. By the time he'd returned to download the photos and print out copies for Margaret and Lara to use as a reference, he'd received so many e-mail messages and calls begging for more information and help, he hadn't known what to do. He'd called his mother, Rachel, and Penny Sledgeman, his friend Jerry's wife, to help reply to the e-mail and return phone calls. As the mayor of Ferryman's Landing, he requested a meeting with Simon Wolfgard—and wasn't surprised to learn that Wolfgard wasn't returning calls.

But all those things were the reason he was driving out to the Gardners' farm a day later to talk with them and the one other *cassandra sangue* who had been brought out of the Midwest compound that had been run by the Controller: Jean, the blood prophet who had helped Meg Corbyn escape.

Parking near the house, Steve picked up the digital camera and got out just as Lorna Gardner walked around the side of the house, followed by her two children. He hadn't expected to see James. Every family had their own allotment of land, but the Simple Life farmers worked together for the sowing and harvesting, and it was the growing season.

Lorna took him to the guest cottage, a smaller version of the main house.

"Jean?" Lorna called, opening the door just enough to be heard. "Steve Ferryman would like to talk to you. Can you do that?"

She took a step back and lowered her voice. "If you have answers . . ."

"I have some," Steve replied. "But it will mean allowing some technology into your home. Not equipment you'll have to use, but you'll need the results."

After a thoughtful moment, Lorna nodded. "If it will help her."

"Come in," Jean said.

"Come to the house when you're done," Lorna said, stepping aside.

Steve entered the cottage, standing in the doorway while his eyes adjusted to the dark room. All the curtains were closed. All the windows were closed. No light. No fresh air.

"Close the door," Jean snapped.

He closed the door and leaned against it.

"How are you?" he asked.

"I wanted this," she said. "From the day I was brought to that compound and given a designation, I wanted to live outside; I wanted to be a person again instead of property. But I didn't realize it would be this hard." She hesitated. "How is Meg?"

"Meg is fine. She and her friends in the Lakeside Courtyard have found some answers that, hopefully, will make things easier for all the blood prophets who have left the compounds."

"She sent me a letter. I haven't opened it yet."

"Why not?"

"Just receiving a letter was one new thing too many that day."

"Maybe you should read it soon."

The curtains didn't block all the light. Now that his eyes had adjusted, he could see her sitting at a simple wood table, turning her silver razor over and over in her hands.

His heart gave one hard bump, then seemed to freeze in his chest for a long moment before it started beating again.

"What I'd like to do is open the curtains and get enough light in here to take pictures of the rooms," he said. "Then I'll take pictures of the Gardners' house and the barn and other buildings. I'll take pictures of the animals."

"So I can stay in here and see outside through images?"

He heard bitter, weary resignation in her voice.

"It's reference so that going outside and seeing the real thing isn't as much of a shock. Meg and the women working with her to create a guide for blood prophets suggested this. We did this for the girls staying at the B and B, and it helped them. Today I'm here to do the same for you, if you'll let me."

"Meg, the Pathfinder," Jean said softly. "Meg, the Trailblazer. All right, Steve Ferryman. Show me the first trail marker." She gave him a strange smile. "I don't know what such a thing is or what it does, but it was one of the training images."

"You never saw it in context?"

Her smile chilled him. "That would have provided too much information."

In the compound, she had been battered and abused in almost every way one person could abuse another. He'd heard, in confidence from one of the island's doctors, that she had a crosshatching of scars over several parts of her body and, in some places, layers of scar tissue.

Was she sane? No one wanted to make a diagnosis one way or the other. As long as she wasn't a threat to the Gardners, the doctors and the *terra indigene* were willing to let her stay in the guest cottage.

Steve held up the camera. "Start of a new life, Jean, and a way to live outside again. Ready to try?"

She pushed away from the table. "I'm ready." She paused. "And while you take the pictures out there, I will write a short note to Meg."

CHAPTER 13

"The two apartment buildings are in pretty good shape," Pete Denby said, sitting at one of the tables in A Little Bite. "Eve says all the apartments need sprucing up—fresh paint and wallpaper, that sort of thing."

"Nothing the new tenants couldn't do for themselves," Eve said. "You might want to hire a professional to check out the buildings, but we didn't see any structural problems."

"Then why sell the buildings?" Simon asked. Elliot, Tess, Henry, and Vlad had joined him in the coffee shop to hear the Denbys' report. Since she was a member of the Business Association, he'd told Jenni Crowgard about this meeting, but she'd expressed no interest in joining them. That troubled him a little, but hearing about something wasn't the same as having the opportunity to poke around someplace new, so maybe it was all the *blah, blah* that wasn't of interest to the Crows.

"Lack of tenants," Pete said. "The current owner of the buildings is behind on the mortgage payments because he's not getting the rental income he needs. Each building has four two-bedroom apartments. Only half those units are occupied now, and *all* the tenants will be out by the end of the month, with no new ones moving in."

"The owner and the real estate representative didn't put it in quite those terms," Eve said. "They talked about potential and a clean sweep—new landlord, new tenants. They were very careful not to say why tenants didn't stay. Like

I said, Pete and I didn't see any sign of insect infestation or water damage or any structural reason why people wouldn't want to live in those apartments."

"Mayor Rogers told me the other day that there was a housing shortage in Lakeside," Elliot said. "If that's true, why are acceptable dens still empty?"

Pete looked uncomfortable. "Location."

"Meaning the humans suddenly object to living so close to the Courtyard?" Vlad asked with chilling politeness.

"The real estate representative didn't say *that*," Eve said. She glanced at Pete. "But we both had the impression that was the reason the apartments hadn't been filled when the previous tenants moved out at the end of last year—and why the existing tenants are leaving."

Pete removed a piece of paper from his inner jacket pocket. "This is the asking price for each building. We did inquire about property taxes and the average cost of utilities. I think we were being told optimistic numbers."

"More like numbers based on having two apartments in use in each building, and none of the tenants having children," Eve said. "I'd double the figures for utilities for each building, minimum."

"When asked, I told the owner that I was the attorney representing a business association that was looking at the buildings for an investment and income property," Pete said. "One question I couldn't answer was how my client intended to pay for the property."

Simon frowned. "We give them money. They give us the papers that say we own the buildings. How else would we pay for it?" Did Pete think they would just take what wasn't theirs? The Others in the Courtyard weren't *that* human, no matter how well they could assume the form.

Then again, even animals fought among themselves to hold on to, or acquire more, territory.

"They were asking how you were going to finance the purchase," Pete said. "Can the *terra indigene* get a mortgage from a bank?"

"Why would we want this mortgage when we have money?" Henry asked.

"Cash? You're thinking of paying cash for both buildings?" Pete blinked. "Do you understand the asking price?"

Simon studied Pete and decided the man wasn't trying to insult his education. "The city of Lakeside and all the farms that support it stand on land that is leased from the *terra indigene* through the Lakeside Courtyard. A quarter of the rent is due each season. We don't need this mortgage thing. We have money."

Eve stared at him.

Pete gave him an odd smile. "The land for a small town, like the one Eve and I lived in before coming here, is leased as a whole. The boundaries are set before the population grows to fill it, and the lease on all that land expires at the same time. But a city like Lakeside would have grown by parcels. Whether you call it willful optimism or a desire not to call attention to a basic truth, I don't think the government ever negotiated with the *terra indigene* to consolidate those leases. Which means the land leases for different parts of Lakeside come up for renewal at different times."

"Yes, they do," Simon agreed.

Eve looked at Pete, then at Simon. "So what would happen if you didn't renew the lease?"

"Humans would have to move off the reclaimed land," Simon replied. "Just like the humans who had to leave the village of Jerzy when it was reclaimed by the *terra indigene* who take care of the West Coast Region."

"Then all you have to do is wait for the lease to expire on the lots across the street. Once you reclaim the land, no one could live in those buildings without your permission," Pete said.

"What you say is true," Henry agreed. "But the land lease that includes those lots doesn't expire for a few more years, and Ruthie and Kowalski need a place to live now. Since the buildings are for sale, we have decided to do this the human way and purchase them."

"In that case, you should know that the woman who lives in the double between the other two buildings asked if my client would be interested in buying her house too," Pete said. "Eve took a quick look while I kept the apartment owner occupied."

"It's a two-family wood house, with one flat above the other," Eve said. "The upper flat had been occupied by the woman's son and his family, but the son recently took a job in a place called Hubbney. Is that really a town name? Anyway, the flats have three bedrooms, living room, dining room, kitchen, and bath. There is off-street parking behind each of the buildings, as well as on-street parking on Crowfield Avenue. Not much land for gardens and such."

"That wouldn't be a problem," Simon said.

"Tenants might appreciate being able to grow a few vegetables. Anyone trying to feed a family will want to grow a bit of food in order to pay for things like bread, which doubled in price in the past week and is becoming a luxury item."

Bread was a luxury item? That didn't sound right. Then again, he ate bread only when it was part of a meal served at Meat-n-Greens or when he picked up a sandwich at A Little Bite.

Simon looked at Tess, but she was studying Eve.

<Is bread a luxury item?> he asked Tess.

<I thought it was a basic food, the sort of thing every human ate,> she replied. <If something has happened on human farms to change that . . .>

<If you hear anything, let me know.> He'd rather eat fresh deer than fresh bread, but Meg should have bread whenever she wanted it.

Eve pulled a piece of paper out of her purse and handed it to Simon. "Anyway, that's what Mrs. Tremaine would like for her house, but she wants to relocate soon to be with her son, so she'll take any reasonable offer."

Simon walked to the windows and studied the buildings across the street. <If we buy all three, we would own all the buildings on that block, except the commercial building that faces Main Street,> he said to the other *terra indigene*.

<That's a lot of humans,> Henry said.

<Maybe.> He turned. "You. Handyman Eve. Could you live in that house?"

"The two-family? Sure," Eve said. "Needs a little work, but nothing I couldn't do. Of course . . ." She looked at Pete. "I doubt we could afford to rent a place that size. Not right now."

"You wouldn't pay rent. You would be the manager who took care of the buildings for us."

Pete and Eve looked like a pony had kicked them in the head. He wished they didn't look that way. He'd feel better about the plan that was taking shape if he was confident that their brains would keep working.

"You're offering me a job as your property manager?" Eve finally said.

"Yes. And Pete could be our attorney when we have to deal with human matters."

<Simon!> That came from Tess, Elliot, and Vlad. But not, he noted, from Henry.

"We will buy the buildings, and you will take care of them," he said.

"What about tenants?" Pete asked. "Are you going to advertise that you have apartments for rent?"

He knew by the look in their eyes that he no longer passed for human.

"No," he said. "We will choose who lives on our land."

Pete blew out a breath. "In that case, let's talk about what kind of offer you want to make for each building."

Henry looked at Simon and nodded. After a moment, so did Tess and Vlad. Elliot wasn't part of the Business Association, but he would have to deal with Lakeside's government. When the Wolf nodded, Simon focused on Pete and Eve. "Yes, let's talk."

After agreeing with what Pete and Eve needed to do next in order to purchase the buildings, Simon walked them to the Market Square, where they collected their children and then drove away. When he returned to HGR, he wasn't surprised that Vlad, Tess, and Henry followed him up to the office, but he hadn't expected Blair Wolfgard to slip in behind them.

"You can tell me about this later," Blair said. "I just wanted to let you know that Nathan is on his way home and wants me to pick them up at the train station this afternoon."

"Them?" Simon said. Human ears just didn't prick properly to show interest. "Nathan found a mate?"

Blair hesitated. "Didn't sound like it. But he is bringing someone with him." The Courtyard's primary enforcer walked out of the office, closing the door behind him.

"Is it wise to become so entangled with humans?" Henry asked.

"Our *terra indigene* ancestors allowed some humans to settle in Thaisia. Were they wise?" Simon countered. "Maybe not. But they made that choice, and we have to find a way to live with the humans who are here now."

"*They* have to find a way to live with *us*," Tess said. "While some pieces of the world belong to humans, Thaisia was, is, and always will belong to the *terra indigene*."

"I agree," Henry said. "And it is the humans who *are* trying to live with us who are under discussion."

"So what choice are we making for Lakeside?" Vlad asked.

"Balance," Simon said. "Talulah Falls has been reclaimed, and the *terra indi-*

gene are now in control of that town. They allowed the tourists who survived the reclaiming to leave. They also allowed the students who were attending the university to leave. But they're holding the adults who live in Talulah Falls responsible for the explosion that killed several Crows and for the insane human who killed one of the Sanguinati. Those people are working, and living, in fear."

"You could say that most humans in Thaisia are living in fear, except those who live in the largest cities and are willfully blind to the truth of what it means to be a human living on *terra indigene* land," Vlad said.

"This is different. There has never been so much anger toward humans that we held some captive." He saw the small, uneasy movements they all made. The *terra indigene* killed humans as meat or killed them as enemies or rival predators. They destroyed cities when humans became too much of a threat. But they had never held humans captive within a town before the troubles in Talulah Falls.

Simon rubbed the back of his neck, trying to ease tight muscles. How human was too human? There was always a risk of absorbing too much of a form. Is that what happened to the Others who accepted the task of controlling Talulah Falls? Had they absorbed too much human behavior?

They're behaving with those humans the way the Controller behaved with Meg and the other blood prophets.

He shook his head, as if that would shake out the thought before it had a chance to burrow. "The Wolves, Crows, and all the other earth natives who live in Courtyards are the buffer between humans and the rest of the *terra indigene*. The humans who are being branded Wolf lovers are a buffer between us and the rest of the humans."

"There aren't that many of them, so it's not much of a buffer," Tess said.

"But those who are trying to work with us are being driven out of their dens," Simon said. "If we don't help them, someone else will offer them what they need for themselves and the young they'll have. Someone else will offer food and shelter and give those humans a reason to feel loyalty."

"And the River Road Community?" Henry asked.

"I don't want to lease any of that land to humans again, but having some humans living there along with *terra indigene* would give humans a reason to protect that land too." He paused, then added, "And I'm going to increase the pay for all the humans who still work for us. They are all doing more work now, and different kinds of work. They should get more money."

"You're making a lot of decisions on your own," Vlad said. "And you're making a lot of changes very fast. Maybe too fast."

"I *am* the leader," Simon snarled. But Vlad did have a point. Once they had secured the River Road land and the human dens across from the Courtyard, everyone needed time to adjust to the changes. Including him.

A beat of silence before Vlad said, "Yes, you are the leader." The Sanguinati glanced at the Grizzly.

"Floodwaters can trap you," Henry said, looking troubled. "Sometimes there is a storm in the distance, and it looks too far away to matter until the water comes raging through your own territory, sweeping away what you thought was safe."

Simon nodded. "A storm in the distance, but we're starting to feel it here. Things between humans and Others have changed in the past few months. The Controller was making drugs from the blood of *cassandra sangue*. The fights between humans and Others that were caused by those drugs were the start of the floodwaters. Now humans are talking about being *entitled* to land, to water, to wood, to whatever they want. And there is that group calling itself the Humans First and Last movement goading humans into doing things that will turn the *terra indigene* against them. And bread is becoming a luxury. Why?"

"Maybe that's something you should ask Meg the next time she makes a controlled cut," Tess said.

Simon and Vlad snarled at her.

Her hair immediately turned red with black threads and began coiling. "Be careful, vampire," she warned, looking at Vlad.

"Yes, the next cut should be a controlled cut," Henry said. Though he spoke quietly, his rumbling voice drowned out the snarls. "It was different from the ones our Meg made when she was upset. It didn't strain her body like the other cuts did."

"How could you tell?" Vlad asked.

Henry smiled. "The weather has warmed enough that she opened the window in the sorting room when she started her work. I could hear her singing." He thought for a moment. "Well, it was a happy sound anyway."

"Fine," Tess said, the black threads fading from her hair. "Humans aren't the enemy anymore."

"Oh, most of them are still enemies and meat," Simon said. "But I think this plan will help us identify the few who aren't."

CHAPTER 14

Firesday, Maius 11

For the second time in two days, Monty joined Captain Burke and Pete Denby for a meeting behind closed doors.

"It's unprecedented," Burke said after Pete told them about looking at the apartments and the subsequent job offers from Simon Wolfgard. "Of course, Wolfgard has been a progressive leader ever since he took over the Lakeside Courtyard."

"Did you have the sense they want to expand the Courtyard?" Monty asked.

Pete shook his head. "No, but I do think he's focused on the survival of the Courtyard's residents. That makes me wonder what he knows that we don't."

Burke opened his hands in a "Who knows?" gesture. "They have a blood prophet. And while Wolfgard has shared information he's gotten from Meg Corbyn, I wouldn't assume he shares all of it. On the other hand, there is no other police force on the whole continent who interacts with the *terra indigene* the way we do, and Lieutenant Montgomery and his team are largely responsible for that. So anything the rest of us can do to keep that communication open is an avenue I'd like to explore."

"Have to admit, I'm kind of curious too," Pete said. "So is Eve."

"You concerned about the children?" Burke asked.

"Some. But I'm more worried about what other humans might do than what the *terra indigene* will do," Pete said. "Anyone else notice how yesterday's news stories about police and Others cooperating to locate and help those abandoned girls have been replaced by reports about the desperate situation in Talulah Falls and how every regional government is reviewing the ration books to determine what foods will be added in anticipation of shortages? Since I doubt there are many Others who pay attention to human news reports, it seems like someone doesn't want us to see any proof that we can get along. And that scares me. Humans don't own so much as an acre of land on this entire continent. We can build or farm on the land that is leased; we can extract minerals and fuels; we can harvest timber. Most of the land leases are twenty or twenty-five years for villages and small towns. They get renewed so quietly I doubt anyone but government officials, and lawyers, even think about it anymore. Or they didn't until the *terra indigene* refused to renew the lease for Jerzy and all the humans were forced to leave that village. The occasional mention of a city land lease during a government meeting is brushed aside so fast you're not even sure you heard the words. People in my old town were shocked when they realized that the Others take those leases seriously and are willing to evict any tenants they view as too troublesome to tolerate."

"Maybe that's partly what's behind the talk about shortages," Monty said. "Maybe some of the leases on tracts of farmland are coming due, and the governments aren't sure that the leases will be renewed this time."

Burke nodded. "That's a possibility. The water tax here helps everyone remember who owns the water that supplies the city. But Pete is right about people forgetting about the leases. Lakeside has been around long enough that most people don't read the fine print that says when they buy a house, they're buying the building and not the parcel of land it stands on."

"Eve and I spent the rest of the morning talking it over," Pete said. "And frankly, we talked about looking at another town in the Northeast or somewhere in the Southeast Region."

"You think those places would be safer?" Monty asked.

"No, we don't. That's why I'm going to accept the job of being the Others' attorney for human concerns and Eve is going to work for them as an apartment manager."

"Smart move," Burke said. "I'll give you what help I can."

Monty looked at Pete. "Before you go, I'd like to ask . . . If you're working for the Courtyard, will you—*can* you—also take on other clients?"

"Lieutenant?" Burke asked, rising to his feet.

"Simon Wolfgard didn't say I couldn't," Pete said. "And I don't think they have enough business for me to make a living if I don't take other clients. Why? Do you need a lawyer?"

Monty nodded. "I'm worried about my daughter. For a while, my ex was talking about relocating to someplace in Cel-Romano to live with Nicholas Scratch and his family."

"Scratch?" Pete looked at Monty, then at Burke. "The HFL speaker?"

"The same," Burke said grimly. "Scratch is still in Toland making his speeches. Gods above and below, you can't listen to a news report without hearing the bastard making one of his speeches."

"Since Scratch is in Toland, it stands to reason that Elayne is there too," Monty said. "But I haven't been able to reach her for the past couple of days." He tried to hold in the words, but they burst out. "It's bad enough that she invited Scratch to move in with her so soon after meeting him, but Lizzy is just as much my daughter as hers, and I do not want Elayne taking Lizzy across the Atlantik to live with a man I don't trust. Gods! Nicholas Scratch is an alias. We can't even find out who he is and if he really is from a wealthy Cel-Romano family as he claims."

"You think he said that to sound more credible?" Pete asked.

"We don't know," Burke replied.

Monty pulled the papers out of the inside pocket of his suit coat and handed them to Pete. "These are copies of Lizzy's birth certificate and the legal papers Elayne had drawn up for child support."

"No other legal agreements between you and Elayne?" Pete asked.

"We weren't married, if that's what you're asking."

Pete tucked the papers in his briefcase. "All right. I'll look into what options you have to gain some kind of custody, or, at the very least, prevent Elayne from taking Lizzy beyond Thaisia."

"Thank you." If he did gain some kind of custody, would his mother be willing to relocate and help him take care of Lizzy? Something else to think about.

Monty's mobile phone rang. "This is Montgomery."

"Lieutenant." Something odd about Simon Wolfgard's voice. "Come to the Courtyard. *Now*. We have something that belongs to you."

Pater,

Payment for merchandise was misdirected. Location known, but re-
trieval will be difficult. First shipment of merchandise will be sent in good
faith.

—NS

CHAPTER 15

Firesday, Maius 11

"Why do I have to play with a human?" Sam asked again as Meg reached for the back door of A Little Bite.

She stepped away from the door and bent over, bracing her hands on her thighs so that she and Sam were eye to eye. The way he was growing, she wouldn't need to do that much longer. Or maybe this growth spurt would plateau soon. None of the Others would talk about what the *terra indigene* looked like before taking on the forms that separated them into various gards and gave each group particular traits, but Meg had the impression that Sam's growth wasn't based on how quickly or slowly wolves or humans grew to maturity; it was based on how the *terra indigene*'s mysterious first form matured.

"We're not playing with her, exactly," Meg said. "We're just going to have a snack and keep her company until Lieutenant Montgomery arrives."

"Because he's her sire?"

"Yes." She touched his arm, a moment of contact. "She's all alone, Sam, and she's too young to have come all that way on a train by herself."

Simon hadn't told her much, but he'd said enough. Lizzy Montgomery might not have reached Lakeside if Nathan hadn't been on that train and riding in the same car.

Sam looked at the ground between their feet before asking in a small voice, "Did something happen to her mom?"

Simon said there's some dried blood on Lizzy's toy bear, Meg thought. *Sam is a Wolf pup. He's bound to smell it.*

"We don't know what happened to Lizzy's mom," she said. "But Simon and Lieutenant Montgomery will find out."

Now he reached out, a fingertip touch on her arm. "Are you going to have to bleed?"

He didn't know about the *cassandra sangue*'s addiction to cutting, but he did know that she cut herself in order to see visions.

"No. Whatever happened has already happened. I . . . cut . . . when it's important to see what *might* happen. Like when those men attacked the Courtyard and I knew before they arrived that you had to stay with Mr. Erebus because you'd be safe with him."

"And you knew when that box of sugar lumps would make the ponies sick."

"Yes."

Apparently satisfied that nothing would happen to *his* pack, he eyed her head with unnerving interest.

"Can I feel your fur?" he asked.

"It's not fur; it's hair."

"Uh-huh. Can I feel it?"

Bad enough she'd shocked herself with this new haircut, but every Wolf, Crow, Hawk, Owl, and Sanguinati she'd seen yesterday had stared at her. Jester Coyote-gard had trotted over from the Pony Barn to get a look—and then gleefully raced back to report to the girls at the lake. Even the ponies, who were the Courtyard's mail carriers and the Elementals' steeds, had been more interested in lipping what was left of her hair than in eating the carrot chunks she had for their treat.

"Why?" she said. "It's the same as it was before."

"Uh-uuuh."

Meg huffed out a breath. "Fine. You can feel it."

"It's soft and thick," Sam said, running his hand over her hair. "Feels like Wolf."

The soft, and deliberate, scuff of a shoe on the ground just behind her.

Meg snapped upright and whirled around.

"Simon." She tried—and failed—to recall a training image that matched the look on his face. Baffled annoyance with a touch of hurt feelings?

"Wait for us inside, pup," he said. "And don't shift in front of the little human."

Big gusty sigh. Then, having made his point about being put upon by entertaining a *human*, Sam opened the door and slipped inside A Little Bite.

"I should . . ." Meg pointed at the door.

"You growl at me because I want to feel your hair, but you don't even grumble at him?"

Definitely some hurt feelings.

"He's a puppy!" she protested.

"So?"

"Well . . . but . . ."

"I don't growl at you when *you* want to pet my fur," Simon said.

"But . . . that's different!"

"How?"

Meg opened her mouth to explain exactly how it was different—and couldn't think of anything to say. It *was* different, wasn't it? He never objected when she ran her fingers through his fur. He was a Wolf. And fluffy. Less fluffy now that he'd shed his winter coat, but still!

Had she been intruding on what a magazine article called personal space without realizing it? He'd never objected, but he'd never actually given her permission to pet him.

She looked at him patiently waiting for an explanation and realized he didn't see a difference between his tactile curiosity and hers. And right now she couldn't figure out the difference either.

"Fine," she muttered.

Not like Sam's touch. Simon's larger hand slowly moved over her head, those strong fingers finding the spot behind her ear where the muscles were tight. Pressing. Circling. Coaxing the muscles to yield and relax.

She swayed. Didn't even realize he'd moved until her forehead rested against his chest.

"Oh," she breathed. "No wonder you just lie there when we're watching a movie."

His breath ruffled her hair when he said laughingly, "Well, yeah."

Too soon Simon lowered his hand and stepped back. "Sam's getting impatient—and curious now that he's gotten a look at the Lizzy. You should go in. The Lizzy wouldn't tell Nathan what happened to her mother, but she might tell you."

Meg nodded and walked into A Little Bite.

Not just Lizzy, *the* Lizzy.

Ruth was the one who had realized the *terra indigene* had a verbal hierarchy they used when talking about humans, a way of indicating the degree of interaction with an individual. Ruth had been the Ruthie when she'd been a customer at Howling Good Reads, but since she'd started working in the Courtyard, she was just Ruthie. Meg was Meg, the Meg, or our Meg depending on who was talking to her or about her.

And humans the Others didn't like had "that" added to their names.

Simon came in behind her and gave her a gentle nudge, which made her realize she'd stopped moving while she pondered name distinctions.

As she walked up the hallway that led from the back door to the front of the shop, she pictured the customer area of A Little Bite with its tables and the counter where Tess worked. She pictured Sam sitting at one of the tables. She hadn't seen Lizzy yet, so she recalled a training image of a young girl. Now she had some idea of what to expect.

Then she heard a young female voice say, "Bad dog!" She heard the *whap* of two things connecting, followed by a yelp. And then Skippy bolted down the hallway and almost knocked her over in his haste to escape.

"You should deal with that," Simon said, giving her another nudge. He turned and went out the back door with Skippy.

Deal with what? How many things had she dealt with because Simon assumed that she could? And how many things had she dealt with because she didn't want Simon to know that she couldn't?

Something to think about another day.

Shaking her head, Meg walked into the coffee shop's front room.

"I'm making grilled cheese sandwiches," Tess said. "You're the referee. You can tell Miss Lizzy over there that Boo Bear does not get his own sandwich. He'll have to settle for a bite of hers."

Since Tess's hair was green and curling, Meg didn't argue and she didn't ask. But she wondered why no one had mentioned that a member of the Beargard was visiting the Courtyard.

Sam, who had been standing near the counter, grabbed Meg's hand and whispered loudly, "She whacked Skippy. With a *bear.*"

The pup sounded impressed. Meg felt confused.

Unable to recall any training image that would match what Sam had said, she whispered, "Come on, let's introduce ourselves." Holding his hand, she walked up to the table where the girl watched them. "I'm Meg. This is Sam. Can we sit with you?"

The girl nodded. "I'm Lizzy. This is Boo Bear."

Looking at Boo Bear, Meg understood why he wasn't going to get his own sandwich. She just hoped Lizzy understood the difference between Boo Bear and a real bear.

Tess came over and set two plates on the table. Both held a grilled cheese sandwich cut in half and a sprig of red grapes. "I'm bringing yours," she told Meg. Then she looked at Lizzy and Sam. "Sit down. Eat. Try not to cause a riot."

Was that supposed to be amusing? Meg wondered.

Sam sat on the edge of a chair, one foot on the floor in case he needed to make a quick escape. He picked up one half of his sandwich and took a bite, all the while watching the girl and bear.

Meg took a seat and thanked Tess when the third plate of food and three glasses of water were placed on the table. For a minute, she savored the experience of eating—the taste and texture of toasted bread and melted cheese, the crisp sweetness of the grapes.

After she'd eaten half the sandwich, she focused on the girl. What to say? What to do? What if something bad *had* happened?

Of course something bad happened, Meg thought. *Lizzy is here, alone. Sort of. The police should be the ones who ask about that. But I need to say something.*

Then she knew exactly what to say because she'd had a similar experience a few months ago.

"How did you like riding the train?" Meg asked. She addressed the question to Lizzy, but it felt like she was talking to the team of Lizzy and Boo Bear.

Lizzy took a bite of her sandwich before pressing the toast and grilled cheese against the spot where Boo Bear's mouth would be. When she raised the sandwich to take another bite, Meg tried to ignore the toast crumbs and dollop of cheese clinging to the fur.

"It was okay," Lizzy said. "Boo Bear was scared for a while because there was a bad man on the train. But the Wolf police chased him away."

Meg blinked. "The what?"

While sandwiches were devoured, the story of Nathan scaring off the bad man segued to Sam talking about the Wolf Team movie he'd watched recently. At first Meg wondered if the story would be too scary for a human Lizzy's age. After all, watching those movies scared *her*. However, after a few minutes of listening to the two children arguing about who was stronger—the Wolf Team or a group of girls who sounded more like tiny Elementals than young humans with special powers—Meg wasn't sure if the term "bloodthirsty" should be applied to the youngster who preferred eating his meat raw.

He had his mobile phone, house keys, wallet, and police ID. Since he couldn't figure out what he'd left at the Courtyard that needed to be retrieved so urgently, Monty focused on his partner.

"What are you and Ruth going to do?" Monty asked, referring to the forced move from the new apartment.

"Store some of our stuff with my folks and some in Ruthie's parents' house. And hope we can find another place quickly," Kowalski replied. "Narrow-minded, shortsighted . . ." He stopped.

Monty waited a beat. "Are you talking about your soon-to-be-ex-landlord or your parents?"

Kowalski didn't reply until they stopped at a traffic light. "My folks will help because we're family and that's what families do. But they aren't happy about why I'm being shown the door. When my brother said he wouldn't want to live in the same building with Wolf lovers, my parents didn't say a thing. That amounts to tacit agreement. And with all the news about troubled girls committing suicide, and with the *terra indigene* being blamed for so many of those halfway houses closing because the administrators were afraid to keep them open, well, that's another reason not to side with monsters, no matter what they look like. And then having the surviving girls taken to undisclosed locations . . . There can only be one reason for that, right?"

"Most people aren't going to want to admit that the monsters in this case not only look human but are human." Monty hesitated but decided he needed to ask, needed to know. "Karl, do you want a transfer?"

Kowalski made the left turn on to Main Street, then turned again to pull into the Courtyard's delivery area.

"No, sir, I don't," he said. "And Ruthie doesn't want to walk away from her job in the Courtyard. We both believe that if push comes to shove, the kind of interaction we have with the Others now could help Lakeside remain a human-controlled city instead of turning into a cage like Talulah Falls. So we'll stick."

"And hope that your parents will come around to your way of thinking?"

"That's not likely. But they haven't said—yet—that they won't be at Ruthie's and my wedding next month."

Monty heard the bitter resignation in his partner's voice and regretted the rift growing in families. What would happen in the city if the allure of the Humans First and Last movement caused a rift between police officers? Would stations polarize to the point where you couldn't count on your own for assistance?

"Come on," Monty said as he opened his door. "Let's find out what ruffled Wolfgard's fur."

They used the back door at Howling Good Reads. Nothing unusual in the stock room, except a noticeable lack of stock. But there was a crowd at the archway leading into A Little Bite.

Simon, Nathan, and Blair turned to look at him. Simon handed a pencil and pad of paper to Nathan, then moved away from the door, tipping his head to indicate Monty should follow.

"Something of interest?" Monty asked.

"The Lizzy," Simon replied.

He must have heard wrong. "Lizzy and her mother are *here*? *My* Lizzy?"

"No, the Lizzy and Boo Bear are here."

He felt the blood drain out of his head. "What about her mother? Where is Elayne?"

"That's a good question, Lieutenant." Simon studied him. "Is it usual for a pup that young to travel alone? We wouldn't do it, but . . ."

"Of course it isn't usual," Monty snapped. He heard a soft growl and wasn't sure if the warning came from Nathan or Blair. "No," he said, struggling to bring his voice back to calm courtesy while his heart pounded. Lizzy here alone? How? Why? "She's only seven years old. A girl that age wouldn't be, *shouldn't be*, traveling alone. Did she say anything about her mother?"

Simon looked grim. "No. But there's some blood on Boo Bear, and it doesn't smell like the Lizzy."

Gods above and below. "Where . . . ?"

"She's in A Little Bite having a snack with Sam and Meg."

"She's not hurt?"

"No." Something in Wolfgard's eyes. "No" wasn't a lie, but it didn't fill in the whole truth.

"Can I ask?" Kowalski stepped up to join them. "How did Lizzy end up here in the Courtyard?"

"Nathan was on the same train. When he realized there weren't any adults with her, he . . . guarded . . . her and brought her here."

His little girl had needed a guard. Would he have received a different kind of phone call if a Wolf hadn't been on the train? How life circled around. He'd been transferred to Lakeside because he had killed a man in order to protect a girl who was a Wolf. And now a Wolf had come to the aid of his own little girl.

He would make a special visit to the Universal Temple and light an extra candle for Mikhos, the guardian spirit who watched over policemen, firefighters, and medical personnel. And, it seemed, watched over their families too.

"I want to see her," Monty said.

"Go ahead."

Bland words that made him stop and consider. He wanted to see Lizzy and needed the reassurance that she was all right, but he wondered why three grown Wolves were crowding around an archway instead of going into the coffee shop and taking a seat at another table.

"Are you standing at the archway to avoid scaring Lizzy?" Monty asked.

Nathan and Blair snorted a laugh.

Simon stared at Monty. "We're standing there because, for a small human, the Lizzy is territorial. She's already whacked Skippy for coming over to take a sniff, and we can hear everything just fine from the archway." He paused. "Besides, Boo Bear really stinks."

Kowalski coughed.

The Wolves made room for Monty to stand in the archway and observe his daughter. She seemed fine, chatting away with Sam and Meg, pausing every so often to relay a comment from that silly bear.

Gods, Elayne had been furious with him when he came back from an outing with Lizzy and had that bear instead of the doll Elayne had said would be a suitable toy. But Lizzy hadn't wanted a doll. She'd focused on that furry brown bear, pulling it off a shelf she could barely reach and holding on so fiercely he'd had the choice of taking the bear or leaving the child.

The dolls were dutifully played with when Elayne insisted Lizzy play with something that looked human, but it was Boo Bear, her bestest friend, who went everywhere with the girl.

Apparently that was still true, despite Elayne's infatuation with Nicholas Scratch and his damn HFL movement.

Meg looked toward the archway. "Lizzy," she said as she pointed.

Lizzy turned and saw him. "Daddy!" She scrambled out of her chair and ran to him, dumping Boo Bear on the floor.

Monty dropped to his knees and wrapped his arms around her.

"Lizzy." He kissed her cheek, her forehead. "Lizzy girl. You okay, baby?"

"We're okay. We were on the train, and there was a bad man, and the Wolf police scared him away!"

Monty looked up at Nathan. "Thank you."

The Wolf shrugged. "Should have . . ." He glanced at the girl and stopped.

"Nathan's teeth got really big," Lizzy said. "I *saw* them!"

One of the Wolves behind him sighed.

"Lizzy, where's your mother?" Monty asked.

Her eyes held a blend of guilt and fear, an expression he knew well. She looked that way anytime something happened because she'd been doing something she'd been told not to do. Lizzy understood that actions had consequences. She just didn't want to believe that applied to her. Of course, his transfer, and the disruption in all their lives, was a powerful example of actions and consequences. "Lizzy?"

"Mommy got hurt. She said I needed to be a big girl and go on the train by myself. Me and Boo Bear."

Hurt could mean a lot of things to a child. "Where did she get hurt?"

Lizzy placed a hand over her belly.

"No!" Meg shouted.

Monty looked up. Lizzy turned and yelled, "Bad dog!" and ran toward the table just as Skippy grabbed one of Boo Bear's stubby front legs and tried to run off with the prize.

"I'll get him!" Sam said. He pushed down his shorts, yanked the T-shirt over his head, shifted into Wolf form, and rushed at Skippy, chasing the juvenile Wolf in and around the tables, both of them banging into chairs.

Lizzy ran back to the table, grabbed the last bite of her sandwich, and threw it at Skippy, distracting him just long enough for Sam to get his teeth into one of Boo Bear's back legs.

The fierce game of tug only lasted a few seconds before seams split and Skippy darted under a table with a fuzzy front leg. Sam dropped the torn back leg, grabbed the rest of the bear, and brought it back to the table. He dropped it at Lizzy's feet before shifting to the form of a naked, grinning boy who was so obviously pleased with himself.

No one spoke. Getting to his feet, Monty felt laughter bubble up at the absurdity along with a father's panic. Lizzy wasn't wailing about Boo Bear being in pieces—yet—but that was probably because she was getting her first good look at a naked boy. Sam didn't look that much older than Lizzy, and he wasn't *doing* anything, but still. Naked boy.

Simon pushed into A Little Bite, followed by Nathan.

"Sam, put your clothes on," Simon said mildly. "Meg? You okay? *Meg!*"

"Can I help?" Kowalski asked, easing around Monty.

"Keep an eye on things," Tess said. She strode to the table where Meg stood frozen and took the girl's hand. "Meg and I need some air and time to settle. We'll be at the Liaison's Office." She led Meg out of the coffee shop.

Watching the two females leave sobered Monty. Meg Corbyn was the key to so many things, and, so far, she was the only *cassandra sangue* who had managed to live outside a compound without having breakdowns. If she was starting to break now, how much would break with her?

Simon scooped up Boo Bear's hind leg, then approached the table where Skippy lay mouthing the front leg and growling.

The Wolfgard snarled. Skippy dropped the mangled front leg and scooted farther under the table.

Nathan went around the counter. He came back out and held up one of the Wolf cookies. "Skippy. Cookie."

Skippy leaped up and thumped his head on the underside of the table hard enough to be momentarily stunned. Nathan hauled the juvenile Wolf away from the table and half carried him out the back door.

Simon looked at Sam. "Go with them."

Sam stared at his uncle for a moment before running to catch up with Nathan.

Which left Lizzy literally hugging the stuffing out of Boo Bear while Simon, Blair, Kowalski, and Monty formed a circle around her.

"Daddy?" Now the tears began to fall. "Boo Bear got hurt."

"I know, Lizzy girl. But . . ."

"I have called the Wolfgard bodywalker," Henry Beargard rumbled as he stepped through the archway and joined them. "She will meet us at the medical office and do what she can."

"But he's a *bear*," Lizzy wailed. A little more stuffing dribbled out from the torn spots.

"So am I," Henry said. "But I am the only Grizzly in the Courtyard, so when I am hurt, the Wolf tends to me." He held out a big hand.

"Henry is the Courtyard's spirit guide," Simon said. "He is wise."

Lizzy hesitated, then gave Boo Bear to Henry.

The Grizzly studied the toy bear. Then he sniffed the face, the places where the legs had been torn off, the seam along the back.

Watching Henry's face, Monty eased Lizzy behind him. He felt Kowalski shift position to provide additional protection.

"There is sickness here," Henry said. "The bodywalker must tend to Boo Bear."

The Others did know Boo Bear was a toy. Didn't they? Now that he considered it, the Wolves *had* talked about Boo Bear in much the same way Lizzy did— as if the stuffed bear was alive in some way.

"Is he going to need another operation?" Lizzy asked, her eyes swimming with tears that tore at Monty's heart.

"Perhaps," Henry said. "But I will stay with my brother bear." He exchanged a look with Simon.

"Where is Ruthie?" Simon asked.

"She wasn't scheduled to work, so she's at home packing," Kowalski replied.

Simon studied Kowalski. "Don't leave until we talk."

Monty bristled at the Wolf's assumption that he could order Kowalski around, but they were all moving toward the back door of A Little Bite and then out to the medical office in the Market Square.

Theral MacDonald was closing up her desk when they walked in. Kowalski greeted her and would have stopped if Simon hadn't growled, "Kowalski, we need you back here. The Lizzy should stay out front with Theral."

"Mr. Wolfgard . . . ," Monty began. Pointless to protest about Wolfgard giving orders to a police officer or making decisions about a human child. This was the Courtyard, and humans had little, if any, say about anything.

The door opened and a female Wolf walked in. She had fur instead of hair, and her ears were Wolf—a bizarre combination with a human face. But not terrifying like the blends he had seen a few weeks ago when a man named Phineas Jones had tried to hypnotize Meg and convince her to leave with him.

The female Wolf hesitated.

"Jane, this way," Simon said, leading them all to the examination room Dominic Lorenzo had put together to provide medical care for the humans who lived or worked in the Courtyard.

Henry put Boo Bear on the examination table. Simon set the detached front and back leg next to the main body.

"There's something inside," Simon said. "Something that doesn't smell like the Lizzy."

Monty was about to point out that Boo Bear had been made by hand and might smell of the person who had stuffed him. But Lizzy had been three when she fell in love with the furry toy, and after four years, would there be any scent beyond the ones in the apartment and the people Lizzy came into contact with often?

"The child mentioned another operation," Henry said.

Jane bent over the bear, sniffing as her fingers moved over the fur on the bear's back. Then she rummaged around in the drawers, no doubt destroying any order Lorenzo had created. Not finding whatever she was looking for, she went out to the front desk and returned with a box cutter.

Monty didn't have time to protest before she slit Boo Bear's back.

Simon leaned over the table, poking at the stuffing. Suddenly all the *terra indigene* focused on the bear, as if they'd heard something.

Simon pulled out a small cloth sack. He opened it and poured the contents on the table.

Emeralds. Sapphires. Rubies. Even a few diamonds. And some kind of designer ring made of white gold or platinum and set with several diamonds.

Kowalski whistled softly.

Simon cocked his head and looked at Monty. "Do humans usually stuff jewels inside bears?"

"No." Monty swallowed the sick feeling in his gut. Gods above and below, where was Elayne? And what was she doing hiding a fortune inside Boo Bear?

Or had she been the one who had hidden the jewels?

"Brown bear eating jewels," Henry said. "That was one of the visions Meg saw yesterday when she made the cut."

"I have to report this," Monty said. "I have to . . ."

"Take care of your pup," Simon said.

Monty looked at the Wolf. "Yes." Lizzy came first. Someone else could call the police in Toland and ask about Elayne. Ask about stolen jewels.

"Maybe Lieutenant Montgomery and Lizzy could stay in the efficiency apartment you set aside for the team?" Kowalski said. "The Courtyard is closer to the station, and Lizzy could rest for a while."

Henry nodded. "A good idea. The child has traveled far enough today."

"What do we do with the bear and . . ." Jane waved a hand over the table, indicating all the bits.

"We leave it exactly as is," Monty said. "I'll call Captain Burke." He hesitated, not sure how Wolfgard would react to the next part. "Police will need to examine this, ask questions of all of us."

"Police who are not connected to you because the Lizzy is your pup?" Simon asked.

"Yes. Until we know what happened, it would be better if it wasn't anyone on my team."

"But one of the police we know and one of our enforcers will watch the unknown police."

That was more of a compromise than he'd expected, so he agreed.

When he walked into the reception area, Lizzy jumped off a chair. She looked at his empty hands, then at the door of the examination room.

"Boo Bear has to stay here and help the police with their inquiries," Simon said, addressing his words to Lizzy. "Theral is kin to police, so she and Henry will stay with Boo Bear. Officer Kowalski will bring your carryall to the efficiency apartment where you and Lieutenant Montgomery will wait and rest while the police do their sniffing. Blair will wait at the delivery entrance and will escort the unknown police back here."

I'm off balance and not being much help, Monty thought as they left the medical office and followed Simon to the efficiency apartments above the seamstress/tailor's shop.

The last time he and Simon had dealt with children, they'd been bringing five girls from the Controller's compound to Lakeside. He'd been overwhelmed by what he'd seen when he, Simon, and Dominic Lorenzo had entered the compound. Savagery and slaughter. And heartbreak when he saw the girls, the *cassandra sangue*, who were being raised and trained for someone's profit.

Simon had looked after the girls, and he'd made the arrangements for the Intuits on Great Island to take care of them. Now he was giving the orders again.

Take care of the pack. Protect the young.

It wasn't quite that simple when you were human.

Jewels inside a toy that Lizzy took everywhere. Blood on Boo Bear. Elayne injured in some way—and feeling desperate enough that she'd told Lizzy to make the trip to Lakeside alone. Why hadn't she called her mother or brother? They lived in Toland and could have fetched Lizzy if Elayne had needed to go to the hospital. Why send Lizzy all the way to Lakeside . . . unless staying in Toland wasn't safe anymore.

Gods above and below, what was Elayne mixed up in?

One advantage to living with predators is we know how to wait, Tess thought as she and Meg sat at the little table in the back room of the Liaison's Office.

Meg didn't seem to be in distress. She wasn't digging at her skin—a sign that she was plagued by a pins-and-needles feeling that indicated something that might be revealed in a vision.

How much was too much? When you thought about how many things had happened to Meg since she stumbled into the Courtyard a few months ago compared to how little had happened to her during her first twenty-four years, was it any wonder that her mind was overwhelmed? Of course, what had happened to the girl during those first twenty-four years might have been repetitive, but Tess didn't think any of it had been kind.

"Merri Lee, Ruth, and I watched a movie recently," Meg finally said. "It had a large dog with lots of hair. Ruth says there are lots of breeds of dog, but we weren't taught breeds, just general identification of animals."

"Makes sense," Tess said. "Why would someone pay for a prophecy about an animal unless it was valuable? Why are you thinking about the movie?"

"The dog kept getting into trouble. It didn't mean to, but it did. It knocked things over or chased a cat through a party so that people fell into a swimming pool or ended up with gooey food spilled over them."

Tess got up, rummaged in the under-the-counter fridge, and found a bottle of cold water. She filled two glasses and brought them back to the table.

"We had enough fuss with a cheese sandwich, a stuffed bear, and an idiot Wolf," she said.

"Exactly!"

She studied Meg. "What exactly?"

"Merri Lee and Ruth said the movie was a comedy, that the dog getting into trouble and getting snobby people wet or dirty was supposed to be funny. But the people weren't laughing. They looked angry and yelled at the dog." Meg sipped water. "Some training images produce feelings. Like seeing bugs crawling on food. I didn't like looking at those images. So that's a bad thing."

"If you're someone who eats bugs, that would be a good image and show what kind of bait should be set out."

Meg stared at her.

Tess shrugged. "For many things, good or bad is how you feel about it. If you see a picture of Wolves killing a deer, you might feel bad for the deer. Or you might understand that the Wolves have fed their family that day, the same as a human who kills a cow or a chicken to feed his family." She considered what she knew about Meg. "You have all these images in your head. Thousands of pictures, and you absorb more images every day. But now that you're having your own experiences, now that you're learning your own likes and dislikes, you're also trying to assign the proper feelings for all those images, aren't you?"

"Yes. Some things are easy. Sam is easy. And working here, and knowing all of you. Those things are easy. I feel good working here. I feel good when I'm learning new things, at least until I get tired. But sometimes I don't know how I should feel."

"For instance, should you feel upset like Lizzy because Boo Bear was damaged, or feel embarrassed like Lieutenant Montgomery because his little girl saw a naked boy, or laugh because it was like watching one of those absurd movies." Tess paused. "Or be like me—grateful that Skippy didn't manage to eat any of the bear so I don't have to deal with barfed stuffing all over the coffee shop."

"One image, but *feelings* change how it can be seen," Meg said quietly.

"I'd say that's true of most things. Wouldn't you?"

Meg took a deep breath and let it out in a sigh.

Relaxed. Balanced. She had provided the answer Meg needed.

"Your hair is brown again," Meg said.

"I'm sitting here talking to you."

Meg was rather like that big dog in the movie. Didn't mean any harm but managed to set all kinds of things in motion.

"Why are you laughing?" Meg asked.

"Just thought of something no one else would find amusing."

Simon filled a few book orders while he waited for Kowalski. Not much else he could do. Vlad was in the office upstairs, hopefully dealing with some of the paperwork that seemed to breed faster than bunnies. Nathan had messages from the Addirondak Wolves, but those would have to wait until the police finished sniffing around Boo Bear and asking their questions.

Which meant the only useful thing he could do right now was fill orders—and consider if he wanted to suggest to the *terra indigene* who ran small publishing houses that they should publish more books, maybe even a few by human authors. It was getting harder to purchase books from the human publishers, and written stories, like recorded music, were two human things the Others really enjoyed and wanted.

Or maybe the Intuits published books? Something to ask Steve Ferryman.

So many things to think about, at least until it was time to go home. Then he could shift and think about good things for a while, like the taste of water and the scents of bunnies and deer, and maybe playing an easy game of chase with Meg. Wolf thoughts.

Kowalski walked up to the checkout counter. He and Ruthie were going to be mates officially next month. Simon wasn't sure why that made a difference since they were already mating—any Wolf could smell *that*—but apparently humans couldn't tell, so Kowalski and Ruthie had to have a ceremony and be given a piece of paper so that other humans would know they were mating.

"Lizzy has her things," Kowalski said. "Officer Debany and Nathan are at the medical office, observing while the bear and jewels are bagged. Captain Burke is there too and would like to talk to you when you're available. And . . . Jane? . . . said to tell you she took Sam and Skippy back to the Wolfgard complex."

And Meg? Simon thought.

He didn't hear anything, even with his superior hearing, but he turned toward the archway when he saw Kowalski tense, then make a visible effort to relax.

"Meg is fine," Tess said. "She's with Henry in his studio. They're talking about wood and listening to earth native music."

He nodded, noting as Tess ducked back into the coffee shop that her hair was brown and the curls had relaxed to waves. So Meg was fine and Tess was calm. Both good things when humans who weren't pack were sniffing around. He'd given his consent, but that didn't mean he liked it.

"You wanted to talk to me?" Kowalski said.

Simon sniffed the air, trying not to be too obvious about it. Nerves. But not fear. That was good.

Since Kowalski was in the way, Simon walked around the counter instead of vaulting over it, flipped the simple lock on HGR's front door, and stepped outside. When Kowalski joined him, Simon pointed to one of the stone buildings across the street. "Two bedrooms. I'm told it needs cleaning and paint. Is that a den you and Ruthie could live in?"

"Sure, but I don't think we could afford it."

"Once the Courtyard buys those buildings, you can afford to live there. The question is, would you?" Eve Denby would have first pick of the dens in the house across the street, and Ruthie could have the other, but he still wanted to know if the human pack would consider the apartments in the stone buildings as suitable dens. No point buying the buildings if their humans didn't want to live in them.

Kowalski stared at the buildings on the other side of Crowfield Avenue. "Any space there for a small kitchen garden?"

"Not much. But for the human pack . . ."

He hesitated. It was his idea, but now that the moment had come to say something, did he really want to expose more of the Courtyard to humans? What if the humans couldn't, or wouldn't, accept the *terra indigene* who couldn't pass for human?

And yet Kowalski was the second human today to ask about land to grow food. Someday he and Ruthie would have pups, so food was important. But why, at the beginning of the growing season, were humans thinking there wouldn't be enough? The ground wasn't quite ready for planting yet, and none of the earth native farms were reporting trouble.

He'd missed something. Maybe Vlad would know since the Sanguinati tended to pay more attention to human prattle.

"We have gardens where we grow vegetables," Simon said. "We can expand some of them. We have fruits and nuts that we harvest. You do your share of the work, you get your share of the food."

"Why are you doing this?" Kowalski asked. "You were pissed off at all of us yesterday."

Simon sighed. "Maybe to say, 'Sorry I almost bit you,' to Ruthie?"

Kowalski stared at the buildings across the street. "We went out to all the farms yesterday, drove around for hours checking anyplace that might have been doing that to those girls. Lieutenant Montgomery, Debany, MacDonald, me. Even Captain Burke. And I'm pretty sure the captain had a quiet word with other patrol captains, because I saw men from other districts on the roads too, looking. It made you angry, hearing about what they did to girls like Meg, to the babies. It made us angry too. Maybe if I'd received a phone call like that, learned about it like that, I might have taken a swing at someone because I couldn't think straight. Would have been sorry for it, and would have been glad that someone stopped me. What I'm saying is, we all understood why you lashed out. You don't have to make up for being upset by offering Ruthie and me a place to live."

He hadn't expected understanding. Somehow that made him feel worse about snapping at Merri Lee and Ruthie.

"That's not the only reason to do this. Maybe we want to find out if it can be done. The Intuits and the Simple Life folk have lived alongside the *terra indigene* for many generations, and each side fulfills parts of the bargain so that all sides have enough without constantly fighting for territory. But we haven't made those kinds of bargains with your kind of human." Wouldn't have even considered making such a bargain until Meg started working for them and they had to allow for her need to have human friends.

"I'll talk to Ruthie," Kowalski said. "It's a decision we need to make together." As mates should.

Kowalski's mobile phone rang. A brief call. "Captain Burke wants to see me." Simon pulled the door open but Kowalski hesitated.

"Thank you. It means a lot that you would do this for us." Kowalski went inside and headed for HGR's back door.

Simon returned to the checkout counter and continued filling orders.

He'd said the words. Hopefully he hadn't made a mistake that would threaten everyone in the Courtyard.

CHAPTER 16

Firesday, Maius 11

Meg sat at the top of the stairs leading to her apartment, a book beside her. Her porch provided shelter in bad weather and shade when it was sunny. It had latticework for privacy. What it didn't have was anyplace to sit.

Some of the apartments in the Green Complex had porches; others didn't. None of the other porches had the privacy latticework. They also didn't have furniture. Too early in the season? Or didn't Hawks, Owls, and Crows bother with furniture since the porch railing was a sufficient perch?

Tomorrow she would look through the ads in the *Lakeside News* to get an idea of what people might buy for outdoor furniture. This evening . . .

"Want to take a walk?"

She looked at Simon standing at the bottom of the stairs.

"Okay," she said. "Aren't you going to shift first?"

"No."

Not the answer she expected. Simon usually shifted to Wolf as soon as he got home, relieved to be out of the human skin.

Taking the book inside, she exchanged the soft house shoes for sneakers. A walk with Simon could mean anything from an amble to a muscle-burning pace, and just because he started out in human form didn't mean he wouldn't be trotting along on four legs by the time it was finished.

She closed her front door, then joined Simon.

"You need to read this first." He unfolded a piece of paper and handed it to her.

Haven't we all faced enough today? she thought as she refolded the paper and handed it back to him.

She started walking, needing a distraction from the prickling around her shoulder blades. Simon fell into step beside her, saying nothing for several minutes.

Plenty of Courtyard residents out and about. Many saw them and hesitated, but no one approached.

"I remember her," Meg finally said. "I remember *cs821*. She was younger than me. I can't tell you her age, but she got her first scar last year or the year before, so the doctor's guess sounds right."

"She said she wants to live. Jackson isn't sure she will. What can he do? What would help you if you were in her place?"

"They took away the silver razor?"

"Probably."

"Return it to her. Return the razors to the girls who had them."

"They'll cut themselves."

"They'll cut anyway." She kept walking, kept moving. "So many things will cut skin, but those razors were designed for it."

"She doesn't want to die."

"Neither do I." Meg stopped and looked at Simon. He couldn't quite pass for human anymore. "Neither do I, but I want to be the one who makes the choice."

He started walking, a fast pace, as if he wanted to run away from the words.

She ran to catch up to him, then had to run every few steps to keep up with him.

"Simon . . . ," she panted.

He slowed but didn't stop.

The *terra indigene* had agreed that it was her choice, but they didn't like the cutting. To them, fresh blood meant a wound, and in the wild country, a wound could be fatal. Add in the fact that *cassandra sangue* blood acted like a drug, and she understood why the Others weren't easy about her cutting. Being thrust in the position of taking care of a girl they didn't know—and who didn't know them—would make everything harder for all of them.

"Tell Jackson to give her a room that contains as little as possible. Give her time to rest." Meg thought about the girl called *cs821*. "Maybe leave one thing that has colors. She liked colors. She would describe training images first by their color and then by their shape."

"I'll tell him."

They returned to the Green Complex in silence. Simon hurried into his own apartment and came out again a minute later. He shook out his fur and ran off, needing something she couldn't give.

Sighing, Meg looked up at her apartment. She felt exhausted and restless, hungry and too listless to bother with food.

"Have you eaten?" asked a voice in the shadows beneath her stairs. Vlad stepped into the fading light, his form still shifting from smoke to human. "We picked up a couple of pizzas from Hot Crust. Tess made a salad. We're gathering in the social room to watch movies."

"Which movies?" Meg asked.

"Does it matter?"

She preferred being able to hide behind Simon during a movie's scary bits—and most *terra indigene* movies had scary bits. "I guess not."

"Then join us." Vlad smiled. "I'll tell Simon where to find you when he finishes his run." He studied her. "Or I can bring you some food if you'd prefer to be alone."

Did she want to be alone? Did she *need* to be alone?

"I'll join you for the first movie," Meg said.

His smiled widened, showing a bit of fang. "Come on, then. Let's get the pizza while it's still warm."

As she and Vlad walked to the side of the Green Complex that held the mail room, laundry room, and social room, Meg heard a wolf howling. She thought he sounded lonely.

The efficiency apartments had shower stalls instead of bathtubs. After many assurances that he would be able to cope with her hair if she got it wet—and equal insistence on Lizzy's part that she could wash herself and would be careful on the slippy floor—Monty left his little girl to shower by herself. While he listened for any sign of distress or, gods forbid, a slip and injury, he unpacked her suitcase, hanging up a few things in the closet and putting the rest in half the drawers in the dresser.

A temporary arrangement until they had more information about what happened to Elayne. A practical choice, since, as Kowalski pointed out, the Courtyard was closer to the Chestnut Street station than Monty's apartment, and it was a safe haven for his little girl, because who would think to look for her here?

Monty picked up Lizzy's folded pajamas and felt something the size of a small book. Unfolding the pajamas, he stared at the pink diary sprinkled with gold stars. It had a latch and a tiny keyhole. He tried the latch, confirming that the diary was locked. A quick feel through the suitcase didn't turn up a key.

He rubbed his thumb over the stars. A diary? What would a seven-year-old write about? School? Friends? Please, gods, no confessions about a crush on a boy. Not yet.

Before he could wonder too much about the contents, Lizzy yelled, "Daddy! Make the water turn off!"

Monty stuffed the diary in the drawer with Lizzy's underwear and hurried to make the water turn off.

CHAPTER 17

Watersday, Maius 12

At seven a.m., Douglas Burke gave the phone his typical fierce-friendly smile and waited until the third ring before picking up.

"Chestnut Street station, Captain Burke speaking."

"Captain," Vladimir Sanguinati said smoothly. "Do you have a minute to talk?"

"Of course."

It was a disappointment, but not a surprise, that the Sanguinati had gotten back to him before the Toland police called to inquire about a missing child.

There were a few reasons why Elayne Borden had sent her child to Lakeside, allowing the girl to travel several hundred miles alone. According to the verbal report he'd received from Officer Kowalski, Lizzy had said her mother was hurt in the belly. Acute intestinal distress could account for Elayne looking hurt or being in pain. It could also account for her decision to send the child to Monty while she sought medical help—especially if she was in enough pain that she wasn't thinking clearly. Or, considering what had been found in the stuffed bear, maybe she *was* thinking clearly and realized she couldn't trust anyone but Monty where Lizzy was concerned.

Or she could have put the child on a train without a backward glance so that she could go off with her new, socially prominent lover unencumbered.

He didn't think Elayne was that cold or callous where Lizzy was concerned, or that any of his speculations were accurate, but they were arguments he could make if anyone asked why he hadn't called the Toland police after Lizzy arrived in Lakeside.

Had Monty called anyone in Elayne's family yet? He didn't think so, but he would check.

"Did your kinsmen hear anything on the news about a woman being injured or taken ill at the train station yesterday?" Burke asked. The Wolves had talked about dried blood on Lizzy's bear, but the truth was, the patch of fur that had brushed against some blood was so small, the blood could have come from a fresh cut on someone's hand, a moment's jostle while people were boarding the train. A human would have overlooked it. Humans *had* overlooked it. If that hadn't been the case, a conductor or *someone* on the train would have questioned the child about a bloody bear and the absence of an adult.

A hesitation. Then Vlad said, "Stavros considers it part of his work for the Toland Courtyard to read the human newspaper and listen to the news. There was a report yesterday evening about a woman being stabbed at the Toland train station. Dead at the scene. Police investigating. Name withheld until next of kin are notified. When I spoke with him, he hadn't listened to the morning news, so I don't know if they've named the woman yet."

"So the police are investigating a suspicious death."

Lizzy had been on the early westbound train. Next of kin would have been notified well before the evening news aired. If the dead woman and Elayne were one and the same, then someone had known Elayne was dead . . . and hadn't called the father of her child.

Hadn't even noticed Lizzy was missing?

Another, longer hesitation before Vlad said, "Train stations are a good hunting ground."

Burke sat up straight. "Are you saying one of the Sanguinati killed Elayne Borden?"

"No. I'm saying that the Sanguinati are often at train stations, especially stations in larger cities like Toland because so many trains come in and go out, and there is usually an abundance of prey. But the stations also provide a way to study humans. The Sanguinati observe as well as hunt. They weren't in that part of the Toland station when it happened, so they didn't see the attack, and they didn't see the Lizzy get on a train. They became curious about all the activity once the police arrived—and then they listened."

Great. Were Sanguinati usually in the crowds around a crime scene, drawn by the commotion and the cluster of humans who would make easy prey? Something to think about. Later. "What did they hear?"

"The restroom where the woman was found had an Out of Order sign on the door. The maintenance staff at the station insisted that the sign had been on the men's restroom door, *not* the women's. It was unclear if the woman moved the sign in an attempt to hide or if her attacker moved it to delay anyone finding her. The woman was wearing a small gold key on a long thin chain hidden under her shirt. It was speculated that the key opened the lock on a jewelry box, but the woman's suitcase wasn't opened at the station, so the Sanguinati couldn't say if the box was found."

Burke scribbled notes. "Anything else?"

"The woman had two tickets for a commuter train going to Hubb NE. She was found shortly before that train left the station, so police searched for her companion among the passengers boarding it but didn't locate anyone who knew the woman."

Burke thought for a moment. Had Elayne purchased a second set of tickets to give herself another escape route? Or had one set been a diversion? If *Lizzy* had both tickets for Lakeside, that could explain why no one had questioned the absence of an adult. Mommy was in the bathroom. Here was her ticket.

Mommy *had* been in the bathroom. Just not the bathroom on the train.

"Thank you for the information," Burke began.

"Captain?" Vlad's voice, which had been conversational up to that point, suddenly chilled. "Has anyone called you or Lieutenant Montgomery to ask about the child?"

Burke felt his heart thump heavy against his chest. "No," he said, swallowing a sour taste he recognized as fear. "No one has called to ask about the child."

"That's what we thought." Vlad hung up.

Gods above and below, he thought, noticing how his hand trembled as he returned the receiver to its cradle. It was one thing for him to condemn that disregard for the child's welfare. It was quite another to wonder how the Sanguinati viewed that disregard.

Considering how the *terra indigene* had reacted to the deaths of *cassandra sangue* babies, he didn't think the Others were going to allow humans to make all the decisions where Montgomery's little girl was concerned.

Burke slumped in his chair but straightened again a moment later when Louis Gresh tapped on his doorway. Waving the bomb squad commander in, he said, "Come in and close the door." He studied Louis and added, "Aren't you off duty today?"

"I was supposed to be, but with Monty being off I thought you could use an extra hand." Louis shrugged. "Did you hear from the Toland police?"

"Nothing from the police yet, but I did hear from the Sanguinati. I called Vlad last night and asked him to make some inquiries with his Toland kinsmen." Burke blew out a breath. "A woman was attacked and killed yesterday morning at the train station. I'm guessing it was Elayne Borden."

"Gods," Louis breathed. "Does Monty know?"

"Not yet." Burke sat back and folded his hands over his trim belly. "You have children."

"A boy and a girl. Both teenagers, may the gods help me."

"It's a seven-hour trip from Toland to Lakeside. The attack happened early in the morning. Police are called in, crime scene investigators begin their work, and someone contacts next of kin. If you were informed of the death of a family member, a single mother, what would you say after you got past the initial shock?"

"'Where's the child?'" Louis rubbed his chin. "Assuming the girl wasn't staying with me or her location was already known."

"Exactly. The woman is dead under suspicious circumstances. Her child is missing, and both the relatives and the police know that well before the train reaches the Lakeside station. And yet *no one* called Lieutenant Montgomery to ask if Lizzy somehow got on a train to Lakeside. No one called to see if she was with her father, if she was safe. Twenty-four hours have passed, and no one has called looking for the child."

Louis eased himself into the visitor's chair. "Monty turned off his mobile phone and he's not in his own apartment. Someone could have tried to reach him."

"He's a cop," Burke said quietly. "If you call the station and tell anyone that something happened to his daughter and he needs to be found, you can be damn well sure we will find him whether his phone is turned on or not."

"True enough." Louis sighed. "But if they haven't been looking for the girl, what *have* they been looking for?"

A jewelry box that goes with a small gold key? A fortune in jewels that someone hid inside a stuffed bear?

"I've answered a couple of calls on Monty's office phone this morning," Louis said. "A man's voice. Wouldn't leave his name. Wouldn't leave a number. Said he needed to make a delivery and wanted to be sure Monty would be home today. When I asked for the name of the store making the delivery, he hung up. The second time he called, he must have recognized my voice as fast as I recognized his because he hung up before making his spiel. Officer Kowalski is here, so I asked him to man Monty's phone. It could be one of Ms. Borden's relatives."

Or it could be the man who needs to find a bag of jewels, Burke thought.

A one-two rap on the door before it opened partway and Kowalski leaned into the office.

"Pardon the intrusion, Captain, but there's a Captain Felix Scaffoldon from the Toland police calling for Lieutenant Montgomery. He says he's from the Crime Investigation Unit. He's holding on line two."

"This should be interesting." Burke wagged a finger at Kowalski to indicate the officer should come in. Then he picked up the phone. "This is Captain Douglas Burke."

A pause before a too-hearty voice said, "Guess your man on the desk hasn't had enough coffee yet. I asked for Crispin James Montgomery."

"Lieutenant Montgomery is taking a couple of days' personal leave. I'm his commanding officer. What can I do for you?"

"It's important that I talk to him. Could you give me his home and mobile phone numbers?"

"Talk to him about what?"

"It's private."

"Then give me your number, and I'll give him the message when he calls in."

"You said he's taking personal time."

"He is. But he's a diligent officer, so he'll call in." Tucking the phone between shoulder and ear, Burke tore off a sheet of paper from a pad and wrote *Call Pete. Custody. ASAP.* He handed the paper to Kowalski, who looked at it and hurried out of the room.

Burke could feel the hostility coming through the phone line.

"Look," Scaffoldon said. "I need to verify Montgomery's whereabouts for the past forty-eight hours."

He waited a beat. "Why?"

"Damn it, Burke!" Heavy breathing before Scaffoldon continued with more control. "He's a person of interest in the suspicious death of Elayne Borden."

"He couldn't be. Lieutenant Montgomery hasn't been off duty enough consecutive hours to make the trip to and from Toland."

"You said he'd taken personal time." Scaffoldon had latched on to those words.

"Which began after his shift ended yesterday." Burke got tired of dancing. "He's taking personal time because his daughter arrived for a surprise visit."

"She . . . She's *there*? *How?*"

The surprise in the voice wasn't genuine. Scaffoldon, or someone he'd talked to yesterday, suspected Lizzy was in Lakeside.

"She had a ticket and got on a train," Burke said.

"No." Scaffoldon's denial bordered on vehemence. "Celia Borden, Elayne's mother, told me Montgomery had been making threats, that Elayne feared he was going to forcibly try to take her daughter. If the girl is there, it's because Montgomery took her and Elayne was killed when she tried to stop him."

"Montgomery couldn't have made the trip," Burke insisted. "If I were you, I'd be looking at the man who moved in with Elayne shortly after Lieutenant Montgomery moved out. He's an unsavory character living under an assumed name."

"What name?" Scaffoldon asked warily.

"Nicholas Scratch."

Silence. Then, "Do you know who Nicholas Scratch is?"

Burke heard fear as well as hostility in Scaffoldon's voice. "No. That's the point. If I were you, I'd see what kind of alibi *he* has for the time of the murder."

"You impugn . . ."

While he waited for Scaffoldon to regain some control, he looked toward his door, waved Kowalski and Pete Denby into his office, then held a finger to his lips to indicate he wanted them to be quiet.

"You have no proof, *none at all*, that Nicholas Scratch was associated with Elayne Borden, let alone living with her," Scaffoldon snarled. "You're trying to smear a man's reputation by connecting his name to a murder inquiry."

"Isn't that what you're doing by trying to drag Lieutenant Montgomery into this? My man is a seven-hour train ride away from the crime scene. Your man is in the same city. I know who I'd be talking to."

Silence.

"Mrs. Borden has custody of the child," Scaffoldon said. "We'll arrange a police escort to bring the girl back to Toland. If she was with her mother in the train station, she'll need to make a statement."

If the first gambit doesn't work, try another, Burke thought. "Once again, you've been given inaccurate information. Lieutenant Montgomery has custody of his daughter. She will be staying here. We'll take Lizzy's formal statement later today, and I will send you a copy of the transcript. Good—"

"Wait! What about the bear?"

Burke gave the three men listening to his every word his fierce-friendly smile. "The bear?"

"Mrs. Borden mentioned a stuffed bear. The girl's favorite toy. Took it everywhere. Is it there?"

"Most of it," he replied pleasantly. "Little girls can be careless, and Wolves have sharp teeth."

Scaffoldon sucked in a breath. "It was destroyed?"

"It lost an arm and a leg but is otherwise intact."

A hesitation. "Where is it now?"

"I tucked it out of harm's way here at the station and was going to have it mended as a surprise for Lizzy. But I can box up the pieces and send it to you if you think it will help your investigation."

"No," Scaffoldon said sharply. Then his voice shifted to something that might be mistaken for courtesy. "There's no need to do that."

"If you change your mind, you just let me know."

"Montgomery is the only one with a motive to kill Elayne Borden. If you try to shield an officer who already has a serious blotch on his record, you're going to step on some important toes, Burke. That won't be forgotten."

"You ever do a tour of duty in the wild country, Scaffoldon?"

"It's a punishment assignment," Scaffoldon snapped. "No sane police officer volunteers for it. So, no, I've never done that kind of tour."

"I have. Twice. Learned a lot from the experience. That's why I'm not intimidated by government officials or businessmen with deep pockets . . . or motivational speakers claiming to come from a wealthy family who conveniently lives on another continent. I've seen some of what's out there in the dark. *Those* are the toes I don't want to step on."

"I guess Montgomery fits in well there."

"Yes, he does." Burke hung up. He rubbed his hands over his face before sitting back.

"I guess I'd better get those custody papers processed before someone asks to see a copy," Pete said.

"I know a judge who owes me a favor."

To his credit, Pete didn't say, *Of course you do*. At least not out loud.

"Problems?" Louis asked.

"Oh yeah," Burke replied. "More than a few—including a CIU captain who most likely belongs to the Humans First and Last movement. He did not want Scratch connected with Elayne Borden in any way."

"Not surprising he belongs to the HFL," Pete said. "You've got to figure some cops are going to like that tune."

"The shortsighted ones." Burke looked at Kowalski. "Anything to tell me about the lieutenant?"

"I went to his apartment last evening and packed a bag for him, brought it back to the Courtyard. Also brought him my sleeping bag. Only one single bed in those efficiency apartments. Figured stretching out on the floor might be more comfortable than sleeping in a chair."

He studied the young man. "What else?"

Kowalski hesitated. "Have you heard the Others are looking to buy a couple of apartment buildings across from the Courtyard?"

Burke tipped his head toward Pete. "I have heard that."

"Do you know anything I should know about those buildings?" Pete asked. "I'm the Courtyard's attorney when they deal with human things like the purchase of a building."

Kowalski eyed Pete. "Simon Wolfgard asked me if Ruthie and I would be willing to live in one."

"It's my understanding that you do need to find another place to live," Burke said mildly.

"Yes, sir, we do. But it's the offer of a share in the gardens that has me wondering."

"Wolfgard called Eve yesterday evening and told her a share in the gardens would be part of her wages," Pete said. "Then he hung up before she could ask him what that meant."

"I know they bring in things like beef and eggs from farms that are con-trolled by the *terra indigene*," Kowalski said. "But it sounds like the Courtyard res-idents grow some of the fruits and vegetables they need. And this year human employees are being given a choice to have a share of the harvest if they help with the work."

"That could mean exposure to more of the Courtyard and interacting with residents who have little, if any, contact with humans," Burke said. "How do you and Ruth feel about that?"

"Excited. A little scared. Simon Wolfgard said the *terra indigene* haven't tried to make a bargain like this with our kind of human, but he indicated that the Oth-ers do work cooperatively with Intuits and Simple Life folk. We're willing to try."

"All right. Pete?"

"The woman who owns the double wants to sell," Pete said. "After doing a bit of research to get an idea of the asking price of other houses in the area, I made her an offer yesterday evening. I went over her asking price. Not by a lot but enough to sweeten the deal. She accepted, so I'm going over to the Courtyard this morning to explain what paperwork needs to be done in order for the Busi-ness Association to purchase a house in the human part of the city." He turned to Kowalski. "I don't want to appear too inquisitive about the Courtyard, but I would like to know more about this share in the gardens, especially because I'm not sure working for the *terra indigene* will qualify me or Eve to receive a family ration book."

"Ruthie will be able to find out more," Kowalski said. "All the girls are meet-ing up this morning for a nature walk or some such thing."

Burke pushed back from his desk. "It sounds like several of us have business with the Others this morning." He eyed them. "Something else?"

"Not from me." Louis stood up. "I'll stay at the station and answer Monty's phone until you say otherwise."

"There is something else, but I'll wait outside," Pete said, giving Kowalski a look before walking out with Louis.

Burke studied the young officer. These past few months of working around the Others had seasoned Karl Kowalski in ways most cops wouldn't experience. In some ways, working around this Courtyard was similar to a tour of duty in the wild country, except here you had a better chance of coming out of an en-counter alive.

That was the kind of seasoning Burke wanted more of his men to have.

"What's on your mind?" he asked.

"Captain Scaffoldon asked about the bear, but he didn't say anything about the jewels?"

"No, he didn't."

Kowalski was one of a handful of people in Lakeside who knew about the jewels in Boo Bear. But word would get out. With a fortune sitting inside that bear, and the death of a police officer's former lover added to the mix, word would get out.

"Do you think he knows?" Kowalski asked.

"He knows. He's not interested in the bear . . . or the child. Elayne Borden got tangled up in some kind of mess, and I'd bet a year's salary that it's connected to Nicholas Scratch and the HFL movement."

"She's dead?"

"Yes."

Kowalski nodded. "Hoped I was wrong, but I kind of figured . . . Lieutenant Montgomery asked me to check his messages when I went to his apartment. There wasn't anything from Lizzy's mom. You'd think, if she could, she would have called to make sure Lizzy got to Lakeside all right."

"With the woman dead, the child is now in the middle of this. Until we have a better idea of what's going on, we all need to stay sharp. You're going to the Courtyard?"

"Yes, sir."

"Then you tell Lieutenant Montgomery to keep his mobile phone turned off. I don't want him hearing about Elayne from anyone but me. Tell him we have to take a formal statement from Lizzy, and I need to talk to him beforehand, so he's to wait in the Courtyard until I get there. And find out if Vladimir Sanguinati will be available to talk to me."

"Yes, sir."

When Kowalski walked out, Pete walked back in.

"You think that Toland cop is compromised in some way?" Pete asked.

"Nicholas Scratch is linked to the Humans First and Last movement. Smear the reputation of one and you damage both. If Scaffoldon does belong to the HFL, I think he'll do whatever it takes to make sure Scratch's name isn't connected with Elayne Borden."

"Humans First and Last is a seductive idea. To have everything you need and also not be afraid of what's out there because it isn't out there anymore."

Burke snorted. "You lived in a small town in the Midwest. How many *terra indigene* did you interact with?"

"You still know they're out there."

"You know there are human muggers and rapists and killers out there too. But you still leave your house and go to work. Eve is out running errands. The kids are in school. Some of the people you see in courtrooms are far more dangerous to your family than a Hawk soaring overhead looking for his dinner or a Crow perched in a tree, curious about something it spotted in your yard."

Pete gave him a crooked smile. "It's still a seductive idea."

"The first humans and the last humans," Burke said grimly. "The last humans in a city, in a region, on a continent? In the world?"

"That's not what Humans First and Last means."

Burke came around the desk and indicated that Pete should precede him out of the office.

But Pete stopped at the doorway and studied him. "That's not what it means."

"I think the meaning depends on whether you're human or one of the *terra indigene*."

CHAPTER 18

Watersday, Maius 12

Monty jackknifed to a sitting position, his heart pounding as he tried to shake off the dream that had scared him out of a fitful sleep.

Hearing the toilet flush and water running in the sink, he ran his hands over his head and tried to steady his breathing.

Safe. His little girl was safe. But Elayne . . .

He dreamed Boo Bear had shifted into a *terra indigene* Grizzly who wanted the bag of jewels for some weird dream-logic reason, and Elayne wouldn't give it up. They struggled, she got slashed in the belly, and the Grizzly grabbed the bag and swallowed it, turning back into Boo Bear before Lizzy came out of the stall and saw him for what he truly was—a killer hiding behind the mask of something she trusted.

Or someone she trusted?

Gods, Monty thought as he got up and looked at his mobile phone. He should have called Elayne's mother or her brother, Leo. Burke didn't want him to make any calls, but surely it wouldn't hurt to turn on his phone and check for messages.

As he reached for the phone, someone knocked on the apartment's door—a quiet yet urgent sound.

Monty glanced toward the kitchen. No gun safe in the efficiency apartment, so he'd put his weapon on the highest shelf in the kitchen. Now it felt so very far away.

But who would know he was here? And who could get into the building without raising an alarm from the *terra indigene* on watch?

He unlocked the door and opened it.

"Morning, Lieutenant," Kowalski said.

A look in Karl's eyes, confirmation of what he'd figured out for himself, even if only in a dream.

"Elayne's dead, isn't she?" he asked.

Kowalski hesitated. Then he nodded. "I'm sorry, Lieutenant."

Monty felt a stab of grief. "Me too. Things were . . . strained . . . between us these past few months, but we were a family up to that point. She was the mother of my child."

"I know." Kowalski shifted his weight from one foot to the other. "Toland police called this morning. Captain Burke will be here soon. He wants you to keep your mobile phone turned off until he talks to you."

Burke wanting him to stay unavailable after the Toland police called made Monty uneasy. "Any message on the answering machine at my place?"

"No, sir."

Monty looked toward the bathroom. Water was still running? What was the girl doing in there?

"Well. I'd better get dressed. Call the captain and tell him there's no reason for him to come to the Courtyard. Lizzy and I can meet him at the station."

"He said you should stay here."

"Call him."

"Yes, sir. Lieutenant? If there's anything Ruthie and I can do, you only have to ask."

"You've done plenty already, but I'll keep it in mind." Monty forced his lips into a smile. "Thank you."

As he closed the door, he heard the water shut off. Then Lizzy came into the living area, dressed in her pajamas. Looking at her bare feet, he noticed that her toenails were painted the shade of red that Elayne had preferred.

Odd thing to do if you were running away from something or someone. Then again, Elayne hadn't been home the night he called—the night before she'd gone to the train station. Where had she and Lizzy stayed? Had painting nails been a way to pass the time and distract a young girl?

He and Lizzy would go to the Chestnut Street station and make a formal statement. After that, he had to consider the practicalities of having her here. He had a one-bedroom apartment, and his rent had been based on one occupant. With the price of water being what it was, his landlord was bound to raise the rent since Lizzy wouldn't be a guest who was staying for a few days. Sure, he could squeeze enough out of his paycheck to pay the extra rent, especially since he'd now have the money he'd been sending Elayne for child support. Sure, he could give his little girl the bedroom and sleep on the couch, but that was a temporary arrangement, just like staying in this efficiency apartment was a temporary arrangement.

"Daddy?"

How long had he'd been staring at her, lost in his own thoughts?

Monty kissed her forehead. "Morning, Lizzy girl. Did you sleep well?"

She nodded, but she looked toward the bed, where Boo Bear should have been.

"You hungry?" Monty asked, wanting to avoid her questions for a little while longer. Wanting to avoid telling her about Elayne a little while longer. "Let's see what Officer Karl and Miss Ruth left for us."

There were eggs in the fridge, as well as bread, milk, butter, and a small jar of grape jelly. The box of cereal in the cupboard wasn't the sort that would tempt a child. Wouldn't even tempt him. So he scrambled four of the eggs and toasted the bread. And since he didn't find any coffee, they both had a glass of milk.

Why make coffee up here when you could go downstairs for Tess's brew? Would she be open at this hour?

"Can you watch TV or read a book while I take a shower?" he asked as he quickly washed the dishes.

"Okay. Are we going to work?"

He looked into those big dark eyes and felt his heart stutter, sure that no man had ever loved a child more. And sure no child should face what Lizzy would have to face today. "Yes. We're going to sit down with Captain Burke, and you're going to tell him everything you remember about going to the train station and riding the train to Lakeside."

"Then we can get Boo Bear?"

Monty dried his hands and hung up the dish towel. "No, honey. Boo Bear has to stay at the station to help the police." And between the jewels hidden inside the bear and the blood on the bear, it wasn't likely that Boo Bear was ever coming back.

He'd avoid telling her that bit of truth for as long as possible.

"If we don't have Boo Bear to protect us, can the Wolf police come with us? Nathan has big teeth. Even bigger than Boo Bear's."

Ah, damn. "Honey . . ."

"*Please*, Daddy."

Defeated, he said, "I'll ask." Then he retreated to the bathroom before Lizzy could think of something else she needed in order to give her statement.

CHAPTER 19

Watersday, Maius 12

*D*o not bite the messenger. If you bite him, he won't work for you. Do not bite the messenger.

Sitting in the Business Association's meeting room with Vlad, Henry, and Tess, Simon refocused his attention on Pete Denby and the excruciating list of papers that needed to be filled in or signed or some other such thing in order to purchase a building.

Why couldn't they just give the human female a bag of money and then pee on the building so that everyone would know it was theirs?

This was one of the reasons a few *terra indigene* went through a human-centric education that exceeded what anyone wanted to know about the clever meat. But even having that education wasn't sufficient for enduring such an irritating process.

"Title search. House inspection," Pete said. "Those have to be done. Since you're paying cash, we might be able to push the paperwork through and close the deal by the end of the month."

"We could inspect the house ourselves," Simon said. "Give it a good sniff."

"You still need the paperwork. And from a legal standpoint, a good sniff just isn't sufficient."

Simon sighed. He'd rather be out with Meg, doing whatever she was doing.

"You get the papers we need," Henry told Pete. "Then we will give the human the money and claim the house."

"About that." Pete smelled nervous. "When you say you'll pay cash . . ."

"We will fill a bag with the correct amount of money," Vlad said.

"You will *not* give Mrs. Tremaine a sack of money," Pete said with a snap in his voice that made Simon growl . . . and annoyed Tess enough that her brown hair acquired broad red streaks and began to coil.

Pete raised both hands, a placating gesture. Not as submissive as exposing his throat, but sufficient that Simon didn't feel a need to enforce his role as the Courtyard's leader.

"We will do this the human way and give the woman money for her house," Henry rumbled.

"Yes," Pete said quickly. "I wasn't indicating that you wouldn't, or shouldn't, buy the house in the human way. But . . ." He studied the four of them. "This money will provide Mrs. Tremaine with food and shelter for the rest of her life. It's a lot of money. Giving it to her in a bag will leave her vulnerable to thieves. They might hurt her, even kill her if she tried to fight them. It's not the proper way to buy a house, even when you're paying in cash."

"Then what do you suggest?" Vlad asked.

"I saw some kind of bank in the Market Square. It's a legitimate bank?"

"Yes," Simon said. Then he paused, uncertain. No one had ever asked that question before, but a bank was a bank. Wasn't it? "The Business Association also has accounts at a human bank located in the Bird Park Plaza."

"That's good." Looking relieved, Pete made notes. "That's a regional bank, so there should be a branch in Hubb NE, which is where Mrs. Tremaine is going. If she also uses that bank, you can take money from your account and she can deposit it into hers. Safe and easy. Or we'll get a cashier's check. That would be even better." He looked up from his note making. "Do you have enough money in those accounts to cover the costs of buying the house? The purchase price and the fees?"

<Fees?> Henry asked, looking at the other *terra indigene*.

"We should have enough," Vlad said. "But we'll make a deposit next week to take care of anything unexpected. What about the other two buildings?"

Pete frowned. "The owner tried to double his price once he realized the Courtyard was interested in the buildings. I told him you weren't in a hurry to acquire the properties and would be willing to wait until the bank foreclosed and put the buildings up for auction. He's behind on the mortgage payments," he explained when the Others stared at him. "He doesn't live in either building. It's rental property that's supposed to generate income, but he has no tenants. The last people in the buildings are packing up. And frankly, once it's known that you own the building in between those two, it's not likely he's going to get any tenants. I made him an offer that matched his asking price, and I told him you were willing to pay cash. And I made sure the real estate representative also heard the offer."

<He has done much in a short amount of time,> Henry said.

<We wouldn't have known to do half of it,> Vlad said. <Pete Denby is being fair to the humans in making these bargains, but he's also being fair to us.>

Tess had made no comments, but Simon noticed her hair was now a wavy brown, which meant she was no longer angry.

"We're agreed," he said. "We'll buy that house and pay the human in the way you suggested."

Pete made another note. "I'll get the paperwork started on Moonsday. Oh. One other thing. Mrs. Tremaine is moving into a smaller place and is leaving a fair amount of her furniture behind. She said she'd call a couple of people who have tables at the stall market to cart the stuff away, but you might want to take a look before she does that. Personally, I think some of it is junk, but Eve thought a few things could be spruced up and look quite nice. It's available for the asking, and it certainly wouldn't hurt to look."

"Junk?" Simon cocked his head. The Crows hadn't gone out for their trash treasure hunts since the day some humans baited a street and tried to kill Jenni Crowgard and her sisters, as well as many other Crows. Meg's warning had saved the Crowgard, but the experience had soured the Crows' pleasure in finding bits of shiny among the trash humans set at the curb each week. Maybe this would be fun for the Crowgard? And they could discard whatever they didn't want.

"We'll look," he said. Then he thought about Pete and his family packing up their car and escaping to Lakeside after Pete had helped Captain Burke search for the Controller. "You owned a house full of stuff."

"Yes. Well, we rented a house."

"But you owned the stuff." He'd never seen the inside of a human house except on TV shows, but he had the impression a real house looked similar to the Crows' shop, Sparkles and Junk—packed with all the bits and pieces humans couldn't seem to live without.

Pete gave him a crooked smile. "Yes, we owned stuff. But stuff can be replaced."

"What will happen to it?"

Pete shrugged. "The rent was paid through the end of this month. After that, I expect the landlord will haul everything out and put it in storage—or more likely keep the furniture and rent the house as furnished and sell everything else, claiming he couldn't find me."

As far as Simon was concerned, territory mattered because territory was about having a place to live that had plenty of food and good water, but a table was a table, a chair was a chair. As long as it functioned, one wasn't any different from the other. But humans were more like the Crowgard. They collected stuff.

"Write down your address," Simon said. "I'll see if there is anything the *terra indigene* in that area can do about retrieving your possessions."

Everyone—human and Other—looked at him in surprise.

"Appreciate that," Pete finally said. He pulled out a ring of keys, removed two keys, and set them on the table. Then he wrote down the address and town. "If your friends have to choose what to transport, tell them personal things first—clothes, toys, the photographs. Those are more important to Eve and me than a piece of furniture."

"I'll talk to them," Simon said. "Anything else you need from us?"

"No." Pete put his papers in his briefcase and walked toward the door. Then he stopped and looked at them. "Thank you."

As Pete walked out, Nathan Wolfgard walked in.

"The Addirondak Wolves want to know if they can send some of the pack to Lakeside for a visit," Nathan said. "They'd like the Wolves who have studied how to interact with humans to have some day-to-day exposure to humans before taking an assignment in a Courtyard."

"There are human settlements in the Addirondaks," Henry said.

"Yes, but the settlements are small and have trading posts where the *terra indigene* go to buy human goods. I went to one of those places, and it had all the basic items we need when we're in human form, but it's a different experience than going into stores like the ones in our Market Square. The humans who live in those settlements and work in the trading posts are Intuits, and they're polite, but they don't really *talk* to the *terra indigene*, not like the humans are doing here." Nathan shrugged. "We have things the Addirondak Wolves have only heard of."

"Like our very own blood prophet squeaky toy?" Tess asked dryly.

Nathan squirmed.

Mine! Simon swallowed the thought—and the accompanying growl—when Henry shifted in his chair.

"We have our own human instructor who can show *terra indigene* details that humans learn when they're young," Henry said. He turned to Simon. "That's why you hired Ruthie, isn't it? So that more than the Lakeside Courtyard can learn what to look for in a human who could be a friend—and how to recognize behavior that indicates an enemy?"

"Yes," Simon agreed. "We need to recognize both kinds of humans." As soon as he could shift out of this skin, he'd give his fur a good shake—and take a quick run to find out what Meg was doing. "I'll talk to the Addirondak Wolves. We have room for a few guests."

That much settled, they went their own ways. Henry went to his studio. Tess went to A Little Bite. Simon and Vlad went downstairs to fill out book orders and open up HGR. They kept the Residents Only sign on the door to discourage humans from coming in, but more of the Courtyard's residents were venturing in now for the experience of buying a book and having a small interaction with one of the humans in Meg's pack.

"I'll be back soon," Simon said.

"If you have any sense, you'll run away from the females, not toward them," Vlad called after him as he walked into the stock room.

Ignoring Vlad's laughter, Simon stripped off his clothes and set them on a chair near HGR's back door. Then he stepped outside, shifted to Wolf, and trotted off to see Meg.

As long as he could outrun them, he wasn't worried about dealing with the female pack.

CHAPTER 20

The female pack—Meg, Merri Lee, Ruth, and Theral—met up at the Green Complex before walking back to the Market Square. It was an experiment to figure out what the *cassandra sangue* could absorb and what triggered overload. Since Merri Lee and Ruth were helping her write up notes for *The Blood Prophets Guide*, and Theral worked in the medical office and might need to know about the triggers, Meg had asked them to join her on a walk from her apartment to the Market Square.

She drove this road every workday and she often took walks with Simon and Sam. So the road was familiar and yet slightly different each time, but she didn't remember experiencing her mind blanking out whenever something changed. So what did overwhelm *cassandra sangue* to the point of panic . . . and self-destruction?

She needed to find out because it wasn't just about her anymore or about upsetting the Others in this Courtyard. The *Guide* wasn't just Simon's way of keeping the female pack busy. There were girls out there right now who wanted to live and might not survive because the people who wanted to help them didn't know how to help them.

So she and her friends would walk, and she would look, and maybe they would find an answer to one question that would help some of the girls live a little while longer. Maybe even long enough for her to figure out the next answer.

"We took the Courtyard bus up to the Green Complex," Merri Lee said as the women headed toward the Market Square. "Henry met us in the Market Square and told the driver that we were allowed to take the bus up to your apartment from now on."

"I think a Hawk was driving," Ruth added. "Or maybe it was an Owl. Anyway, just before the bus stopped at the Green Complex, I saw the big patch of overturned earth that must be the kitchen garden. And there were wooden stakes with string beyond what's already turned, so it looks like the Others really are planning to expand it enough for all of us to have a share."

"I hope we can all participate," Merri Lee said. "But even if Mr. Wolfgard is only making that offer to tenants of the apartment buildings, the vegetables and fruits sold at the Market Square grocery store are always very fresh—and they cost less than in the human grocery stores."

"What about the butcher shop?" Theral asked. "I went in to buy some meat a few days ago, but that shop seemed a little . . . strange."

A hesitation. "Just remember to be specific about what you want," Merri Lee finally said.

"Maybe that's why my aunt said the beef tasted a bit odd, and why Lawrence turned pale when I said I bought the meat at the Market Square."

"If it tasted gamy, it wasn't beef, which isn't always available," Ruth said. "The grocery store is a bit hit-or-miss too. You can find a jar of spaghetti sauce and a box of pasta, but no boxes of cereal. Lots of things sold in canning jars that you're expected to return, but not much sold in cans."

"Canned foods taste like metal, and the *terra indigene* tend to eat fresh foods that are in season," Meg said. The pins-and-needles feeling filled her cheeks, tongue, and jaw.

She stopped and studied a cluster of plants that hadn't been in bloom a couple of days ago.

The other girls stopped too.

"How are you doing?" Merri Lee asked, eyeing Meg while Ruth took a picture of the plants.

"All right," Meg replied. Now that they had stopped talking about food, the prickling faded. Should she mention that? Or would her friends feel uncomfortable about talking to her at all, afraid that they would trigger the need to cut?

"What kind of flower is that?" Ruth asked as Merri Lee waited, pen poised over a small notebook.

"Wildflower?" Meg offered. "I don't recall a training image that matches it."

"It is a herald of Summer," said a female voice behind them. "What other name does it need?"

"Good morning, Spring," Meg said, turning to face the Elemental. "Hello, Mist."

"You are not working today?" Spring asked.

"I am. We all are. But we're taking a walk first."

"Very wise. It will rain later. Not a storm. A soft rain for all that is blooming. But some things need a small drink now." Spring smiled at them before she and Mist cantered away.

Theral pointed to the spot where the Elemental and steed had been. "The road is wet there. Just there."

"That's because Mist was standing there," Meg said.

The girls stared at her. Finally Merri Lee said, "So the ponies really are their names?"

"Yes."

"Wow."

Theral didn't know the names of all the ponies and didn't understand the significance, but Ruth and Merri Lee, who had witnessed the storm in Febros, looked a little scared.

"That explains some things," Ruth said.

Meg didn't remember much about the storm that struck Lakeside after she'd fallen through the ice on the creek. But she remembered being stuck in the hospital, along with Simon and Jester, because the whole city had been trapped by a record snowfall.

She also remembered waking up at some point to find Simon in Wolf form, scrunched into that hospital bed with her to keep her warm.

"Better get moving," she said.

Crows followed them as they continued down the road. Hawks soared overhead or found a convenient observation perch. A couple of Owls, who should have been home by now, flew over their heads.

A small rabbit hopped across the road, watched by a Hawk. Would the Hawk have done more than watch if the girls hadn't been passing his perch?

Grateful she didn't have a new image of a bunny being killed, Meg looked at the flowers and grass and trees. Would Simon let her work in the garden? If she wore gloves and was careful to protect her skin, she could plant and weed like the other girls. Couldn't she?

"Do ponies talk to each other?" Merri Lee asked.

Meg turned away from the flowers that had caught her attention and smiled. All the ponies except Mist were at the junction where the Courtyard's main road met the road leading to the Pony Barn. Even Whirlpool, the newest pony, was there, although he still hadn't quite achieved the "I'm a harmless, chubby pony" form.

Meg waved at them. "We have carrots for the treat today."

"Is that significant?" Ruth asked when they were far enough down the road not to be overheard.

"Everyone comes for the treat on Moonsday because it's sugar lumps," Meg said. "But not everyone will show up for carrots."

"Makes sense," Merri Lee said.

"So does that," Ruth said quietly.

A Wolf with a dark coat shot with lighter gray hairs raced toward them—big, fast, lethal. And happy. Maybe that meant the meeting had gone well? More likely, Simon was happy to be outdoors and furry, even if it was only for a few minutes.

"I didn't bring the rope, and I'm not going to run and get all sweaty before starting work, so don't even think about playing herd the human," Meg said.

He laughed at her—she could tell he was laughing—and eyed the woven hat Merri Lee had brought for her to wear so her head wouldn't get sunburned.

Meg clamped a hand on the hat, which seemed to amuse him.

Wolves could make a game out of almost anything, and playing snatch the hat could go on for weeks before they became sufficiently bored to look for something else.

Having achieved whatever he came to do, Simon turned and loped in the direction of the Market Square.

He would have stayed if she'd been walking alone.

"You could call him back, walk on ahead of us," Merri Lee said.

Meg shook her head. "We're doing an experiment."

But she wished she could have run a hand through his fur, just for that moment of connection. Just to say *I am here.*

———

Simon pulled on the clothes he'd left at HGR: jeans, canvas shoes, and a dark green polo shirt. Not the kind of outfit he used to wear during bookstore work hours, but he didn't have to worry about making the correct impression on human customers anymore. Besides, now that it was warmer, these were the same kinds of clothes Kowalski, Debany, and MacDonald wore when they weren't on duty. For the *terra indigene* who kept watch on the humans, blending in on a city street was just as important as moving unseen in the wild country.

Meg looked fine. He'd caught the scent of fear when he'd caught up with the girls, but it hadn't come from her. Someone else in the gaggle had feared the Wolf because he looked like a Wolf.

He grinned. Gaggle of girls. Female pack had a sound of teeth and power. But gaggle? Easier to deal with a gaggle as long as he remembered a gaggle could change into a pack pretty damn fast.

As he reached the archway between HGR and A Little Bite, he noticed the lattice door was still closed. When he tried to open it, he discovered it was locked.

<Tess?>

<Fucking monkeys. Wither their eyes. Squeeze their hearts into black pulp. Turn them into festering cesspools contained in a weeping bag of skin.>

Simon stepped away from the lattice door. The voice sounded like Tess, but not the Tess he knew.

Plague Rider.

Harvesters were a rare form of *terra indigene*, loners who could kill with a look when their true nature was revealed. He'd invited Tess to live in the Lakeside Courtyard when he'd taken over as the leader. He'd known she was a dangerous predator, but he hadn't known *what* she was until recently. And he'd never felt that he'd put the rest of the *terra indigene* in Lakeside at risk by letting her live here—until now.

<Tess? What's wrong?>

<Go away, Simon. Just . . . go away. I'll talk to you later.>

Hurrying to the stock room, he found the cloth they sometimes used to cover a table for an extra display. He tucked it over the lattice door. He suspected that Tess was somewhere in the back of her shop, out of sight of anyone looking in the windows, but if that wasn't the case, he didn't want any of his own being struck down by catching sight of her.

"Simon? Something you should know before you meet with the police." Vlad approached him and eyed the covering. "What's that?"

"Something's wrong with Tess. Lieutenant Montgomery and the Lizzy will be coming down from the apartment anytime now. I *think* Tess locked all the doors into A Little Bite, but wait by our back door and make sure everyone comes into HGR."

"You going to call Henry?"

Simon nodded. Not that a Grizzly could do any more than a Wolf against a Harvester, but Henry had been the first to recognize Tess's form of *terra indigene* by the way she'd killed Asia Crane during the attack on the Courtyard. And Henry could help him keep everyone else away from the coffee shop.

While Vlad went out back to keep watch, Simon called Henry, Blair, and Nathan.

Lieutenant Montgomery walked in first, followed by Kowalski. Blair and Nathan arrived moments later.

"Where is the Lizzy?" Simon asked sharply.

Montgomery hesitated. "I needed a minute to talk to you, and Mr. Beargard kindly invited her to see his garden totems."

The girl hadn't slipped past Vlad and stumbled into Tess. Good.

Montgomery and Kowalski looked at the cloth covering the lattice door.

"Is there a problem?" Montgomery asked.

"Tess needs some quiet time," Simon replied. And as soon as it was safe to approach her, he'd find out what had angered her so much.

"I need a favor," Montgomery said, looking uncomfortable. "Lizzy has to make a formal statement this morning, and she'd like the Wolf police to go with her."

"Wolf police?" Blair said.

Nathan huffed. "I didn't think she'd know what an enforcer was."

"Why does she want Nathan?" Simon asked.

"Lizzy believes that Boo Bear protects her from bad things, and now he's not with her when she has to talk about what happened to her mother. That's why she'd like Nathan to come with us. She says he has big teeth, even bigger than Boo Bear's."

They stared at Montgomery. Finally Simon said, "Boo Bear doesn't have *any* teeth, so *everyone* has bigger teeth."

"I know that." Monty hesitated. "Lizzy's mother was stabbed at the train sta-tion yesterday morning. She's dead."

Had I looked that tired and confused the night Daphne was shot? The night Sam watched his mother die? Simon glanced at Vlad. <You knew?>

<Captain Burke asked me to check with the Sanguinati in Toland for news,> Vlad replied. <Stavros called early this morning with information. It sounds like the lieutenant has learned enough to know why the Lizzy was on the train alone.>

"I'll go with the puppy," Nathan said.

"A lone Wolf in a building full of humans with guns?" Blair growled.

"Not alone," Kowalski said. "Nathan won't be alone."

Simon nodded to acknowledge that promise.

"I'll go with her," Nathan said. "But the Lizzy is a squeezer, so I won't shift to Wolf form."

"It's a sign of fear," Simon said, pleased to share a nugget of information about human females—and relieved to think of something besides a death that stirred up too many memories. "When Meg watches a Wolf Team movie with Sam, I end up being squeezed."

Should he mention the nervous fur plucking? Nah. That might just be Meg. Besides, Nathan wasn't going as Wolf, so it shouldn't matter.

"I've got the car," Kowalski said. "We can go whenever you're ready, Lieu-tenant."

Montgomery looked at the covered door. "Anything I can do to help with that?"

Simon shrugged. "When I find out what upset her, I'll let you know."

Montgomery, Kowalski, and Nathan left the store to fetch Lizzy and drive over to the station.

Simon studied the doorway, then went to the counter to work on whatever orders he could fill.

When Tess was ready to talk, she'd let him know. He just hoped she didn't kill anyone before then.

CHAPTER 21

Watersday, Maius 12

Nathan didn't like the police station. Too many walls, too many people, too much noise. He didn't like the way some of the men watched him as he walked by with the Lizzy and Lieutenant Montgomery. Hard not to snarl a warning for them to keep their distance.

Hard not to notice the way some of the men looked at Kowalski—as if he no longer belonged to the same pack.

Then he caught the scent of Captain Burke before the men realized the captain was there. And he wondered how Burke would settle this potential conflict within the police pack.

"Mr. Wolfgard," Captain Burke said. "Thank you for coming in with Lizzy and Lieutenant Montgomery. If you would follow me?"

Burke led them to a small room.

Someone had been sick in here not that long ago. Should he tell Captain Burke that the humans hadn't cleaned up all the sick? The room held the stinging scent of cleansers, so maybe humans thought the room was clean and couldn't smell what was still there.

He hoped the Lizzy didn't take a long time to tell her story. He did not want to stay in that room.

He tried to look as if he wasn't paying much attention. After all, his job was to guard the Lakeside Courtyard, not fuss about something that had happened in Toland, so why would he be interested in such things?

Easier to pretend he wasn't interested when he was in Wolf form. The deliverymen who came to the Liaison's Office talked to Meg. It didn't occur to them that the Wolf who looked like he'd lost interest as soon as he recognized them still listened to everything they said.

He had a feeling police weren't as easy to fool as deliverymen. Especially someone like Burke.

After assuring Lizzy that Boo Bear was getting the best care and still needed to stay at the station and help the police, Captain Burke turned on a tape recorder. Then he just wiggled his pen and stared at the paper in front of him.

What was Burke waiting for? How long was he going to wait? They didn't need to sneak up on the answers like some kind of skittish prey. The Lizzy had the answers. They just needed to ask the damn questions so they could all get out of this room!

"Why now?" Nathan asked. He ignored the sharp looks from Burke and Montgomery and focused on the Lizzy. "Why did your mother want you to come to Lakeside now?"

Lizzy fiddled with a button on her shirt. "Mommy and Mr. Scratch had a fight because Mr. Scratch went to a sleepover at a lady's house, and Mommy didn't like that. She yelled at him, and he slapped her face. Then he packed his suitcase and left. Then Mommy called Grandma Borden and cried, and when she hung up, she cried some more. Then Boo Bear's stitches broke because Uncle Leo didn't do it right the last time we played doctor, and I tried to fix Boo Bear with the sticky bandages, and then Mommy looked at Boo Bear and found the secret."

Nathan studied the two men. At the word *doctor*, they had stiffened as if they'd scented danger, which made no sense since a word didn't have a smell.

"Did your mommy call anyone?" Captain Burke asked.

Lizzy shook her head. "She said we had to keep the secret until we could talk to Daddy."

"Do you remember what day that was? Did you go for the train ride the next day?"

"No. We went to the bank and got money. And Mommy packed a suitcase for each of us. And when Uncle Leo came over, she told me to stay in my room because our trip to see Daddy was a *big* secret, and Boo Bear might blab."

Nathan considered this additional information. He didn't understand why play would be bad. Play was how the young learned skills. Maybe playing with the Uncle Leo was the bad part, that the male was a danger? Since the mother was so concerned about the Lizzy talking to the Uncle Leo, it sounded like human young didn't know enough to stay quiet and hidden when a predator came sniffing around the den. Didn't seem fair to blame Boo Bear, though, since *he* wouldn't have blabbed to anyone.

"Then what happened?" Captain Burke asked.

"As soon as it was dark, Mommy and I went to a hotel for a girls' night out. We painted our toenails and watched TV and ate dinner in our room. And she didn't make her mad face when I didn't eat all my vegetables." Lizzy kept fiddling with the button.

"Lizzy?" Montgomery said quietly.

"Mommy kept saying that the train ride had to be a secret from everyone, even Grandma Borden and Uncle Leo." The look she gave Nathan made him want to whine in sympathy. "I didn't tell the *secret* when Uncle Leo called. But . . . maybe I said I knew a secret."

"When was this?" Captain Burke asked. "Do you remember?"

"In the morning," Lizzy replied. "Mommy was in the bathroom. That's why I answered the phone."

"Did Mommy tell you not to answer it?" Montgomery asked.

She turned to him. "But it was the *phone*, Daddy. And it kept ringing and ringing."

Montgomery nodded. "What did Uncle Leo say?"

"He asked what we were doing at a hotel, and I told him we were having a girls' night out, and he said we'd packed a lot of stuff for one night and were we going somewhere? And I said I couldn't tell him because it was a secret. Then Mommy came running out of the bathroom and hung up the phone and said we had to leave *right now*. I told her I didn't brush my teeth yet and Boo Bear needed to make poop, but she said right now meant *right now* and Boo Bear would have to wait until we got to the train station because I had blabbed to Uncle Leo after she'd told me not to answer the phone." Tears filled Lizzy's eyes. She sniffled.

"You made a mistake, Lizzy girl," Montgomery said. "But the man at the desk would have told Uncle Leo that you and Mommy were staying at the hotel. That's why he called your room. So the man at the desk made a mistake too."

Burke quietly cleared his throat. "Then you went to the train station?"

Lizzy nodded. "Mommy bought two tickets. Then we went to another window, and she said I could be a big girl and buy the tickets for Lakeside. She stood right behind me, and the man smiled and winked at her, and then I gave him the money and he gave me tickets, and Mommy told me to put the tickets and the extra money in the special zip pocket inside my summer coat. Then she said we were going to pretend we were being chased, like in a movie. Boo Bear and I had the secret that we had to bring to Daddy, and she would be the decoy. If she could, she would get on the train with me. If the bad men were already looking for us, she would lead them away and catch the train to Hubb's Knees, and then call Daddy."

"Your mommy put you on the train?" Burke asked.

"She showed me where I was supposed to stand when it was time; then we went to a restroom so Boo Bear could make poop before getting on the train. And I had to . . ." Lizzy stopped, her cheeks flushing red. "Mommy got mad because Boo Bear didn't keep his mind on his business and took a long time and we were going to miss the train. But when we left the restroom, she looked around and made a sound, like she was going to be sick. She told me to get on the train, to find a family with children and act like I belonged with them, like a girl would do in the movies. She told me to go *now*, and she pushed me. Then she went back into the restroom."

"Did you get on the train?"

"I didn't want Mommy to be a decoy! I did what she told me, sort of, but then I went back to the restroom because I didn't want to go without her. But she was on the floor, holding her tummy. I shook her arm, and she looked at me and told me to run. She told me she would be all right in a minute, but I had to run before the bad man hurt me too."

The button Lizzy had been fiddling with the whole time came off the shirt. She looked at it for a long moment, then set it on the table.

"There was a boy and girl with their mommy and daddy getting on the train. The boy was crying and stamping his feet and all the people were looking at him. While the daddy was scolding him and picking him up, I got on the train with the mommy and then found a seat by myself."

Silence. Then Burke said, "Thank you, Lizzy. That was a very good report. Why don't you and your father get something to drink and wait for me in my office? I'd like to get Mr. Wolfgard's statement about the train ride."

Nathan would have preferred getting a drink with the Lizzy, but he remained seated and watched Montgomery and the Lizzy leave the room.

"What happened on the train?" Burke asked.

"I had spent some time in the Addirondak Mountains and was on my way home," Nathan replied, shrugging. "Took a seat. Noticed the Lizzy and Boo Bear by themselves. A human male kept walking through the car and looking at her. She's just a pup, and Boo Bear doesn't have teeth, and no adult members of her pack had shown up, so . . ." Another shrug.

"So you stepped in," Burke finished. "Lizzy might not have reached Lakeside if you hadn't."

Nathan shifted in his chair. "This room stinks. Can we leave now?"

"Stinks because you don't like being here?"

"It *smells* of sick and cleansers."

"Ah. I'll let maintenance know."

The moment Burke stood up, Nathan was on his feet too.

"Officer Kowalski will drive you back to the Courtyard. Would you mind taking Lizzy with you, just for an hour or two? Lieutenant Montgomery and I have some work to do."

Nathan studied the human. The voice. Too casual. Like when a Wolf trotted past a herd of deer pretending not to notice them.

"Why do you want her there?" Nathan asked. "This building is protected. You have many humans with guns."

"I've been told that Celia Borden wants custody of Lizzy," Burke said quietly. "Leo Borden knew where Lizzy and Elayne were staying. Not a big leap to think Leo told someone, and that person wanted to make sure Elayne Borden didn't leave Toland while her daughter's toy held a fortune in gems."

"What does that have to do with the Lizzy staying in the Courtyard?"

"Human law doesn't apply in the Courtyard. I want to make sure our laws can't be used against Lizzy and put her in danger. I don't want to be compelled to hand her over to the enemy."

Nathan thought trying to force Burke to do something that made him angry would be like trying to force Henry Beargard, with pretty much the same result. "That's Simon's decision, not mine."

Burke didn't mention that he and his police had helped Simon protect Meg, had done more to be helpful than humans had done before. Smart of Burke not to mention it and to keep the choice with the *terra indigene*.

"Tess is angry, so I'm not sure the Courtyard is the safest place, but the Lizzy can come back with me," Nathan said. And he'd just hope some of the human pack were around and knew what to do with a human pup.

CHAPTER 22

Watersday, Maius 12

There had been the sound of dripping, and blood on the floor, and the other girls. . . .

She stood next to the bed and focused on the man who blocked the room's doorway.

A different place. A new keeper. But he didn't look like a Walking Name. It wasn't just the jeans and blue shirt that made him different from the ones who had controlled her in the compound. He seemed . . . wild . . . and his amber eyes made her certain that he wasn't human.

Why had one of *them* brought her to this place?

"I'm Jackson Wolfgard. You said you wanted to live. The Intuits couldn't keep you in their village, so we brought you here to the Wolfgard camp in the *terra indigene* settlement."

She had said she wanted to live. Had screamed the words. Yes. She remembered that much. Her memories of how she had gotten from that room to this one were veiled.

She recalled training images of expressions in an attempt to figure out what she saw in his face. Reluctance. Resignation.

He moved to the desk and chair, the only other pieces of furniture in the room besides the bed and small table with a lamp. When he stepped away, she stared at the silver razor he'd left on the desk.

"Meg, the Trailblazer, says you should have the razor, that cutting should be your choice. She says this kind of room will help quiet your mind." Jackson watched her, just as she watched him. "We don't know how to take care of the sweet blood, but we'll try to help you stay alive, if that's what you want." A hesitation. "You should choose a name."

"I'm called *cs821*," she whispered.

"That's not a name."

She didn't know what to say.

"If you want something, ask us."

When she nodded, he left the room and closed the door.

She waited, but nothing happened. When she got tired of waiting, she explored the room. Wood walls, wood floor, wood ceiling. Wood desk, wood chair, wood table, wood headboard. Wood shutters that were open, but the screened window was covered on the outside with white paper that allowed light to come in but prevented her from seeing out.

The adjoining room had a toilet and sink and another small covered window.

Returning to the bedroom, she went to the desk and reached for the razor gleaming silver on the dark wood. The euphoria that came from a cut would make her feel good. So good.

But something Jackson said finally clicked. Meg, the Trailblazer, had told her new keepers that this is what she needed to stay alive. *Meg.*

Could it be . . . ?

She looked around the room again. Nothing but wood and a covered window.

She walked over to the bed and studied the cover, sorting through training images until she came up with an identification. Patchwork quilt. Different colors, different patterns of fabric stitched together.

Gingerly, she sat on the bed. Timidly, she touched the quilt. Quietly, her finger traced the patterns. Intrigued by the shapes, she forgot about the razor.

CHAPTER 23

Watersday, Maius 12

" 'The terra indigene *demanded full disclosure of the whereabouts of these so-called blood prophets, publicly exposing already troubled girls who, according to medical experts, require the quiet life of private institutions. And once these institutions admitted to having some of these troubled children, the Others removed the girls from sheltered environments and took them to undisclosed locations. Everyone willing to stand up for human rights and human dignity should insist that the government in every village, town, city, and region in Thaisia demand the same full disclosure from the terra indigene that they demanded of us. If the Others truly mean these girls no harm, let us see them, let us know they're safe. And let humans take care of humans without fear of reprisal.'*

"Nicholas Scratch's speech was heard by a standing-room-only crowd at an HFL fund-raiser in Toland. Closer to home, Mayor Franklin Rogers told reporters that he would assist Governor Patrick Hannigan in creating a medical task force for the Northeast Region. The task force will be charged with inspecting all facilities that care for at-risk girls who have life-threatening addictions."

"Turn that off," Burke said as he drove up Main Street toward the Courtyard.

Monty turned off the radio. "So-called blood prophets. Do you think someone like Nicholas Scratch doesn't know about the existence of *cassandra sangue* and what those girls can do?"

"The Cel-Romano Alliance of Nations has developed an airplane—a new form of transportation that gives humans an expansive look at the land around them. The Humans First and Last movement bursts onto the scene in Thaisia, coming over from Cel-Romano. A speaker for the movement arrives in Toland to spread the message that humans should come first, last, and everything in between when it comes to having the resources available in this world. Drugs show up in various human communities and either render the user completely passive or so aggressively violent that self-preservation isn't a consideration. Is it a coincidence that all these things have happened in such a short time? I don't think so. Developing an airplane would take months, even years. Now that there's a machine that works, it would be time to put the other pieces in place. I wouldn't be surprised to hear that Scratch had had contact with the Controller or men like him. I wouldn't be surprised to hear that the drug problems in Thaisia were tests of potential weapons. The last message I received from my cousin, Shady Burke, indicated that Cel-Romano still shows signs of preparing for war. Living in the human part of Brittania, he's concerned that Cel-Romano's leaders may decide that it's too risky to fight the *terra indigene* and will attack other human-controlled parts of the world in order to acquire more land and resources."

"And Brittania is the closest place." Monty bobbed his head. "Either way, having some idea of what the future might look like and being able to adjust military plans could make the difference in winning or losing a battle."

"Drugging troops to turn them berserk is also helpful when facing an enemy that humans have feared since our first encounter with the *terra indigene*."

"Do you think the Others found all the blood prophets who were taken away from compounds and breeding farms?" Monty's stomach did a slow roll as he considered the possibilities. The drugs gone over wolf and feel-good were made from the blood of *cassandra sangue*. Wouldn't Cel-Romano leaders want to have the source nearby if troops needed to receive a dose just before battle?

Maybe that was something he should mention to Simon Wolfgard. Ships were the only way to cross the Atlantik. If the girls were being taken from Thaisia, they would have to travel by ship. And what eastern city had ships coming and going daily to ports in other parts of the world?

"You think the Toland police know where Scratch is staying?" Monty asked.

"I'd be surprised if they weren't the ones providing protection," Burke replied. "And if you're looking for someone to stir up trouble, Scratch is a persuasive bastard. He's got everyone so focused on what's happened to the *cassandra sangue* over the past few days that no one is asking what had been happening to those girls for generations. As for this medical task force, the *terra indigene* might allow unknown doctors to go into the settlements where the girls are residing. Letting them leave is a whole different story."

Monty watched a white car turn into the Courtyard's Main Street entrance. "I think that's Dominic Lorenzo's car. Must be his morning to work in the Courtyard." Or Meg Corbyn needed medical treatment and Lorenzo had been summoned.

Burke turned into the Courtyard and continued down the access way. Pulling into the employee parking lot, he parked in a space beside Lorenzo's car.

"What brings you here this morning?" Burke asked as the three men walked toward the back door of Howling Good Reads.

"I need to talk to Simon Wolfgard about the medical task force," Lorenzo replied.

"You're not going to try to convince him that letting doctors into settlements tucked in the wild country is going to be beneficial?"

"May the gods help me, yes, I am." Lorenzo looked uneasy. "As of this morning, I'm the task force for Lakeside and the surrounding area. I'm on paid leave from Lakeside Hospital in order to gather information and provide medical care for blood prophets. I've been given a grant from Lakeside's government to hire one assistant. I'm hoping I'll be allowed to make use of Ms. MacDonald's administrative skills in exchange for sharing anything I learn with the Others. Right now, I'm one of four doctors covering the entire Northeast Region."

"Couldn't you decline the appointment?" Monty asked.

"I could have. I didn't. Helping these girls will have an impact on everyone. And thanks to my exposure to the Others here, I have a little experience dealing with the *terra indigene*, which is something the other doctors can't say."

"At least you won't spend half your time traveling across the whole region."

"Not in the beginning, anyway. First we have to locate the girls, and I doubt we'll be successful unless the *terra indigene* choose to help." Lorenzo eyed Monty. "You okay?"

"Been better." He hesitated, but there *was* a medical office in the Market Square, and Lorenzo was here. "After you talk to Wolfgard, I'd appreciate it if you could give my daughter a quick checkup."

"Is she sick?"

When Monty hesitated, Burke said, "Lizzy's mother was murdered in the Toland railway station yesterday. The girl boarded the train on her own to come to Lakeside to be with Lieutenant Montgomery."

"Gods," Lorenzo breathed. "Sure, I'll take a look. The girl wasn't injured?"

"No," Monty said. Then he tipped his head toward HGR's back door. "Doctor, you go ahead. I need a word with the captain."

Burke raised his eyebrows and waited.

"Someone close to Elayne and Lizzy slipped a bag of jewels into a stuffed bear that was seldom out of Lizzy's reach," Monty said.

"Unless it was Elayne herself, the short list is her mother, her brother, Leo, and Nicholas Scratch," Burke said.

"Using Boo Bear was a desperate choice or hasty one. Scratch strikes me as being smarter than that."

"Maybe. But if Leo playing doctor with Boo Bear and Lizzy meant operations—opening seams and sewing them up again—then planting the jewels in the bear had been part of a plan all along, although I would guess that the jewels had been hidden somewhere else in the apartment most of the time."

"It doesn't explain where the jewels came from," Monty said. "Elayne's family is sufficiently well-to-do, but I don't think they could afford that many jewels unless they liquidated all their assets."

"Not an impossible action if her family is committed to the Humans First and Last movement and is willing to support it to that extent. The other possibility is the bag of jewels represents contributions from many families or supporters." Burke opened HGR's back door. "And you're forgetting the third possibility—that the jewels were stolen and Scratch or Leo Borden is involved."

Instead of going forward, Monty rocked back a step. Despite the years he and Elayne lived together, and despite being in the same city, he'd never gotten to know her family. There was a coolness whenever he made an appearance at a family gathering that had kept him at a distance. Could he say with any certainty that her family *wasn't* involved in stealing jewels?

"If the jewels were stolen . . ." Monty swallowed hard.

"Using Lizzy as a courier would have made Elayne the fall guy if something went wrong—especially if the investigating officer didn't want anyone looking at Nicholas Scratch or other members of HFL. But Scratch hadn't anticipated Elayne throwing him out for sleeping with another woman, and he hadn't expected her to run."

"Thaisday night, when I called Elayne, someone answered the phone. Just heavy breathing. I thought she was messing with me."

"Someone could have been sent to retrieve the jewels," Burke said grimly.

"If Elayne and Lizzy had been home . . ." Monty couldn't finish the thought. "Would the Toland police tell us if any jewels had been stolen recently?"

Burke gave him that fierce-friendly smile. "The police aren't the only ones who have an information network. And we know people who know people, don't we?" He walked into HGR, leaving Monty to follow.

On busy days, HGR had had more humans in the store than there were right now, but they hadn't been gathered around the counter wanting to talk to *him*.

"What?" Simon growled, eyeing Burke, Montgomery, and Lorenzo.

He decided to take the same approach as he'd take with vultures covering a kill: scatter them.

He pointed at Monty. "Meg asked the girls at the lake if the Lizzy could see the ponies, so Meg, the Lizzy, and Nathan have gone to the Pony Barn and should be back soon." He pointed at Dominic Lorenzo. "Merri Lee, Ruthie, and Theral are at the Liaison's Office, watching for deliveries and making notes to add to *The Blood Prophets Guide*. If you want to talk to them, I'll have Henry go over with you."

"That's fine," Lorenzo said. "I would appreciate any information. But I did want to talk to you about the task force that's now responsible for ascertaining the mental and physical well-being of blood prophets in Lakeside and the surrounding areas."

Stay human, Simon told himself. Tess had finally calmed down enough that she wanted to talk to him. It wouldn't help anyone if he damaged the one doctor he was willing to have around Meg.

Besides, Vlad had just slipped into the front part of the store.

"I don't think the task force will have a problem around here as long as *you* are the doctor making these visits," Vlad said with a smile that showed a warning fang. "I think we can arrange for you to visit Great Island and talk to the people who are taking care of the blood prophets. Then you can assure the humans who didn't care a week ago that the girls are being looked after properly. Make your report about their physical and mental condition. Just remember that it would be very unhealthy if the girls' *location* ever showed up in a report."

"One of the things I've been asked to decide is if a girl is an alleged blood prophet or a girl with other problems that manifested as some kind of self-harm," Lorenzo said. "I'd like to talk to Meg Corbyn and get any insights she can offer."

"Steve Ferryman might have someone who can provide you with some insights," Vlad said.

<Ferryman?> Simon asked, using the *terra indigene* form of communication.

<A female showed up at Ferryman's Landing, driving a car that was loaded with all her possessions, including a dog. She's worked at several houses that took care of troubled girls. After being fired, again, because she isn't afraid to share her opinions with anyone, she packed up and started driving. She told Ferryman she had a feeling this was the place she'd been looking for, the place where she could really help.>

<A feeling? She's an Intuit?>

<He thinks she is, but he's not sure *she* knows what she is. He still wants to take her over to the island and see how she responds to the girls. He wants your approval. So does Ming.>

A few weeks ago, a man named Phineas Jones had tried to reach Great Island to find girls who might be *cassandra sangue*. He had been an enemy. The Controller was dead, and so was Phineas Jones, but other men running compounds could have sent other humans to find the girls.

<She doesn't stay on the island, and she's never alone with the girls,> Simon said.

<Ferryman said the same thing.>

Simon realized the humans had been watching this silent exchange, knowing something was being discussed. "If the woman who came to Ferryman's Landing is acceptable to us, then you can talk to her."

He didn't think Lorenzo liked having decisions made for him, but an Intuit who hadn't lived in one of their communities might understand *outside* better than individuals who had been accepted for their abilities their whole lives. And that was the person Lorenzo should see.

The lattice door between A Little Bite and Howling Good Reads opened. Tess gave no sign of noticing the cloth Simon had used to cover the lattice. Her wildly curling hair had streaks of brown, green, red, and black, as if she didn't quite know how she felt.

Since he suspected her hair had been the death color an hour ago, Simon took all the other colors as a good sign that the rest of the Courtyard most likely would survive.

"When you're done talking with each other, there's something I want the four of you to see," Tess said, looking at Vlad, Montgomery, Burke, and finally Simon. Then she retreated into the coffee shop.

"I'll go over to the Liaison's Office now, if that's all right with you," Lorenzo said. He looked at Montgomery. "If I finish up there before your daughter returns from visiting the ponies, you can find me in the medical office."

Montgomery nodded.

"That takes care of the doctor," Simon said. "Now what do you two want?"

Burke turned to Vlad. "We would appreciate a little more information from your kinsmen in Toland."

"Ah." Vlad looked at Monty. "We've heard nothing more about the death of your former mate."

"I'm wondering if they've heard anything about stolen jewels or jewelry," Burke said.

"Wouldn't the Toland police have heard about such things? Why can't they tell you?"

"The Toland police captain I talked to doesn't like me, so I doubt he'll tell me anything," Burke replied. "Unlike the police captain, I don't think the Sanguinati have any interest in the jewels that were found in Boo Bear. That makes them an unbiased source of information."

Simon studied Burke. The police captain thought the Others would be more honest than his own kind? What did the Sanguinati think about the police in Toland?

"I'll give Stavros a call and see what he or Tolya has heard," Vlad said.

"I'd like to stay in the efficiency apartment with Lizzy one more night, if that's all right with you," Montgomery said.

"We set one apartment aside for the police, so you can stay," Simon said. When the humans didn't speak, he added, "Shall we find out what Tess wants to show us?"

He walked into A Little Bite. Vlad and the two policemen followed him.

Tess stood behind the glass display case, her hair now solid red coils. Angry again. But why?

He glanced at the food in the display case—the pastries, cookies, sandwiches, and other items that were delivered that morning. When he leaned down for a closer look, he understood, and shared, Tess's anger.

Spoiled. All of it. Mold on the bread. Dried-out or moldy cheese in the sandwiches. Even with the lesser human sense of smell and the glass between him and the food, he could scent meat going bad.

"Is something wrong with your refrigeration system?" Burke asked.

"No," Tess replied in a rough voice. "Something is wrong with the humans in this city."

The bakery they had been dealing with had stopped making deliveries a few weeks ago. Trying to give the humans another chance before informing the mayor that the agreements between humans and *terra indigene* had been broken, Tess had contacted another bakery in Lakeside that provided the kinds of foods she sold in A Little Bite.

"This is what I was given this morning," Tess said. "It was packaged in a way that I couldn't see the rot, so I paid the invoice *in cash*, as required." She came around to the front of the display case and jabbed a finger toward the food. "Would you eat that? Would you feed that to your child?"

"No," Montgomery said.

"We're not open to humans who aren't connected to the Courtyard anymore," Simon said.

"That's not the point," Tess snapped. "That was never the point. The agreements with the city are clear enough: we are entitled to anything available to humans. If they can buy it, so can we."

"And if we can't, neither can they," Simon said.

"Are a few pastries and sandwiches that important?" Montgomery asked, sounding alarmed.

Simon looked around. "This coffee shop was modeled on the ones humans use. It provides the same beverages and foods. Most of those shops don't bake their own products; they buy them from bakeries. So we did the same in order to understand why such a place would have any value. When the bakeries all close tomorrow because the agreements with the *terra indigene* were violated *twice* with regard to supplying food for the coffee shop, how important will the lack of those pastries and sandwiches be to the humans who go into those coffee shops?"

"I'm not sure the government will tell the bakeries to close or require the police to enforce those closings," Burke said, sounding as wary as a coyote who'd just caught the scent of a grizzly.

"You won't have to enforce anything," Tess said. "The Elementals can take care of closing the bakeries. I'm sure Fire would oblige once I show her what the monkeys sent us as food for Meg and the other girls."

Simon blinked. Ask one of the Elementals to burn all the bakeries in the city? That seemed . . . harsh. Better to burn down the troublesome ones, especially the one that sold Tess rotten food to give to Meg.

Burke and Montgomery looked shocked—and sufficiently afraid.

Vlad smiled. "Or, rather than burning down all the bakeries, we can redirect the food grown in *terra indigene* settlements and offer it only to human businesses that *will* honor the agreements they make with us. That would cut the food supply coming into this city." He looked at Simon. "Perhaps we can build our own little bakery and hire someone to make what we need."

"Steve Ferryman said the bakeries in Ferryman's Landing would sell to us," Simon said. "And we will need to adjust supply allotments for Ferryman's Landing anyway to accommodate the Wolf cookies they're already making. Redirecting the food is more practical than burning down buildings." But he would give some thought to asking Fire to visit that one bakery.

"Would you be willing to try one more Lakeside bakery?" Montgomery asked. "There's a place on Market Street that I frequent. I'll talk to the owner and see if she would be interested in supplying items for your coffee shop."

Simon hesitated. None of the Courtyard's stores were going to be open to the general public anymore, but the coffee shop would still be a useful learning experience for the *terra indigene* who didn't have access to such a place—or a chance to interact with humans like Meg's pack.

"All right," he said. "One more. If that doesn't work, we'll give our business to Ferryman's Landing—and give them the extra supplies as well."

"We'll do that now," Burke said. "The lieutenant needs to stop by his apartment and check his mail anyway."

<One more thing after the humans are gone,> Tess said to Simon and Vlad.

"I'll tell Jester that Meg and the Lizzy should come back now," Simon told Montgomery. "You can wait for her at the medical office."

"Do you mind if I take a quick look around the bookstore?" Burke asked.

"Go ahead." He watched the men go through the archway before turning to Tess. "What?"

"Even if that food had been good, I wouldn't have placed another order with that bakery," Tess said.

"Why?" Vlad asked.

Black threads appeared in her hair. "Because Jake Crowgard noticed an HFL decal on the delivery van's back window."

CHAPTER 24

Watersday, Maius 12

"**W**hy can't I ride a pony?" Lizzy whined.

Such an annoying sound. If she ever whined like that, Meg hoped Simon bit her. Really hard.

But Wolves whined too. Why didn't it bother her when they did it?

"Because the Courtyard's ponies aren't riding ponies," Meg said for the third time. Her skin prickled every time Lizzy asked to ride a pony, making her feel odd, overwhelmed. She *had* to make Lizzy understand that, in the Courtyard, puppies were supposed to obey adults, and *no* meant *no*. But what more could she do? What more could she say?

When she'd first met the ponies, she hadn't wanted to ride them, and it hadn't occurred to her when she offered to take Lizzy to the Pony Barn that the girl would want to—or be so persistent about getting her own way.

And the ponies, who had been curious enough about the small human to allow Lizzy to pet their noses, now wore their grumpiest faces as they trotted away.

"We have to go back to the Market Square," Meg said. Had anyone heard her? Had she spoken out loud?

Jester Coyotegard growled at Lizzy. "Meg said *no*, and being the one who looks after the ponies, *I'm* saying *no*. So that's the end of it, pup."

"That's not fair!" Lizzy stamped her foot. "Grandma Borden would let me ride a pony!"

Lizzy's voice changed the pins-and-needles feeling into a painful buzz. Meg dug her fingers into her side just above the waistband of her jeans, scratching at her skin through the T-shirt. Needed to think. Couldn't think, not with Lizzy's voice buzzing in her ears. Too much. Too much! Had to . . . what?

"Typical human," a female voice said. "Grant them one thing and they always want more."

Meg stared at the Elemental whose red hair was tipped with yellow and blue, at the female face that could never pass for human. But sometimes danger could hide quietly . . . and so easily.

"Meg?" Nathan's voice.

Nathan. In danger?

The buzz turned into an agony she needed to tear out of her skin before it ate her alive.

Have to stay in control, she thought. *Have to . . .*

She pulled the silver razor out of her pocket.

"Meg!" Nathan snarled, grabbing the hand that held the closed razor. "Meg, what's wrong?" Should he have sensed something? Distracted by the Lizzy, had he missed a sign that Meg would cut?

"I want to ride a pony!" Lizzy shrieked.

He released Meg, whirled around and snapped at Lizzy, his teeth just missing her nose and shocking the girl into silence. Then he grabbed Meg again, trapping the hand with the razor and pulling her other hand away from her side.

"Has the little human hurt our Meg?" Fire asked, looking at Meg and then at the Lizzy.

<Jane!> Nathan called. <Come to the Pony Barn. Meg needs help. Hurry!> More to the point, *he* needed help.

"Let me go!" Meg struggled to free herself. "Need to cut. *Need to.*"

"Meg?" Now the Lizzy sounded scared.

<I'll take the pup back to her sire,> Jester said. The Coyote grabbed the girl, stuffed her into Meg's BOW, and drove off.

"Too much," Meg cried. "Too much danger! I have to cut. I have to cut *now.*"

"You cut a couple of days ago," Nathan protested. "It's too soon."

"Have to," she panted. "Lizzy. Have to."

He wasn't supposed to be around her when she was bleeding. None of the

Wolves were supposed to be around her. *Cassandra sangue* blood was an almost irresistible temptation, as well as a drug humans called feel-good. Simon had learned that the hard way when he licked one of Meg's cuts and suffered an overdose, becoming so passive he'd been helpless for hours.

"Meg," Nathan growled. "Meg!" If he kept holding her, he would end up hurting her. If he let go, she would make the cut when she was acting crazy, and that might kill her.

Meg cried out as if she were in terrible pain. What if she was? What if not letting her cut was damaging her in some way he didn't understand?

Howls from the Wolfgard Complex. Help was coming . . . but not in time.

Nathan looked at Fire. "The only way to protect her is to cut her. But I'll have trouble once she starts bleeding."

Fire stared at him. Then she nodded. "I will protect Meg. Even from you, Wolf."

Nodding, Nathan pulled Meg into the barn. Grabbing a blanket, he tossed it over the straw in the first stall and pushed her down.

Crying. Begging. Was it always like this? He didn't think so.

He pulled the razor out of her hand and opened it. Her hands, now freed, clawed at the skin just above the waistband of her jeans, trying to cut the skin with her fingernails.

Nathan pinned one of Meg's hands under his knee. Fire grabbed her other hand.

How long? How deep? No time to wait for answers.

Sharp steel kissed the skin she'd been scratching. She shuddered, and her face was filled with such terrible pain, Nathan was sure he had killed her. Then her face changed, and he caught the strong scent of lust as Meg began to speak.

The delicious scent of fresh blood filled the air. Sweet blood. Hot. Rich. More potent than any other scent around him.

Nathan's mouth watered and he craved a taste of that blood. Just one little taste.

He shook his head, trying to clear it. Had to listen. That was his job now, to listen.

"Happy mask," Meg said. "Angry face. Ice chest. Heart. Rotting meat."

She said the same words twice. Then she sighed . . . and relaxed.

Nathan leaned closer. He should lick the blood, clean the wound.

"Wolf." A hot warning.

He looked up, startled. He'd been so drawn to the scent of Meg's blood, he'd forgotten about Fire.

"Go outside," a voice said.

Snarling, he sprang to his feet and spun to face the intruder, who held out a hand dotted with feathers.

Owl. Male. Bodywalker. Not a threat.

"Go outside," the Owl said again.

Nathan bolted out of the Pony Barn.

The euphoria passed quickly, and with its passing, Meg became aware of her surroundings again. Her face was wet, someone was pressing on her side too hard for comfort, her jeans and T-shirt were soaked, and Nathan was howling—a sound so full of misery she wanted to cry in response.

Swiping a hand over her face, she opened her eyes and looked at the gray pony nose. A fine mist continued falling over her face.

"I'm awake now, Mist," she said, blinking water out of her eyes.

"Which just proves you've got less sense than a chick still inside the egg."

She turned her head and looked at a male she didn't recognize.

"I'm Welby, the Owlgard bodywalker," he said. "Jane Wolfgard is on her way, but I don't know if she knows how to fix this either."

"Fix . . . ?"

Meg lifted her head to look at the hand pressing a cloth against her side. As she brushed against Mist's muzzle, he lipped her short hair before taking a step back.

Welby pushed her down, none too gently. "You and the little human caused enough trouble today without you hurting yourself even more."

"I . . ." Lizzy. Where was Lizzy? "We caused trouble?"

"You hurt the Wolves and upset the Elementals and Sanguinati." Welby's hair changed to feathers, a sign that he, too, was distressed to the point where he couldn't hold the human form.

She struggled to think of a safe question. "Why am I so wet?"

"Fire got upset and the hay started to smolder. Water came and soaked everything."

Jane Wolfgard rushed into the barn. "Simon says the human bodywalker is at the Market Square office. Blair is outside with a BOW. He says he can stay human long enough to get Meg to the office."

"Where is my razor?" Meg asked once they wrapped her waist to hold a folded cloth over the cut.

"Simon and Henry said all of this straw and the blanket need to be burned," Jane said as she and Welby lifted Meg and took her to the BOW. "Anything with fresh blood on it needs to be burned."

They wouldn't speak to her directly as they settled her in the passenger seat. And Blair just snarled at her, making it clear *he* wouldn't talk to her either.

Just as well, she thought as she pressed a hand over the cut. She was certain Simon would have plenty to say when she saw him.

Would he be able to tell her what happened?

Henry held out a hand. "Give it to me."

Hateful thing, Simon thought, turning the silver razor over and over in hands that were furry and clawed.

"Simon," the Grizzly rumbled.

He gave Henry the razor. "I thought Meg liked Nathan. Why would she do that to him? What am I supposed to say to her?"

He couldn't bite the Lizzy, who had started the trouble, because it was Montgomery's duty to discipline the pup. And he couldn't bite Meg because she was Meg. But he was so scared and furious right now, he really wanted to bite *someone*.

"You will say nothing," Henry said. "I am spirit guide for this Courtyard, so *I* will deal with Meg."

Jester had pulled into the area behind HGR howling for Simon and Vlad and anyone and everyone. Since Burke and Montgomery were still there, they'd come running too.

Something about the Lizzy not being allowed to ride the ponies. Of course she couldn't ride any of the Elementals' steeds, no matter what form they were in! But the Lizzy's whining had caused Meg to try to make a cut when she was out of control. If Nathan hadn't been there . . .

If it was anyone but Meg, she'd get such a bite for upsetting a pack member like that!

"Yes," he said, feeling his canines lengthen. "You deal with Meg. I'll see what I can do for Nathan."

Nathan had run to HGR as soon as Jane Wolfgard ran into the Pony Barn. The moment he handed the folding razor to Simon, he stripped off his clothes and shifted to Wolf. At Tess's insistence, he'd eaten part of a chamomile cookie, but even with that much of a calming effect he was still so upset he couldn't stop shaking or whining.

After Dr. Lorenzo gave the Lizzy a quick check and assured Montgomery that the girl was fine, the lieutenant took the Lizzy back to the efficiency apartment. Now the doctor waited for Meg.

<I'm taking Meg into the medical office now,> Blair said.

<All right,> Simon replied. He hesitated before adding, <Henry will deal with Meg.>

<Good. Right now, I really want to bite her. And that idiot police pup too.>

<Once Meg is with Dr. Lorenzo, come to HGR and help me with Nathan.>

Simon looked at Henry. "Maybe it was a mistake to let humans into the Courtyard. If the Lizzy hadn't gone to the Pony Barn with Meg, this wouldn't have happened."

"Maybe," Henry said. "But we all agreed to try something that hasn't been done before. We are all learning, and that means there will be mistakes. This time, it is Meg who made the mistake, and she must understand what she has done. Go tend Nathan, and let's hope today has not completely soured his willingness to work with humans."

CHAPTER 25

Watersday, Maius 12

"**S**he'll be fine," Ruth said, giving Monty a strained smile. "We'll watch a movie or read a book until you get back."

Monty studied her. "Karl told you?"

"Yes." She glanced at Lizzy, who was sitting in the stuffed chair with her arms wrapped around her legs. "Does Lizzy know?"

Monty shook his head. So much had already happened this morning, there hadn't been the right time to tell his little girl that her mother was dead. And he needed time to consider the questions she might ask. Could they both have gotten away if she hadn't lost track of time in the bathroom, playing her silly game with Boo Bear? Would Elayne have died if Lizzy hadn't answered the phone in the hotel room, confirming their location?

He didn't have answers. Would never have answers. But he needed *some* kind of answer so that Lizzy wouldn't carry guilt as well as grief.

He walked over to the chair and crouched, resting a hand on Lizzy's feet.

"I just wanted to ride a pony," she whimpered, breaking his heart with those big eyes swimming with tears.

"I know, Lizzy girl, I know. But those aren't ponies people can ride, and you should have respected Miss Meg when she told you that."

"Did Miss Meg get hurt because I didn't listen?"

How to explain a blood prophet's addiction to cutting? How to tell his little girl that Meg's new cut was, in some way, her doing? How to say that without Lizzy confusing Meg's cutting with Elayne being stabbed—and dying?

At least the Others had taken the child away before Meg made the cut. But based on the reaction of the Wolves, this had not been a typical cut, and Meg's life had been at risk.

"Miss Meg is a special kind of girl," he said carefully. "And she can get hurt when something is more upsetting than she can handle."

"Nathan doesn't like me anymore."

Probably true, but he said, "We'll see. We'll have time to talk later about all the scary things that have happened. But right now, Miss Ruth is going to look after you while I take care of something with Captain Burke. Is that okay?"

Lizzy nodded.

He wanted to stay with his little girl. She needed him. But he had to balance that need against the welfare of the entire city of Lakeside. So he had to get the bakery issue settled before the Others settled it in their own way.

He kissed Lizzy's forehead, then nodded to Ruth as he left the efficiency apartment to join his captain.

Sitting on the bench in Henry's studio, Meg stared at the fur on the back of the Grizzly's hands. The studio didn't feel peaceful the way it usually did. And the Bear in human form didn't look peaceful. He looked big and powerful . . . and angry.

"I had to cut." She hoped Henry would understand since Simon wouldn't talk to her. She hoped *someone* would understand and help *her* understand, because the pain that had overwhelmed her had been too much to keep inside herself.

"Had to." Nodding, Henry wandered around his studio, looking at the sculptures in various stages of creation. "Had to cut when you were out of control because you're too stupid to try to understand what is around you without cutting?"

She stared at him, shocked. "Henry . . ."

"We've seen enough of these cuts since you came to live with us to know you have warnings, those prickles that tell you something is wrong." Henry towered over her. "You must have had those prickles at the Pony Barn, but you didn't tell Nathan so that he would know something was wrong, didn't walk away from the Pony Barn to see if the prickles would fade. Isn't that what you've done before to determine if a cut was necessary?"

"Yes, but—"

"Instead you stayed, trying to talk to a cub who thought she should get her own way. You stayed when you had already said everything there was to say about her riding the ponies."

"But Lizzy is in danger!" Meg protested.

"Who among us didn't already know that?" he replied with a curtness that wounded her. She expected Simon to snap and snarl at her, but not Henry.

"And Nathan was in danger too!"

"Because of you and the Lizzy!" Henry roared. "*You* put a Wolf who thought you were a friend in the position of being around fresh blood you know is a danger to him. Did you know Nathan had to make the cut? You were so out of control, *he* had to make the cut to stop you from slashing your belly open."

Meg froze, shocked so deeply she could barely breathe. She remembered Nathan howling, so much misery in the sound. "No," she whispered. "No, I didn't do that."

"You did," Henry growled. "Fire helped hold you down, and that experience has sharpened her feelings about humans in general and the Lizzy in particular."

"But it was worth it," Meg insisted. What she had seen had to be worth all this hurt she'd caused to beings she cared about.

Henry pulled a piece of paper wrapped around her folding razor out of his pocket. He tossed both into her lap. "Was this worth the distress you caused?"

She unrolled the paper and stared at the words.

> Happy mask
> Angry face
> Ice chest
> Heart
> Rotting meat

"There must have been more." She watched her hands shake.

"No. That was all you said."

"Maybe . . . maybe the cut wasn't long enough or deep enough." The cut *felt* long enough and deep enough.

"Maybe men like the Controller were right and the *cassandra sangue* can't survive outside of cages. Maybe blood prophets can't experience the world like other beings because everything and everyone can be an excuse to use the razor. Is that what we should tell the Intuits and other humans who are struggling to help these girls survive? That the blood prophets need limited contact with other people, limited experiences, a limited *life*? Otherwise you'll cut yourselves to death over any little thing."

"No! Henry, I did it for Lizzy!"

"None of us believe that."

She stared at him, stunned.

"It is said you have a thousand cuts before the one that kills you. How many scars do you have now, Meg? How many years do you have left if you cut yourself every three days? You say you did this cut for the Lizzy? What do you want us to tell Sam when you bleed out one day from a cut you didn't need to make?"

"Henry . . . ," she sobbed. His words battered her like fists.

"You hurt all of us. You hurt Sam and Simon and Nathan. You upset the Elementals and the ponies and the Sanguinati. You're supposed to be the Pathfinder, the one who will consider alternatives to the razor so that blood prophets *can* live in the outside world."

Pressing a hand to the cut at her waist, she wept. And when Henry sat down beside her and put his arms around her, offering grumbling comfort as he might do for a cub, that hurt worse than his angry words.

CHAPTER 26

Watersday, Maius 12

*L*izzy is fine, and Ruth is well able to look after her for a couple of hours, Monty thought as he and Burke walked into Nadine's Bakery & Café after the lunchtime rush. *Stay focused on the work now.*

Nadine didn't give him her usual smile. Instead she said, "Are you here to ask me to choose a side, Lieutenant?"

"Choose a side?"

"Maybe this has been bubbling under the surface for a long time, but it seems like, all of a sudden, people are expected to declare themselves one way or the other. Either you're for humans and against the Others, or you're a traitor to your own kind. Neutral as an option hasn't been eliminated completely, but it's getting there. There's talk that we'll be seeing shortages of pork and beef by the end of summer because animals are dying due to lack of feed. There's already a limit on how much flour and sugar bakeries can purchase each week, and prices for some items have already gone up—have doubled in some cases." Nadine sighed. "You know Chris from Fallacaro Lock and Key?"

"He works with the *terra indigene* in the Courtyard," Monty replied.

"His father and I are cousins. Last night Chris slept on my couch because his father joined the Humans First and Last movement and declared that the business is humans only from now on, and if Chris does another job for the Others he'll not only be tossed out of the business; he'll be disinherited. And any other employee who doesn't join HFL will be out of a job." Her dark eyes held an equal measure of anger and worry as she focused on Monty. "You usually come in on your way home from the Universal Temple. Somehow, I don't think you're here to pick up a late lunch."

"No, we're not," Monty said, regretting that Nadine was right—he was going to ask her to choose a side. He just hoped that she would understand that choosing the Others *was* a way to help humans. "There's a coffee shop in the Courtyard. It's no longer open to the general public, but it does supply food for human employees as well as the *terra indigene*. Two bakeries in Lakeside that were supposed to supply the coffee shop with baked goods and other foods have broken their agreements with the Courtyard."

"Then the Others should learn to bake or do without," Nadine replied.

"There are bakeries on Great Island that will supply them with anything they want for the coffee shop," Burke said. "But there will be penalties to Lakeside if *no* bakery in the city honors the agreements."

Nadine studied them. "What kind of penalties?"

"Some of the food needed by the people in this city is grown on farms run by the *terra indigene*," Burke said. "All Simon Wolfgard has to do is inform those farms that, from now on, the surplus they had sold to businesses in Lakeside now goes to businesses on Great Island or to other human settlements who do not support the HFL movement. And if Wolfgard, who is the most liberal *terra indigene* leader I've ever met, takes that stand, other *terra indigene* leaders will adopt that stand as well. And then, Ms. Fallacaro, we *will* know shortages."

Nadine stared at Burke. Then she turned to Monty. "Is that true?"

Monty hesitated. "Captain Burke has more knowledge of the *terra indigene* than I do, so I would take his words as truth."

She let out a brittle laugh. "So much for wanting to be neutral."

"You can refuse to supply goods for the Courtyard coffee shop," Monty said.

"How many other bakeries are you going to ask? Or will you just look for the HFL decal in their windows and not even bother to ask?" Her smile was as brittle as her laugh. "Chris's father thinks humans will soon have the capability to rise up against the *terra indigene* and lay claim to every corner of this world. Do you think that can happen?"

Monty looked at Burke, who looked at Nadine.

"I think," Burke said quietly, "that if we were able to visit some parts of the wild country, we would find the remains of great civilizations that once thought the same thing—and were wrong."

They waited, giving her time to consider.

"I don't want to advertise that I'm selling to the Courtyard," she finally said.

"They have unmarked vehicles. Picking up an order could be arranged," Monty said.

"I'm not even sure why I'm agreeing to this," Nadine muttered.

"To keep the peace," Burke said. "You're helping to keep the peace."

"Thank you," Monty said.

"Wait." Nadine quickly assembled two bakery boxes and filled them with a variety of pastries. "I have some quiche left from the afternoon lunch hour. I'll get it for you. Might as well find out if the Others will like what they'll be getting."

She went into the back and returned a few minutes later with another box that held pieces of quiche as well as a few sandwiches. She packed those into a small lightweight cooler that Monty promised to return.

"This could put her in danger," he said after he and Burke stowed the boxes in the backseat of Burke's car and headed for Monty's apartment to pick up the mail and a couple more changes of clothes.

"Yes, it could," Burke agreed. "But this is a precarious time for all of us, whether the majority of people realize it or not."

Since he agreed with that, Monty lapsed into silence during the short drive to his apartment, his thoughts going back to Lizzy. She'd been very upset when Jester brought her to the Market Square medical office. Part of that had been an excessive display of emotion for what should have been a small disappointment when she couldn't ride a pony. More had been real fear when Meg Corbyn spun out of control because of her tantrum.

And may the gods help him, she still didn't know Elayne was dead.

That excessive display wasn't typical of Lizzy. At least, it hadn't been a few months ago. He hoped this wasn't a new pattern of behavior.

Right now he hoped a lot of things.

Burke parked across the street from Monty's apartment. When they went into the building, Monty stopped to check his mailbox before going up the stairs.

He opened the apartment door, took two steps inside, and stopped.

"Lieutenant?" Burke said quietly, drawing his gun.

Monty stepped carefully into the kitchen, set his mail on the table, and looked around. Nothing out of place, and yet . . .

He checked the living room, bedroom, bathroom.

"I think someone searched my apartment," Monty finally said.

"You think?" Burke looked around. He holstered his gun and took out his mobile phone. "This is Burke. I want a list of all trains between Toland and Lakeside yesterday and this morning. And I want a list of every train that arrived in Lakeside between yesterday morning and now. Don't leave those lists sitting on my desk. Hold on to them until I get back to the station."

"This would be the first place someone would look for Lizzy," Monty said. "If they figured out she was on a train to Lakeside, this is where they would look."

"Did someone travel to Lakeside to make a search, or did someone call a person who was already here? There are some police officers in Lakeside who think Humans First and Last is a mighty fine idea." Burke blew out a breath. "The search didn't turn up the bear or the jewels. That could be the reason Captain Scaffoldon called this morning."

Monty looked at Burke. "Scaffoldon? From the CIU unit in Toland?"

"One and the same. Someone called the station early this morning, trying to confirm if you would be home. Shortly after that, Scaffoldon called, claiming to want to know your whereabouts for the time of Elayne's murder. Would have been enough time for someone to search your place and report back to Scaffoldon that nothing was found."

He needed to think clearly, so Monty ignored the burn of anger at being accused of Elayne's murder—and the deeper burn that he and Lizzy could have been here, could have been attacked by whoever was searching for the jewels. More trauma to Lizzy, if not something worse. And for what? Boo Bear and the jewels were already at the Chestnut Street station.

Of course, no one would have known that.

"Are Boo Bear and the jewels in the evidence lockup?" Monty asked.

"Boo Bear, the jewels, and the photographs taken of the evidence are in a safe place," Burke replied.

An evasive answer. Right now, he didn't care about the bear or the jewels, so it was a sufficient answer.

Monty went back into the bedroom and pulled the lockbox off the top shelf. He set it on the bed and opened it. Pete Denby had the copy of Lizzy's birth certificate and the legal papers for the child support, so the lockbox held Monty's checkbook and savings account. His will. A copy of the rental agreement for the apartment. A few other personal papers.

Nothing missing. Nothing out of order.

When Burke stepped into the bedroom doorway, Monty said, "I can't ask an investigating team to dust the apartment for fingerprints when I can't even be sure anyone has been in here." And as soon as he asked, the news would surely travel and, quite likely, reach the ears of the person who had conducted the search.

"That's the human way of looking for an intruder," Burke said. "You have another option."

It took Monty a moment to realize what Burke meant. Then he sighed as he pulled out his phone and called Howling Good Reads.

"Mr. Wolfgard? I realize this isn't a good day to ask for a favor, but I need some help determining if someone has been in my apartment looking for Lizzy."

CHAPTER 27

Watersday, Maius 12

"I'm sorry, Meg," Merri Lee said. "But I think Henry is right. You shouldn't have made that cut, especially when you were feeling out of control."

They were sitting in the back room of the Liaison's Office making a record of what had happened to precipitate Meg's need to make the cut, including everything Lizzy had said while the pins-and-needles feeling escalated to the painful buzz. Now Meg pushed away from the table and went into the sorting room, looking for something to do that would give her an excuse to end this discussion.

"That's not what you wanted to hear." Merri Lee followed Meg into the sorting room and set the pad of paper and pen on the counter.

"I *had* to cut!" Meg shouted. "Why doesn't anyone understand that?"

"Maybe no one understands it because no one else sees it that way," Merri Lee replied hotly. "You screwed up, and now you're trying to justify your actions."

"Lizzy . . ."

"Threw a hissy fit and tried to get her own way. Maybe she's a spoiled brat and thinks she should always get her own way. Maybe she's been misbehaving—and getting away with it—because her mother caved when she started whining and Lieutenant Montgomery wasn't there to insist on good behavior. Or maybe she's acting up because she's only six or seven years old and has been through a lot in the past twenty-four hours." Merri Lee blew out a breath. "Look,

Meg, you tried to do something nice by showing her the ponies. They're chunky and they look kind of cute in a grumpy sort of way. And everything was fine until she started going on about *riding* a pony, right?"

Meg laid a hand against her waist, feeling the bandage over the cut. "Yes, but then . . ."

"Then you got that prickling warning that something was going on," Merri Lee interrupted. "Which escalated into feeling so bad and desperate that you would have done who knows how much harm to yourself if you'd been alone with the razor."

Tears stung Meg's eyes. She'd expected support, not someone else telling her she was wrong, that she couldn't cope with the world outside a sterile cell.

"I did it for Lizzy," she insisted.

Merri Lee made a face. "All right, let's take a look at that. You did it for Lizzy because you were absolutely sure the prickling you felt was a prophecy about Lizzy. But if you told me everything you remember, Lizzy wasn't the only person with you. You focused on Lizzy, so the visions you saw were about Lizzy. But maybe the initial prickling had really been a warning about trouble for Nathan or Jester or the ponies or one of the Elementals, since Fire was standing there when Lizzy made the grand statement that Grandma would have let her ride a pony. Which may or may not be true, by the way. You can't exactly call Grandma and ask, can you? That prickling might have been about *you*, warning you that you needed to get away from Lizzy and the Pony Barn because something might happen to *you* if you stayed. Did you even consider that?"

Meg stared at Merri Lee. "You think I should have walked away."

"Yes, I do. Your skin prickles several times a day. We've all seen you rub your arms or legs. But you don't cut yourself every time you get that feeling. Why are those times different from what happened today?"

"Sometimes the pins-and-needles feeling fades away." Meg rubbed her arm, not because she had that feeling, just as a way to recall what she usually did. "When the sugar lumps were poisoned, I knew the danger was in the back room of the Liaison's Office, but I had to cut in order to see the vision that would tell someone *what* was wrong."

"How did you know the danger was in the back room?"

"The feeling went away when I left that room and came back when I went in."

Merri Lee picked up the pen and began scribbling on the pad of paper. "So the prickling goes away when you put some distance between yourself and a person or an object, giving you an indication of *what* might be important. That means the prickling is a kind of dowsing rod. A tingle might mean misplaced car keys—a minor thing that's not worth a cut—while a buzz that causes physical discomfort usually means something really important. Is that accurate?"

Meg nodded.

"So if you'd walked away and then had each person approach you, you might have realized what you were feeling wasn't about Lizzy at all." Merri Lee put the pen down and took Meg's hands in her own. "Lizzy was on overload, which is understandable. But so were you. Going with her on your own wasn't the best idea. And having Nathan with you doesn't count because he didn't know what to do with a human child throwing a hissy fit."

"He would have nipped a puppy. He's nipped Skippy plenty when the two of them are the office watch Wolves."

"There you go."

Meg sighed. "What should I do?"

"If I were you, I'd call that bakery in Ferryman's Landing and buy Nathan his own box of Wolf cookies as an apology for upsetting him. And then . . ." With a tight smile, Merri Lee released Meg's hands and stepped away.

"And then?"

"And then Meg, the Trailblazer, should think about what you would want other blood prophets to learn from what happened today. I made some notes. You add your thoughts; then Ruth can fix it up a bit and give it to Vlad to send out."

After Merri Lee left, Meg looked at the clock. Too early to close the office. Deliveries had dwindled, but there was still a chance something might arrive.

Sighing, she went into the front room and saw Simon in the passenger seat of the minivan right before it pulled out of the delivery area and drove away from the Courtyard.

CHAPTER 28

Watersday, Maius 12

"The sign says 'Do not park in driveway,'" Blair said.

"There's nothing close on the street, so we're parking here," Simon replied. "I don't want too many humans seeing a Wolf." He looked back at Nathan, who had refused to shift out of Wolf form once someone else could take care of Meg. "You still want to come in with us?"

<Yes.>

Still sounds shaky, Simon thought. But he gave Nathan credit for resisting the temptation to lick Meg's blood once the cut was made. He hadn't been able to resist when he'd found her after she'd made an uncontrolled cut last month. Then again, he hadn't had Fire standing there, ready to scorch him for his own good.

Blair pulled into the driveway next to Montgomery's apartment building. Simon got out and opened the side door for Nathan. Then the three of them went into the building and up the stairs.

None of the Wolves were feeling friendly toward humans right now, so Simon didn't bother to suppress the growl when he saw Montgomery and Burke waiting for them just inside the apartment doorway.

"Thanks for coming," Montgomery said. "I appreciate it."

"The lieutenant suspects that someone searched his apartment after Lizzy arrived in Lakeside yesterday," Burke said. "I'm guessing it was sometime early this morning."

Simon stiffened, insulted. "We're not some damn sniffer dogs!"

"No, sir, you're not," Montgomery said, his usually courteous voice sounding strained. "But you can confirm if someone was here without me going through any official channels."

Simon thought that through. Like wolves, *terra indigene* Wolves maintained territories where they hunted for food or grew foods their human forms enjoyed. But Wolves living in different territories would work together to protect themselves and the wild country from an invader. He'd thought of the police precincts in those terms: different packs who guarded a specific territory but would work together to guard the whole city of Lakeside. "You don't trust the other packs of police."

Neither human spoke. Finally Burke said, "That will depend on what you can tell us."

<Since we're here, I'll give Montgomery's den a sniff,> Nathan said as he pushed past the two humans.

Simon and Blair stepped inside. Montgomery closed the door.

While Nathan systematically explored the living room, Simon stepped toward the kitchen and sniffed. Then he looked at Montgomery. "Something stinks in there."

"I meant to take out the kitchen waste when I got home yesterday," Montgomery said, looking embarrassed.

<Old smells here,> Nathan reported as he sniffed the back and sides of the sofa.

When Simon relayed the remark, Montgomery nodded. "The sofa was here when I rented the place, left by the previous tenant. I haven't replaced it yet."

<Kowalski's scent on some of the books,> Nathan said as he checked out a bookcase before returning to the sofa.

"Kowalski was here?" Simon asked.

Montgomery nodded. "He packed a bag for me yesterday." He blinked. "You can tell he was here? You recognize his scent?"

"Of course," Simon replied, watching Blair check out the kitchen, including fridge and cupboards. No reason for intruders to look in those places for the Lizzy or Boo Bear, but Wolves didn't get invitations to look at human dens. Why waste the opportunity?

<He lives lean,> Blair said. Then he paused near the waste container. He

crouched and sniffed around the top before getting down on his hands and knees to sniff the foot pedal that lifted the lid.

Simon watched Blair but noticed how Monty winced, probably thinking it was the garbage that was interesting . . . and noticed how Burke focused on the Wolf.

<Someone who isn't Montgomery or Kowalski touched this container,> Blair said.

<Some new scents on the edges of the cushions,> Nathan reported.

Simon relayed the observations as the other two Wolves checked out the rest of the apartment.

"Ah . . ." Montgomery hurried forward when even human ears could hear Blair rummaging in the medicine cabinet in the bathroom.

The three of them reached the bedroom in time to see Nathan shift his forepaws enough to pull open dresser drawers and poke around. Abandoning the dresser, the Wolf sniffed the clothes in the closet before standing on his hind legs in order to sniff the shelf above the clothes rod.

Finished with the closet, Nathan poked his head under the bed, then pulled back, sneezing. <Dusty.>

Judging by the look on Montgomery's face, Simon didn't have to relay that comment.

Montgomery sighed. "If it was my mama noticing the dust, she would have said, 'Crispin James, you are disrespecting your home.'"

"Crispin James?" Simon said. "Not Montgomery?"

"Mama calls me Crispin or Crispin James. The rest of the family calls me C.J., and my friends call me Monty."

"Why do humans need so many names?"

"I do not know." After a moment, he said, "Sometimes names represent a different aspect of the same person. Crispin James is the son of Twyla and James Montgomery. Lieutenant Montgomery is a police officer. Same person, but the people around me have different expectations, need different things from me."

"We each have one name," Simon said.

"That's not quite true," Monty said. "I've heard you referred to as the Wolfgard when other *terra indigene* talk about you as the leader of the Courtyard. And then you have Meg Corbyn and *cs759*. Same person."

"*No.*" Simon showed his teeth to emphasize the denial. "One was property. The other is *Meg.*"

"Same person, but what she was, and is, called carries weight and meaning, for herself and for the people around her," Monty countered.

The blood prophet pups on Great Island need to have names to help them learn they aren't property anymore, Simon thought as Nathan gave the bathroom and kitchen a quick sniff while Blair went into the bedroom. Something to discuss with Steve Ferryman since the Intuit might already know some suitable names.

That settled, at least momentarily, Simon watched the humans without making it obvious. Burke remained focused on the Wolves. Montgomery, on the other hand, looked like he regretted calling the Courtyard and letting those sensitive noses poke into every corner of his life.

Blair and Nathan returned to the living room.

"Two scents that aren't Kowalski or Montgomery," Blair said. "We don't recognize them, so it's no one who has been around the Courtyard."

Simon saw the tension drain from both men. Not a betrayal from someone Montgomery would trust.

"Thank you for your help," Burke said.

Simon looked around the apartment. No pack here to help guard the young. No one to protect the Lizzy when Montgomery had to do police things.

Humans were like sticky vines. If you didn't escape at the first touch, you got more and more tangled up.

Most of them were meat, would always be meat. But, damn it, now when he looked at some of them he just didn't see them as meat anymore, even when he wanted to bite them for a transgression.

"Predators have found your den," he said reluctantly, remembering how Montgomery and Burke had helped him protect Meg. "The Lizzy can't stay here." Hearing Nathan's soft, distressed whine, he added with some heat, "But I don't want her playing with Meg or Nathan until she understands how much trouble she caused today by being a whiny human."

Judging by the way Montgomery stiffened, his hackles would have risen in defense of his young—if humans had hackles.

But Simon heard more regret than anger in Montgomery's voice when the man said, "I am sorry that Meg and Nathan were harmed by Lizzy's actions. Young humans will misbehave and make mistakes."

"Young Wolves misbehave and make mistakes too," Simon said. "But for the well-being of the pack, the young must learn from mistakes and be disciplined when they misbehave."

<The Lizzy *is* just a pup,> Nathan grumbled. <We won't nip her *that* hard.>

<But we *will* nip,> Blair said.

<If the Lizzy stays in the Courtyard, of course she'll get nipped for misbehaving, same as any other pup,> Simon agreed. They just wouldn't tell Montgomery. And if the Lizzy was smart, she wouldn't tell him either.

"I appreciate you allowing us to stay in the Courtyard while I sort things out," Montgomery said. "I'll make sure Lizzy understands she has to follow your rules."

"We've been here long enough," Blair grumbled.

Simon nodded.

"We talked to a bakery on Market Street and have some samples of the food Nadine Fallacaro can offer for Tess," Montgomery said. "If the food meets with Tess's approval, she can talk to Ms. Fallacaro about placing an order for A Little Bite."

"I'll help them load the bakery boxes and the cooler, Lieutenant," Burke said. "Why don't you pack what you'll need for a few more days?"

"And don't forget to take out the waste in the kitchen," Simon said. "In a couple more days, even other humans will be able to smell it."

They went out. Blair opened the minivan so that Nathan could get out of sight while Simon walked across the street with Burke to fetch the food.

"The food in the cooler should be put in a fridge as soon as you get back to the Courtyard," Burke said as they walked back to the minivan.

Something in Burke's voice reminded Simon of an annoyed Grizzly.

"When Wolves are hunting, they'll follow the scent of prey a long time," Simon said. "You didn't think the predators would follow the Lizzy?"

"They're not after Lizzy," Burke growled as he and Simon placed the bakery boxes and cooler on the floor behind the front passenger's seat. "They're after the jewels. And these people have already killed a woman and broken into a police officer's apartment because of those jewels."

"Can't you keep Boo Bear in the cage?" Just saying the word *cage* made Simon's canines lengthen, but he tried not to make any other shifts.

"Arrest the bear as a jewel thief?" Burke sounded amused.

Not making fun of me, Simon decided. *Just amused by the idea.* Still, it was an opportunity to ask questions. And if Burke wouldn't tell him, he'd just ask Kowalski or Debany why it was amusing.

"On TV shows, the police have a cage for evidence," Simon said. "Doesn't your police station have a cage like that?"

"It does." Burke no longer looked amused. "But I think those jewels need to be tucked away in an undisclosed location until we find out where they came from—and who wants them back. Whoever killed Elayne Borden shouldn't profit from it."

Simon studied the police captain. Then he took out his mobile phone and called Jester Coyotegard, someone who delighted in mischief.

"Pony Barn," Jester said.

"It's Simon. If you wanted to keep a bag of jewels away from bad humans but didn't want them to know you kept the jewels, what would you do?"

"Go to Sparkles and Junk and replace the jewels with sparklies that are about the same size and color," Jester replied promptly. "Of course, if I was planning to give the real jewels back to someone in the future, I wouldn't leave them with the Crows."

Good point. "Thanks, Jester." Simon ended the call and looked at Burke. "Maybe, after the Lizzy is asleep, someone could drive Boo Bear to the Courtyard to visit his kin. And maybe that someone could pick him up again before the Lizzy is awake."

"Maybe someone could," Burke said, smiling. He stepped away from the minivan. "Thanks for all your help."

As soon as Simon got in and closed the door, Blair backed the minivan out of the driveway and drove back to the Courtyard.

He'd had enough, and all Simon wanted now was to get out of this skin. But as they pulled into the Courtyard's Main Street entrance, Meg rushed out of the Liaison's Office.

"Is Nathan with you?" she asked, sounding breathless. "I haven't been able to find him anywhere."

"He's in the back," Blair said.

"Can I talk to him?"

Simon turned enough to look in the back of the van. <Nathan? Up to you.>

Nathan sighed, but he stood up. <You have to open the door and move the boxes.>

Simon made room for the Wolf to hop out of the minivan. He watched Meg go back into the office with Nathan. Then he sighed, closed the doors, and said to Blair, "I'll meet you at A Little Bite."

He walked down the access way and over to the coffee shop's back door, resigned to being human a while longer. He might as well check in with Vlad after talking to Tess.

There were plenty of things he still needed to do before going home. So no one would think he was waiting around to find out why Meg wanted to talk to Nathan.

Meg let Nathan out the back door of the Liaison's Office and watched him hustle over to the back door of Howling Good Reads.

Reporting to Simon, naturally.

After closing the door, she went into the bathroom to wash her face.

Anger. Wariness. Distrust. She didn't have any training images to identify emotions on a Wolf's face, but she spent enough time around Nathan that she could interpret his expressions.

Had the cut been unnecessary? Everyone else thought so.

Meg turned on the taps, splashed water on her face, then remained bent over the sink.

The pins-and-needles feeling was irritating, often painful. But it *was* a kind of dowsing rod that had been evolving since she'd come to the Courtyard. So maybe if she had walked away . . .

No. No, no, *no*. There *had* been danger for someone at the Pony Barn. That painful buzz *had* been a warning about an enemy. . . .

Meg clenched her teeth against the sudden buzz that filled both her arms. She jerked upright and saw her face in the mirror above the sink.

The buzz faded.

Meg stared at her reflection.

"It was me," she whispered. "I was the enemy."

She took a step back from the sink, laid a hand over the bandage at her waist, and thought about what Merri Lee had said: *And then Meg, the Trailblazer, should think about what you would want other blood prophets to learn from what happened today.*

"No one else has the right to decide if or when we cut our skin, but if we don't learn to interpret the warning signs that tell us if we really need to cut, we can become the enslavers as well as the enslaved. We can become our own enemy."

That was the second lesson Meg, the Trailblazer, had learned today. The first lesson—the harder, more important lesson—was that she wasn't the only one who was hurt when she cut.

Simon came around the desk when Nathan appeared in HGR's office doorway.

"That didn't take long."

Nathan approached him slowly, reluctantly. Not typical behavior for the enforcer—unless he'd done something wrong.

Simon leaned over the other Wolf, but he didn't have to lean far to catch the scent. "Why do you smell like Meg?" he demanded.

<She *cried* on me,> Nathan said. <I couldn't understand most of what she said, but she *cried* until my fur was wet.> He sounded baffled and upset.

"I guess she feels bad about making a cut and scaring you. Scaring all of us."

Nathan said nothing for a moment. Then, <There's nothing in my fur, is there?>

Simon gave the other Wolf a careful look. "No boogers."

<Good. I *hate* washing boogers out of fur.>

"Who doesn't? What comes out of human noses is *disgusting*." Simon sat on the floor, his back against the desk. Nathan sat next to him. "Do you want Blair to assign someone else as the watch Wolf for the Human Liaison's Office?"

<No. Watching the humans is interesting, and I like Meg. But we need rules about the razor. Today . . . That was wrong. Meg was wrong, and the Lizzy was wrong. It wasn't fair that I couldn't nip either one of them when they both deserved it.>

"I know." Simon closed his eyes and waited until he sensed the tension draining out of both of them. "Do you still think it's a good idea to have some of the Addirondak Wolves visit the Courtyard? We've got humans doing work for us who don't know how to behave, but we can't attack them and drive them off like we would an enemy."

<If it hadn't pushed Meg into cutting, the Lizzy's mistake would have been annoying but nothing more. And our pups make mistakes too.>

Of course, who could say how long it might have been before anyone discovered the jewels inside Boo Bear if Skippy and Sam hadn't pulled off an arm and a leg? That had started some of the trouble. Then again, Burke and Montgomery wouldn't have known why the Lizzy was in danger if the jewels hadn't been found.

Simon climbed to his feet. "Go home. Go run. Tomorrow is Earthday, and we'll pretend humans don't exist."

<Except Meg.>

"Except Meg."

Nathan rose, shook out his fur, and left.

Simon shut down the computer, turned off the lights, and felt like a weight had lifted off him as he walked out of Howling Good Reads. He couldn't shake off everything human. He wouldn't shake off Meg, who waited for him at the back door of the Liaison's Office, her eyes all puffy and skin all blotchy.

He ran a hand over her short black hair and gave her a scritch behind the ear.

"Simon?" she said in a small voice. "Can we go home?"

"Sure. Let me get the BOW."

He found one of the bakery boxes in the back of the BOW. Since he didn't think Meg had eaten much today, he welcomed Tess's thoughtfulness.

As he backed the BOW out of the garage and waited for Meg to shut the garage door, he glanced toward the efficiency apartments, then shook his head.

He'd had enough. They'd all had enough. The Owlgard would keep watch tonight, but for the rest of this day, Lieutenant Montgomery would have to take care of the Lizzy on his own.

CHAPTER 29

Watersday, Maius 12

While Monty had been at his apartment dealing with the break-in, and Ruth Stuart had been watching Lizzy, his team had brought a mattress from one of the other efficiency apartments so that he wouldn't have to spend another night in a sleeping bag on the hard floor. They'd brought enough food for him and Lizzy for the next couple of days. And someone had selected five movies that he hoped would be suitable for a seven-year-old human girl.

Distractions. Diversions. Care.

Monty sat in the stuffed chair and put his arms around Lizzy when she settled on his lap.

She looked at him with those big eyes. "I just wanted to ride a pony."

Why was she so stuck on that? Of course, he wasn't sure he could explain to a child how dangerous the ponies were when they shrugged off that harmless-looking form.

"Grandma Borden would have let me," Lizzy said.

He knew what to say about *that*. "I don't think Grandma Borden would have allowed you to ride a pony. She would have said they were smelly and you'd get dirty."

But the woman might have raised a fuss because someone had denied her granddaughter, and denying a Borden *anything* was not acceptable. Fortunately, the family didn't have the wealth or status to live up to their pretensions.

"And Grandma Twyla would have called you on being discourteous and making a fuss when Miss Meg had already told you the ponies were special and weren't for riding."

"But—"

"No, Lizzy."

She pouted, and he noted the calculating look in her eyes, as if she was waiting to see what effect it would have.

Lizzy hadn't done that a few months ago. She hadn't been like that before he'd been transferred to Lakeside and had to leave her—had to leave both of them—because Elayne had refused to come with him.

But Elayne had been like that. Funny how he'd never allowed himself to see it. Oh, Elayne was far more subtle about it when she wanted to get her own way, but when the behavior was presented in a child's broad strokes, he couldn't deny that Lizzy was mimicking her mother.

Have to tell her, he thought. "Lizzy . . . You were very brave to ride the train by yourself and find me. Some bad people were looking for you and Mommy, and she did the right thing, having you ride the train without her."

"Will Mommy be here soon?"

"No, baby." Tears stung Monty's eyes. "No. Mommy was hurt very badly and . . . she died. She can't be with us anymore."

Lizzy put her head on his shoulder. "Is Miss Meg going to die because I was bad?"

"No. Miss Meg will be fine in a couple of days." How could he put this to her without scaring her too much? "One of the bad men followed you to Lakeside, so we need to stay in the Courtyard for a while."

Her head came up. "What about Boo Bear?"

"He's with Captain Burke. He's helping the police with the investigation. He misses you, but he's being very brave. Like you."

She nodded, settling down again.

Did she understand? Maybe she understood as much as she could handle. Maybe it would be easier being in a place that held no reminders?

Gods, did he even have a photograph of Elayne so that Lizzy would have *something*?

"You'll be safe in the Courtyard," he said. "But staying here means brushing off your good manners and minding the grown-ups who are looking after you when I can't be here." He looked at her, his darling girl. "Do you know the difference between human police and Wolf police?"

"The Wolf police bite you if you're bad?"

"Yes," Monty said. "They bite you if you're bad. Today you got off with what my captain would call a caution, meaning now you know you did a bad thing, so the next time . . ."

Lizzy clicked her teeth together to demonstrate biting.

Monty nodded. "That's exactly right."

"Daddy? I'm hungry."

They ate sandwiches from Nadine's Bakery & Café, then watched one of the movies. He wondered if whoever had chosen the movies had picked them because of viewing age or to show Lizzy a few truths about the beings who surrounded her. Whatever the reason, the story about the Wolf Team provided some sharp lessons for both of them.

CHAPTER 30

Late that night, as a quiet, soaking rain fell over the Courtyard, the Owlgard watched Douglas Burke tuck a paper bag against Howling Good Reads' back door.

Responding to the Owls' call, Vladimir and Nyx Sanguinati retrieved the bag and flowed over to Sparkles and Junk, where Jenni Crowgard, Jester Coyotegard, Jane Wolfgard, and Blair Wolfgard waited for them.

One by one the jewels in the bag were stored in a small, velvet-lined wooden box, replaced by sparklies they found in the shop. After studying the fancy ring, Blair made a fair copy using fine wire and bits of glass that Jenni removed from a piece of costume jewelry.

Their tasks completed, they replaced the bag inside Boo Bear, and Jane, being the Wolfgard bodywalker, stitched up the back seam. After some discussion, they didn't restore the arm and leg, leaving the bear looking the same as when it arrived.

At the first hint of daylight, Vlad placed the paper bag outside of HGR's back door, shifted to his smoke form, and waited in the shadows. A few minutes after that, the Owls reported a car parking across the street from the Courtyard. A minute after that, Douglas Burke quietly made his way to HGR's back door and retrieved the paper bag.

As soon as Burke drove away, Vlad joined Nyx, who had waited for him in the Market Square. Together, they took the small box to Grandfather Erebus's marble home in the Chambers, a place where no human could search for the jewels and survive.

Setting two candlesticks on the gleaming wood of an antique table, Vlad lit the candles and watched Grandfather Erebus tip the box and gently spill the jewels over the dark wood.

"A shining fortune," Erebus said. "Humans have killed each other for a single gem. They wouldn't hesitate to kill a woman and child for what these pretty stones could buy."

"Things," Vlad said, revealing his fangs. "They kill for *things.*"

Erebus stirred the stones. "That could be said of us too."

"We kill for food, to protect our land and homes. To protect our kin."

"Food, land, homes. Those are important things that are worth protecting, but they are still things, Vladimir. How much food do you think these pretties could buy?"

"You can't buy what isn't there." Vlad considered what he'd just said. When, exactly, had this talk about food shortages started?

He stared at the jewels. "Maybe the food isn't there because it's already been purchased. Maybe the jewels were the payment. But why hoard food and let people think they and their young will go hungry?"

"We will see the answer soon enough. Hunger can be a sharp master." Erebus swept the jewels back into the velvet-lined wooden box. "Now. Tell me about the humans who were breeding the sweet blood. Have they been found?"

"No." Vlad swallowed bitterness. "I've talked to Sanguinati who live in the regions where the abandoned girls were found or where the bodies of the babies were discovered. As far as they can tell, no one is searching for the farms. No one is searching for the humans who ran those farms."

"What about the police, the government here?"

"You'd have to ask Elliot about the government. The police here *did* search. This I know as truth. They searched and confirmed there wasn't such a place anywhere around Lakeside. No abandoned girls. No dead babies."

Erebus said nothing. Then, "It is not just things that have a price, Vladimir. Loyalty also can be bought." He touched the box with a thick yellowed fingernail. "Since humans won't search for the farms, then we will. Tell the Sanguinati to find the humans who hurt the sweet blood and killed their young."

"Should I talk to the girls at the lake? Their kin could destroy the buildings once they're found."

"Wood. Stone. Glass." Erebus shook his head. "Leave the buildings untouched. They mean nothing. Find the humans who worked in those places and kill them."

"Should the bodies be left where they can be found?" Meaning, did Erebus want humans to know that the Sanguinati had delivered their own form of justice?

Erebus looked at him. Vlad wasn't sure if the astonishment was real or feigned.

"After the Sanguinati have fed, there is no reason to waste the meat, Vladimir," Erebus said, his voice a quiet scold. "No, no. Take the meat into the wild country where it will be useful. There are many there besides the *terra indigene* who will welcome easy food for their young."

CHAPTER 31

Earthday, Maius 13

The girl huddled under the patchwork quilt and listened as the Wolves on the other side of the door woke up. Big yawns, soft vocalizing that reminded her of the howls she'd heard the night before. Then a female voice saying, "Jackson, make some toast. I'll scramble a couple of these eggs for the sweet blood."

They meant her. They wouldn't call her *cs821*. They said it wasn't a name.

Sweet blood wasn't a name either, but calling her that didn't offend them.

The female, Grace, had brought her pajamas yesterday and another change of clothes. Underpants and socks were tucked into one of the drawers in the desk. The rest of the clothes hung on pegs on the wall, including a long, thick sweater.

The girl slipped out of bed and dashed for the bathroom. She shivered while she peed, while she washed her hands and splashed cold water on her face. Hurrying, she stripped off the pajamas and put on jeans, a long-sleeve shirt, and the thick sweater. She had one sock on when the door opened and Grace and Jackson walked in.

"We don't know how to cook many human foods," Grace said. "But I have learned to scramble eggs, and Jackson made you some toasted bread." She set a plate on the desk. Jackson set a glass of white liquid beside the plate.

Grace left the room. Jackson lingered, studying her.

He said she could ask. Did she have the courage to ask? It could be a trick to see if she was still tempted to do the thing she wasn't allowed to do. The Walking Names always tried to trick her. But Jackson was a Wolf. He knew Meg.

A test, then. But this time, she wouldn't be the only one being tested.

"Could I have a pencil and some paper?"

A thoughtful silence before Jackson said, "A black pencil or colored pencil?"

She felt her breath catch, felt a tingle in her hands. But she wasn't brave enough to ask for both. "Whatever no one else is using."

Another thoughtful silence. "The trading post isn't open on Earthdays. I will see what we have here. Eat your breakfast, sweet blood."

He left, closing the door. She turned on the lamp beside the bed. Wolves might not have trouble seeing in barely daylight, but she wanted a better look at the food before she ate any of it.

Sitting at the desk, she picked up the glass. Sniffed. Cautiously tasted. She was pretty sure it was milk, but it tasted different, more potent than anything she'd been given in the . . . in that place.

The toast was a little burned at the edges; the scrambled eggs, like the milk, didn't taste quite like what she'd had before, but it was good and she was hungry.

After the meal, she went into the bathroom to wash her hands and brush her teeth. When she came out, Jackson stood in the doorway, holding a wooden tray. He set it on the bed, revealing six sheets of paper and a set of colored pencils. Red, green, blue, yellow, orange, brown, black, pink. From training images, she identified an eraser and a small handheld pencil sharpener.

"This is what I could find." Jackson stepped away from the bed.

"Thank you."

He picked up the used dishes and left.

Sitting on the bed, she examined each pencil, touched the paper.

No one burst into the room, yelling at her. No one took away the pencils and paper. No one bound her hands as punishment, leaving her dependent on the Walking Names for every personal need.

Feeling bolder, she studied the patchwork quilt. Then she picked up a pencil and filled one sheet of paper reproducing the patterns in the quilt's material.

She stood up, stretched, got a drink of water, sharpened all the pencils.

Maybe she should do something else for a while. But . . . what? The room held nothing. Could she ask for a book? But she didn't want to read, she wanted . . .

A howl. Distant. Another howl. Closer to this building.

They had howled last night. She closed her eyes and remembered how the sound had seemed to rise like smoke, painting ghostly shapes on the night sky.

Returning to the bed, she took a clean sheet of paper, picked up a pencil, and began to draw.

CHAPTER 32

Earthday, Maius 13

Simon, all four-footed and furry, stared at Henry. Not only was the Grizzly in human form; he was awake and bringing a request.

<But it's Earthday.> Simon did his best to stifle a growl. <It's supposed to be a human-free day.> His ear canted back at the sound of Meg's laughter and Sam's happy yips in the kitchen. <Except for Meg, but she doesn't count as human in *that* way anymore.>

"You were the one who told the humans they could share in the harvest if they also shared in the work," Henry rumbled. "The vegetable gardens have to be expanded, and they're willing to do the work."

<But . . .> Simon stopped. Thought. Sighed.

He was the one who had made the decision to let humans in, both to reward the ones who didn't want to be enemies and to learn more about humans from informal interaction. Maybe the *terra indigene* had tried this before in the centuries since the first humans came to Thaisia. Maybe it was a mistake.

A gamble, at any rate. For everyone.

<All right, fine.>

"I will stay in human form," Henry said. "And Vlad will be there."

<Is Montgomery going to be there with the Lizzy?>

Henry nodded. "Pete and Eve Denby are bringing their young as well. And the police who have use of the efficiency apartment and our human employees will be here."

<All of them?> That was a big pack of humans to mingle with Wolves, Crows, Hawks, Owls, and whoever else decided to watch the visitors.

Then Meg came out of the kitchen with Sam bouncing around her, his gray eyes fixed on the hat she held out of his reach.

Couldn't grab the hat once she put it on because it had ribbons that she tied under her chin to keep the hat from blowing off, and she might get hurt. But if someone happened to chew off one of the ribbons, and Air was willing to cooperate a little bit, they could play catch the hat.

Not today, Simon thought with regret. Too many onlookers today, so *someone* would notice who deribboned the hat.

"Are we ready?" Meg asked, her eyes so happy-bright, if she had a tail, it would be wagging.

Sam *arrooed.* Henry opened the front door. And Simon gave Meg's hand a quick lick as he passed her to help him remember why there was a human pack in the first place.

Meg closed Simon's door, then frowned at the area under her second-floor apartment. Simon's apartment was two stories. Her place and his shared a back hallway on the second floor and stairs that led to the outside door. From what she had gathered, since she hadn't found anything in her apartment that matched training images she had studied, the heating system and hot-water tanks for both apartments were in a utility room on the ground floor of *his* apartment.

So what was under her apartment? It was boarded up, like images of abandoned buildings, only neater. And there was a door that was also boarded up where a window might be.

During the winter, she had noticed it occasionally and dismissed it because it wasn't part of what she needed to absorb in order to live on her own and keep her job. Now . . .

The Green Complex was shaped like a U, with apartments on the two sides and the laundry, mailroom, and social room taking up the back, along with the archway that led to the garages.

Meg looked across the open area. Henry's apartment was across from hers, and it, too, had a boarded-up space under it.

"Henry, what's under my apartment?"

He gave her a big smile. "That's the summer room that you and Simon share. It's been boarded up for the winter, but now it's time to open it up and clean it out."

She looked at Henry, then at Simon, who gave her a Wolfie grin. "Summer room?"

"A screened room to keep out bugs," Henry said. "A cool place to sleep during hot, muggy weather. Come. It's time to meet the rest of the diggers." He started walking, clearly expecting her to follow.

When Simon paw-whacked her butt to get her moving, she hustled to catch up to the Grizzly, glancing back at the Wolf, who looked way too pleased with himself.

She hadn't experienced hot, muggy weather yet, but Merri Lee and Ruth had told her the kind of clothing she should purchase for Lakeside's summer. Which reminded her of the other thing she was supposed to ask someone.

"Henry? Should I buy a bathing suit?"

"Why would you need one?"

"Merri Lee wasn't sure if there was a place to go swimming in the Courtyard. She said I should ask."

"We have the small lakes and the creeks. In hot weather, plenty of us spend some time in and around the water. The Wolves especially like to swim. So do I."

"So what do they wear when they go swimming in human form?"

He looked so baffled, she blushed and wished she'd waited to ask Tess about bathing suits and swimming.

Of course, Henry might be baffled because the Others *never* went swimming in human form. But she didn't think that was the part of her question that puzzled him.

She hadn't realized she'd stopped walking until Simon licked the back of her knee. She leaped forward and squealed, "Simon!"

Meg, if we're going to be working outside today, you can't wear long pants and long sleeves, Merri Lee had said. *You'll end up with heatstroke or something.*

Ruth had partially agreed with Merri Lee, expressing concern about possible scratches as well as sunburn. They compromised on the choice of outfits, which was why Meg wore a pair of shorts, a tank top, and a long-sleeve gauze shirt. The clothing definitely suited the warmer weather. But Meg hadn't considered the amount of skin now available to be licked—or what the unexpected swipe of a wet tongue would feel like.

Stealth licking, she thought with a sigh. *A new game for summer.*

Fortunately, the kitchen garden wasn't that far from the Green Complex, and Vlad was already there with officers Kowalski, Debany, and MacDonald; Ruth, Merri Lee, and Theral; the Denbys; and Lieutenant Montgomery and Lizzy. Even Lorne from the Three Ps had come to help.

The humans eyed the Wolves, who were also there. Meg didn't think all the Wolfgard had come to help, but there were enough of them. Then the Crows and Hawks arrived.

Would some of them have been in human form if the humans hadn't been there?

She didn't know, couldn't care. This wasn't a thousand new images, but one moving image full of new experiences. Making a garden. Working with friends. Finding the path that would allow other *cassandra sangue* to live in the outside world without being overwhelmed.

She wanted to take in as much of this experience as she could before she had to retreat and let mind and body rest.

Meg blew out a breath. Her eyes met Simon's. This was a new experience for him too.

She smiled at him. "Let's plant a garden."

Simon gave them credit for one thing: these humans did know how to work. And humans and *terra indigene* had experienced each other in a new way as they combined skills to expand the garden.

Kowalski, Debany, MacDonald, and Henry cut the sod for the expanded area. Montgomery and Pete Denby used a tool with curved prongs and a long handle to break up the soil.

The Wolves, of course, used paws and claws to achieve the same results. But Simon noticed Blair sniffing around the garden tools the humans had brought with them and figured Meg would be given a list of tools to order for the Utilities Complex.

"Good thing we had a light rain last night," Montgomery said as he broke up the soil while Pete stacked the squares of sod that had been cut.

All the other humans stopped and looked at him.

"It didn't rain last night," Kowalski finally said.

"Guess it was a localized shower," Montgomery said.

A laughing grunt from Henry had the humans turning to the Grizzly.

Henry sank the spade into the soil, his movements easy and powerful. "We talked to the girls at the lake yesterday evening and told them we were expanding this garden—and that our Meg wanted to help with the digging and planting the seeds."

"So it just rained in the Courtyard last night?" MacDonald said.

<That disturbs him.> Puzzled, Simon paused in his digging to study Lawrence MacDonald.

<Yes. I find that interesting.> Henry went back to cutting sod.

Simon glanced at the three children. The Lizzy was still petting the Wolf pups, but the Robert and the Sarah were playing with some of the juvenile Hawks by hitting badminton shuttlecocks into the air for the Hawks to catch and then drop for the next player with a racket to hit back into the air.

Eventually the pups would grow bored with being petted and run over to see what Sam was doing, since he had stayed close to Meg. Eventually the Hawks would tire of the game and fly off to see what else was happening in the Courtyard. Eventually the Crows would find the humans less entertaining and fly off to work on their own garden—the cornfield especially.

And Meg, who had never dug into soil or smelled freshly turned earth, who had never had to be reminded to drink water when she worked outdoors or to put a cream on her skin to avoid sunburn . . . Meg was entranced by everything.

Simon kept a watchful eye on her and listened to the female pack as they talked about the garden and some of the vegetables and herbs they would like to plant. He wasn't sure any of the *terra indigene* would care about the herbs. After all, deer was supposed to taste like deer, and you didn't sprinkle anything on a rabbit before you ate it. But Tess wandered by and expressed an interest in the herbs, so herbs would be planted, along with corn, lettuce, broccoli, peppers, tomatoes, beans, peas, and something called zucchini, which Merri Lee said tasted good with tomato sauce and pasta.

"Enough for today," Henry said as he began to collect the tools that belonged to the Others. "Tess, Vlad, and Jester are saying it's time to eat."

A moment's tension as the humans looked at the Others.

"Is this the picnic?" Meg asked.

"Not quite a picnic, if I understand what humans mean by that word," Henry replied. "But something we hope you will enjoy."

Nathan arrived in the pickup used by the Utilities Complex, loaded up the Wolf pups and juveniles, including Sam, and took them back to the Wolfgard Complex for their own kind of meal. Hawks, Crows, and a couple of sleepy Owls also headed for their own places, which left the humans and the residents of the Green Complex, who were walking back to the meal Tess had set out.

Simon trotted ahead of them, leaving Henry to watch over Meg. If he was going to eat with them, better to look human. And better to shift in private. Being *terra indigene*, he didn't respond to female bodies the way human males did unless the female smelled like she wanted to mate. But naked wasn't something done around human pups—although he wanted to ask the men why naked from the waist up was all right for them but females remained covered. That didn't seem fair.

Shifting a paw just enough to form stubby fingers, he opened his front door, then rushed up to his bedroom to shift all the way and put on denim shorts and a T-shirt. Sandals. Reviewing his mental checklist for human grooming, he decided everyone else was going to be sweaty and leaving a strong scent, so he didn't have to mask his own scent and could keep his grooming to a minimum. He splashed water on his face, combed his hair, brushed his teeth, and was back outside before the humans straggled into the open area that formed the center of the Green Complex.

A potted tree provided some shade for a water trough that someone had filled with fresh water. A couple of benches provided places for birds to perch or Others in human form to sit if they didn't want the privacy of their own porches.

Henry picked up the sponge resting in the raised area of the trough and washed his arms, chest, and face before squeezing out water to run down his back.

Kowalski and Debany arrived next.

"Soap?" Kowalski asked when Henry offered the sponge.

"Not in this water," Henry replied.

Before they could ask why, Jake Crowgard flew over to the trough. He took a drink, then had a quick splash in the raised area before flying off.

"Right," Debany said, wiping down with the sponge after Kowalski finished with it.

Simon stepped in front of Meg. She looked tired, her eyes a little glazed.

"Too much?" he asked quietly, noticing how the other girls gave him a look before moving toward the trough. Was the look supposed to be a warning, a message, or just the curiosity human females and Crows seemed to have in common?

"Yes, but in a good way." She smiled. "No pins and needles."

"Tess, Vlad, and Jester opened up the summer room. Nathan brought over sawhorses and planks to use as a serving table. There's not much furniture to sit on, but there are a couple of benches."

She closed her eyes. She frowned a little, but the smile still curved her lips.

"I have training images of sawhorses and benches, but I can't put them together to make an image of the summer room."

"I can bring you food. You could eat on your porch, or inside."

She looked at him, and her smile warmed. "No, I'm all right. I'd like to see the summer room. I'd like to see how the food is put out for a picnic that's not quite a picnic."

"Okay."

Meg looked at the water trough. "But I'm going to wash up in my own bathroom."

Simon stepped aside.

As soon as Meg went inside her apartment, Montgomery approached him.

"Is Meg all right?" Montgomery asked.

"She's fine."

"No problems with yesterday's cut?"

"No. She was careful today." And he'd stayed close enough that he would have caught the slightest whiff of blood if the cut had reopened.

Montgomery looked around. "This is something new, isn't it? You and us."

Simon shrugged. "Don't know if it's new, but I don't think it's been tried for a long time. Not with your kind of human."

Montgomery hesitated, as if he wanted to say something else. Instead he smiled. "Guess I'd better get washed up."

Simon watched the humans. Cautious but not afraid. Even the newest humans, the Denbys, weren't afraid. Not like they would have been a year ago.

He hoped they stayed cautious, especially if the Courtyard started having guests.

<The food's in here,> Vlad said.

<I'm waiting for Meg.> He heard the toilet flush. Hard not to hear water

whooshing through the pipes with the summer room open. Since humans pretended they didn't know about each other's pee and poop, he'd let her figure that out on her own. He had something else on his mind. <Why is having a share in this garden so important to the human pack?>

<They like to eat same as us?>

<It's more than that. They're *too* relieved about having another source of food besides what they can buy in human stores.>

<Then it will be interesting to find out.>

Simon said nothing more because Meg returned. He followed her into the summer room to see what kind of food he was eating instead of a deer.

Now that he'd eaten, all Monty wanted was a hot shower and sleep. He had at least a decade on every member of his team, and today he felt those years.

Were they going to work this hard *every* Earthday until harvest?

On the other hand, the *terra indigene* expected to work hard for every meal, so today was just a different kind of work.

"Fresh corn on the cob is great," Kowalski said as talk flowed about what everyone wanted to plant.

"Why?" Simon asked, puzzled.

"Corn is good," Jenni Crowgard said.

Kowalski grinned. "Oh, yeah. Steamed until it's tender and then brushed with melted butter. Only way to eat it."

Baffled silence.

"Steamed?" Jenni said. "You *cook* corn?"

Kowalski, Debany, and MacDonald exchanged looks.

"Yes," MacDonald said. "We cook lots of vegetables, including corn."

"I never cared for the taste of it, but it might be appealing if it was cooked properly," Vlad said.

Jenni huffed. "Maybe. But it's fine just the way it is."

If you're a Crow, Monty thought. "How do you protect your crops?" They weren't likely to put scarecrows in their gardens.

Henry laughed. "Didn't you see the Hawk post? What comes to raid a garden is also food for many of us, so this is a season of plenty."

"And protecting a garden is good training for the juvenile Wolves," Simon added.

Forks paused. Eve Denby stopped chewing and eyed the dishes that Tess had contributed to the meal, no doubt wondering about the ingredients.

"There's nothing here that you wouldn't find in a human store," Tess said, amused.

"Your pups have stopped eating," Jester said. The Coyote pointed at the three children, who were fading after an active day. "I could take them to the social room to watch a movie."

"Go ahead," Simon said.

"I'll give him a hand," Theral said.

The rest of the women refilled their glasses and went outside. After a moment, Jenni Crowgard joined them, leaving Tess as the only female still at the table.

"We were wondering why having a share in the garden is so important to all of you," Vlad said with a casualness that made Monty wary.

"You did offer," Monty replied.

Vlad nodded. "We did. Why did you accept?"

Tension filled the room.

"Speaking for myself and Ruthie, being able to grow some vegetables means a smaller bill at the grocery store, and lots of foods are going to be more expensive, including fruits," Kowalski said. "The price of anything made with flour has also risen in the past couple of weeks."

"We have fruit as well as the vegetable gardens," Simon said. "We have strawberries, raspberries, blackberries, grapes. There are some apple trees in the Courtyard, as well as pears and peaches."

"Walnut trees too." Henry smiled. "While a particular form might have acquired a taste for certain foods, the *terra indigene* can, and will, eat much of what Namid provides. So our Courtyards have some of everything that grows in this part of Thaisia."

"Why is fruit going to be expensive?" Vlad asked.

After a look around the table, it was Pete Denby who answered. "Shortages. Several of the regional governments are predicting food shortages this year, and prices are already going up. The loss of the farms in Jerzy—"

"The farms weren't lost," Simon snapped. "The farmers might be working for the *terra indigene* now that the land was reclaimed, but the work is the same. They keep what they need to feed their own and provide the food for the Intuits who moved into the hamlet to run the businesses that those farmers also need. The rest of their crops are sold to the markets in human cities, same as last year."

"Crops were lost in the Midwest," Pete said. "At least, that's what the news reports are saying."

"The Elementals weren't interested in farmland. The enemy wasn't hiding in the fields. They struck what they intended to strike."

Another look exchanged around the table.

Pete leaned forward. "They're saying we've lost a lot of our surplus crops because of damaged silos. We've lost feed for animals, and some livestock has died because of it. There's talk of shortages of flour and grains for cereals."

"The ration book had coupons that allowed a family to buy a dozen eggs per month at a fixed price," Kowalski said. "When my mom went to buy eggs the other day, the same coupon is now for half a dozen eggs for the same price."

"I heard bakeries will get dibs on ingredients like flour and sugar in order to stay in business, and everyone else will only be able to buy a pound bag of each per month, *if* it's available," Debany said. "That means families won't be able to bake their own bread or make biscuits."

"A bakery down the street from us told Theral each household needs to register with certain businesses to guarantee the availability of some items. Anyone registered with that bakery will be guaranteed one loaf of bread each week," MacDonald said.

Debany nodded. "Doesn't mean everyone who registers will be able to afford to buy a loaf a week in six months' time."

Monty listened, becoming more and more uneasy. Had all of this escalated in the past couple of days while he was focused on Lizzy's arrival and Elayne's death?

Simon seemed to be wondering the same thing. "That doesn't answer the question. Last year, there was enough food. Why isn't there enough this year? The *terra indigene* haven't reclaimed that much land, and what needs to be grown is still being grown."

Pete Denby shook his head thoughtfully. "I haven't heard of any infestations that would account for lost crops."

"There has been one," Vlad said. "The Humans First and Last movement."

Simon nodded. "We hadn't caught any scent of them last year. This year, they're howling everywhere about everything."

"Maybe we should pay more attention to what they're saying," Tess suggested as her hair turned green and began to curl.

"Maybe we should," Simon agreed.

Monty suddenly had the feeling his team really wanted an excuse to leave. He looked hard at Kowalski. "What aren't you saying?" It wasn't a good question to ask, not with the Courtyard's leaders present, but information was also a crop to be tended.

Kowalski winced. "I've been hearing from other officers that some of the butcher shops and bakeries will display an HFL decal. Customers who want limited items will not only have to register at a particular shop; they'll have to show their HFL membership card."

"And if they don't have a membership card?"

"I don't think nonmembers will be welcome. Or safe."

Something to tell the captain in the morning, assuming Burke didn't know about it already.

Simon, Vlad, Henry, and Tess looked eerily calm.

Then Simon shifted in his chair. "Enough. It's time to rest."

"I'll second that," Pete Denby said.

They agreed to let Tess store the remaining food and bring it to A Little Bite in the morning, since most of the humans would be working around the Courtyard anyway. Kowalski, Debany, and MacDonald headed out together, and their voices mingled with those of the women who were still sitting outside.

After bidding the Others good night, Monty and Pete walked over to the social room to fetch their children.

"They say the eye of the storm is the safest place to be," Monty said.

"Is that where we are?" Pete asked. "The eye of the storm?"

"Maybe. We're going to be able to feed our families, and that's not something everyone will be able to say."

"You think the Others are responsible for the shortages?"

"No. And that's a worry, because if it's not them . . ."

"Then it's us," Pete finished.

Monty pushed aside the grim feelings, but he didn't need to put on a smile for his little girl. The children, and Jester, were sprawled on furniture, sound asleep. Only Theral was still awake, and she gave them a distracted wave before turning her attention back to the Wolf Team movie.

"Almost over," Theral whispered.

Jester jerked upright at the sound of her voice and blinked at Monty and Pete. With a grunt, he scrubbed at his hair and sat back when Theral hissed a warning for him to be quiet before he had a chance to speak.

So they all stayed quiet.

Not a human-made movie, Monty thought as he watched the Wolf Team's successful attack and rescue—and listened to Pete suck in a breath as the Wolves dealt with the bad humans.

"Are there more of these movies?" Theral asked, turning down the volume as the credits began to roll.

"A few," Jester said. "You might have to put your name on a list at Music and Movies since the Wolf Team is very popular. There are books about them too."

Nodding, Theral stood and stretched. Then she yawned. "Is Lawrence ready to go home?"

"I think he forgot you were up here and is looking for you," Monty said, smiling. He picked up Lizzy, then waited for Pete to pick up Sarah and shake Robert awake enough to have the boy follow him back to the car.

As they walked outside with the children, Monty glanced toward the summer room. No light, so he couldn't be sure Simon Wolfgard was still in there. But the Others wouldn't need a light.

"Where's Meg?" he asked.

"She went up." Merri Lee tipped her head to indicate Meg's apartment. "She's tuckered out. So am I."

They piled into the cars they'd left in the visitors' spaces across the road from the Green Complex. Kowalski and Ruth dropped off Merri Lee and Debany, as well as Monty and Lizzy.

Bidding them all good night, Monty climbed the stairs and went to the efficiency apartment he was using. He woke Lizzy sufficiently for her to use the toilet and put on pajamas. As he tucked her in, he wondered how long Merri Lee and Debany would stay outside, and if Merri Lee would come in alone.

No need for a candle or lamp. The *terra indigene* saw quite well in the dark.

"What do you want to do?" Vlad asked quietly.

"We've never concerned ourselves with the human ships that travel on the Great Lakes or what those ships bring to the port here," Simon replied. "Our supplies from other regions are brought in on earth native or Intuit ships. Humans will notice if we start sniffing around their ships now."

"A few of the Sanguinati who live in the Courtyard often hunt around the docks. They might know something they didn't think would be of interest to Grandfather."

"Ask them. But there's one form of *terra indigene* who can find out more."

"If they're willing," Henry said.

Simon nodded. "If they're willing." He stood. "I'm going to check on Meg. Then I'll pay the girls at the lake a visit."

"Tonight?" Tess asked.

"Yes." He looked at the three of them. "Will you be here?"

Henry and Tess nodded. Vlad said, "I need to visit Grandfather Erebus, but I'll wait until you get back."

He went upstairs and found Meg on the sofa, sound asleep, despite the television being tuned to the show she watched every Earthday. Crouching, he ran a hand over her fuzz of hair. She couldn't growl about it if she didn't know.

Fairly sure she wouldn't wake anytime soon, he stripped out of his clothes and shifted. Then he left her apartment and ran to the Elementals' part of the Courtyard.

Except for Winter and Autumn, who slept during the warmer seasons, all the girls were around the lake. They watched him approach. Air rustled the leaves in the trees. Water lapped the bank, flowing over Earth's toes. Fire, Spring, and Summer sat a little farther away from the lake's edge.

"Is something wrong with our Meg?" Spring asked.

<No. She had fun today. She's looking forward to planting more seeds and tending what grows.>

"No planting tomorrow," Water said. "Rain is coming from our kin who live near Lake Superior."

"Since our Meg is happy, what does the Wolfgard want?" Fire asked.

<I want your help. I think you and your kin can find answers to some questions.>

CHAPTER 33

The questions were the pebble dropped in a pond, and the ripples were whispered in the wind to the Elementals throughout the continent of Thaisia. They flowed through the Great Lakes and down the streams and rivers, and they were part of the rain. They became a scent in the earth that was picked up by more than the shifters and Sanguinati willing to reside near human settlements.

That scent did not please the earth natives who lived in the most primal, and pristine, parts of the wild country.

And when the ripples became surf, Ocean took the questions into herself and sent them far beyond Thaisia.

CHAPTER 34

Moonsday, Maius 14

"**S**imon, it's Tess. Blair is driving me up to Nadine's Bakery and Café. She said she can sell me some of what she has ready, but she would prefer we pick up the order before she opens for human customers."

Simon growled at the answering machine and continued to rub a towel over his hair. He'd heard the phone ringing when he got in the shower. The damn phone had done nothing but ring from the moment he'd turned on the water. But Tess could have used the *terra indigene* way of communicating to tell him she was leaving the Courtyard and chose not to, preventing him from voicing an opinion.

"*Simon, this is Steve Ferryman. Remember me telling you about the woman who showed up to work with the girls? I'd like to hire her if I can figure out how to stretch the village budget to pay her. Anyway, I'd like you to meet her. And I wanted to go over some things about the River Road Community. Any chance you could come up to Ferryman's Landing today?*"

"How should I know?" he grumbled. "I'm not even dressed yet." And if he didn't get moving, Meg would growl at him for making her late for work—or leave without him.

"*Simon, this is Pete Denby. I need to talk to you about the two-family house you want to purchase. And I wanted to ask . . . do you have a spare desk and computer in one of the offices that I could use?*"

Humans. Couldn't be satisfied with being considered not edible; they also wanted to *talk* to him. And talk. And talk.

He took two steps away from the answering machine when the phone rang again.

Pouncing on the phone, he picked up the receiver and snarled, "What?"

"*Arroo!*"

"Sam?"

"Uncle Simon! The Wolf pups are going on a field trip with Miss Ruth!"

Simon blinked. "You're going on a trip to see a field?"

Sam laughed. "No. We're going to visit Howling Good Reads and learn how to buy a book!" A pause. "Can I stay with Meg after the field trip? Nathan gets to stay with her."

"Nathan's the watch Wolf." Since the Lizzy was still in the efficiency apartment with Montgomery, he'd have to check and make sure Nathan was going to be in the office with Meg. The enforcer was still upset with the Lizzy for misbehaving and causing so much trouble on Watersday.

"Uncle Simon?"

"Okay, sure. But don't whine if Meg doesn't have time to play with you."

"See you later!" Sam hung up.

Simon put the phone down and ran up to his bedroom to get dressed. Then he let himself into Meg's apartment through her kitchen door and found her with her hands braced on the table.

"Meg?" He hurried over to her.

She blinked at him. "I am so sore. Even my butt muscles are sore. I didn't do anything with *them*. Why are *they* sore?"

"Don't know." He hadn't done as much snoozing as he usually did on Earthday, but he felt just fine.

He ran his hand over her puppy fuzz hair. When she didn't growl at him, he wasn't sure if he should be pleased or concerned.

"Did you eat breakfast?" he asked.

"I tried to reach for the milk. It was too far."

He gathered up her work things and then gave her a quick once-over to make sure she was sufficiently dressed for the office. That much accomplished, he herded her out her front door and was entertained by watching Meg whimper her way down the stairs.

She wasn't sick; she wasn't injured. Before he called Dr. Lorenzo to come look at her, he'd see if the other females were whining this morning.

Probably best not to point out that the human males and the Wolves had done the digging yesterday, which was harder work than planting. And none of *them* were whining.

Well, the Wolves weren't.

He waited until they were driving to work before he mentioned the morning field trip.

"Why do a field trip?" Meg asked.

"Because someone untied its shoes?"

Meg frowned. "That makes no sense."

"It makes as much sense as most human jokes."

"That's true."

Simon carried Meg's things into the Liaison's Office, then wondered if he should offer to carry her. But she came inside on her own, so he put the BOW in the garage and walked over to Howling Good Reads to tell Vlad about the field trip—and find out if anything else wanted to bite his tail that morning.

Meg sagged against the front counter and stared at Nathan, who was stretched out on the Wolf bed under one of the big windows.

She felt relieved to find him in the office. After upsetting him so much when she'd made that cut—or, more honestly, forced *him* into making the cut because she'd been out of control—she wasn't sure he'd be willing to work as the watch Wolf anymore.

She eyed him lying there, looking so lazy and comfy.

Of course, "work" could be a flexible word.

"If Earthday is supposed to be a rest day, why did we all work so hard yesterday?" she asked.

He raised his head just enough to look at her, grunted, then flopped back down on the Wolf bed.

She watched a delivery truck pull in. "It's Harry."

Letting out a gusty sigh, Nathan rolled onto his belly, then stood up and performed the stretch that, in her Quiet Mind class, was called playful wolf, although Merri Lee had told her that the move was usually referred to as down dog.

Meg watched him for a moment before bracing her hands on the counter and stepping back far enough to perform a modified version of the stretch.

Nathan changed positions, now stretching his back legs and hips. Then he gave himself a good shake.

"Show-off," she muttered.

He just yawned, displaying all his teeth.

Harry walked in with a couple of packages, looked at the two of them, and grinned.

"Guess everyone was working outdoors yesterday," Harry said. "The wife and I turned the soil and planted some vegetables. Then she wanted to have a couple of pots of flowers for some color, so we went to the garden center. You couldn't turn around there without making new friends."

She didn't know what that meant and was too tired to ask.

"We planted some vegetables too." Meg took out her clipboard and slowly wrote the information for the delivery.

"You should take aspirin or something to help those sore muscles," Harry said. "And remember to drink plenty of water."

"I'll remember." She waited until Harry drove off, then wandered into the sorting room to see if there was anything she could do that didn't require standing, bending, lifting, sitting, or reaching for something.

Drink plenty of water? She didn't think so. Drinking meant peeing, and peeing meant getting her thigh muscles to bend enough so that she could sit on the toilet. She'd already done that once this morning. She wasn't eager to try it again.

"Meg?" Merri Lee walked in from the back room, carrying an insulated container from A Little Bite and a small bag. She opened the container and set the food on the sorting table. "Coffee, sandwich, and a couple of cookies." Then she opened the small bag and removed two bottles. "I wasn't sure if you usually took aspirin or acetaminophen, so I brought both."

"I don't think we were ever given anything like this in the compound," Meg said, taking a moment to recall training images of medications.

Merri Lee looked thoughtful, then opened the bottle of acetaminophen and shook two pills into Meg's hand. She went into the back room and returned with a glass of water. "They probably didn't give you aspirin because that reduces blood clotting. Wouldn't be the best idea for a *cassandra sangue*."

Meg swallowed the pills and drank all the water. "Don't you hurt?"

"I don't *hurt*, but I'm plenty sore, which is one or two levels below *hurt*. And being sore is why I made an appointment with Elizabeth Bennefeld today to get a massage. I made an appointment for you at four fifteen, when you finish the afternoon shift here. Ruth and Theral also made appointments. And Eve Denby did a butt wiggle when I told her there was a massage therapist who worked a couple days a week in the Market Square."

"What do I do in the meantime?"

"Stretches. Just don't overstretch. I have to go. Ruth is bringing the Wolf pups to HGR as a field trip to learn about bookstores and the proper way to behave when you're in one, and I'm working the checkout counter today."

As soon as Merri Lee left, Meg bent forward. In Quiet Mind class, she could touch her fingertips to the floor. Today her fingers dangled just below her knees.

The Crows who were perched on the shoulder-high wall that separated the delivery area from Henry's yard started cawing moments before Nathan quietly *arrooed* a warning that another delivery truck had pulled in.

She grunted when she straightened up and walked into the front room. Then she frowned as she pulled out the clipboard and wrote the name painted on the side of the small delivery van. "Blooming Blossoms. That's a new one."

It was nothing more than a comment, but Nathan moved closer to the counter.

The man opened the door but didn't quite enter the office. He gave Meg a nervous smile. "I've got a delivery for Theral MacDonald. Am I in the right place?"

The pins-and-needles feeling swept over Meg's ribs, then felt like it wanted to burrow into the bones.

Nathan looked at her, then growled at the deliveryman.

"I can sign for that," she said, struggling to stay calm.

"So she does work here? I was told to confirm that before handing over the delivery." He held up the flower arrangement.

The prickling filled Meg's hands now as well as her ribs. "She'll be able to pick up the flowers here."

"I guess that's all right as long as I get a signature." He strode to the counter, keeping an eye on Nathan. "That's some pet."

"Uh-huh." She glanced at the man's shirt as she signed for the flowers. The dark green shirt had the Blooming Blossoms logo on the left side. No name tag, though.

"You should keep your dog on a leash."

She gave the deliveryman a vague smile and wondered what kind of employer would send someone to the Courtyard and not tell the person anything about who lived there.

Put a Wolf on a leash!

Of course, Sam used to wear a harness and leash when he came to the office with her. Could the man have heard about that from another deliveryman? Or did he really not know the difference between a dog and a Wolf?

The deliveryman studied her, and she studied him. He had blond hair and blue eyes. Nothing unusual about that combination. She couldn't recall a training image that would fit his overall look. Not handsome. Pleasantly attractive?

But something about him made her skin prickle. *Go away, go away, go away!* she thought fiercely.

The mail truck pulled up.

"Busy place." He sounded annoyed about that.

"Yes, it is."

"Well, you have a nice day." He walked out and held the door for the mailman.

"Anything going out?" the mailman asked as he set a mailbag on one of the handcarts that was used for larger packages.

"Not today, thanks."

She waited until he'd walked over to retrieve the mail from the blue mailbox positioned outside the consulate. Then she bolted into the sorting room. She wasn't surprised when Nathan leaped on the counter and came in right behind her. But she was surprised when he shifted to his human form.

His *naked* human form.

"What's wrong?" he demanded.

She scurried to the other side of the big sorting table so that she couldn't see him from the waist down. *Naked* naked wasn't as disturbing as when Nathan shifted into that weird blend of human and Wolf that made him look like both and neither.

When he started to come around the table, she squeaked and scampered to the doorway of the back room. "You should put on some clothes when you're in human form."

He snarled at her.

Okay, not interested in clothes, she thought, trying to ignore her curiosity and not peek at his parts, since that could be construed as sending a signal. At least, according to *The Dimwit's Guide to Dating* that she'd been reading ever since that . . . confusion . . . with Simon the night he'd shifted from Wolf to human form and she kicked him off the bed. But the kicking was because of the dream she'd been having and not because of Simon being naked . . . and human.

Since Nathan didn't seem to care one way or the other if she saw him naked, maybe Wolves and humans didn't read the same signals?

The office's back door opened. Nathan, looking satisfied, shifted to Wolf form and returned to the front room.

Okay, *that* signal was clear enough.

"Tattletale," Meg muttered as Simon and Vlad rushed in.

"Meg!" Simon said. He bared his teeth. "Nathan says you're itchy. Why are you itchy?"

"I'm not." She didn't feel even the slightest tingle anymore.

"*Arroo!*" Nathan said, his forelegs on the front counter so he could watch what was going on in the sorting room.

Meg turned and glared at him. He stared back.

"I was itchy, but now I'm not," she amended when Simon growled, clearly more inclined to take Nathan's word over hers right now.

She held out her hands. "No more prickles. When that deliveryman showed up, the pins-and-needles feeling started and kept getting worse. I got away from the front counter as soon as I could."

Vlad hissed. Simon *and* Nathan growled.

Meg decided she didn't like being growled at in stereo.

"We're not upset with you," Vlad said.

Funny, it sure sounded that way.

"What was delivered that caused the prickles?"

"A flower arrangement," she replied.

As soon as she moved toward the door with the PRIVATE sign, the prickling began again around her rib cage. When she reached the door, the pins-and-needles feeling became a painful buzz along her ribs and a fierce prickling in her hands. She'd been focused on what she was feeling and hadn't realized Simon and Vlad were standing so close. When she tried to back up, she stepped on Simon's foot, making him yelp.

Simon grabbed her and hustled her to the back room.

"Is she all right?" Vlad asked, rushing to join them.

"I'm fine," she said, shaking her hands. "The prickling is fading again, so there must be something about the flower arrangement that is causing the reaction. The flowers came from a company called Blooming Blossoms. They've never delivered here before." She stopped, thought.

"Meg?" Simon said sharply. "You turned pale."

"Delivery for Theral," she whispered. "The flowers are for Theral."

Vlad slipped out of the back room. She heard him pick up the phone and say, "Come to the Liaison's Office." Pause. "Fuck waiting for someone to watch the cash register. Get over here *now*."

Meg blinked at him when he returned to the back room. "You swore at Merri Lee?"

"How did you know I was talking to Merri Lee?" he asked.

"She told me she was working the checkout counter at HGR this morning, so it had to be her, and you said . . . something bad."

Vlad rocked back on his heels. "It seemed appropriate. Should I apologize?"

"At any other time, you would have yelled at her for leaving the cash register unattended, so, yes, you should apologize." Meg wasn't sure if a human employer would have apologized, but if she'd been yelled at unfairly, *she* would want an apology.

Vlad sighed.

Merri Lee arrived at a run. So did Tess, whose brown hair had green and red streaks and was starting to curl. The rumbling voice in the front of the office announced Henry's arrival.

"What's wrong?" Tess demanded.

"Something to do with flowers," Simon replied. "But we don't know why they're causing trouble."

Determined to find an answer, Meg headed for the front room with Merri Lee on her heels and the three *terra indigene* close behind. But she stopped before she reached the Private doorway and wrapped her arms around her herself, wanting to claw and claw until she could reach the buzzing.

Meg backed away from the door. Merri Lee slipped past her and stepped up to the front counter.

"Nathan says it doesn't smell like anything but flowers and a little bit like the human who carried it in and someone else," Simon said.

"Probably the deliveryman and the florist." Merri Lee studied the flowers. "Nice arrangement of seasonal flowers. I don't see anything here that looks strange or dangerous, although I suppose most flowers could be dangerous if someone tried to eat them."

"Where's Skippy?" Meg asked.

Nathan and Simon sighed, but it was a valid question. Skippy was willing to eat anything that looked or smelled vaguely edible—and other things as well.

Merri Lee turned the vase. "There's no card."

"That's unusual?" Tess asked.

Merri Lee nodded.

Meg rubbed her arms, edged close enough to the doorway to see what was happening, and looked at Merri Lee. "The deliveryman said they were for Theral."

"You both smell afraid," Simon said. "Why?"

Merri Lee hesitated. "You know why Theral is living in Lakeside with her cousin's family, and why Officer MacDonald escorts her to work and home again?"

Simon nodded. "Montgomery said she ran away from a mate who hurt her."

"His name is Jack Fillmore. He could have sent the flowers just to confirm where to find her."

"The deliveryman called Nathan a dog," Meg said. "And he was annoyed that the office was busy."

"What did he look like?" Merri Lee asked, then held up her hand. "Wait. I'll call Michael and ask him to have a quiet word with Lawrence. Maybe the Mac-Donalds have a picture of Jack Fillmore. The rest of the family might have tossed out the photos, but I'll bet Lawrence kept one in case the police need it."

"Theral thought she would be safe here," Meg said, then added silently, *Like me.*

"She is safe," Simon growled. "Is Montgomery still at the efficiency apartment?"

"No," Merri Lee said. "He had to go to the station. Lizzy is taking the bookstore field trip with the Wolf pups. Eve Denby said Lizzy could spend the day with Robert and Sarah, but Lieutenant Montgomery doesn't want her to leave the Courtyard without him."

"Sensible," Henry rumbled.

"We need to know more, but Henry and I have to leave for the meeting with Steve Ferryman," Simon said. He studied Meg. "Is that all right?"

"I'm fine." She retreated into the sorting room, moving to the other side of the table. That far away from the flowers, the prickling was nothing more than a mild annoyance.

Simon followed her.

"I'm fine," she said again. "You go to your meeting." She waited to see if there might be some kind of prophetic response to the words.

Nothing.

"Okay," he said after studying her. "Henry will take the flowers over to the consulate so they won't bother you. Vlad is calling the police."

"Human law doesn't apply in the Courtyard."

"No, but the threat isn't in the Courtyard. Besides, Officer MacDonald is family to Theral, so the police will know anyway and want answers."

She nodded. Then she gave him a wobbly smile. "I didn't cut."

"That's good." He hesitated, shifting from one foot to the other.

"You shouldn't keep Henry waiting."

But he still hesitated. Then he sighed and walked out of the office.

"You sure you're okay?" Merri Lee asked quietly after Nathan curled up on his bed and the rest of the *terra indigene* had returned to their own work. "I'll stay if you need me."

"I'm okay."

Meg thought for a moment. Simon was a Wolf, and human rules didn't always apply because even when he looked human, he didn't think like a human. And yet . . .

"He seemed . . . disappointed . . . when he left. Simon, I mean."

Merri Lee leaned on the sorting table. "When Michael and I are together and one of us has to leave, we kiss good-bye. Maybe Simon would have liked the Wolf equivalent."

Meg frowned at her friend. "I'm not going to lick his face."

Merri Lee laughed. "Okay, but if he's in human form, I think a kiss on the cheek would give the same message."

"I am here." Connection. Companionship. Touch.

"Touch of a hand works too when you've got an audience."

Something to think about. Meg smiled. "Are you going to leave Vlad at the checkout by himself?"

"He yelled at me, so I'd let him fend for himself, but I think Ruth could use a hand right about now."

After Merri Lee left, Meg opened the delivery door and pulled the handcart into the sorting room. She needed to get the mail sorted before the ponies arrived to have their mail baskets filled.

But after she dumped the mail on the table, she just stood there, making no effort to work.

Connection. Touch. *I am here.*

Definitely something to think about.

CHAPTER 35

Moonsday, Maius 14

While Simon drove up River Road to Ferryman's Landing, Henry answered one phone call after another. When a full minute passed without the mobile phone squawking at them, he said, "Problems?"

"Messages," Henry replied. "A policeman has arrived from Toland and wants to interview the Lizzy. Captain Burke asked if the meeting could be held at the consulate."

"Smart move. Why didn't Lieutenant Montgomery ask? He's the one who usually works with us."

"Perhaps because the Lizzy is his child and his asking would cause some trouble we do not understand. Stavros Sanguinati also arrived this morning. He and the policeman from Toland must have taken the same night train."

"Do you think Stavros insisted on riding in the private executive car?"

Henry bared his teeth in a smile. "If one of those cars was part of the night train, I'm sure he was riding in it."

In Thaisia, the *terra indigene* could travel by train anytime, anywhere, in exchange for the railroads being allowed to build tracks through the wild country to connect human communities. But until Simon, Lieutenant Montgomery, and Dr. Lorenzo had gone to the Midwest during the hunt for the Controller, the Others hadn't known there was usually a car that had luxuries, like leather seats and its own little kitchen and shower, and didn't stink of so many humans. Now the Others did know, and the humans who used those cars could no longer count on the travel time between cities to privately plot and plan against each other—or against the *terra indigene*.

Even when there wasn't a vampire or a shifter in the car, the *terra indigene* now watched the humans who used those cars. It was fortunate for humans that the Elementals, and some of the usually unseen forms of earth natives, paid little attention to the clever meat unless provoked.

"After the police talk to the Lizzy, Lieutenant Montgomery will talk to Meg about the flowers and the human who delivered them," Henry said.

"The bad mate." This male had driven Theral away from two other jobs in another city. Being kin to Officer MacDonald and living with his parents in Lakeside provided her with some safety. Working in the Courtyard provided her with more.

Was it enough?

Simon wanted to shake off the human business that stuck to him these days like burs in fur. He knew why things had changed, and he didn't regret Meg's presence. She not only made it easier to deal with other humans; she provided entertainment for everyone in the Courtyard, making the press of all those humans living in Lakeside more bearable.

But that didn't mean her presence wasn't confusing.

Take her friendship with Nathan. He was glad they got along. The Liaison's Office wouldn't run smoothly if Meg and the watch Wolf didn't get along. But sometimes Simon resented looking out the window and seeing *his* squeaky toy romping outside with another Wolf when he had to deal with stupid human paperwork.

But Nathan was what humans called a work friend. Meg didn't spend much time with him away from the Liaison's Office. She didn't cuddle up with him to watch television or movies. She didn't share a bed with Nathan whether he was human or Wolf.

Those were things she did only with *him* because he was a different kind of friend. It was almost . . .

A scent, a *feeling* in the air, caught Simon's attention, scattering his thoughts and reminding him of why he'd made some of the choices he'd made over the past few years.

"If the *terra indigene* who work in Courtyards become too human, do we become the enemy?" he asked softly.

Henry turned his head, his shaggy brown hair whipped by the air coming in the windows. "Are you asking for yourself or for another reason?"

"Do you smell it?"

Henry looked away and said nothing. Then, "Yes, I smell it. Their scent wasn't here the last time we drove to Great Island. It's a reminder of how far removed we are now from the earth natives who live in the wildest part of the wild country."

It also meant that the ripples caused by rash actions the humans had made over the past few months had reached the primal wild country, disturbing the kinds of earth natives who usually didn't come this close to human habitation when their intentions were still benevolent.

The wild country was a term for all land that humans weren't allowed to use, but the wild had different levels, like the circles of a target. The center was a human place. The first circle contained the *terra indigene* who could shift and pass for human, at least long enough to interact with the interlopers and receive the agreed-upon goods that were payment for use of some land—that is, the Others who worked in the Courtyards or lived in their own settlements near human villages in order to keep watch. The next circle were *terra indigene* who liked some of the things humans made but didn't want contact with them. Those two circles made a buffer of a few miles between humans and the wild country that was unmarked by human influence in every way. Beyond that buffer . . .

The forms they took when they didn't walk in their true earth native form had no names. Their footsteps were a silent thunder felt beneath stone and grass. Even powerful shifters like the Wolves, Bears, and Panthers were no match for them. They were Namid's teeth and claws.

The rest of the *terra indigene* referred to them as the Elders.

"Log cabins," Simon said. "Wells. Farms. Spinning wheels and looms. Windmills and water wheels. Years ago, when humans were erased from a part of Thaisia, what was left behind became homes for other beings or quietly became part of the world again. The absence of humans made no difference. The *terra indigene* had learned how to build their own log cabins; how to spin and weave the cloth and blankets we wanted; how to farm in our own way and store the harvest for hungry days. We could do all that without absorbing too much from this form. But now . . ."

Henry blew out a breath. "Now, if humans weren't around to tend what they've made, those things would not quietly become part of the world again. At least, not for a long time." He turned his head so the air blew his hair out of his face. "Is that why you're so interested in this River Road Community and nurturing a pack of humans at our Courtyard?"

Simon nodded. "It's going to happen again. Humans are going to push until the *terra indigene* destroy them. The drugs that were being made from the blood of the *cassandra sangue* were just the beginning of the trouble. Even without the drugs, trouble is still spreading. It's like catching the scent of smoke but not being able to locate the fire. None of the *terra indigene* who work around the farms we control can understand why humans are claiming there is a shortage of food or why they're going to go hungry this year. There is no reason why they *should* go hungry, at least most days."

"That is true of all of Namid's creatures, including us."

"We *know* not all days end with a full belly. Everything in the world *except* humans knows that. But fear of hunger has humans looking toward *our* lands, and the anger that they can't take what isn't theirs is building. At least some regions of Thaisia are heading for a fight for territory."

"So you're trying to figure out if *terra indigene* can be sufficiently human to replace humans without losing who we are?"

"Yes."

Silence. Then Henry said, "This explains why you're interested in helping the Intuits on Great Island and the Courtyard's human pack. They're an experiment." He paused. "Is the time you spend with Meg also an experiment?"

"No," Simon said, swallowing the desire to snap out an answer. Wouldn't be smart to piss off Henry when they were in a moving vehicle and he couldn't dodge a swat. "Maybe it is. She's learning from us; we're learning from her. And she and I . . . We're learning together."

Another silence. "Good," Henry said.

CHAPTER 36

Moonsday, Maius 14

Jackson Wolfgard took a couple of steadying breaths before he opened the door to the scarred girl's room. When he didn't catch any scent of blood, he entered and set the plate of food on the desk before he studied the girl sprawled on the bed. She blinked at him, then yawned, showing a mouthful of dainty, healthy teeth.

"I brought you something to eat." He took a step toward the bed, curious about the pictures she had made. The first one looked like a drawing of the patchwork quilt. He wasn't sure what the second one was supposed to be. But the third picture . . .

"What is this?" he asked, pointing to the third picture.

"It's what I heard last night."

Jackson looked at land lit by moonlight. Two Wolves had their heads raised in song. Smoke drifted out of their mouths, rising to the night sky, where it took the shapes of bison and elk, moose and deer, mountain goats and rabbits.

"You drew our song."

The girl tucked her hands into her armpits, as if needing to protect them. "Did I do wrong?"

"No." He picked up the drawing and saw her eyes fill with regret. "I'd like to show this to the Wolfgard elders. I'll bring it back."

"Could I . . ." She wouldn't meet his eyes. "Could I put it on the wall?"

"Yes."

Now she looked at him. Just a puppy frightened of being punished for following her instincts. Which meant the humans in the compound *had* punished her for drawing pictures. Why?

He needed to say something. "Grass is not the same color green as leaves, and water can be different shades of blue. I can go down to the trading post today and see if they have more pencils . . . if having more colors wouldn't be upsetting to you."

"I like colors."

He turned to go.

"They were going to cut off my fingers. In that place. They were going to cut off my fingers because I needed to draw pictures and they wanted me to need the cuts instead."

He walked out of the room and gently closed the door.

Grace looked at him, her smile fading as she studied his face. "What's wrong?" She sniffed the air.

He turned the drawing around so she could see it.

"How did she know?" Grace asked, staring at the drawing.

"That's something I'll ask Meg, the Trailblazer. Right now, I want to show this to our elders. Then I need to make a trip to the Intuit trading post."

"You should buy a frame for the sweet blood's picture."

"Come with me to pick it out?"

Grace was a white Wolf who had come down from the High Northwest as a juvenile and eventually found her way to Sweetwater. She could pass for human, but her hair remained white with strands of light gray. Combined with a youthful face, she looked distinctive and drew attention that made her uneasy.

"There were strangers at the trading post when I went there last week," she said. "I didn't like their scent. I don't think the Intuits liked it either."

He stepped closer. "You should have told me."

"I told the elders. I think the Crows are keeping watch on the village, and the Hawks and Eagles are paying attention to the road and the vehicles coming our way." She ruffled her hair. "I'll go with you. I don't think any of us should visit the trading post alone. Not for a while."

He wanted to be her mate, and she was thinking of accepting him. He'd hoped she would go with him to spend time with him, but he didn't want her to go because she thought a lone Wolf would be in danger. If there was trouble at the Intuit village, she would be in danger too.

But the Intuits had said nothing about strangers in their village when he'd responded to their plea for help with the scarred girl. That was something else to think about.

Jackson carefully rolled up the drawing and left with Grace. He stopped long enough to assign another Wolf to stay in the cabin so that the sweet blood wouldn't be alone. Then he and Grace went to see the elders before taking one of the settlement's two vehicles and driving down to the trading post.

When he returned, he would send a message to Simon Wolfgard, asking if the sweet blood could reveal visions and prophecies in other ways besides cutting their skin.

CHAPTER 37

Moonsday, Maius 14

Monty moved quickly when he heard the raised voice coming from Captain Burke's office.

"I just spent seven hours on a train, stuck in a car with a freaking vampire. I expect some cooperation, Burke."

"Cooperation I can give you. As for the rest, I can't give you what I don't have," Burke replied as he glanced toward the doorway. "Lieutenant, come in and meet Captain Felix Scaffoldon of Toland's Crime Investigation Unit. Captain, this is Lieutenant Crispin James Montgomery."

Monty stepped into Burke's office. "Do you have some news about what happened to Elayne?"

Scaffoldon gave Monty a cold once-over. "Just strolling in now, Lieutenant? I guess getting cozy with the Wolves here has its perks if you don't have to report to work on time. We'll talk further." He turned away from Monty—a sharp, dismissive gesture—and looked at Burke. "Right now, I want to see the girl."

Monty stepped forward, forcing Scaffoldon to include him. "You came all the way to Lakeside to interview Lizzy? Weren't you sent a copy of the interview that was already conducted?"

"He was," Burke replied before Scaffoldon could. "But the captain is really more interested in retrieving the physical evidence, which I have already offered to hand over to him for his investigation."

"Yes, I need to bring that bear back to Toland," Scaffoldon snapped. "Having it sit here doesn't help us find a killer." When he said "killer," he didn't look at Monty, and he did it in a way that made it clear he believed Monty *was* the killer, despite the physical impossibility of being able to travel to and from Toland in the time frame. "But the child's family wants her returned to Toland, so I'll take her back with me."

"My daughter is staying with me," Monty said with quiet heat.

"Alleged daughter. Ms. Borden's mother is questioning if you are, in fact, the child's father."

Monty pulled a document from his inner suit coat pocket and handed it to Scaffoldon. "Here. You can pass this on to Celia Borden."

"What is it?" Scaffoldon didn't bother to look.

"When the legal documents for child support were written, Elayne expressed no doubt that I was Lizzy's father. She had no doubts when Lizzy was born and the birth certificate was filled out. She had no doubts, and neither did Celia Borden, during the years when Elayne, Lizzy, and I lived together in Toland. I *know* I'm Lizzy's father, regardless of what Celia Borden is saying now. I'm Lizzy's closest relative, and I can support her. So *my daughter* is staying with me. What I gave you was a photocopy of the custody papers that were signed and witnessed this morning."

The relief he'd felt when he'd signed those papers had staggered him. Celia Borden had never shown any real interest in Lizzy, and Monty didn't think her wanting custody now was sparked by feelings of affection for the girl. Celia just wanted the girl within easy reach for some reason, and whatever the reason, he was sure it wasn't for Lizzy's benefit.

Scaffoldon's face was suffused with anger. He looked like he wanted to rip up the papers and throw them on the floor.

"I want to see the girl," Scaffoldon said.

Burke's fierce-friendly smile turned icy. "She's at a safe house. Since you insist on seeing her, I've arranged for you to interview her there. I'll have the bear brought up from the evidence lockup. You can take it with you so you won't have to stop back here after the interview." He made a show of looking at his watch. "She'll be available in an hour."

"I'll interview her here."

"No, you won't."

Scaffoldon stared at Monty and Burke. "By all the gods, where did you stash her?"

The icy glint in Burke's blue eyes matched his smile. "In the Lakeside Courtyard."

CHAPTER 38

Moonsday, Maius 14

They met in the government building on Great Island, in the conference room Steve Ferryman had reserved for this meeting.

Simon studied the woman sitting across from him, but he didn't know the proper way to describe Pam Ireland. Plump? Solid? Compact?

Those were human terms. Since he wasn't considering whether she'd have enough meat to feed a pack, he thought of other words that were relevant.

Sincere. Yes, that was a good word for what he was sensing. And . . .

"You smell like dog," he said.

"That's Ben," she replied with an easy smile. "He's a golden retriever. He's still young, so he's a little goofy, but he's great with kids."

Simon cocked his head. "Small humans or young goats?"

She laughed. "He's never seen a young goat."

"He will if you stay here," Steve said, taking the seat beside her. "Along with Foxes, Bears, and Coyotes, to name a few. There are some dogs and cats on the island. Mostly working animals." Looking at Simon and Henry, he waved a hand to indicate Ming Beargard. "Until Ben arrived and made it clear that, to him, a Bear smells like a Bear whether he's wearing fur or human skin, it didn't occur to us that the animals here don't respond to the *terra indigene* in the same way as an animal who didn't grow up around their scents. Poor Ben has spent half his time hiding."

"Despite that, he's been a kind of furry security blanket for the girls," Pam said. "Mr. Ferryman indicated that there are a few people who need to decide about my employment here . . ."

"But I wanted to see how Ms. Ireland interpreted the information Ms. Corbyn had already provided," Steve interrupted. "So I gave her permission to work with the girls for a few hours."

"And?" Simon said.

"I wish I'd known even this much in a couple of places where I worked," Pam said. "More to the point, I wish I'd had outside confirmation for my own impressions as I worked with some of the girls in those halfway houses. I had a feeling some things would work, would relieve the distress some of the girls experienced, but I didn't have any proof, and feelings weren't enough for the administrators."

Simon thought the sudden bitterness in her voice was interesting. "The girls died?"

"A few of the suicide attempts were successful. But after being told a little about the *cassandra sangue*, I'm wondering if those girls really were trying to kill themselves or had cut themselves for a different reason and were unlucky enough to bleed out before someone found them."

Opinionated. That was another word for this female. He'd bet she'd expressed a lot more opinions to her employers than the female pack did to him. Of course, her former employers most likely didn't have a good set of fangs between them.

"The young prophets cannot continue to live in the bed-and-breakfast," Ming said. "Even after simplifying their rooms as your Meg suggested, the place is too busy for them."

"And Lara and Margaret need to make a living," Steve said. "The village has been paying for the girls' board, but we can't do that forever either."

"You can't cut them for profit," Simon growled.

"Of course not!" Steve scraped his fingers through his hair. "But our village doesn't have a lot of resources to spare."

Simon sat up straighter. The Lakeside Courtyard had plenty of money. Pam Ireland could be hired by the Courtyard's Business Association but work for Steve Ferryman as the blood prophets' caretaker. And she could meet with Dr. Lorenzo at the Market Square medical office to talk about the girls and decide what would be put into his task force reports.

Yes, that could work for all of them.

"You have some ideas?" Henry's question to Ming pulled Simon back into the immediate discussion.

The Black Bear nodded. "The *terra indigene* have talked among ourselves, and we've talked with the Intuit leaders. We will give thirty acres to build a home for the *cassandra sangue*."

"Thirty acres?" Simon said, surprised. "What are five young girls going to do with thirty acres? They don't know how to hunt or fish or even dig to plant food."

"We'll build housing, starting with just what we need but planning for a total of a hundred girls living on the campus," Steve said.

"Campus." Simon bared his teeth—and realized his canines weren't close to human size when Pam's eyes widened. "Is that another way of saying *compound*?"

"No. Well, yes, in a way." Steve blew out a breath. "Not a place with walls and locked doors. We're not talking about anything like that. But a place where the *cassandra sangue* can live and receive schooling. A place that will be more like a private school, but will have walking trails and water. Gardens where they can grow some of their own food and have an active connection with the world. A small farm with a couple of dairy cows and a handful of chickens that the girls can help take care of. Maybe a goat or two. And Jerry Sledgeman said he'd talk to the Liveryman family about donating a couple of ponies."

"Hopefully many of the girls will be able to move beyond the campus and work in a small community like Ferryman's Landing when they reach adulthood," Pam said. "But I think you have to prepare for the fact that some of those girls will never be stable enough to live outside of a supervised facility."

"And some will die, regardless of what anyone tries to do to help them," Henry finished, nodding.

"You have the workers who can build this campus?" Simon asked. What would Meg say about blood prophets being moved from one kind of confined place to another? *Would* it feel confined? Thirty acres wasn't much to a Wolf. On the other hand, the three hundred acres that made up the Lakeside Courtyard was surrounded by a fence that defined the boundaries. Did *Meg* feel confined?

Something to ask her this evening.

"We have the workers," Steve replied. "We have an architect working to design the buildings—clean lines with an eye to blending privacy with protection. Not as basic a design as the houses the Simple Life folk prefer, but more in keeping with the rest of Ferryman's Landing."

When Steve hesitated, Ming said, "What the Intuits and the Great Island *terra indigene* don't have is money to buy lumber and pipes and the other things that go into making human dens."

<That is something to discuss among us,> Simon said, glancing at Pam.

<The girls like her,> Ming said. <I think Steve would like to put her in charge of the campus once it is built.>

<Has she met Jean?>

<We have told her about Jean, and Steve went to the Gardner farm to tell Jean about Pam Ireland. But they have not met. Jean is not ready.>

Simon turned toward Pam. "You're hired to work with the girls living in Ferryman's Landing. Now go away."

She blinked at him several times before looking at Steve, who nodded and said, "Thanks, Pam. We'll talk more as soon as I'm done here."

She left the room in a controlled hurry.

"That was rude," Steve said.

"No," Simon corrected. "Threatening to eat her if she didn't leave would have been rude, since employees are not edible. But decisions need to be made, and she isn't part of that."

"River Road Community," Henry rumbled, cutting off anything Steve might have said. "Simon had to deal with other things these past two days, so Vlad and I have talked to the *terra indigene* who have heard about that land."

Simon looked at the Grizzly. So did Ming and Steve.

"There are some Sanguinati living in one of the houses," Steve said cautiously. "When I went with a crew to check out the houses and make a list of what would be needed, they came out to investigate and said you'd given them permission."

"We did," Simon said. "And Erebus Sanguinati has also given them permission. Tell me about the houses."

"Not in bad shape," Steve said. "Need some basic care and all of them could use a few repairs. The industrial building would need significant work to convert into something we could use—once someone figures out how it will be used."

"The main concern, for us, is that humans who manage to escape from Talulah Falls might try to claim those houses and that land," Ming said.

"Which is why we need to get more than a handful of juvenile vampires into those houses," Simon said.

"What kind of humans did you have in mind?" Steve asked.

"A mixed community. Intuits, the humans the HFL movement calls Wolf lovers, and *terra indigene*." Simon studied the other four males. "Right now, Talulah Falls is a dangerous place."

"The Crowgard have told me the *terra indigene* who have taken the duty of keeping that city under control have said they are separating the useful humans from the meat. And most of what is in the city is meat," Ming said.

"The animosity between humans and Others is fuel for the HFL movement." Simon frowned. Something Ming had said created an itchy thought. "How are humans escaping from Talulah Falls?" The *terra indigene* who controled that town had brought in a Harvester for their main enforcer. How were humans getting past him?

"A group of humans create a distraction," Steve said. "They cause enough of a ruckus so that when the Others go to deal with them, another group of people on the other side of town can escape on foot, taking only what they can carry." He fidgeted. "Personally, I think the Others are letting people escape. Now that the initial anger toward humans has passed, I have a feeling that if they could find a way to keep the necessary industries running, they would let everyone else leave. What they aren't considering is that people in the HFL movement probably consider every escape as some kind of victory over the *terra indigene*, even if the people don't survive long enough to reach another human village."

"Victory implies a fight, and there is nothing to be gained by fighting with us," Henry said. "The humans can't win."

Simon held up a hand, signaling they should all be quiet.

Distractions in one place so that something else could happen in another place. Something being claimed as a victory even if no one survives. Catching the scent of a fire so distant you can't do anything about it, and yet knowing that a shift in the wind could bring that fire right to your den with little warning.

"The humans in Thaisia can't win a fight against the *terra indigene*," he said quietly. "So why is the HFL movement trying to start a fight here? What do they gain when they have to know they'll lose?"

Steve's eyes widened. "Distraction. Creating a ruckus and pulling everyone's attention away from somewhere else—or something else."

"Wolves will attack another predator to draw it away from the pups. It's not a serious fight, although it can turn into one. They just pester and nip, forcing the predator to deal with them while other members of the pack get the pups to safety."

"The HFL movement here could be the nip and pester to keep us, and other humans, focused on them," Henry said. "But what are they protecting? Every time you stand against another predator, you run the risk of being hurt or killed. What is worth that risk?"

"Being able to control all the food, all the water, all the resources," Steve said.

"The humans can't win a fight against us," Simon said. "Not here, where cities are separated by miles and miles of wild country. But someplace else where the humans would need extra food and supplies to sustain a fight?"

Steve leaned forward. "You think the HFL movement here is a distraction and resource for the HFL in Cel-Romano? That they've been conned so they'll send as many supplies as possible—so many, in fact, that they're creating food shortages here? Gods above and below, if they truly believe that anything that happens in Cel-Romano will benefit them, you'll never convince them that they're being set up."

"It doesn't matter if the humans in Cel-Romano win or lose their fight with the *terra indigene*; the humans in Thaisia will lose," Ming said.

Simon nodded. "They will lose. But the HFL movement is like an invasive weed that has taken root and spread through human communities across the continent. We're not going to be able to convince the humans who are ensnared that they are being set up or that they will lose. We need to protect our own packs as best we can—and we both have a better chance of doing that if we work together."

"Agreed," Steve said.

"That's why we need the River Road Community inhabited by a group of humans and *terra indigene* who will help us defend the route between Ferryman's Landing and Lakeside." *And will be tolerated by the earth natives in the wild country who have been disturbed by the humans' recent actions.*

"Okay, what do we do?" Steve asked.

"I have been talking to *terra indigene*," Henry said. "Word has traveled that the Lakeside Courtyard is going to be a training ground for Others who need more detailed lessons for interacting with humans. I have talked to Panthergard leaders from the western regions, as well as Lynxgard from the Northeast and High Northeast regions."

"Some of the cats want to come to Lakeside?" Simon tried not to whine. A Wolf would take on a Lynx or Bobcat if necessary, but one of the cats known as Panther or Cougar? Not if there was a choice. They were bigger, heavier, and meaner than Wolves.

Ideal as enforcers for the new community?

"They asked about training at Lakeside, not living there," Henry said. "But at River Road, some houses could be set aside for various gards that wanted to spend more time here before returning to their old territory."

It took them an hour to come up with a working plan. The River Road Community had forty-five semidetached, two-bedroom doubles with the garages sharing a common wall. Fifteen of the doubles would be set aside for the *terra indigene*. Twenty-five would be available to humans who wanted to help build this community and who met the approval of both the Intuits and the *terra indigene*. The other five buildings, the ones closest to River Road, would become the business center. For the time being, the industrial plant would be used for storage.

The Intuits would supply the labor to get the houses in shape as quickly as possible. The Lakeside Courtyard would supply the money to purchase needed materials. Some acreage would be set aside to create allotments so that residents could grow some of their own food, and there would be a fenced common pasture for livestock. But there would still be plenty of open land for those who preferred to hunt for their food instead of grow it.

Officer Roger Czerneda, the official police officer in Ferryman's Landing, would be offered a house in the River Road Community in exchange for expanding his territory to include the community and the road that ran between it and Great Island.

It would not be easy for humans and *terra indigene* to live so close to one another. Even in a place like Great Island, where Intuits and Others had worked together for generations to provide food and shelter and protect the island's residents, they had not tried to live side by side. No one had considered such a thing—until Meg began living in the Green Complex and showed some of the *terra indigene* that it could be done.

None of them said it, but Simon understood that part of the Panthergard's and Lynxgard's interest in Lakeside was the blood prophet who retained the sweetness of a child's heart. Meg was the kindling that had started a different kind of fire among humans and *terra indigene* alike—a fire that burned just as bright as the blaze the HFL movement kept fanning.

Hope or hatred? Which fire would light Thaisia?

CHAPTER 39

Moonsday, Maius 14

Alone in the back room of the Liaison's Office, Nathan tucked the blue checked shirt into his jeans. A T-shirt would have been easier to wear in warm weather, but Michael Debany had told him that would be too casual for an official meeting. And this was business with a Toland police officer who was a stranger and, while not yet confirmed, might well be an enemy.

That was the reason he was attending this meeting: because the Toland police officer might be an enemy. Since Nathan was the enforcer the Lizzy knew best, the Courtyard's Business Association thought she'd be able to tell her story honestly if she felt safe.

At least he wouldn't be confused this time if the Lizzy turned into a whiny puppy. Meg wouldn't be at the meeting, wouldn't need his protection from the stranger—or from the Lizzy. Not totally the Lizzy's fault that Meg had needed to cut. But fault or not, being forced to make the cut for Meg had scared him badly, and that made him wary of the Lizzy.

"Why are you growling?" Meg asked as he entered the sorting room.

"I'm not."

"Yes, you are."

He shrugged, not willing to admit that humans were more difficult to deal with when you couldn't give them a lethal bite or even a sharp nip.

Then he caught something in Meg's scent and focused on her. "What's wrong?"

"Nothing."

"You—" Probably shouldn't say she didn't smell right. In the books he'd read recently, human females got snappish when a male commented about her smell—unless he said it was a *good* smell. "You look upset."

Nathan came around the table, eyeing the catalogs and envelopes. Nothing there that looked dangerous. But the envelope Meg was holding had her name on it. No one wrote to Meg.

"Let me see that." He held out a hand. Couldn't grab it from her. Paper could cut too.

Meg gave him the envelope. "I've never received a letter before. Not one that was mailed. It's a new thing."

"A scary new thing?" He watched her think, could tell by the look in her eyes that she was remembering training images in an attempt to match one to her own experience.

"A little," she finally said. "Not because I received it, but because I don't know what is inside. Some training images showed a person holding an envelope and looking excited or happy. Other images show a person looking scared or sad."

"How do you feel?" He asked partly out of curiosity and partly so he could report a potential danger to Meg.

"Excited and scared," she decided.

Nathan studied the envelope. The return address was Gardner Farm, Great Island, NER, and the postal code for Ferryman's Landing. He sniffed the envelope, picking up the scent of chickens, cows, humans, hay.

"Smells like a farm," he said, handing it back to her.

She looked at him, then sniffed the envelope. "If you say so."

"Want me to open it?"

Meg shook her head. "Not ready for what's inside."

The Crows on the outside wall cawed a warning.

"The police are here," Nathan said. "I have to go." He hesitated. Something wasn't right with her. "The letter is a new thing, but it's not why you smell . . ." Back to smells again.

"Did I do the right thing, not making a cut when the flowers were delivered?" Meg asked.

Worry. A little fear. *That's* what he smelled on her. Did she really think he'd say anything that would encourage her or give her an excuse to cut? Simon would rip him apart. And if Simon didn't, the Sanguinati surely would. Vlad had made that *very* clear.

Neither of those things was important in the end. He worked as an enforcer. He protected the residents of the Courtyard. He'd gotten a little complacent as the watch Wolf because he hadn't fully understood that Meg had one enemy that was always nearby: herself.

"What could you have learned from a cut that we didn't learn just from your skin prickling?" he asked. "We know the flowers are for Theral, and we suspect they came from the mate she ran away from because he hurt her."

"We don't know that for sure," Meg said.

"We don't need 'for sure,' Meg. We're on guard now. We'll keep watch. Theral is protected here. And she is kin to police. MacDonald's teeth aren't much use in a fight, but he has a gun, so he'll protect her too." When she didn't say anything, he pressed because he couldn't leave until he was sure Meg wouldn't become her own enemy. "Is your skin still prickling?"

Meg shook her head. "Not since the flowers were taken away."

He tapped the envelope. "No prickling about that?"

She looked surprised by the question. "No. I don't feel anything that indicates there is a prophecy connected to the letter."

<Nathan,> Elliot said. <The police have arrived. Lieutenant Montgomery is bringing the Lizzy to the consulate's meeting room.>

<When?>

<Now.>

Nathan turned to Meg. "I have to go." He opened the Private door, vaulted over the counter, and went to the front door. Then he stopped and returned to the counter, remembering what Crystal Crowgard had told him that morning. "Meg? Do you remember Charlie Crowgard?"

She smiled. "Of course I remember him."

"Remember when that Phineas Jones came to the Courtyard, and you and Merri Lee saved Skippy by hitting that human with a teakettle and broom?"

Now she paled. "Yes, I remember. Sort of remember."

"Crystal told me that Charlie Crowgard wrote a song about the fight. It's called 'Teakettle Woman and Broomstick Girl,' and it's so popular with the *terra indigene* who have heard it, he's going to record it so the rest of us can hear it too."

As he hurried out of the office, he heard Meg yipping for him to come back.

As a police officer, it took Monty less than a minute to realize he didn't like, or respect, Captain Felix Scaffoldon of the Toland Crime Investigation Unit. As a father, it took him half that time to realize he didn't want his little girl in the same room as the man.

Something about Scaffoldon was . . . off. Not a sexual predator vibe, but Monty had the impression that Lizzy didn't count in some way, was considered acceptable collateral damage.

A chill went through him. What did Scaffoldon know about Elayne's death that he wasn't sharing? Had she been considered collateral damage too?

No one had asked for his consent before arranging this interview. Monty had thought it had been high-handed of Burke to make such arrangements. Now he had to admit he wouldn't have thought to make *these* particular arrangements.

Scaffoldon had been prepared to have Monty and Burke present, one as the police presence representing the city of Lakeside and the other as the child's father. But the man hadn't been prepared for the *terra indigene* who had seemingly invited themselves to the interview. Elliot Wolfgard, consul for the Lakeside Courtyard and the Wolf who dealt with the city's government, stayed near the door of the conference room. Nathan Wolfgard stood behind Lizzy's chair, making it clear to everyone that the Wolf was here to guard the child. Then there was Vladimir Sanguinati, representing the Courtyard's Business Association, wearing black slacks and a black T-shirt. And last was Stavros Sanguinati, one of the vampires who ran the Toland Courtyard, wearing a black-on-black suit that made everyone else in the room—including Elliot Wolfgard—look like they were wearing secondhand cheap.

"Shall we get started?" Captain Burke asked pleasantly.

The door opened and Pete Denby walked in. "Sorry I'm late. Had to get the children settled at A Little Bite." He took the seat next to Monty, opened his briefcase, and removed a notepad and pen. "Whenever you're ready."

"Feel the need for an attorney, Lieutenant?" Scaffoldon asked.

Pete looked surprised. "I'm not here as Lieutenant Montgomery's representative. I'm here as Miss Elizabeth's attorney and advocate."

"I, too, am trained in human law," Stavros said. "So I can advise Lieutenant Montgomery if that is required."

Scaffoldon barked out a laugh. "A vampire attorney? Isn't that redundant?"

Stavros smiled, but his dark eyes remained cold. "Perhaps."

"Should be having this interview at the station." Scaffoldon had been voicing that complaint all the way to the Courtyard. At least Monty wouldn't have to listen to the man's complaints on the way back from the Courtyard. Burke had asked Louis Gresh to follow in another car and drive Scaffoldon to the train station after the meeting.

"Have you apprehended the person or persons responsible for the death of Elayne Borden?" Stavros continued to smile. "No? Then Elizabeth is safer here. Ask your questions, if you have any."

Whatever questions Scaffoldon really had, he didn't want to ask in the presence of the *terra indigene*. He covered the same ground that Burke had covered in the initial interview with Lizzy, but Monty noticed Scaffoldon didn't ask about anything that happened *before* Elayne and Lizzy's arrival at the train station.

Had Burke sent the part of the interview about Elayne and Lizzy staying in a hotel the previous night, or about the phone call from Leo Borden that precipitated the flight from the hotel to the train station?

Had the transcript that had been sent to the Toland police mentioned finding the jewels inside the bear?

A strange thought bubbled up.

Was Scaffoldon wondering if the *terra indigene* were staring at him with such focused attention because of what he was saying or because they were thinking about dinner?

Scaffoldon ran out of questions about the same time the novelty of being the center of so much adult attention wore off for Lizzy. In another minute, she would start pestering or pouting, sure that whatever Sarah and Robert were doing at A Little Bite was much more exciting than talking to police officers.

Scaffoldon couldn't read Lizzy's signals, but apparently Vlad could.

"I think that covers everything, don't you?" Vlad asked, looking at Stavros.

"Everything," Stavros agreed with a chilling smile directed right at Scaffoldon.

"Mr. Denby," Vlad said. "If you and Nathan could escort the Lizzy to A Little Bite, she can join the other children for a snack."

Pete looked at Monty and Burke before putting his notepad and pen back in his briefcase. "Sure."

Man, Wolf, and child left the conference room.

Burke slapped his hands on the table. "Now that that's settled . . ."

"Nothing is settled," Scaffoldon snapped. "The child needs to be returned to Toland and her family. She's a witness."

"To what, exactly?" Stavros asked. "As she just told you, she didn't see who hurt her mother, and she's already answered all of your questions. At least, she answered the questions you chose to ask."

"Meaning what?"

"I, too, have a few questions. Not for the child, but for you."

Scaffoldon went so pale, Monty wondered if the man would faint.

"I don't have to say anything to you," Scaffoldon said.

"Which says everything I needed to hear." Stavros stared at Scaffoldon. "There is no reason for you to return to Lakeside. There is no reason for you, or anyone you work with, to speak with the child again. If you stay focused on her, the Sanguinati are going to become focused on you. And your associates."

Oh gods, Monty thought, noticing the color draining from Burke's face while Scaffoldon's face filled with dark fury. *Is Stavros threatening to have the Sanguinati square off against the Toland police force?*

Getting to his feet, Scaffoldon looked at Burke and didn't try to hide his animosity. "You're backing the wrong side."

"No, I'm not," Burke replied.

"I'll escort Captain Scaffoldon to his car and see him out of the Courtyard," Elliot said, opening the conference room door in a silent command.

Giving all of them one last look, Scaffoldon walked out.

"Mr. Wolfgard." Burke fished his car keys out of his pocket. "Captain Scaffoldon needs the box of evidence that is stored in the trunk of my car. Since he won't be returning to Lakeside, we wouldn't want him to leave without it."

Elliot took the keys and walked out, and that left two vampires and two cops in the room.

Vlad looked at Burke and smiled. Burke, regaining some color in his face, returned the smile.

Monty breathed a quiet sigh of relief. Then he looked at Stavros. "Would the Sanguinati really attack the Toland police force?"

Stavros looked surprised. "Why would we? They have not provided sufficient provocation for such a decision."

"You said you would focus on Scaffoldon and his associates."

"I wasn't referring to the police. Not all the police," Stavros amended.

Burke nodded. "Humans First and Last movement."

Stavros turned to Vlad. "Why did you and Captain Burke find that human's departure amusing?"

Vlad smiled, showing a hint of fang. "Because he's scurrying back to Toland with a battered toy bear he was sent to retrieve."

"Why?"

"Because that bear has a bag of jewels hidden inside it," Monty said, reminded of the most likely reason that Elayne was dead and Lizzy had been in danger.

"Ah." Stavros gave Vlad a curious look. "Is that why Grandfather Erebus waved away any discussion of jewels yesterday? Because he was allowing the gems to be returned to Toland, despite . . ." He stopped, then studied Vlad and Burke.

"Where would a young girl get a bag of gemstones?" Burke said. "It's more likely that she was pretending to be a jewel thief or some other such thing that she'd seen in a movie and had stashed a bag of colored glass inside her partner in crime."

Stavros looked delighted. "Colored glass?"

"Such pretty colors," Vlad murmured. "Blues and greens and ruby red."

Stavros laughed, long and loud.

Monty felt queasy. "When the HFL find out . . ."

"The Wolves tore off an arm and a leg, but the bear's torso was untouched," Burke said. "Scaffoldon didn't say one word, didn't ask one question about jewels. He has no reason to think we found them. That being the case, he certainly wasn't going to tell *me* about them."

"Especially since there have been many reports of jewelry being stolen from the Toland elite," Stavros said. "And news reports have droned on about a couple of jewelry stores also being robbed. Humans were trying to blame the Crowgard, which is ridiculous. If an earring or a ring is dropped on the sidewalk that borders the Courtyard, a Crow won't resist claiming it. But they don't go into human houses and steal—and they don't remove the gems from a piece of jewelry and discard the setting."

"The police have no leads?" Burke asked blandly.

"The police investigating the thefts all wear little HFL pins on their lapels. So do the humans who were robbed. So do the owners of the jewelry stores that reported the theft of loose gems."

"Elayne might have been caught up in the glamour of being with Nicholas Scratch and rubbing elbows with society people who wouldn't have acknowledged her otherwise, but she would not have stooped to stealing jewels, and she certainly wouldn't have put Lizzy at risk by hiding them in Boo Bear," Monty said hotly.

Vlad leaned forward and said gently, "She found the secret, and she tried to run. They had to stop her."

He rubbed his face, suddenly tired. "She should have left the jewels. Dropped them in a closet, scattered them over the floor so someone would waste time finding them."

"It wouldn't have made any difference. She still had the secret. So did the Lizzy."

"Unlike the Toland police, we don't think anything has been stolen." Stavros pitched his voice to be low and soothing. "We think these were arranged . . . donations . . . for the HFL movement."

"With the added benefit of pointing a finger at the Crows and feeding the animosity growing between humans and *terra indigene*," Burke said.

"Exactly."

Sickroom voices, Monty thought. *Do they think I can't, or won't, handle the truth, whatever it may be?*

"Someone should question Leo Borden," he said. He couldn't picture Leo being able to pull off a jewel heist, but he could see the man as a courier—and he could easily imagine Leo thinking that Boo Bear would be a good hiding place for a fortune in gemstones. After all, who would look for them in a child's toy, especially a child living under the same roof as Nicholas Scratch?

She doesn't have anything else Scaffoldon or Scratch would want, so Lizzy is safe now, Monty thought. The father wanted to believe it. The cop knew it wasn't true, could *feel* it wasn't true.

"What will happen when the HFL discovers the gems Scaffoldon brought back are fakes?" he asked.

"I believe you humans call it a domino effect," Stavros replied as Elliot slipped back into the room. "Which brings me to the reason I came to Lakeside. I will, of course, talk to Simon directly, but Grandfather Erebus decided select humans as well as the *terra indigene* should be prepared."

"Gods above and below," Burke muttered. "Prepared for what?"

"According to humans, Toland is Thaisia's center of commerce," Stavros said. "Many ships dock there, and a great flow of goods comes into the city from other parts of the world. Just as great a flow of goods goes out."

"Do *terra indigene* ships also dock there?"

"No. We have other harbors for our little ships, harbors we share with the Intuits."

A sharpness in the words made Monty wonder if there had been trouble in the past: fights, sabotage, other kinds of incidents that had encouraged the Others to keep their distance.

"Our ships don't dock in the Toland port, but we still pay close attention to what comes into Thaisia . . . and what goes out."

Monty wondered if the weight suddenly clinging to his bones was a feeling of dread.

"What is going out?" Burke finally asked.

"The Crowgard can probably tell you more than the Sanguinati since they like to poke around in everything, and my kin tend to visit the area around the docks at night," Stavros said. "I can tell you that ships coming in from Brittania aren't receiving all the cargo they expected to load, but they're still being charged for the full amount. Any captain who protests is threatened with being struck off the trade list."

"What happens to the cargo that isn't loaded?" Monty asked.

"We noticed that ships bound for the Cel-Romano Alliance of Nations are now loaded late at night when there are fewer observers. We suspect the cargo that is held back from Brittanian merchant ships finds its way into the holds of Cel-Romano ships."

"Another form of piracy," Burke muttered. "With your permission, I'd like to have a quiet word with a cousin of mine. He's a police officer in Brittania, and he keeps me informed of rumors coming out of Cel-Romano."

"Would he also be willing to use his influence to provide discreet assistance?" Stavros asked.

Burke stared at the vampire for several heartbeats. "I think that would depend on what he was asked to do."

"Very soon, a storm in the Atlantik will blow a Cel-Romano ship off course. It will run aground off the coast of Wild Brittania and everything will be lost."

"Including the crew?"

"Oh, especially the crew, since it was the Sharkgard who passed the message along to the Sanguinati with the understanding that *that* bounty will be shared." Stavros smiled, showing his fangs. "However, the ship will run aground in such a way that the cargo, and the ship itself, will not be damaged and can be claimed as salvage, divided equally between the humans who assist and the *terra indigene*. With one exception, which is where your cousin, the Brittania police officer, would come in. As that particular ship was loaded the other night, the Sanguinati who were watching heard some of the boxes crying—boxes with air holes."

Monty braced his hands on the table. "You think they're shipping *humans* to Cel-Romano?"

"We think they're shipping *cassandra sangue*. Cargo worth thrice its weight in gold," Stavros said. "Especially to leaders of the Humans First and Last movement." He looked at Vlad, his eyes full of unnerving sympathy. "Those girls . . . Most are not like your Meg. At least, not the ones who are already addicted to cutting. They don't want the challenge of having a life. Many have found another way to be sheltered."

"Prostitution?" Burke asked, his voice stripped of emotion.

"Of a sort. A few prime establishments have sprung up in Toland. Or rather, the same establishments are now calling themselves by a different name. The blood prophets are now paid for each cut. They are pampered, indulged, and want for nothing—as long as they can pay for the care they receive."

"But they're still being used," Monty protested.

"A girl provides the service she was hired, and paid, to provide," Stavros said. "No coercion, no talk of ownership, benevolent or otherwise. The transition was done so smoothly, and so quickly, we suspect the men who run the establishments had warning that this might happen, even if they didn't know what would start the chain of events." He paused. "The girls in those establishments . . . Being there is their choice, and since they are on land that is currently under human control, we will not interfere with them. But the girls who were packaged like cargo . . . Humans have no say when they enter Ocean's domain."

After an uncomfortable silence, Burke said, "When that ship goes aground, what is my cousin supposed to do with the girls?"

"That is something the humans in Brittania must decide," Stavros said. "But the message I was asked to convey is this: Ocean will not be pleased with Brittania's humans if those girls end up in Cel-Romano."

Vlad listened while Elliot escorted Burke and Montgomery out of the consulate. Then he turned to Stavros, who said, "Do you think your police officers understand the significance of the *terra indigene* not docking ships in Toland?"

"Montgomery is thinking of his child and keeping her safe, which is only right, but I think Burke will understand eventually," Vlad replied. Thaisia's center of commerce could disappear overnight if an Elemental like Ocean unleashed her wrath on Toland.

"Whispers around the docks," Stavros said. "Thaisia is not the only land dealing with shortages. A lot of things are in short supply in Cel-Romano too. Especially food."

"A bag of gemstones could have bought a lot of wheat and corn. I wonder if the shortages in Thaisia will disappear now that the real gems are being stored in the Chambers."

Stavros gave Vlad a brilliant smile. "Know what I'm wondering? How many bushels of wheat and corn will the HFL movement be able to buy with a bag full of colored glass?"

Meg looked at the envelope, picked up the envelope. Sniffed the envelope.

"Doesn't smell like a farm," she muttered.

Carefully opening the envelope to avoid a paper cut, she pulled out the single sheet of paper.

Dear Meg,

I tried to write a couple of letters to you since arriving on Great Island, but I couldn't write them, couldn't send them. It feels like getting here ate up my ability to do anything.

It's so hard living outside the compound. I didn't remember it being so hard. I sent you out in this, so sure it was better. Now I'm not sure of anything. Some mornings Lorna Gardner brings me food because I can't face even the simple life and people beyond the walls of the guest cottage.

Some nights I remember the things I've seen in prophecies when they were using me to make gone over wolf. Terrible things.

Some nights I wonder if I started what's going to happen by helping you escape.

But this morning, I managed to go outside and watch the sun rise—and I wondered
if, by helping you, I did the one thing that might save some humans from what is
coming.

    Take care of yourself, Meg.

Your friend,
Jean

Meg read the letter twice, then returned it to its envelope and tucked it in the drawer where she kept the notebook that held her lists. Taking out the five postcards she'd gotten at the Three Ps, she set them on the counter and studied the pictures.

The red rocks, the plateau? No. Too different and out of reach.

The pictures of Talulah Falls? Also out of reach.

She looked at the picture of the deer half shrouded by mist. She turned it over, then picked up a pen.

Dear Jean,

    I have seen a deer. I have petted a pony. I helped plant a garden. I have smelled
earth and felt it in my hands. You watched the sun rise. These things are worth the
struggle to live outside.

Your friend,
Meg

Simon,

Can the *cs* see visions without cutting? The scarred girl drew a picture of a Wolf song, so we wondered. Ask your Meg what safe toys we can give the girl. We bought her drawing paper and many colored pencils. She hasn't cut since she's been here.

—Jackson

Jackson,

Meg says maybe about the visions. The *cs* weren't given a chance to try anything besides cutting. Your girl may be finding a new path. Books are good toys. Give the girl photos of the settlement and surrounding land. That will help when she is ready to go outside.

—Simon

N,

Ship blown off course during storm. Search found nothing. Ship, merchandise, and all hands declared lost.

—Pater

Douglas,

Half of the aunties' gifts arrived broken beyond repair. Am taking the next ship to Thaisia to discuss with you in person.

—Shady

CHAPTER 40

Windsday, Maius 16

On Windsday afternoon, Steve Ferryman and Roger Czerneda pulled up in front of one of the semidetached houses in the River Road Community. As he got out of the car and waited for Roger, Steve spotted the six columns of smoke gathered near one of the houses farthest from the entrance to the community.

He raised a hand in greeting. The Sanguinati's only response was to shift to human form—four males and two females.

Steve didn't recognize any of them, wasn't sure how much contact they'd had with humans. Enough that, from a distance anyway, they looked like human teenagers, but looking human and being able to act human were very different things. While the Sanguinati in Lakeside had made it clear that residents from Ferryman's Landing were not to be harmed, it was obvious to him that six against two were *not* good odds—especially if the vampires were hungry and willing to overlook their promise to behave.

He heard cawing and felt the tension in his shoulders ease a little. Crowgard. He and Roger weren't alone with the Sanguinati. Then he considered the warning tightness between his shoulder blades and wished they *were* alone with the vampires and Crows.

As Steve lowered his hand, one of the Sanguinati males raised a hand, imitating the greeting.

With that much acknowledgment, Steve turned to Roger and said, "What do you think?"

Roger studied the house. "Do I think I could live in one of these houses? Do I think it's a good idea to have a community that includes Intuits running small farms and businesses, and *terra indigene* doing the gods only knows what as their contribution? Or do I think Simon Wolfgard is a little bit crazy for proposing this in the first place?"

"He's not crazy," Steve replied. "He's implementing a lot of new ideas in a very short amount of time, and I think he knows he's moving a bit too fast. But I think he's pushing to get this community and the changes in the Lakeside Courtyard started because he's worried. There's—what?—a couple hundred *terra indigene* in the Lakeside Courtyard surrounded by two hundred thousand humans. If things swing out of control in the city, I'd want some kind of escape route for my people, wouldn't you?"

"Yes, I would," Roger said quietly. "And I know firsthand what can happen when things swing out of control."

Steve swore. "Sorry. I didn't think about Jerzy."

"That was a case of a human-controlled hamlet surrounded by miles of wild country controlled by the Others, and the humans started the conflict. Didn't make the result any easier to accept." Roger studied Steve. "You got a feeling about all of this?"

Oh, yeah, he had a feeling. The skin between his shoulder blades had been twitching and twinging since they pulled in here.

"About the community? Yes. But right now, I have a feeling we're being watched," Steve said quietly.

Roger nodded. "By more than vampires and Crows. Yeah. I feel like I have a target painted on my back."

Steve looked around and saw nothing unusual. Saw nothing, actually. The Sanguinati had disappeared—and the Crows were silent.

"When I was a boy, Douglas Burke came to visit for a couple of weeks," Roger said. "Old friend of my father's."

"I figured that, since he paved the way for us to hire you."

Roger kept his eyes on the houses in front of them. "You know how men will tell stories about their lives when everyone else is off doing something, and it's just them and memories? They know when a kid sneaks back to listen, but they pretend they don't, and they tell the kind of stories mothers wouldn't want a child to hear."

Steve smiled. "The Intuits have a winter tradition called an 'I Remember' night when grandfathers and grandmothers talk about how things were when they were young. Same kind of thing. Knowledge passed along from memories. Children aren't invited, but nobody banishes you if you slip into the room and stay quiet."

"Uncle Doug talked a bit about his time as a young police officer, serving in human settlements surrounded by the wild country. I remember him saying that there is a buffer of *terra indigene* land that separates human places from the wild country, and how very few humans have ever seen the true wild country and survived."

"Ming told me once that there is no wild country on Great Island. Most of the island is untouched land that belongs to the Others, but all the *terra indigene* are aware of us, and even the ones who don't interact with us directly participate in hunting or harvesting that benefits both sides."

"Intermediaries, like the Others who live in the Courtyards." Roger paused. "I've never forgotten something Uncle Doug said during that visit. He said humans only thought of the wild country in terms of uncultivated land and distance from human dwellings. But when the Others talk about the wild country, they're talking about who lives on the land as well as the land itself. He said people think the buffer between human land and wild country is always measured in miles, but sometimes the buffer between one and the other can be measured in yards, and it's when that truth is ignored that people die and human places disappear."

Steve nodded. "That fits with what I've observed about the Others. I think there are tiers of earth natives. The first tier is the one that deals with us. When our ancestors came to this continent, those earth natives watched us and saw skills they wanted to acquire. Maybe they already used simple tools and saw ours as an improvement of what they had. Sure, humans were invaders who were both rival predators and a new source of food, but we lived in packs and were understood to some degree. And some of the *terra indigene* were curious enough or committed enough to their own kind to study us, to become . . . contaminated . . . with our shape and some of the behaviors that make us human.

"The second tier are the earth natives that live in the buffer land and the edge of the wild country and are the same forms as the ones who live in the Courtyards. Maybe they can approximate a human shape enough to use our tools, and they like some of the things humans make. So they'll harvest some trees in their territory in order to make paper for books, and they'll allow some mining for coal and gold and silver and whatever else might be on their land. Some. And they don't usually deal directly with humans; they deal with the first tier of *terra indigene*."

"And the third tier?" Roger asked.

"The third tier isn't touched by humans in any way, and lives on the land that is considered the true wild country—that is most of Thaisia. Those earth natives don't want us here, have never wanted us here. As long as we don't draw too much attention to ourselves, as long as we aren't a threat to their own kind, we'll be tolerated. But when they decide that they'll no longer tolerate us . . ." Steve shuddered.

Roger looked at Steve. "That's what you're feeling? That it's the third tier of earth natives who are out there watching us?"

"Yeah. I don't think Simon Wolfgard likes or trusts most humans. If I were a Wolf, I guess I would feel the same way. And six months ago, he wouldn't have cared if he woke up one morning and all the humans had disappeared. Now he has a vested interest in *some* humans surviving, and we need to help him believe that we should be among those humans."

"Gods above and below," Roger breathed. "Is that why those earth natives are here? To watch us?"

"No," Steve replied slowly, guided by feelings. "They're not interested in us. If you believe some of the old stories, earth natives have been around in one form or another since the beginning of the world. They were the top predators then and they're the top predators now because they change as the world changes, absorbing qualities from new species of predators without losing the essence of what they are." Certainty settled between his shoulder blades. "They're not here because they're curious about a species that isn't part of their own. They're curious about Simon Wolfgard and what he's trying to do here and in the Lakeside Courtyard."

"Because they're wondering if he represents the next adaptation of *terra indigene*?" Roger asked. "A Wolf who can take the place of humans but still remain a Wolf?"

Steve looked around the community, the houses and the land beyond them. "There are more storms coming. Big storms. Bad storms. We need to make this place work. We need to prove to the *terra indigene* that we can share the work and the world peacefully. And that *is* a feeling."

Roger said nothing. Then he nodded. "I'm in." He pointed at the house. "I'd like to take a look inside that one."

"Then let's take a good look before we head back to Ferryman's Landing and work up a proposal for what a self-sufficient community would need."

CHAPTER 41

Thaisday, Maius 17

Simon opened the door to one of the rooms above the Liaison's Office, then stepped aside to let Pete Denby enter first. The man wanted a little den of his own in which to work. After some thought and discussion among the members of the Business Association, it was decided that an office above an office made sense—as long as Denby's clients were young enough and healthy enough to climb the stairs.

"Do I want to know what this room has been used for?" Pete asked as he looked around.

"It was used for sex." Simon thought that was obvious since the main piece of furniture was a bed, but humans didn't always see, or smell, the obvious.

"I'd heard there were rooms above the social center for that."

"Yes, but these are . . ." Simon frowned, not sure how to explain the difference.

"The executive suites?" Pete didn't sniff everything the way a Wolf would have, but he was checking out every part of the room.

Simon nodded. "More private. But they haven't been used much, and we don't need both rooms for sex anymore." Actually, he couldn't remember a time when both rooms had been needed on the same night.

Pete eyed him but said nothing. Instead, he checked out the bathroom, even flushed the toilet and ran water in the sink and shower, before going over to the windows that looked out over the delivery area and the Main Street entrance. "You don't have any office space in the Market Square?"

"We have some, but here you could have human clients who weren't connected to the Courtyard."

"You're optimistic."

"Why?"

Pete shook his head and smiled in a way that made Simon think the man had tasted something bitter.

"I'd like to put a fresh coat of paint on the walls, and I'll need to replace the furniture that's here with office furniture," Pete said as he turned in a slow circle. "I'd also like to put up a partition of some kind to create a reception area and a private office."

"We can move these things and store them. The consulate might have a desk and other things you could use. You would need to buy filing cabinets for your papers, but we can find humans or Others who can help build a wall."

"Appreciate it. I'd like Eve to take a look at this space. She and some of the girls are helping Mrs. Tremaine this morning."

"Tremaine?"

"The woman who sold you the two-family house. She's leaving behind some of the furniture, and one or two pieces might suit an office. And speaking of houses, I think the owner of the two apartment buildings will be accepting your offer in the next day or two. Eve said he and the real estate representative did have a couple of people looking yesterday, and they were talking it up as good income property."

"Eve must have good hearing."

Pete laughed. "Not as good as the Crows who were perched on the roof, but the windows in Mrs. Tremaine's house were open and the apartment owner wasn't keeping his voice down. Anyway, the prospective buyers were getting enthusiastic about the coffee shop and bookstore and fitness center right across the street, and the convenience of a park close by. Definitely a selling point to tenants with children. Which is when the Wolves started howling and the prospective buyers realized they were looking at the Courtyard."

"That explains why Jake Crowgard asked the Wolves to howl," Simon said.

"I called the real estate representative a little while later and reminded her that there was an offer on the table for the asking price of both buildings, and my client would pay in cash. I think I'll get a call very soon. We won't be able to close by the end of the month on those two buildings, but you'll be able to take possession of the double by then."

"Good. Eve can decide which den she wants. Ruthie can have the other one."

"What about Lieutenant Montgomery and Lizzy?" Pete asked. "They can't keep living in an efficiency apartment."

He hadn't figured on them staying there. But none of the humans seemed eager to take the Lizzy outside of the Courtyard. "Why isn't the Lizzy safe now?"

Pete ticked off the items on his fingers. "She heard something, saw something, knows something that can implicate the person who murdered her mother."

Simon huffed. "She was in a stall teaching Boo Bear how to poop in the toilet. Then she went to the train, which she was supposed to do, and came back to find her mother, which she wasn't supposed to do." That last part could have gotten the pup killed. "And she's short, even shorter than Meg. What could she have seen with all those grown humans rushing around to catch their trains?"

"You're probably right about Lizzy being safe now." Despite saying the words, Pete didn't sound like he really believed that. Then he added, "However, I've heard that Celia Borden may challenge Monty's right of custody. And sometimes when there is a fight like this, one of the people will hire someone to snatch the child away from the parent who has custody."

Simon stiffened. "That female would take the pup away from her pack?"

Pete hesitated. "I'm not saying Celia Borden would try, but you have to admit, you have excellent security, which is something I'm sure Lieutenant Montgomery values right now."

What they had was a lot of sharp teeth and a taste for special meat.

Probably best not to mention that.

He would have to talk to the other members of the Business Association to figure out where Lieutenant Montgomery and his pup could live—temporarily. He and the rest of the residents weren't ready to have humans *living* in the Courtyard beyond the area designated for business.

Except Meg.

"Here." Simon held out a key. "This opens the outside door and both doors upstairs."

Pete pocketed the key. "Thanks." He hesitated. "Do you wish you hadn't started this, hadn't changed the dynamics between the Others and humans?"

That was a bit like wishing you had taken another path through the trees and caught the deer instead of taking a tumble and landing in a creek. He hadn't wanted to become this tangled up with humans, but the choices he made now were still aimed at benefiting the *terra indigene*, and Meg, first.

He didn't think Pete wanted to hear that. Still, it was better if the human understood now. "Some of you have become like the Intuits—you're considered not edible because you have made a bargain with the *terra indigene* that will benefit both sides." He looked at Pete and let a hint of the Wolf show through the human form. "But most humans are clever meat. They are also predators that came to *our* land and keep trying to encroach on *our* territory. We won't allow it. We never have. That's something humans tend to forget."

Vlad pushed his chair back when Merri Lee, Ruthie, Theral, and Eve Denby walked into HGR's office and lined up on the other side of the desk.

"If this is another girl intervention thing, go talk to Simon," he said. "If this is about Meg and Simon, let them work it out for themselves." The last time the fluffballs ganged up on him for one of these interventions, the topic was sex and the result was all kinds of confusion.

"Nothing to do with Meg or Simon," Merri Lee said.

"It's more to do with furniture," Eve Denby said.

"And the Crows," Ruthie added.

Theral just smiled at him, as if to say no other information was required.

If only that were true.

"I'm listening." Vlad didn't see any way out of it that wouldn't cause more trouble.

"We were helping Mrs. Tremaine pack up some of her things, and she said it was too bad there wasn't time for a yard sale so she could sell off what she wasn't going to take," Eve said.

"And then I said maybe the Crowgard would like to take a look since they aren't going out anymore to look for treasures," Merri Lee said.

"And that made me think of the stall market that's open on the weekends," Ruthie said. "In good weather, some of the tables are outdoors, but most of the tables are in a big building that is rented out for different events. And there's also a farmers' market set up outside during the summer. Anyway, some people sell craft items and other people sell household items and things they pick up from moving sales and estate sales. Karl and I are going to take a look around this weekend. And I thought, as long as the merchants were agreeable, that it might be a fun field trip for some of the Crows. Maybe Jenni and her sisters could be the designated shoppers, and the rest of the Crowgard could purchase the items at Sparkles and Junk or some other store in the Market Square."

"So you want to take Crows on a field trip to a place that has lots of little things they can buy," Vlad said. He studied each woman in turn. Their eyes were bright with excitement, but none of them looked crazy sick.

"Yes. But we wanted to check out the idea with you before mentioning it to Jenni," Ruthie said.

The idea made him uneasy. Lots of humans in the same place with a small group of *terra indigene* was never a good combination. By agreements with human governments, the Others were entitled to attend any public event. But experience had taught them that it wasn't safe to attend a human school, or go to a concert, or see a play or a sporting event. "It sounds like a place where there would be a lot of humans milling around."

"Not as many people on a nice day as there would be if it rains," Ruthie said. "And Karl and I would talk to the merchants first."

The other customers would be more of a concern than the merchants. Then again, the Crows had been acting subdued since they stopped going out on their trash treasure hunts. Maybe a short visit to this stall market would be safe enough, if they were there and gone before too many humans noticed them.

"I don't see a problem with you and the Crows going across the street to buy whatever Mrs. Tremaine doesn't want. As for going to the stall market, I'll talk to Simon and Henry. Get their opinions first." He picked up a pen and moved a couple of papers on the desk. He'd seen a human in a movie do that as a way to end a meeting. Apparently, the females hadn't seen that movie. "Don't any of you have work to do?"

They beamed at him before they filed out the door.

Vlad watched them go, relieved he didn't have to make this decision on his own.

A pack of human females and some Crows in a building full of things to buy. He sat back and sighed. "And humans think vampires are scary."

Douglas,

Trip delayed. Concerns at work. Overseas connections erratic due to storms in Atlantik. If possible, will call. Aunties request instruction manual for gifts you sent.

—Shady

Shady,

First part of instruction manual already on its way. Will wait for information about your travel plans.

—Douglas

CHAPTER 42

Firesday, Maius 18

Hearing the radio in the station's cafeteria—and realizing he heard it because everyone had stopped talking to listen—Monty paused in the doorway.

"'. . . *we cannot ignore the plight of these girls who, having been expelled from facilities designed for their special needs, are now unable to cope and are at risk because of the Others' callous behavior toward humans in general and these girls in particular. Therefore, the people of Cel-Romano have opened their homes and their hearts to these girls and will do everything in their power to give the girls the care they need.*'

"*Nicholas Scratch made that impassioned speech at the Toland port as thirty at-risk teenage girls were escorted onto a passenger ship known as an ocean greyhound. These ships are the fastest oceangoing vessels in existence, and the captain told reporters he is confident his ship will be able to outrun any of the storms that have been responsible for the loss of several merchant ships over the past few days.*"

Several men noticed Monty standing in the cafeteria doorway, but only Louis Gresh came over to talk to him.

"I heard an earlier report," Louis said. "Big to-do with Scratch and Toland's mayor making speeches. The girls weren't available for comment, but the reporter described them as walking sedately up the gangplank and waving to everyone once they were on board."

"I wonder how heavily the girls were sedated in order to cope with that much stimulus," Monty said quietly. "And I wonder if these girls are more valuable, or if someone decided to change tactics after smuggling *cassandra sangue* out of Thaisia didn't work."

Louis frowned. "Say that again?"

I shouldn't have said it the first time. But Louis was on Burke's short list of people who could be trusted with such secrets. He was on Monty's list too, since he had worked with Monty and Burke to help the Others find the Controller. "Some girls were smuggled out as cargo. The ship was blown off course in a storm and was lost. No trace of it."

"That's the official version?" Louis asked.

Monty nodded. "Arrangements were made to pick up the cargo." He felt relieved when Louis didn't ask about the ship's crew.

"If the Others don't want any of those girls going to Cel-Romano, what difference will it make having Scratch splash this voyage all over the media?"

"To the *terra indigene*? None whatsoever. But it will give Scratch more ammunition to use in his humans-versus-Others speeches when the water-dwelling *terra indigene* sink the ship." Monty held up the newspaper folded to a small inside article. "I have something else to talk to the captain about this morning."

"Monty. Do you really think the Others will sink that ship, knowing those girls are on board?" Louis asked.

"They may try to save the girls, but even if they can't, that ship won't reach Cel-Romano. The Sharkgard and an Elemental known as Ocean will make sure of it."

Monty walked to Burke's office. Seeing his captain on the phone, he hesitated in the doorway until Burke waved him in.

"You got the bear," Burke said. He held the phone away from his ear far enough that Monty recognized Felix Scaffoldon's irate voice but couldn't make out the words. When the yelling started to wind down, Burke put the phone up to his ear again and said, "What jewels?" He held the phone away from his ear for another minute before responding. "So the bear had a secret compartment where a little girl could stash whatever little girls stash. Be happy you found some bits of colored glass. If the bear had belonged to a boy, you might have found a couple of rocks and a desiccated frog. No . . . No, I'm not trying to wind you up. I'm telling you that we weren't asked to look for anything inside the bear, so we didn't look. Why did you expect to find something?" He nodded as he listened. "Oh, really? Do you think the murder was a falling-out among thieves? I thought the Crowgard had been accused of taking . . . Ah. They might be *fencing* the stolen jewelry. Well, if the thefts are being carried out by humans, the brother would be the most likely accomplice, although the thefts didn't start until—"

Burke looked at the phone. "Huh. Scaffoldon hung up." He leaned back in his chair, his smile a lot more fierce than friendly. "Sit down, Lieutenant. Let's talk about Elayne Borden."

Monty sat, the newspaper in his lap. "What is there to say?" He thought about the part of the phone conversation he had heard. "Scaffoldon found the substitute jewels?"

"He did. He was quite upset. Now the theory is that Elayne Borden was holding the stolen jewels for the as-yet-unknown thief and tried to abscond with the whole take instead of just her share."

"If he keeps floating theories, he'll sound like a fool," Monty said.

"Well, he can't exactly come out and say that Toland's society darlings *gave* their jewelry to Nicholas Scratch in order to help finance the HFL movement but claimed the jewelry was stolen in order to collect the insurance money. But the stones are gone because someone put them in the bear, and the bear ended up in Lakeside with Lizzy, and that means Scratch doesn't have the fortune he expected.

"And that brings us back to Elayne Borden," Burke continued. "How does a woman go from being the lover of a disgraced police officer to the lover of a public figure like Nicholas Scratch?"

"I've thought about this since I first learned about Elayne's involvement with Scratch," Monty replied. "Elayne, or I should say Elayne's mother, was always fixated on social status, but her family doesn't have the money or the clout they want to believe they have."

"But they do have, or had, something that Scratch wanted," Burke argued. "They provided him with some kind of connection. Otherwise, why would he get involved with Elayne or her family?"

Why would he? Monty thought. "So someone has decided that if Elayne didn't have the jewels on her at the train station, then Lizzy has them. Why not assume that they were hidden in the apartment and left there?" Monty paused, then answered his own question. "Because the apartment had been searched even before the police became involved. Whether Elayne was in on acquiring the jewels or had found them and realized who was involved, she knew too much and she was running. Therefore, she was a liability."

"Someone knew where the gems were supposed to be, and Scaffoldon was sent to fetch them. It isn't likely that he thinks Lizzy still has them. If he was going to believe anything, it would be that I found the jewels and kept them." Burke smiled. "I didn't, but I could have hidden them in the evidence lockup or in a desk drawer." The smiled faded. "That being said, I think it would be a good idea for Lizzy to stay in the Courtyard unless she's with you. Now, what did you want to tell me?"

Churned up about Elayne, and feeling he had forgotten something, Monty set the newspaper on the desk and pointed to an article about a woman being killed in a random attack while out shopping with her family.

"Heather Houghton?" Burke said.

"She worked at Howling Good Reads. Resigned last month after Meg Corbyn . . ." Monty's throat tightened.

"Ms. Corbyn saw this?"

"Saw something. Meg reads the *Lakeside News*. I don't know if anyone else in the Courtyard does."

"You should make Simon Wolfgard aware of this." Burke sighed. "It's so seductively easy to think that using the *cassandra sangue*'s pronouncements will make the bad things go away, that we'll be forewarned about anything and everything and will avoid being in the wrong place at the wrong time. But it's not always true."

"No, sir. It's not always true."

Monty met up with Kowalski in the parking lot. The younger man glanced at the newspaper, then got in the car, saying nothing.

"You saw the article?" Monty asked.

Kowalski nodded. "Heather's family had been pressuring her to quit her job, had threatened to disown her if she didn't quit. If she'd still been working at Howling Good Reads, she wouldn't have been in that store, and she'd still be alive."

"You don't know that," Monty said gently. Since Kowalski was feeling the same kind of pressure from his own family to distance himself from the Others, Monty didn't offer platitudes. But he wondered exactly what was said before Meg saw that vision.

CHAPTER 43

Firesday, Maius 18

At least she had stopped crying.

Simon didn't mind when Meg cried on him during a movie. Well, he minded but he accepted that this was typical of human females, and she shook off feeling bad once the movie ended. But this was something else, a deeper pain, as if she'd swallowed a splinter of bone that was tearing her up inside.

"It's my fault," she said.

He'd lost count of the number of times she had said that since Nathan howled that something was wrong with Meg. "How could it be your fault? You weren't there. You didn't hurt Heather."

"I gave her the wrong advice, told her the wrong thing," Meg cried. "That's why she died."

"She died because a human turned rabid and attacked other humans who were shopping in that store." Had someone gotten hold of a dose of gone over wolf? Something he would ask Lieutenant Montgomery.

"That day we were all doing research to locate the compound where I'd been kept, Heather was upset because her family was going to disown her if she continued to work at Howling Good Reads. I remember thinking, *What will happen to Heather if she makes the wrong choice?* I must have hit my hand at the same time I was thinking that because I had a vision about Heather. There were magazines scattered around her, covered in blood. I saw a date. Not the current issue." She frowned. "Not even the current year. But what I saw had to be wrong. I must have mixed up the numbers."

"Is that all you saw? Magazines scattered around Heather?"

"You sell some magazines at HGR, so I thought . . . There was so much blood, I thought it meant she was going to die in the store if she stayed."

There hadn't been many details about how Heather died, but the newspaper article hadn't mentioned anything about magazines. Something else to ask Montgomery. And whether Meg mixed up a date hardly mattered now.

"Meg?" Simon moved until he was right next to her, then rested his forearms on the sorting table, matching her position. "Would that store have had magazines?"

She blinked at him. "What?"

"That store Heather was in. Would it have magazines?"

"I don't know." She had that look in her eyes that meant she was reviewing her training images to see if she could find a match. Then she shook her head. "I don't know."

"Heather was a bunny," he said gently. "She was nice for a human, and a good worker, but she was afraid of us in a way that Merri Lee and Ruthie aren't. Vlad and I recognized the signs and knew she wasn't going to stay much longer, even before the *terra indigene* leaders came here for that meeting. Even before you had that vision."

"But if she had stayed a little longer . . ."

"She would have been driven out of her pack, and when she left HGR, maybe they wouldn't have taken her back, and she would have been alone."

"But alive."

"Would she?" He touched her hand. "Maybe Heather did avoid the death you saw because she quit when she did. She was with her family, and that's what she wanted. If they hadn't gone to that store on that day, or if they had been delayed, or if Heather had decided to stay home and do some chores, she would have been reading about someone else who was killed in that attack. You can't know about what you don't see, Meg."

Meg sighed. "You're right. I couldn't know. And I can't make a cut to see what might happen every time a friend has to make a choice."

"No, you can't." He ran a hand over her head and gave her a light scritch behind one ear. "You feeling better now?"

"A little." She gave him a wry look. "Better enough that I won't put another knot in Nathan's tail."

<I was *concerned*,> Nathan said from the front room.

<And rightly so,> Simon replied. <But Meg looks embarrassed, like a squirrel who fell out of a tree and is trying to pretend she intended to do that.>

With a huff of annoyance, Nathan went back to the Wolf bed.

"I'm fine," Meg said. "I don't want my friends to get hurt, and it's hard knowing that what I saw wasn't enough to save Heather when I was able to save the ponies and Sam. And maybe she did live longer than she would have if she'd continued working at HGR."

And maybe she died much sooner, Simon thought.

CHAPTER 44

Firesday, Maius 18

Not only had Jackson returned her drawing of the Wolf song; he and Grace framed it and hung it in her room. They brought her more paper and more pencils in different colors. They spent time telling her that this shade of green was grass and that shade was tree that shed its leaves when Autumn walked the land and that shade was pine. They described, as best they could, the shades of water, but they knew water as shallow and sun warmed versus the coolness of a deep pool, not the *color* of the water.

She listened, soaking up what they said and wondering what was outside her room. Jackson and Grace weren't the only Wolves here. She knew that from the song. But she wasn't brave enough to ask if she could leave her room.

She thought about her new keepers. They refused to call her *cs821*. Once each day, they asked if she had chosen a name. They didn't punish her for not choosing. They fed her, cleaned her clothes, made sure she had what she needed to wash herself and use the toilet. And they seemed pleased that she liked to draw.

Jackson and Grace. But as she thought of them, she didn't see Grace. She saw Jackson and . . .

Taking a clean sheet of paper, the girl began to draw.

Jackson walked into the scarred girl's room with a plate of food for the midday meal.

She sat at the head of the bed, her arms wrapped around tucked-up legs, her chin resting on her knees.

"What's wrong?" he asked, only realizing how sharp he sounded when she winced. He set the plate on the desk and approached the bed, sniffing lightly so that she wouldn't know he was trying to catch the scent of blood.

No blood, but something was wrong.

"I wanted to draw a picture for you and Grace, but I drew that." She pointed to the paper at the end of the bed.

Holding it carefully by one corner, he turned it around. Then he sucked in a breath.

"Have you ever seen these places? Seen . . . images?" he asked.

She shook her head.

She'd never seen him in Wolf form, but she'd drawn his head, muzzle raised to the sky, the Rocky Mountains in the background. That filled the top left section of the paper. The bottom-right section was filled with the head of another howling Wolf. Filling the center of the paper was a human dwelling like nothing he would find around his home territory, an Eagle's view of an island, and the thundering water known as Talulah Falls.

"That other Wolf isn't Grace," she said, sounding worried.

"No, it's my friend Simon. He lives in Lakeside, a place on the eastern shore of Lake Etu." He studied the girl. Her shaggy hair was a golden brown, and her eyes were green with flecks of gold. If she were a shifter, he'd think she belonged to the Panthergard with her coloring. "You drew this for me?"

She nodded. "It means something." She looked at the desk, at the drawer where she kept the razor. Then she looked away.

"It means something," he agreed. "A strong friendship always has meaning."

She looked surprised, then relieved.

No, Jackson thought. *I won't ask you to use the razor.*

He picked up the drawing, careful not to smudge it. "Thank you." Then he saw the drawing under it.

"It confused me, so I didn't finish the picture." She hesitated, then added softly, "I used up a lot of my blue pencils."

"I'll go down to the Intuit village later today and see if they have more."

There was power in the drawing she'd made of him and Simon, but this other one disturbed him. A wheat field. He knew it was wheat because she had drawn stalks with ripe grain in the foreground. But it was underwater. Sharks swam above the wheat field, and in the background, at the edge of the paper, was something that looked like a sunken ship.

He took that drawing too.

"Eat your food," he said.

"Wheat doesn't grow underwater. I remember that from the training images." A glance at the drawer that held the razor.

"You don't have to cut. You've given us answers. It's up to us to figure out the questions."

Jackson left the room and closed the door. Then he listened.

Soft footsteps crossing to the desk. A drawer opening.

He counted to ten before the drawer closed again and the chair scraped over the floor. When he was sure she was eating instead of using the razor, he silently stepped away.

Only one telephone in the *terra indigene* settlement. There wasn't any need for more. The phone, along with the computer, was in the cabin at the edge of the settlement, next to the road that led to the Intuit village. Mail and packages were delivered there as well because there were too few who lived in the settlement who could pass for human.

He looked at the drawing of two Wolves who lived in different parts of Thaisia but were connected by more than friendship.

He would show the drawings to the elders, then leave them with Grace for safekeeping while he walked to the cabin with the phone and placed a call to Simon.

CHAPTER 45

Firesday, Maius 18

Simon reviewed the lists in his hands, then looked at the books on the shelves. Early in Maius, he'd asked the gaggle of girls and the police who had become part of the Courtyard—including Lieutenant Montgomery—what kinds of books they read and what authors they liked. They'd given him lists, and based on those lists, it was time to cull the stock.

Setting a cart within easy reach, he began pulling books off the shelves.

"Is this something I should know about?" Vlad asked, leaning against the shelves.

"We've closed the store to humans who aren't part of the Courtyard's pack, so it's time to remove books that aren't of interest to them or the *terra indigene*."

Vlad pulled a book off the shelf. The cover showed a muscular male who was partially clothed, looked menacing, and was meant to be some kind of *terra indigene*. At the male's feet was a partially clothed female, probably human, who, despite cowering, had her chin lifted in a defiant attitude and had her back arched in a way that displayed an impressive pair of breasts.

"Do you think humans will ever realize breasts have no attraction for us once we're weaned?" Vlad asked, opening the book to a random page.

"Why should they?" Simon tipped his head toward the book. "None of us would be interested in that story, so none of us would think to mention it, and *terra indigene* publishers already know that cover wouldn't attract us." The better question, as far as he was concerned, was how had that book gotten on the shelves in the first place?

Vlad read a couple of pages, then put the book on the cart. "Some of us might read it if you shelved it as a comedy."

Simon eyed him, then looked at the book. "Or put it in with the cookbooks?"

"Too obvious what our interest in the breasts would be."

Laughing, he handed half the lists to Vlad. "These are books our humans enjoy reading. I want to keep those authors in stock, as well as similar books. It seems Heather was the only one who was interested in straightforward kissy books, but the gaggle likes romance thrillers or adventures. For now, I'm keeping one of whatever we have in stock, kissy books and all, and removing the extra copies. Henry can take his pick for our library, and we'll pass along the rest."

"What are we going to do with the shelf space?"

"Add books written by *terra indigene*. Instead of a shelf tucked way in the back or an occasional display in the front of the store, we'll sell the books next to their human counterparts."

"Simon? Is turning the Lakeside Courtyard into a kind of academy really a good idea? Especially now?"

"When humans came to Thaisia and we made the first bargains long ago, their settlements were small, and it was easy to study them despite little actual contact beyond what was owed to us for use of the land. That's the way it still is in most places. Even the Others who keep watch over the largest human cities only interact with a handful of humans, and then it's a formal meeting, or it's with the Human Liaison, and that interaction is formal too. They can hide things from us now."

"Like the compounds that held, and still hold, the *cassandra sangue*?"

Simon nodded. "We knew about the blood prophets for as long as humans knew about them. Maybe longer. But they slipped out of sight because we didn't concern ourselves when humans dealt with humans. For the most part, humans have kept the peace, but they're an invasive species—a two-legged kudzu—and will take over as much land as they can if they aren't held to the agreed-upon boundaries. Now trouble is stirring everywhere because of that Humans First and Last movement."

"You think the answer is learning to become more human?"

Simon pulled a few more books off the shelves. "Not exactly. I think the answer is learning to recognize the enemy when it's hiding within the herd. Once we do that, we can kill the enemy and keep ourselves, and Thaisia, safe." He looked at

Vlad. "We call them clever meat, so it's easy to forget that the reason some of our ancestors learned this form was because the *terra indigene* recognized the first humans who came to Thaisia as a new kind of predator, something we needed to understand in order to remain dominant. Now we need to understand more in order to decide what kind of humans should be allowed to remain in Thaisia." *While earth natives like you and me still have some say in that decision,* he added silently.

"I wonder how Lieutenant Montgomery would feel, or Kowalski or Debany for that matter, if they heard that."

"There's no reason for them to know, is there?"

"No reason at all."

After Vlad went to the next group of shelves to pull books from his lists, Simon stared at the titles in front of him, seeing nothing.

He liked the humans who were interacting with the Courtyard. And he liked Steve Ferryman and the other Intuits he'd met at Ferryman's Landing. But lately he'd come to realize that words could be a weapon as devastating as a gun, and that was something most of the Others didn't understand yet. The *terra indigene* hadn't continued to learn enough from humans because so much of what humans wanted held no interest for them.

Vlad returned, his hands full of books. "Simon, do you want to keep these?"

Before he could respond, Jenni Crowgard came rushing in from the stock room and said, "The Crows know why humans are running out of food!" She paused for a moment, then added, "Well, so do the rest of the *terra indigene.*"

"What do—" Simon snarled when the phone started ringing.

Vlad set the books on the cart and led Jenni toward the back of the store, saying, "Tell me what you've heard."

Simon grabbed the ringing phone. "Howling Good Reads."

"Simon? It's Jackson."

He froze for a moment. His friend sounded . . . odd. "Is everything all right?"

"Yes. Maybe." Jackson hesitated. "The scarred girl drew a picture of me in the Rockies and you in Lakeside, with Talulah Falls in between us. Does that mean anything to you?"

"Maybe." He thought about the land between Lakeside and Talulah Falls. He thought about the new community the Others and the Intuits would make together. He hadn't thought Jackson would be interested in leaving the Northwest, but a lot of things were changing throughout Thaisia. The other Wolf might be feeling it was time to move on. Would Jackson want to live in the River Road Community?

"She drew another picture."

"Okay." Did the scarred girl rub her skin the way Meg did when a prophecy started prickling and buzzing? Was that why Jackson sounded disturbed?

"A wheat field underwater. Sharks swimming over the field. A sunken ship. Mean anything?"

Simon looked toward the shelves of books and noticed that Vlad had returned alone and was watching him. Waiting for him. He repeated what Jackson said about the wheat field.

Vlad nodded.

"Yes," he said, answering Jackson's question. "It means the humans tried to send food across the water while claiming there wasn't going to be enough food for the humans living in Thaisia. They lied to their own kind in order to cause trouble for us."

"What can we do?"

"Wait. Keep watch. Let me know if the scarred girl makes other drawings that are visions." After receiving an assurance from Jackson that he would be kept informed about the scarred girl's visions, and promising to talk to Meg about the girl, Simon hung up.

"Are you going to tell Lieutenant Montgomery?" Vlad asked.

Simon shook his head. "The wheat is gone, and some foods will be scarce because of it. He already knows that."

"He doesn't know why."

"Does it matter?"

"Wouldn't you want to know why your pup will be hungry?"

"Yes, I would. But Montgomery isn't going to have a say in any of this. Neither are we. There's no point telling him the why until we can also tell him— and Captain Burke—what will happen next."

Vlad took a deep breath and let it out slowly. "In that case, let's make some decisions about these books. That much we can do." He reached for the books he'd dumped on the cart, then stopped. "Oh, and Ruthie is going to talk to the merchants at the stall market tomorrow. If they're agreeable about having some of us there, Ruthie and some other females will take the Crows shopping next Watersday."

"Won't that be fun," Simon muttered.

Vlad smiled. "I'm glad you think so, since you'll need to talk to Blair about who will be going with them."

Simon picked up the book with the cowering, defiant, large-breasted female on the cover. Maybe he would tuck it in with the cookbooks after all.

CHAPTER 46

Watersday, Maius 26

Hand in hand, Meg and Sam walked along the road from the Green Complex to the Market Square.

The Courtyard bus had left right after lunch to go to the stall market—the experimental field trip for Jenni, Starr, and Crystal Crowgard. Ruth and Merri Lee had invited her to join them, but they were quick to point out that the quantity of merchandise, not to mention the crowds and noise that were typical on a Watersday afternoon, might be overwhelming for her.

She took their word for it. Besides, taking a leisurely walk back to the Liaison's Office—or as leisurely a walk as a human could have with Sam and Skippy for company—suited her.

"*Why* can't I mark trees the way Skippy is doing?" Sam asked.

"Because you're in human form," Meg replied.

Skippy, who seemed to be paying no attention to their conversation, lifted his leg and gave them a Wolfie grin.

"Humans pee on trees too," Sam said, glaring at Skippy as the juvenile Wolf trotted off to sniff at something else.

Unable to recall any training images that would confirm or deny that statement, Meg said nothing and kept walking. Tipping her head up so that she could see past the brim of her hat, she spotted the Hawk soaring above them, keeping watch. If Sam ran off to prove that a boy could pee on a tree, he wouldn't be completely on his own, even if she kept walking. And, really, all he had to do was follow the road to the Market Square, so it wasn't like he'd get lost. They might have to hunt up his clothes later if he stripped and shifted to Wolf, but apparently finding abandoned clothes in the Courtyard was pretty common during the warmer months.

Not abandoned, Meg reminded herself. *Left where they can be found again—as long as a human doesn't come along and take the clothes somewhere else.*

She'd learned *that* lesson yesterday when she spotted a pile of clothes near the road while making a few deliveries. Since they were coveralls and work boots, she dropped them off at the Utilities Complex—and then had seen a little too much of an annoyed Blair, who had come looking for the clothes he'd set aside when he'd shifted to Wolf to do whatever it was he'd needed to do in his furry form.

Maybe she should talk to Eve Denby since Sarah and Robert played with some of the Courtyard's youngsters. After all, if Sam was going to grumble about not being allowed to pee on a tree when he was in boy form, would Robert grumble about not being allowed to strip off his clothes and run around naked just because he wasn't going to shift to something with feathers or fur?

She had no training images that matched what young males of any species thought about or found interesting. Apparently such things were not considered useful knowledge when speaking prophecy.

By the time they reached the Market Square, Meg was warm and dewy—a phrase Ruth said her grandmother used because the old woman insisted that ladies didn't sweat.

Ruth's grandmother obviously never had Wolves for playmates. When you played with *them,* you weren't dewy, you *dripped.*

"The whole Courtyard is here," Sam said, sounding impressed.

She knew that wasn't true, but it sure looked like every resident had crowded into the square.

Focus on one or two things, she thought. *Let the rest be a busy background, as if you were seeing a vision occurring in a crowded place instead of a deserted place.*

Feeling steadier after making that decision, Meg looked around and focused on Jester Coyotegard, who pointed to various stores and seemed to be explaining something to a man with red hair and a face that looked sufficiently Foxy not to pass for human. She hadn't delivered any mail to anyone who was Foxgard, so this male was either a visitor or a new resident.

She noticed Blair, who looked like someone was chewing on his tail, which wasn't likely because he was in human form. Then she forgot about the Wolf when she spotted Julia and Marie Hawkgard coming out of Chocolates and Cream, licking ice cream cones.

Had she ever tasted ice cream? She wasn't sure. But she knew she'd never experienced eating an ice cream cone. And Sam hadn't had ice cream in years, if he'd ever had any when he was a little puppy. They would go over to Chocolates and Cream, and she would buy ice cream cones for both of them. And Skippy too, so he wouldn't be left out.

She looked at Sam. "Would you like to get . . ."

The harsh buzz began in her chest, quickly spreading to her left shoulder.

"Get what, Meg?" Sam tugged on her arm. "Meg?"

Meg looked at the Market Square. Crowded place. Too many people, too little room to move, to escape.

The Market Square looked familiar, but it didn't *feel* familiar anymore. And the certainty that she needed to escape grew stronger the longer she stood there.

"Something's wrong," she whispered. She patted the right cargo pocket in her shorts. Empty.

How could it be empty? How could . . . ?

She pressed her hand against the left pocket and felt the shape of her folding razor. She'd put it there—and buttoned the pocket—so that the razor was with her but harder to reach.

"Meg?" Sam whined as he tugged on her arm again.

Meg worked to steady her breathing. She should turn around and walk away from the Market Square, walk back to the Green Complex or as far up the road as she needed to go until the painful pins-and-needles buzz under her skin stopped.

She looked at Sam and Skippy, intending to tell them they had to leave.

But what if the prophecy was about one of them? Could she take that risk? Could she live with the pain if either of them got hurt?

Be sure, she thought. *The last time you didn't walk away, you upset so many friends. You hurt Nathan. And Simon. Be sure.*

She hurried away from the Market Square, intending to reach her office and call . . . who? Simon was at the stall market with Jenni Crowgard and her sisters. Nathan, Vlad, Henry, and the human pack were with them. Except Theral, who was working at the medical office this afternoon because she didn't want to go to a crowded place where her ex-lover might look for her.

Could Theral be the reason for the prickling? There had been no sign of *that man* since the flowers arrived as a way to confirm that Theral could be found in the Courtyard. But no human could reach Theral in the medical office. Especially not today with so many of the *terra indigene* gathered in the Market Square.

Crowds and the sting of sharp, unpleasant smells. Pushing and shoving. Shouts and screams. No room to escape if . . .

"Meg?" Sam said. "Where are you going?"

She ran to the Liaison's Office. *Get inside and call* . . . Blair, the Courtyard's dominant enforcer. No, he was in the Market Square, close by. She would call Nyx. The Sanguinati would help her.

She stopped, barely able to breathe.

The buzzing had gotten worse, not better. She was moving *toward* the reason for the visions building in her skin, not away from it.

Can't cut when I'm not in control. Can't frighten Sam the way I frightened Nathan. Can't. But the danger is here. I know it's here.

Meg looked around, focusing on the buildings that surrounded her as she turned in a slow circle. The garages that stored two BOWs and also held various tools and equipment for seasonal work. The Three Ps and the access way that provided egress to the Main Street entrance to the Courtyard. The back of the Liaison's Office and Henry's yard. The back entrances to Howling Good Reads and A Little Bite.

Meg looked at the stairs leading to the efficiency apartments above the seamstress/tailor's shop—and grabbed at her arms as the buzzing became brutally painful.

Four apartments up there. And this buzzing under her skin was the dowsing rod that would pinpoint which apartment, *which friend*, might be in danger. She would figure out which apartment produced the buzz, which people were the subject of the prophecy, and then she would run away until the buzzing stopped.

She could do this. She *would* do this.

"Meg?" Sam sounded scared.

Couldn't do this with just the boy here. If anything went wrong . . .

She raised her head. *"Arroo! Arroo!"*

Sam cocked his head. "What is that?"

"It's a warning," Meg panted. "Something's wrong at the efficiency apartments. Bad wrong. Have to warn."

"Arroo!" Sam howled. *"Arroo!"*

"Arroo!" Skippy howled a moment later.

A moment after that, a deeper howl answered them.

Meg bolted up the stairs. Halfway up, she stumbled and fell, hitting her knee.

"Meg!"

She twisted around to sit on the stair, barely noticing Elliot as he ran toward her from the consulate. She stared at the torn skin on her knee as her body filled with the agony that was the prelude to prophecy.

Then Tess was beside her, one strong hand bracing the back of her head, and Elliot was on her other side.

"Have to," Meg gasped. "Have to . . ."

"There's no time to fetch paper and pen," Tess said. "We'll have to listen carefully and remember."

Elliot nodded.

Tess turned Meg's face so their eyes met. "Speak, prophet, and we will listen."

A jumble of images. "Pink book, gold stars . . . secrets . . . apartment . . . thief, more thief . . . Lizzy book . . . train . . . train . . . shinies . . . man holding a length of pipe . . . Crows . . . bags of shinies . . . Run!"

Images scalded her mind, burned into her memory. Instead of the euphoria that would protect her from the visions, Meg felt fear gathering until it filled her—a different kind of agony.

Then she saw her own arm rise, stiff and straight. She saw her forefinger pointing and the thumb straight up. She saw the other fingers curling into her palm so that her hand looked like . . . *"Simon!"*

As Meg collapsed, Tess cushioned the girl's head with her hand and looked at Elliot.

"I'll call Simon," Elliot said. He leaped off the stairs and moved a few feet away, pulling his mobile phone out of his pocket.

"She fainted?" Blair asked.

Tess nodded. Not a surprise that the dominant enforcer would have come running, especially if he'd been close enough to hear those odd howls. Not a surprise to see Julia and Marie Hawkgard or Jester Coyotegard responding.

Rushing to join their little group were Lynn and Jane Wolfgard, the toother and bodywalker respectively.

"Simon is in danger?" Jester asked. "He needs help?"

"All the help he can get," Tess replied grimly, hoping the Coyote would understand the kind of help Simon needed.

"I'll tell the girls at the lake." He looked at Meg and hesitated. "Our Meg will be all right?"

"We'll take care of her," Jane said. "I've dealt with one of her cuts before, and I won't lick the blood."

"You hear anything in what Meg said to indicate that they shouldn't take care of her, that we need to wait for a human bodywalker?" Blair asked Tess.

"No," she replied as Meg began to stir. In fact, everything she'd heard indicated they should get the girl away from this part of the Courtyard as fast as possible. "They can take Meg to the medical office and then to the Green Complex." She studied the door at the top of the stairs, then looked at Blair. "You and I need to decide what to do about the efficiency apartments."

Elliot returned, gave Meg a sharp, quick study, then pulled out a clean handkerchief and handed it to Jane. "So she doesn't drip blood."

Jane deftly wrapped the handkerchief around Meg's knee. Then she and Lynn hauled her up and carried her to the Market Square.

"Simon's on his way," Elliot said.

The keening howls had been an annoying background noise that Tess had ignored while she concentrated on the warnings Meg struggled to convey. When the howls abruptly stopped, she realized who was missing. "Where are Sam and Skippy?"

"John grabbed Sam and took both youngsters to the Market Square," Blair said. "They'll go back to the Green Complex with Meg as soon as she's fixed up. John will stay with them to keep the youngsters from worrying Meg's bandages."

"So that leaves us to find whatever is up there that someone wants to steal," Elliot said, pointing toward the efficiency apartments. "I'm assuming that's what Meg meant when she talked about a thief."

Tess nodded, having assumed the same thing. "We take all of the possessions—everything our humans brought in that's personal. Lizzy still has something that someone wants badly enough to enter the Courtyard. If we strip all the apartments, the thieves won't know for sure that *we* know they're after Lizzy's possessions."

Besides, the thieves might be spiteful enough to destroy Merri Lee's possessions when they didn't find what they wanted, which was the main reason for taking all the personal items the Courtyard's humans had brought.

The *terra indigene* didn't need all that stuff in order to figure out what the thieves wanted. Meg had already told her what she needed to find.

"Both BOWs are in the garage here," Blair said. "We'll toss everything into the back of them and sort it out later." He strode to the garage that held the first BOW.

By the time Julia ran up to Howling Good Reads' office and fetched the keys for the efficiency apartments, Nyx Sanguinati had joined them. The four females split up. Julia and Marie packed up Merri Lee's possessions; Nyx checked the apartment that Lorne from the Three Ps and Montgomery's team of police officers were using; and Tess took the apartment Montgomery and Lizzy occupied.

Alone, with the door locked so that no one would walk in on her, she allowed her true nature to show through the human mask. Meg had mentioned a mask when she spoke prophecy at the Pony Barn a couple of weeks ago. Happy mask, angry face. Could apply to a lot of humans right now, but her own interpretation was that the image stood for deceit.

Simon was walking into some kind of danger at the stall market. There were thieves coming to the efficiency apartments at the Courtyard. Two kinds of threat happening at the same time. Coincidence or intentional? Was one meant to be a deception that was supposed to pull their attention away from the other threat until it was too late?

Tess found two suitcases stored under the single bed. Hauling them out, she dropped them on the bed and began emptying drawers, pulling them out of the dresser and upending them over the suitcases, moving as quickly as she could.

But when something from Lizzy's underwear drawer fell into the suitcase with a thud, Tess set aside the drawer to take a closer look.

Pink book with gold stars. A gold clasp and a tiny keyhole.

Tess shook out a few pieces of clothing, but she didn't find the key that fit the lock. Didn't matter. Meg had seen the book, not the key.

She set the book aside while she finished clearing out everything that belonged to Montgomery and Lizzy. Then she wrapped the book in a clean kitchen towel, hid her true nature enough that she wouldn't endanger the other earth natives, and unlocked the door.

Nyx stood on the other side.

"Marie and Julia cleared out Merri Lee's things," Nyx said. "They're driving that BOW to the Green Complex and will park it in the garages there. Blair is waiting to haul whatever you have up here down to the other BOW."

A locked door would have meant nothing to a Sanguinati, and yet Nyx had waited outside. It was that respect for Tess's need of a private moment that made her hand over the wrapped book.

"Keep this hidden from everyone until I ask for it," Tess said.

Nyx took the book. "Is it dangerous?"

"I think so." After all, secrets could be very dangerous.

Blair came around the corner. "You ready? Let's get this stuff out of here so I can bring up the Wolves for defense."

"You're not going to defend the apartments," Tess said, her hair turning solid red and coiling.

Blair took a step back and snarled. Nyx looked curious.

"We're going to let the thieves break in," she continued. "We're going to let them start searching the apartments so that other humans will know they were enemies."

"And then?" Blair asked.

"And then I'll kill them."

CHAPTER 47

Simon glanced at the merchandise on another table, then looked away, uninterested.

Too many people, too much noise, too many *things*. Why did humans need so many things?

Nathan had stayed inside the big metal building that sheltered the stall market for a whole fifteen minutes before claiming that someone needed to guard the Courtyard's small bus against vandals or thieves. Simon would have gladly joined him, but the leader needed to stay and keep an eye on the rest of the pack. Sure, Henry and Vlad were there to help keep an eye on Jenni, Starr, and Crystal. Kowalski, Debany, and MacDonald were there too, but they had their hands full—literally—with being two-legged packhorses for Ruthie and Merri Lee.

"I guess Crows and humans have something in common," Kowalski said as he came up beside Simon. "They like filling their homes with trinkets."

Simon studied Ruthie, who seemed to be cooing over some kind of jar. "You're going to let your mate purchase a jar that looks like a sick cow?"

"What makes you think the cow looks sick?"

"Because I've never seen a healthy cow sit *that* way." He wasn't sure cows—or any other kind of four-legged prey—*could* sit that way. "What is she going to do with it?"

"Put it on the kitchen counter and use it as a cookie jar or something."

"But you'll have to look at it too."

Kowalski shrugged. "She's my mate. I can live with it if it makes her happy."

Simon looked at the bulging carry sacks Kowalski had in each hand. "Couldn't you just give her the best parts of a bunny?"

"Doesn't mean the same thing to a human female."

He sighed. He'd had a feeling that would be the answer.

"Jenni and her sisters are having fun," Kowalski said. "They really like hunting for treasures."

"Can they stop having fun soon?" A Wolf could travel a hundred miles in a day when he needed to. But after an hour of this noise and confusion—and all the *stinky smells!*—he was tired and wanted to go home and nap. And see Meg. He really wanted to see Meg. He wanted to play with Sam. He wanted . . .

He ignored Kowalski's laughter since the human was laughing at him, and answered his mobile phone. "What?"

"Simon, get out of there now," Elliot said.

"We're almost—"

"Now! Meg had a vision, and what she saw about you being in the stall market scared her so much *she fainted*."

Simon stiffened. He watched Kowalski study him, then set the carry sacks aside and motion to Michael Debany. "Meg cut herself?"

"She fell on the stairs leading up to the efficiency apartments. Something bad is going to happen up there too, but you—"

"Keep her safe." He ended the call and looked around for the rest of the *terra indigene*. <We have to leave *now*.>

"Problem?" Debany asked, joining Simon and Kowalski.

"Danger," Simon replied. "Meg says we have to get out of here."

"Should we call Lieutenant Montgomery?" Debany asked Kowalski.

Kowalski shook his head. "The lieutenant and the Denbys took the children to the movies this afternoon. His phone will be turned off. You call the station. I'll call Captain Burke."

As the two men made their calls, Kowalski headed for Ruthie and Merri Lee, while Debany made his way back to the table where Lawrence MacDonald stood, a questioning look on his face when he noticed his partner heading toward him.

Simon looked around and swore silently. Henry was easy to spot, even with so many humans. Jenni, Crystal, and Starr were spread out at different tables and kept disappearing as humans crowded the tables and blocked the Crows from his line of sight. Jenni and her sisters had heard his order, but their attention was too caught by the objects filling the tables. He was going to have to talk to the Crowgard leaders about this obsession with shiny objects. It was getting in the way of survival.

He tried to avoid bumping into humans as he moved toward Jenni, but it seemed a couple of the men deliberately shouldered him, delaying his approach to that merchant's table. When he reached her, something about the shifty, nervous way the merchant looked at him made his fangs lengthen. Fur suddenly covered the upper part of Simon's chest and back, and his hands were no longer even passing-glance human.

Jenni glanced at him and immediately stepped away from the table—a silent admission that she had ignored his command.

"What about this?" the merchant said quickly, flipping a cloth out of the way to reveal a flat piece of metal that, as far as Simon could tell, didn't do anything except shine.

"Ooooh," Jenni said.

Before she could step close to the table again, Simon grabbed her arm and pulled her away, ignoring her protests.

"Simon!" Jenni cried.

"Meg says we need to leave now."

"Just one more thing. Please, Simon. Just one more—"

He turned on her. "We're in danger," he said with quiet menace. "Whatever Meg saw scared her so much she fainted. She didn't faint the last time she saw Crows in danger, so this is bad, Jenni. This is very bad. Stay if you want to, but I'm not going to risk the rest of us because *you* can't resist grabbing another bit of shiny."

"Our Meg says?"

"Yes." He began moving toward the front of the building.

Jenni wouldn't let go of the damn carry sack, but she hurried to keep up with him, darting and dodging around humans as they headed for the front doors of the big building.

<Nathan?>

<I've got the bus started and ready to go. Simon, move fast. Men are gathering in the parking lot. They all have clubs and crowbars, and they're watching the bus.>

He kept moving, kept watching. The shoppers and merchants at nearby tables looked around as he passed, like deer that sensed there was something wrong but weren't sure if they should run. Humans a couple of aisles away paid no attention. But the *feel* of the place had changed; an ugly scent now drifted in the air ahead of him, a scent Wolves recognized as a threat.

Kowalski and Debany were on his right, keeping pace with him. Ruthie and Merri Lee, along with Starr, were a step behind them, each lugging a carry sack. The men were still talking on their mobile phones, but their shirts were rucked up to reveal the badges attached to their belts.

<Henry?> Simon called.

<I'm here, on your left and a couple of steps behind. Keep moving.>

<Vlad?>

<Behind you. Crystal and MacDonald are just ahead of me. But there is a pack of humans behind us who . . . Simon, I think one of the merchants was selling weapons in secret. Some of the humans might have guns.>

<If they fire at us, they'll injure or kill some of their own.>

<Do you think humans care about such things?>

No, he didn't think they cared.

Jenni stopped and looked back when Crystal cried out. Simon looked over his shoulder and snarled. A man had snatched one of the Crow's carry sacks and waved it above his head, taunting her to try to get it back.

Crystal dropped her other carry sack and tried to reclaim the sack that had been taken from her, leading her away from the rest of the Others.

<Let it go, Crystal,> Simon snapped.

<I gave the humans money. Those shinies are mine!>

MacDonald caught Crystal around the waist and lifted her off her feet. Ignoring her cries about her lost treasures, he headed toward the rest of their group, pushing aside humans who didn't have enough sense to get out of the way.

<Simon!> Nathan shouted. <Hurry!>

Looking toward the front of the building, Simon saw the men standing between him and the building's open doors. At first he thought there were only six men looking for a fight. That made it an even number of males, with the *terra indigene* and police officers having the advantage of teeth, claws, and training. Then more men joined the first six enemies. And more. And more.

And all of them carried some kind of weapon.

Simon stopped. Kowalski and Debany stopped with him, forming a line.

"These are not good odds," Debany whispered.

"We're police officers," Kowalski said, his raised voice both a warning and a challenge. "You men step aside and let these people leave."

"They aren't people, and you're nothing but a fucking Wolf lover," one man said. "Don't care if you're a cop. We're going to teach you a lesson."

"You don't want to do this," Simon warned.

The man bared his teeth. "Yeah, we do."

Kowalski shouted, "We're police officers! Put your weapons down *now*!"

"Humans first, last, and always!" the man shouted, rushing toward Simon.

As the man swung a length of pipe at Simon's head, Henry yelled "Simon!" and swatted the Wolf, knocking him to the ground at the same moment the Grizzly roared with rage and pain—and the man who had swung the pipe fell to the ground, his shirt turning wet and red.

Shouts. Screams. Gunshots behind them.

People ran toward the doors or to another part of the building or anywhere that would take them away from the fight. But the men with clubs and knives rushed toward Henry and Simon while others attacked Kowalski and Debany.

Instinctively, Simon shifted what he needed as he sprang up to meet the attack. Wolf head with teeth that could slash and jaws strong enough to break bone. Hands with claws that could tear flesh.

He fought hard, biting and clawing, until he broke through the human wall, providing an escape for his pack.

<Simon!> Nathan howled.

A Wolf alone had no chance against a mob.

More shots and screams and . . .

"Officer down! Officer down!"

Simon hesitated. Nathan was a Wolf, one of his own. Nathan needed him. But as the Courtyard's leader, his pack included Crows and Grizzlies and vampires . . . and even a few humans.

Sorry, Nathan. Sorry, Meg.

Turning away from the doors, Simon leaped back into the fight.

A car pulled into the Courtyard's customer parking lot. Two young men, college age, got out and walked toward Main Street. As they passed Howling Good

Reads, they looked in the windows and paused when they spotted an old man standing near the counter. Not knowing, or caring, who he was, they laughed and gave him the finger. When he smiled, revealing the fangs of the Sanguinati, they shuddered and hurried to cross Main Street before the traffic light changed.

Another car pulled into the lot. A man and a woman, a little older than the other two humans, walked up the street and went into the Stag and Hare.

Two more cars pulled in, as if the Courtyard's lot was suddenly public parking. Humans walking or driving past wouldn't have thought there was anything unusual when a van pulled into the lot. Three men exited from the van's back door and casually walked a few steps to the glass street door that led to the efficiency apartments above the seamstress/tailor's shop.

Tess didn't hear anyone in the hallway, but she *felt* the presence of someone outside the efficiency apartment being used by Lieutenant Montgomery and Lizzy.

Her coils of hair turned the pure black of death as she stepped out of the apartment, but she kept her eyes lowered, just in case the presence wasn't an intruder. A direct look from her—eyes meeting eyes—would kill her prey, but even looking *at* her when she was in her true form would damage flesh.

Looking at the floor, Tess saw smoke that gradually became an old-fashioned black velvet gown. "Nyx," she warned.

"My eyes are closed."

No reason to doubt Nyx, but Tess still focused her eyes on the wall next to the Sanguinati's shoulder, allowing her to see without actually *looking* at the other female.

"While it's possible to harm us in our smoke form, it's very hard to kill us," Nyx said. "An earth native like you might succeed in killing one of us, but you wouldn't survive the fight."

Harvester. Plague Rider. For years she had kept her secret from the rest of the Lakeside Courtyard. Now it seemed there were many who knew what she was. What bewildered her was that they didn't seem to care that one of Namid's most ferocious predators lived among them. Normally her kind lived on the fringes, avoided and feared. Acceptance, *true* acceptance, was a rare and valued gift.

"What do you want, Nyx?"

"A van pulled into the customer parking lot. The enemy will be here at any moment."

"Then you should leave."

"No, I should stay. A bullet can hurt you, even kill you, if the enemy is able to fire a gun before you can harvest enough life to incapacitate him."

True. And if the enemy knew anything about her kind and fired without looking at her, she would be at risk. "What are you suggesting?"

Nyx smiled. "That sometimes it's more practical, and more fun, to hunt in pairs."

Grab the human weapon to block a blow while his teeth tore into flesh. Dodge the blows that could break bone and leave him helpless.

Simon couldn't keep track of his pack. Humans and Others didn't know how to fight as a unit to bring down the enemy, and their defense of the weaker among them was more like adult bison bunching together to protect the calves. That worked well enough for big animals with hooves and horns, but it wasn't going to work for the pack. Despite the number of humans they had already wounded or killed, more enemies were closing around them. They had lost the chance to run, and when there was no longer enough room to fight . . .

<I hear sirens!> Nathan shouted.

Help. Maybe. But would it come in time to save any of them?

The Crowgard watched from the trees and rooftops, memorizing the faces of the humans who had left their vehicles in the lot. The Sanguinati watched from the shadows, waiting for the right moment to snatch the van's driver.

Moving casually and acting as if they belonged, the three men picked the lock on the glass door and went up the stairs.

Stealth and speed. One picked the lock on Merri Lee's apartment and slipped inside. The other two went to Montgomery's apartment. But when they went inside, they had one startled moment to look at Tess's face, to look into her eyes. In that moment, in that one look, she harvested enough of their life force to cause legs and arms to fail and hearts to flutter. The two men collapsed, twitching on the floor, too weak to reach for their weapons.

Tess collected two guns and a short, flexible, leather-covered club. She looked toward the doorway and the column of smoke hovering on the other side.

<Safe?> Nyx asked.

<Not yet.> With effort, Tess hid her true nature behind the human mask. When her coiled hair relaxed a bit and green streaks broke up the death color, she looked at Nyx. <Now it's safe enough.>

"Blair can take them?"

Tess nodded. She bent and patted their pockets again. "No identification."

Nyx smiled. "No identification, no obligation to any human." She sniffed delicately. "At least yours didn't make a mess. Mine peed on the rug. We'll have to figure out how to clean it—and how to explain the urine smell."

"Blame Skippy," Blair said, joining them. "We'll say he got into the apartment somehow and peed on the rug while he was sniffing around for cookies. I doubt a human nose can distinguish between Wolf and human urine, so the human pack won't know the difference."

"The pack will know we expected trouble," Nyx said.

"Thieves broke in, found nothing, and went away," Tess said. She wagged the short club. "Don't know what this is. A weapon of some kind."

Blair took it, slapped it against his palm, and winced. "Meat tenderizer?"

One of the men made a sound.

Tess studied him, then said, "This one's tongue is starting to blacken and rot. If you want him to tell you anything, ask your questions very soon."

Three things happened at once. Something slammed into the back of the building hard enough to shake the structure; half the roof tore off and went flying; and Nathan yelled, <Some cars just exploded and are burning!>

A hesitation in the fighting as a fierce and furious wind entered the building through the open roof and hurled tables and merchandise at humans—a wind that, curiously, didn't touch the tables that might injure the Courtyard's pack.

Despite the screams of people throughout the building, Simon heard the sirens getting louder. And he saw Fire walk through the open doors, her hair and gown fanned out as she approached. The floor smoked in her wake.

That explains the burning cars, Simon thought, shuddering as the Elemental moved closer. Nothing would escape her if Fire wanted to burn, especially if Air fanned her sister's rage through the building.

Fire looked at the men who had been fighting with the pack and said, "Either we all leave or all the humans burn."

A sudden gust of air caught Fire's gown. It flared out and found the leg of one man's jeans. With a cry, he dropped the pipe he'd been holding and smacked at the burning fabric.

"Police! Drop your weapons!"

Many voices made that demand as men rushed through the open doors, then came to a fast stop when Fire turned toward them.

"They're here to help, and we need help."

Hearing the quiet words, Simon glanced at Kowalski. The man's face and clothes were bloody, but the hands holding a small gun were steady.

Yes, they needed help, but he didn't recognize any of these police officers.

Then Captain Burke walked through the door. He didn't say anything. He just looked at Simon and waited.

Time to make a choice.

<Fire,> Simon said. <These police humans will help us.>

She turned back to him, and he realized it hadn't been whim that had brought her and Air to the stall market to rescue him and the rest of the pack. The Elementals hadn't even done it for him; they came here for Meg.

<You trust them?> she asked.

Not all of them. He didn't want to think of what she might do if he answered her question that honestly, so he settled on, <Enough of them. I trust the humans that Meg trusts, and those humans trust the other police officers.>

Sensing that she was too close to expressing her full fury and burning everything in sight, he said the one thing he thought might sway her. <Tell Meg I'll be home soon.>

He didn't care if Fire charred the entire building and everything in it, but he wanted to get his pack away from here first, and there were still too many humans between him and the door.

A heated silence. Then Air said, <Twister and I will remain to keep watch.>

Simon nodded, relieved the Elementals would compromise that much.

<Very well.> Fire tipped her head . . . and disappeared.

Police rushed toward them, restraining the men who had attacked them. At least, restraining the ones who weren't dead or badly injured.

Kowalski lowered his gun but had trouble moving one arm and ended up tucking the gun in the waistband of his jeans. Simon did his best to shift enough to look passably human. Then he heard two voices.

Ruthie saying, "Hang on, Lawrence. Hang on. The paramedics are here."

And Jenni crying, "Crystal? Crystal, wake up! Simon says we have to leave now."

He stepped aside as men from the ambulance rushed in, guarded by police. He looked at his pack.

Henry had a deep, bloody furrow along his right cheek from the bullet that had struck him when he swatted Simon out of the way. Michael Debany was limping and couldn't seem to bend one knee. Ruthie was all bloody, but he couldn't tell if she was wounded or if it was all Lawrence MacDonald's blood. Merri Lee had bruises already blooming on her face, arms, and legs—and a bone sticking through the skin of one finger on her left hand. Vlad appeared un-harmed. So did Jenni and Starr. But Crystal . . .

The back too arched. The feet pointed so hard they were almost curling. The eyes that should have been dark and shining were already dull. And feathers had partially sprouted along her stiff arms.

He looked at the bloody magazines that had fallen around her and thought, *This is the vision Meg had seen about Heather. If the human bunny had been working in the Courtyard, she would have come here with the other girls. Would Crystal have lived if Heather had died here?*

He didn't know how much of a prophecy could change and how much was going to happen, regardless of what someone did. All he knew right now was he hurt and he wanted to go home.

<Nathan?> he called.

<Cut from broken glass and hurt from the rocks they threw at me. The mon-keys pushed the bus over. Don't think I can get out. I smell gasoline.> A hesita-tion. <The police out here are saying they'll help. They say *hurry*.>

<They'll help. Get away from the bus.>

Too much noise. Too much confusion. He felt dull and sick as he watched the paramedics rush MacDonald to the ambulance. He watched police lead the attackers with minor injuries out of the building. And he watched Captain Burke speak briefly to Kowalski and Debany before approaching him.

"Mr. Wolfgard? What can we do for you and your people? You and Mr. Bear-gard are wounded. So is the Wolf who was in the bus."

"Our bodywalkers will take care of us," Simon said. "We just want to go home."

"Your bus is too damaged to drive, but we'll get you home."

"Crystal too."

Burke nodded. "I'm sorry for your loss."

He wanted to get away from this place. He wanted a chance to rest and heal. Then he remembered the other part of Elliot's message. "Tell Lieutenant Montgomery to keep the Lizzy away from the Courtyard. Something bad is going to happen there . . . or has happened."

"What kind of bad?"

"Don't know. Meg saw . . ."

"Simon is hurt," Henry said. "He needs to go home."

"Captain Zajac and his men also responded to the call for backup. Give me a moment to talk to him; then I'll make arrangements to get you all home. We'll need statements from all of you, but that can wait."

As Burke walked away, Kowalski walked up to Simon and Henry, his arm around Ruthie.

"I'm sorry," Ruthie said, crying. "I am so sorry."

"We talked to the merchants' association last week and asked them if there would be a problem with *terra indigene* visiting the stall market to shop. We were told it wouldn't be," Kowalski said.

"I'm so sorry."

"Wasn't your fault," Simon said. "You wanted to give the Crows a treat. Other humans took the opportunity to try to kill us."

No, this wasn't Ruthie's fault. Allowing himself to be lured to a place where the *terra indigene* had so little chance of surviving an attack was *his* fault. As the leader, he should have remembered why the *terra indigene* didn't go to movie theaters or concerts or any other place where a mob of humans could attack a small number of Others. He should have heeded Vlad's concerns about going to the stall market instead of relying on Kowalski's and Ruthie's trust in these humans. Crystal Crowgard had died because of that trust, and Lawrence MacDonald was badly wounded.

Burke returned as Debany and Merri Lee joined them. "Officers, you and the ladies are going to the hospital for treatment. I've left messages for Lieutenant Montgomery and Pete Denby, so they'll be aware of the situation and will take precautions. Mr. Wolfgard, there's transportation waiting for you and the rest of the *terra indigene*."

"We're ready."

Vlad joined them, carrying Crystal and trailed by Jenni and Starr.

Nodding to Burke, Simon walked outside, followed by Vlad and the Crows, with Henry bringing up the rear. Nathan waited for them near some kind of police van. The Wolf was still bleeding from some of the deeper cuts, and judging by the way Nathan moved, Simon suspected there were other, deeper injuries. He just hoped those injuries were things Jane Wolfgard could fix.

As they drove away from the stall market, more ambulances were turning into the parking lot—and Simon wondered if the humans who started this had any idea how much damage they had done.

Blair growled and looked over his shoulder, but the warning ended quickly as Elliot joined them and said, "I have news."

"Simon?" Blair asked.

"He's hurt," Elliot said. "So are Nathan and Henry. Crystal is dead. Jenni and Starr are upset but don't appear wounded. Vlad is unharmed. They'll all be here in a few minutes. The human pack is being taken to the hospital. Various injuries. One of them is badly wounded."

"Let's move these carcasses." Blair hesitated. Then he looked at Tess. "Are these meat?"

She considered the two men, who were already beyond answering questions, and acknowledged to herself that she'd harvested more than she'd intended. She shook her head. "They're rotting too fast."

"Mine is weakened, but the meat and blood are fresh," Nyx said.

Blair nodded. "We've also got the van's driver. Two will provide enough special meat for everyone who wants some."

<Sirens,> Jake Crowgard reported from his position on the roof. <Police are coming.>

"Then we need to hurry," Nyx said.

Blair fetched the drop cloths he'd left at the end of the hallway. The four *terra indigene* wrapped up the three bodies and hauled them down to the Utilities Complex's pickup, which he had parked near the back stairs. They also took the soiled rug.

As soon as Blair and Elliot had driven off with the meat, Tess opened windows in all the apartments—even the ones that hadn't been invaded. Then she wiped the floors while Nyx arranged to have the personal belongings returned after the police left.

By the time Nyx returned and police officers were coming up the stairs from the street door, Tess had everything sufficiently tidy.

She let the officers look around. She answered the questions she chose to answer, and the officer in charge, a Commander Gresh, who had provided assistance on previous occasions, was smart enough to be satisfied with the answers he'd been given.

She told him he could do the smudging thing on the street door to check for fingerprints. The cars in the Courtyard's parking lot? Not customers of any of their shops, so the officers were welcome to seize them, detain them, tow them, or do whatever else they pleased with them.

"A police van just drove in," Nyx said once the police were sniffing around the parking lot. "Vlad says the police will take Simon and the others to the Market Square medical office."

"I don't think our humans will be returning soon, but let's put everything back as best we can."

"Everything?"

Tess looked at Nyx, knowing the Sanguinati was asking about the pink book. "Not everything."

CHAPTER 48

Watersday, Maius 26

Smiling as he listened to the children's excited jabbering, Monty pulled his mobile phone out of his pocket and turned it on. Not that he expected anything. Captain Burke knew he'd taken the day off to spend time with Lizzy. Now that the question of custody was settled, at least for the time being, he had decided it would be safe to take Lizzy to the movies as a treat and had invited the Denby family to join them.

"Do we all want something to eat?" Pete Denby asked.

"Pizza!" Lizzy said.

"Pizza, pizza, pizza," Sarah said.

"Hamburgers," Robert said. "I'm so hungry I could eat a hamburger the size of a cow!"

"A whole cow?" Eve Denby gave her son a disbelieving look. "Even the hooves?"

Before Robert could reply, Lizzy looked at Monty. "Daddy! You turned on your phone."

"I have to check in, Lizzy girl." And what he saw made him uneasy. Three messages from Burke's phone number while he'd been in the theater? That wasn't good.

"You always put work first. Mommy said—"

"That's enough," Monty snapped, stung to not only hear the same words but Elayne's disapproving tone of voice coming out of his own daughter. He looked at Pete. "Check your messages." Then he listened to his own.

"*Lieutenant, there's been an incident at the stall market. Call me when you can.*"

"*The Courtyard is under attack. Do not, I repeat, do not take Lizzy back there until you talk to me.*"

"*Lawrence MacDonald was shot. He's in surgery. Come to Lakeside Hospital as soon as you can.*"

"Mikhos, watch over us," Monty whispered. As he put his phone away, he looked at Pete's pale face and grim expression.

"We'll take Lizzy with us back to the duplex," Pete said.

"Can you drop me close to Lakeside Hospital?"

"Sure."

"What's going . . . ?" Eve looked at both men and didn't finish the question.

"One of my men," Monty said, knowing he didn't need to say more.

They hustled the children to the car. Monty wondered if he looked hunted. The gods knew, he felt that way.

"Gods above and below." Captain Zajac shook his head as he looked at the destruction outside the stall market, which was in his precinct.

The older patrol captain had brushed against the Others when a former Courtyard employee named Darrell Adams died under mysterious circumstances—and a lot of people in the same area ended up in the emergency room with sudden ailments. Since then, Zajac had been fiercely insistent that he be kept informed about the "doings at the Chestnut Street station."

"A third of the vehicles in this lot destroyed in seconds," Zajac said. "I saw them burst into flames and felt the explosions as we were pulling in. Saw that female running past the cars just before they went up."

"It could have been a lot worse," Burke replied. He watched as the Courtyard bus was righted and attached to a tow truck. The bus would go to a garage that serviced police vehicles. If it could be sufficiently repaired, they would do that. If it couldn't, he'd be sitting down with the mayor and the city's comptroller, doing his best to persuade them of the necessity of purchasing a new bus for the *terra indigene*. The Others could afford another bus, and it wouldn't be a hardship on the Courtyard's annual budget—provided, of course, there were buses in the appropriate size for sale. A shortage of steel was starting to make itself felt in several industries, including the manufacture of vehicles. He'd heard from a couple of his sources that public transportation like cabs and buses would be given priority, and individuals might end up waiting six months or more to purchase a family car—and would have to choose from whatever models were available at the time or do without.

What his sources couldn't tell him was why there was a shortage of steel when the *terra indigene* were selling the same quantity of raw materials to the manufacturers as usual.

A problem for another day, Burke thought when he heard the older man sigh.

"I know it could have been worse," Zajac said. "Two exits for the whole damn building, and the back exit blocked by debris that had been thrown against the door. And people stuck behind a barricade of tables and merchandise blown around by a freak wind, with no chance of getting out if a fire had started in that part of the building."

"That wasn't a freak wind," Burke said quietly. "That was done by an angry Elemental. The debris wasn't blocking the back doors by accident, the roof wasn't torn off this place by a chance gust of wind that just happened to find a weak point, and those cars didn't explode because of a leak in someone's gas tank and the heat of the sun on the pavement. That would be a plausible explanation—maybe—and if we're smart, we won't offer a different explanation, because if Fire had entered the building first instead of burning the cars as a way to disrupt the attack on the Courtyard bus, we would have had a lot of corpses and very few survivors."

"Is this going to spoil things?" Zajac gave Burke a bitter smile. "Besides paying attention to what is happening at your station, I do keep my ear to the ground, Douglas. I've heard the Courtyard stores aren't open to humans anymore. I've heard Wolfgard has bought at least one building outside the Courtyard to use as rental property. And I've heard from a couple of friends who serve on the Talulah Falls police force, what's left of it, so I have some idea of just how bad it can be for us humans when the *terra indigene* truly hate us."

Burke had heard a few rumors about Talulah Falls too. If anything like the attack in the stall market had happened there, the Others would have killed *everyone*, and it wouldn't have mattered that the majority of those people hadn't been involved in the attack. "Simon Wolfgard wants to use the Lakeside Courtyard as a kind of graduate school for *terra indigene* who need to interact with humans in one capacity or another. The shops might be closed to the general human population, but *all* their stores are open now to a select group of humans who are interacting with a lot more of the Courtyard's residents. That gives us a chance to show the Others that humans *can* work with them for the benefit of all of us."

"All of that would have been gone if Wolfgard had died today?"

"All of that would have been gone. And the next leader would not have looked favorably on any of us."

They stood in silence for a couple of minutes, watching people absorb the loss of property. Watching people follow paramedics to the ambulances that would take loved ones to one of the city's hospitals.

Watching the medical examiner's van take away the dead.

"Douglas? Don't know if you've seen the alerts yet, but there's a lot of people who have gone missing all of a sudden." Zajac stared straight ahead. "Not from Lakeside, thank all the gods. Closest to us is a dozen people in the Finger Lakes area, all from the same town."

"Maybe they ran off together."

"A fair number of alerts have come in from all the regions," Zajac said as if he hadn't heard Burke's comment. "Groups of people all gone missing around the same time. Almost like someone had decided to put a company out of business by eliminating the employees. Doesn't it strike you as odd that so many people can disappear and no one has caught sight of any of them?"

"Did the missing people live close to roads where the pregnant blood prophets were found?"

"Close enough." A beat of silence. "What are you thinking?"

I wonder who gave the order to hunt down the people who ran the breeding farms. "I think those people are truly gone, and we shouldn't look too hard for them or ask too many questions."

They watched their men escorting people out of the building. A few people were taken out on stretchers, but most walked out on their own.

Yes, things could have been a lot worse.

Finally Burke stirred. "I have to go. I'll get the statements from Wolfgard and the rest of the *terra indigene* who were here and send you a copy of the report."

"Appreciate it. I hope your officer pulls through."

"So do I."

Burke got in his car and drove toward the Courtyard. The Lakeside Hospital was on the way, but he needed to ascertain what else the Others might know about why Lieutenant Montgomery should keep Lizzy away from what had been a safe place. Once he knew that, he'd go to the hospital to check on his men and begin a vigil while waiting for news about MacDonald.

And while he was waiting, he would consider whether these two attacks had happened at the same time by chance or design.

When Monty reached the small, private waiting room, he found Burke at the door talking to Louis Gresh.

Gresh nodded as Monty joined them.

Burke said, "Tell him."

"At the same time that Captain Burke was apprised of the need for backup at the stall market, the station received a call about a possible attack at the Courtyard," Louis said. "Captain Burke was on his way to the stall market and you were off duty, so I responded at the Courtyard, figuring a familiar face would be a better choice."

Monty nodded. "It would be, especially if the Others felt any of their more . . . vulnerable . . . residents were in danger." Meaning the youngsters and Meg Corbyn. Or had this been some kind of attempt by Theral MacDonald's ex to get to her? "Did the intruder damage one of the stores?"

Louis shook his head. "Person or persons unknown entered two of the efficiency apartments, with the probable intent of taking items of value. Ms. Lee is residing in one of those apartments, and you're currently using the other."

Monty felt sick. Someone was still after Lizzy? Why? The Toland police had Boo Bear, and only the *terra indigene* knew where the real jewels were now hidden.

"Did they take anything?" he asked.

"Nothing," Louis replied. "They didn't tell me why, but the *terra indigene* had cleared out all the personal possessions from both those apartments right before the attempted burglary. Since nothing was stolen and there was no sign of the burglars, there wasn't much we could do. The street door was dusted for fingerprints. We took down the license plates of the four vehicles parked in the lot and tracked down the owners. Wasn't hard. They were all having drinks and nibbles at the Stag and Hare."

"Together?" Burke asked.

"No, but I'd bet they knew each other and had parked in the Courtyard's lot as a kind of provocation. And one of the men kept fingering an HFL pin and smirking, as if he knew some big secret—especially after being asked if he'd seen any other vehicles in the parking lot."

"Those cars were camouflage," Monty said. "A single vehicle in that lot would be noticed. Several vehicles parked where they shouldn't be looks more like mooning the Wolves and daring them to make a big deal out of a minor transgression."

"That sounds idiotic enough to be true, but there wasn't another vehicle in the lot when we got there," Louis said. He looked at both of them and added slowly, "And neither of you think we'll find the vehicle."

"Oh, we might find the vehicle," Burke said. There was something in his tone that warned about asking any questions about the occupants of that vehicle.

"Well," Louis said after an awkward silence. "I'd better get back to the station. I'll stop by again later. Hopefully we'll all have good news by then."

They waited until Louis was out of sight. Then Burke blew out his breath in a gusty sigh. "All right, Lieutenant, let's talk to your boys and find out why a simple outing went so very wrong."

His boys, Monty thought as he followed Burke into the waiting room. Not his men, not his officers. His boys.

When he saw them, he understood Burke's choice of words.

Kowalski and Debany sat on the outside chairs, bookending Ruth and Merri Lee. They all looked young and scared and exhausted. Blood on their clothes. Bruises and bandages. One of Merri Lee's fingers was splinted and the hand wrapped. She looked groggier than the other three, and Monty guessed she'd been given a painkiller.

Burke moved some magazines and sat on the table in front of them, ignoring the way it creaked from his weight.

Monty crouched next to Kowalski's chair. "Karl?"

Kowalski made an effort to steady, although he couldn't quite stop his hands from shaking. "MacDonald is in surgery. Ruthie did what she could to apply pressure to the wound, but he lost a lot of blood before the paramedics arrived. Michael called Lawrence's folks. They're on their way. Haven't reached Theral yet. She's not answering her mobile phone."

"There was some trouble at the Courtyard," Monty said quietly. "She may have left her phone somewhere."

"Is Theral all right?" Merri Lee asked, rousing for a moment.

"I'll find out." He'd also have to tell her that her cousin had been shot.

"We'll get a formal statement from each of you later," Burke said. "Right now, I'd like to know what happened."

"I'm so sorry," Ruthie whispered. "A field trip, a treat for the Crows. Karl and I asked the people who run the stall market as well as some of the merchants if there would be any objections to the Others shopping there. We *asked*."

"The impression we got is the merchants would welcome anyone who wanted to spend money," Kowalski said. "But . . ." He looked at his friends.

"Just say it," Burke said.

"It's just an impression," Debany said.

"That's fine. In fact, impressions are good if we're going to do effective damage control."

"The people who run the stall market rent that building every weekend," Kowalski began. "Then they rent out floor space for the merchants' tables. You can rent up to three tables, either together or in different areas of the market. The center cross—the wide main aisles that divide the building into four quarters—are the prime locations and cost the most to rent."

Ruth shifted in her chair. "A lot of shoppers never go beyond the center cross unless they're looking for a specific item or looking for the people who are trying to unload a lot of little stuff from a moving or estate sale and will sell cheap."

"What we noticed was that a number of merchants we recognized as usually having tables on a side aisle had tables on the center cross today," Kowalski said. "And they had the kind of merchandise that would appeal to Crows. Windup toys. Sets of blocks, gaudy crap."

"Jenni and her sisters were so excited, so happy," Merri Lee said. "And they had so much money."

Debany nodded. "Jenni did most of the buying, and she had a money belt around her waist that was *stuffed* with cash. I thought a couple of merchants were going to faint when she pulled out a wad of bills to pay for what they wanted."

Burke pursed his lips. "So you made slow progress down the main aisle of the market, and everyone was having a good time."

"Yes," Kowalski said. "We had just reached the center of the market. The Crows were still going strong, but I had the sense that Simon Wolfgard had had more than enough noise and people. Michael was going to talk to the girls about calling it a day. Before he could do that, Wolfgard got a phone call, and suddenly we were on the move, in danger, had to get out *now*."

"So he stopped you all before you reached the back half of the market?" Monty asked.

"Yes, sir. He grabbed Jenni and began hauling ass for the front entrance where the bus was parked. Ruthie and Merri had Starr with them, and Lawrence was escorting Crystal. Henry Beargard was to Simon's left. Don't know where Vlad was. Behind us, I think. We could see the doors when a group of men blocked our way. They all carried weapons—clubs mostly, but a few had knives. Michael and I identified ourselves as police officers and ordered the men to step aside."

"Is that when you called the station?" Burke asked.

Kowalski shook his head. "Before. We called the station and called you as soon as Wolfgard indicated we were in danger."

Burke took them through the rest, confirming that the humans attacked their group *after* Kowalski and Debany identified themselves as police officers; that the shots that killed Crystal Crowgard and injured Lawrence MacDonald came from behind them; that they had fired their off-duty pieces to protect themselves and the people with them.

That Simon Wolfgard had broken clear and could have gotten away, but turned back to help them when MacDonald went down.

When they finished, Burke looked at Merri Lee and Ruth. "Ladies, could you give us a minute?"

Ruth helped Merri Lee to her feet. The two women slowly left the room.

"Will Merri be able to stay at the Courtyard tonight?" Debany asked.

"The lieutenant and I will be going to the Courtyard soon. We'll assess the situation and let you know." Burke leaned closer. "Now. I want a straight answer. When MacDonald went down and you called for more backup, was there any delay before officers arrived to help you?"

Monty saw the shock on Kowalski's and Debany's faces. They looked at each other, hesitated, then shook their heads.

"It felt like the fight went on for hours, but I don't think the whole thing lasted more than a few minutes," Kowalski said. "The Elementals got there first, but backup was right behind them, and you were right behind the backup."

Burke slapped his hands on his thighs and stood. "All right. Good. We'll check out the Courtyard and then we'll return."

Monty walked out with Burke. Holding the door for Merri and Ruth, he looked at his men, then said quietly to Burke, "I know why you had to ask the question, but did they need to wonder about that today? The question came as a shock. They've had enough shocks."

"Help arrived before they had a chance to wonder if it would arrive. I think that's going to matter a lot in the days ahead. Come on, Lieutenant. Let's find out if Simon Wolfgard also believes help arrived in a timely manner."

CHAPTER 49

Watersday, Maius 26

The driver of the police van did his best to make careful turns and avoid quick stops, but just the motion of the van as they drove back to the Courtyard made Simon hurt. He hurt and hurt and hurt. He wanted to shift to Wolf and find a safe place to hide. Then he could whimper like a little puppy because he hurt and hurt and hurt.

When he was a juvenile Wolf living in the Northwest Region, he'd spent a year with other youngsters learning to work and hunt with a pack that wasn't family—a first step to working in a Courtyard where you would have to work cooperatively with many forms of *terra indigene*. That's when he'd met Joe and Jackson. Working with them had felt easy, natural, and that bond had made the three of them a collective leader of their pack.

But one juvenile Wolf didn't fit in with the rest of them. He wanted to be leader, but there was something about him that made the other Wolves wary, and they wouldn't follow him. He resented Simon, Joe, and Jackson, and that resentment grew until the day they were hunting a half-grown bison. The pack was hungry and motivated to bring down game. Instead of working with the rest of them, the Wolf turned the animal at the moment when Simon would be unable to get out of the way.

He'd been lucky that day. Instead of being trampled, he'd dodged the hooves and received nothing more than a glancing blow that had slowed him down and prevented him from hunting for a few days. But it had hurt, just like the betrayal had hurt.

The resentful Wolf disappeared that same day. The day Simon rejoined the pack for a hunt, they found that Wolf. He'd been trampled, his hip bones crushed. He also had deep claw marks that had torn up his sides. He'd tried to crawl, looked to be heading toward the area where the juveniles were settled. And then something had crushed his skull.

The adult Wolves had said the juveniles were on their own that year—within howling distance if they got into bad trouble, but essentially on their own and not under the watchful eyes of other Wolves.

Whether that was true or not didn't much matter. When they'd searched for scents to figure out what kind of animal had killed the Wolf, they smelled nothing but other *terra indigene*. Not Wolves. Not anything they could name.

It had been the only time during that year that any of them had smelled those forms of *terra indigene*. All of them hoped they never caught those scents again.

Some of those scents had been in the air the day he and Henry drove past the River Road Community on their way to a meeting with Steve Ferryman, which meant some of *those* forms of *terra indigene* were now close enough to watch the humans and the Others who lived around Lakeside.

The lesson the juvenile Wolves had learned that day when they had found the body of the resentful Wolf was this: certain actions angered the earth natives who lived deep in the wild country, and they were the ones who should not be provoked.

Would today's attack be considered provocation? He didn't know. He just knew that, right now when he was hurt and unable to defend himself, he feared other kinds of *terra indigene* more than he feared humans.

<Simon?> Vlad said. <We're home.>

Home. Meg.

He growled about being helped out of the police van, but he couldn't have stepped down on his own. Humiliating, and frightening, to be that vulnerable. Vlad stayed close to him as he shuffled to the Market Square's medical office while Henry helped Nathan.

Jake Crowgard, in human form, ran to meet the van, embracing Jenni and Starr when they emerged.

As Vlad opened the door of the medical office, Simon looked at the humans standing near the van. Strangers in police uniforms. Who could be trusted? And what would happen to any who were deemed untrustworthy?

A white car pulled up behind the police van. Right behind it was a black sedan.

"We're protected," Vlad said quietly. "Let's go inside."

Protected, yes. He spotted several Sanguinati in their smoke form. He saw Blair and a few other Wolves in Wolf form moving along one side of the market's inner square. In the center of the square was Air astride Twister—warning and threat.

Dr. Dominic Lorenzo, Lieutenant Montgomery, and Captain Burke passed under one of the Market Square's archways and strode toward the medical office. Tess and Nyx also headed toward the medical office, but they were coming from the direction of the Liaison's Office.

"I thought you were helping humans deal with the *cassandra sangue*," Simon said to Lorenzo, surprised at how slurred the words sounded.

"I am," Lorenzo replied. "But I'm still putting in some hours here for the Courtyard's residents. I heard a news bulletin about the trouble at the stall market, and I thought I might be needed here."

He was about to refuse. He didn't want any human touching him.

Then Meg appeared in the office doorway. She looked at Henry, then at Nathan, then at him—and burst into tears.

Jane Wolfgard caught Meg before her legs buckled.

"No bending that knee," Jane said sternly.

Lorenzo shook his head. "Enough of this." He looked at Jane. "Take Ms. Corbyn to the examination room. While I'm sure you did an excellent job of cleaning and tending the cut, I'll examine the knee and make my notes for her file." Then he turned to look at Nathan. "You. Do *not* lick those cuts. Even from here I can see there's glass in some of those wounds. If you swallow any of it, it can cut you up inside." Finally he turned to Henry and Simon. "I'll examine both of you and make my recommendations for your human forms. Then you and your healer can decide the best course of action."

Having given his orders, Lorenzo walked into the office and headed for the examination room.

As they hobbled after Lorenzo, Simon noticed Theral, who was standing out of the way. When she saw Burke and Montgomery—and none of the humans who had left with the Others a couple of hours ago—she turned pale and swayed.

"Ms. MacDonald," Montgomery said gently. "We need to talk." He led her into the room Elizabeth Bennefeld used for massages and closed the door.

"Mr. Wolfgard," Burke said, ignoring Simon's warning growl. "I'd like your perceptions of what happened at the stall market."

"We were warned to leave," Simon replied. "Danger. Humans blocked the way and attacked before we could get out. Attacked Nathan too." He tried to turn his head to look at the Grizzly. "Henry knocked me down." And probably had that furrow in his right cheek from the bullet that would have killed Simon.

"Captain, I can give you enough for your report," Vlad said.

Jane stepped out of the examination room. "Nathan?"

"Simon first," Nathan said.

Lorenzo may have wanted to see them in order of visible injuries, but leader came before enforcer. So Simon hobbled into the examination room.

Since he hadn't seen her leave, it shouldn't have surprised him that Meg was still there, sitting in a chair.

He grumbled at Lorenzo and Jane when they cut off his shirt, wasting a usable garment, but he couldn't raise his arms for them to lift it off, so there wasn't much choice. He growled about them removing the shoes, socks, and jeans. He would have bitten at least one of them if they'd tried to remove the briefs. No one was taking those while Meg was in the room.

"Oh, Simon." Meg started crying again.

"Don't cry, Meg," he pleaded. It hurt in a different way to hear her crying.

Lorenzo poked and prodded, gently enough, all things considered, but Simon still yelped a few times.

"Well, even in this form, you're a lot tougher than a human," Lorenzo said. "You're battered and deeply bruised, no question about that. You might have some hairline fractures that I can't detect without taking X-rays, which I can't do here. But I'm not feeling any obvious broken bones or anything that's dislocated. All I can prescribe is rest. Give yourself time to heal."

"Once Simon shifts to Wolf, I can tell if there are problems inside," Jane said.

"Can't shift to Wolf," Simon muttered. "Have to talk to humans about—"

Meg sprang out of the chair and was in his face so fast, he jerked back . . . and then whimpered because the move hurt, hurt, hurt.

"You do *not* have to stay in human form," she yelled. "You do *not* have to talk to any humans until you're better. You need to be a wolfy Wolf! And if you get stupid about this, I'll . . . I'll paint your tail orange!"

He thought of pointing out that he wouldn't have a tail if he stayed in human form, but Jane nodded and said, "That's a good threat. Come on, Meg. Let's step out so Simon can shift and the human doctor can look at Nathan."

After giving him an "I whack bad Wolves" look, Meg limped out of the examination room.

"Let me give you a hand down," Lorenzo said, bracing a hand under Simon's elbow. "I won't offer a painkiller because I don't know how a *terra indigene* would react."

Simon didn't know how he would react to human painkillers either, but he thought giving Meg a couple of licks would make him feel better. He always felt comforted when he gave her hand a couple of licks while they watched a movie. But what about Nathan?

"Tell Jane to have Meg hold one of the chamomile cookies for a minute and then give a bit to Nathan," he said.

Lorenzo studied him. "So the sedating quality isn't just carried in *cassandra sangue* blood? Just having Meg hold something provides enough contact to transfer some of that calming effect?"

Cassandra sangue blood had been used to make the drug feel-good, which could make someone so passive he couldn't respond to any kind of threat. It was easy to argue that taking blood from the girls was a bad thing, especially when the girls were treated like livestock. But Simon was suddenly reluctant to tell anyone, even Lorenzo, that a blood prophet might slip a mild tranquilizer to someone just by handling food.

After all, the comfort *he* felt might just be from giving his friend an "I'm with you" lick.

"The cookies always taste better if Meg handles them," Simon finally said.

Lorenzo seemed to consider that for much too long. "That's definitely something to think about. Now, you shift and get out of here so I can look at your friends."

He hurt just as much in Wolf form, and his forelegs didn't want to take his weight because his shoulders weren't working quite right. But he hobbled out of the examination room, swiftly replaced by Nathan.

<Have to stay Wolf until I heal,> he told Vlad.

<Considering what Meg had done to her hair, you do not want her to paint your tail orange.> Not having a tail, Vlad sounded amused instead of sympathetic. <Montgomery has taken Theral to the hospital. Burke is going to talk to

us about what happened here and at the stall market. I'll interpret for you. Or Elliot can.>

<Elliot?> He didn't see his sire. <Where's Sam?>

<At the Green Complex with John and Skippy. They're well guarded. Blair will bring the Wolf bed from HGR's office to your apartment.>

Yeah, he wasn't going to be jumping up on a bed for the next few days, and sleeping on something cushiony would feel better than sleeping on the hard floor.

Meg stood by the open office door, staring out at the square. But when Nathan, in Wolf form, limped out of the examination room, she turned and stomped back to where the three of them were standing.

At another time, it would have been funny—Meg in a stompy-bison mood with her puppy-fuzz hair and a determined look in her gray eyes. Now . . .

Please don't whack me, Simon thought, grateful when Vlad stepped between the Wolves and the blood prophet.

"Nathan is coming home with us," Meg said. "He needs quiet and rest as much as Simon, and if he's in the Wolfgard Complex, the puppies will pester him."

Vlad knew the adult Wolves wouldn't allow that. But the Sanguinati was oddly silent. Of course, all Simon could see at the moment was Vlad's back and not Meg's face.

"Nathan is coming home with us."

A moment of surprised silence. <Did Meg just growl at you?> Simon asked Vlad.

<Yes. So make up your mind about who is going where before she decides to do more than growl to make her point,> Vlad replied.

Simon thought about Nathan, trapped and alone in the overturned bus, cut by glass and the sharp rocks that had been thrown at him through the broken windows. Which would be more comfort, being with the pack at the Wolfgard Complex or being with a smaller pack that included Meg?

He looked at Nathan. <Do you want to come with us?>

<Yes.>

<Tell Blair to bring Nathan's bed to my apartment too,> Simon told Vlad. <He can stay with me . . . with us . . . until he heals.>

<You sure?>

<Meg is sure, so I'm sure.>

Even though he wasn't going to participate, Elliot felt the interview with the police would have more weight if it was held in the consulate's conference room, and Tess agreed. That was why she and Nyx were sitting across from Captain Burke—and why they'd chosen the seats that would keep Burke from noticing Vlad, in his smoke form, blending into the shadows in a corner of the room.

<Burke looks nervous about being in a room with us,> Tess said.

<He should be nervous,> Nyx replied.

Burke held up a small notebook and pen. "All right if I take notes?"

"Of course," Tess replied. She saw the flash of alarm in the man's eyes when her hair began to coil, but the hair remained brown, a sign that she wasn't feeling angry or threatened.

After a moment's hesitation, Burke opened the notebook. "Mr. Wolfgard said he'd been warned to leave the stall market, that they were in danger. I'm assuming that warning came from Ms. Corbyn?"

"Yes," Tess said.

"What can you tell me about what happened here?"

Tess told him what she knew. She'd been in A Little Bite. John Wolfgard had been unpacking books in HGR's stock room, and Elliot Wolfgard had been doing some paperwork at the consulate when they all heard a weird-sounding howl. Then Sam and Skippy howled a warning that brought them running in time to see Meg dash up the stairs to the efficiency apartments and fall, cutting her knee. John grabbed the youngsters and took them away before Meg began to speak, leaving Elliot and Tess to hear the prophecy.

No, they didn't take notes. They'd been unprepared, and there was no time. Meg had held on for as long as she could before speaking. The prophecy? Thieves entering the apartments to search for something. Danger to Simon, to everyone who had gone on the field trip to the stall market. Meg had fainted out of fear of what she'd seen. By then many of the *terra indigene* who had been in the Market Square had gathered in response to the howls.

Elliot called Simon. Meg was taken to the medical office. Tess, Nyx, and Blair removed the personal belongings from the apartments to thwart the would-be thieves. They were in the process of moving the belongings to a safe place when the thieves must have broken in. As far as the Others could tell, none of the furnishings provided with the apartments were taken. There was some urine on the floor of Merri Lee's apartment. Assuming it was some kind of gesture of contempt, Tess had cleaned it up.

No, she hadn't seen a vehicle and could only assume there had been at least one human.

<He knows enough about us to know that Blair could sniff the area and tell him how many thieves had come up the stairs from the street-side door,> Nyx said. <Could even tell him how many intruders had entered each apartment.>

<Which is one reason why Blair isn't at this meeting,> Tess replied. The other reason being that the dominant enforcer was too furious about the attacks to be trusted around any human, even one who usually would be tolerated.

"That's it," Tess said, looking past Burke. "Anything *you* want to add about the attack at the stall market?"

Burke jerked as Vlad shifted to human form and joined them.

Watching Vlad, Tess thought the decision to close their stores to the general human population was a good one. She didn't think the Sanguinati or the Wolves were going to have much tolerance for human misbehavior for a long time.

Vlad placed his hands flat on the table and leaned toward Burke. "The rallying cry of the humans who attacked us was 'Humans first, last, and always.'"

"That sounds like an HFL rallying cry, but there is no proof that the HFL movement planned the attack," Burke said.

"The shots came from behind us," Vlad continued. "Two guns, two shooters. I heard four shots. I don't know who else was hit. I don't think they'd intended to shoot across that much distance and take the chance of hurting humans. I think they had planned to lure us to the back half of the building and wait until we were close to the table where men were selling what looked like trinkets but the packages they handed to their customers made me think weapons were being sold."

"Which would be illegal at that stall market," Burke said. "There are knife and gun shows where weapons are bought and sold, but selling weapons at the weekly stall and farmers' market is a violation of permissions granted to the building's owners by the city." He sighed. "But in the chaos that followed the shootings, and the amount of . . . merchandise . . . that was rearranged by gusts of wind, it's not likely we'll find the guns."

Burke's mobile phone rang. "Excuse me for a moment."

Tess watched sadness fill Burke's eyes as he said, "I'll be there as soon as I can."

"Problem, Captain?" Vlad asked when Burke ended the call.

"That was Lieutenant Montgomery calling from the hospital. Officer Mac-Donald didn't survive his wounds."

The three *terra indigene* exchanged a look.

"We're sorry for your loss," Vlad said.

"We liked him," Tess said.

Burke put his notebook and pen in his pocket, a sign he was preparing to leave. The sadness had burned out of his blue eyes, leaving behind a fierce fire. "I may not be able to find the guns used to kill my officer and the Crow, but I will damn well find their killers. That's a promise."

Tess looked at Vlad, who straightened up as Burke pushed away from the table and rose.

"You won't have to look far," Vlad said. "You'll find them among the dead."

Burke stared at him.

Vlad smiled, a bitter yet satisfied expression. "I wasn't close enough to stop them from shooting, but I caught them before they could blend in with the other humans and escape."

Burke continued to stare. "Anything I should know about those deaths? Anything that would make someone think a Sanguinati was responsible?"

Vlad shrugged. "Lots of things flying around when Air blew to the rescue. Sharp things that might slice a person's throat. Easy enough for someone else to slip in all that blood and fall the wrong way, breaking his neck."

Burke nodded. "That's plausible. I imagine quite a few people had similar, if less fatal, injuries."

"Quite a few, according to the special news report I heard," Vlad said.

In other words, nothing that would point to one of us killing "innocent" humans, Tess thought. *Of course, there were attackers who were killed by tooth or claw. But that's a problem for the city and the police.*

Burke pulled out a card and handed it to Vlad. "I need to get to the hospital. If you think of anything else, let me know. Or give Lieutenant Montgomery a call."

"Tell Lieutenant Montgomery and Merri Lee that we tidied up the apartments and put things back as best we could remember," Tess said. "We don't want them to be alarmed if they notice that something isn't exactly the way they left it this morning."

"I'll tell them."

Someone knocked harder on Simon's front door.

Meg jerked awake and caught the book sliding off her lap before it conked Simon on his already sore head. She set it aside, pushed herself off the sofa, then stepped around tails and limbs in order to answer whoever was knocking on the unlocked door.

Simon and Nathan stirred, even looked like they were going to try to stand up and challenge the intruder.

"You two." She pointed at them. "*Stay.*"

Grumbling and limping, she reached the door and opened it, saying, "It wasn't locked for a reason."

Steve Ferryman stared at her. "You cut your hair."

Meg huffed. "Yes, it looks like puppy fuzz. No, you can't pet it."

He worked hard not to smile. Then they both heard at least one Wolf trying to get to his feet.

"Simon, stay!" Meg snapped.

The whine sounded more like an annoyed protest, but it was still a whine.

"He needs to rest, so I won't come in," Steve said. "What happened at the stall market is all over the local news. I came by to let you know that the Intuits and Others on Great Island will give you any help you need. And to bring you this." He set a large basket just inside the door. "Wolf cookies for them, including freshly baked chamomile, and a couple of sandwiches and bakery treats for you."

"Thank you."

He looked at her knee. "You okay?"

She looked at her heavily bandaged knee, which was wrapped that way to prevent the Wolves from licking the wound. "It's not a serious wound. I was trying to locate the source of the pins-and-needles feeling and fell on the stairs."

"And spoke prophecy."

"Yes." Meg shuddered. She couldn't recall the images she'd seen, which was for the best right now, but she still felt residual terror because of what she'd seen.

She jolted when Simon and Nathan howled. So did Steve.

"Are they hurt?" he asked. "I mean, freshly hurt?"

"No, that's the 'We want the cookies' howl," Meg replied.

"Gotcha." Steve took a step back. "You take care, Meg. And call us if you need anything."

"I will." She hesitated, but he was here. "The girls who were rescued from the compound. How are they doing?"

"Better now that we've lessened the visual stimuli in their rooms. The girls have a very fine line between enough and too much stimulation or information. The woman we hired to help them has a good feel for where that line is. The more successful outings the girls experience, the easier it is for them to let someone know when they've had too much. Hopefully they'll learn other ways besides cutting to cope when they're feeling overwhelmed."

"They're *cassandra sangue*," Meg said. "Eventually, they're going to cut."

"But not as soon, and even once they start, maybe not as often."

She thought of the information Jackson Wolfgard had sent about *cs821*. "Wait. Another *cassandra sangue* who is living with the Wolfgard in the Northwest is revealing visions through drawings." She rubbed her left arm, trying to quiet the prickling. "Maybe that is something other girls could do to delay cutting."

"Other girls," Steve said softly. "But not you."

"No, not me." The prickling faded with the words, confirmation of a truth.

Steve took another step back. "Thanks for the suggestion. Get some rest, Meg."

She closed the door, hefted the basket, and limped to the kitchen, ignoring the soft, whiny howls coming from the living room.

Were injured Wolves usually this whiny, or were they trying to play the sympathy card to get more attention . . . and more cookies? She'd ask Jane when the bodywalker dropped by this evening to check on the patients.

After putting away the food that needed refrigeration, she limped back to the living room with a tray that held a sandwich, two small plates with various flavors of cookies, and a pitcher of water for all of them. She filled Simon's and Nathan's water bowls halfway, then poured the rest of the water into her glass.

She didn't want to watch television while they ate. And the radio kept talking about the attack at the stall market, so she couldn't listen to that either, especially after hearing the one report. . . .

No. Simon was hurt, and Nathan was hurt, his face all cut up from the broken glass and whatever else the people had thrown at him while he was trapped in the bus. So, no, she wasn't going to tell anyone yet that hearing Nicholas Scratch commenting about the attack in Lakeside had made her skin buzz.

CHAPTER 50

Watersday, Maius 26

Monty rubbed his hands over his face and looked around the efficiency apartment.

Long day. Long, terrible day. There would be physical and emotional repercussions. There would be the potential for reprisals. Local members of the Humans First and Last movement were loudly blaming the Others for the deaths, injuries, and destruction of property. If the Others had stayed in their designated piece of the city, where they belonged—if they belonged in *any* part of Lakeside—the incident wouldn't have occurred, turning a friendly place like the stall market into a battleground. Mayor Rogers had waffled when interviewed, refusing to acknowledge that members of the HFL movement had incited the conflict and had been responsible for the shooting death of a police officer.

Nicholas Scratch, on the other hand, hadn't waffled. Speaking from a safe location in Toland, he had been heavy on condolences for the families of the slain and emphasized how the HFL movement was rallying the whole Northeast Region to provide emotional support and physical assistance to those families. And he laid the blame on the *terra indigene* in the Lakeside Courtyard for making the people at the stall market feel so threatened, they had lashed out. And while it was regrettable that a police officer had been killed, along with several other humans caught in a senseless fight, such a reaction should have been expected.

The most chilling statement was made by Elliot Wolfgard when reporters cornered him after a meeting with the mayor.

"The earth natives who reside in Courtyards are property managers, the middlemen between humans and the rest of the terra indigene. *We may speak for the earth natives who live in the surrounding wild country, but they are Thaisia's final voice, and they will decide what happens next."*

And they, whoever they were, could not be bargained with, because anyone who managed to find them didn't survive. That was assuming humans could communicate with them at all.

Tess had done a fair job of putting all the personal belongings back where she'd found them. If he'd walked in unprepared, he would have known someone had gone through his things, would have sensed differences before he searched out the confirming details. Something folded a little bit off or put in the drawers in a different order. Since he'd been told the Others had taken his and Lizzy's things and then put them back, he'd given drawers and closet no more than a cursory look.

Going into the little kitchen, Monty cracked open a bottle of whiskey and poured himself a healthy glass. He didn't drink much, but tonight he wanted something to smooth off the edges, especially since Lizzy wasn't here.

When he called the Denbys to tell them about Lawrence MacDonald, Eve had insisted on Lizzy staying with them overnight. There were unanswered questions about the attempted break-ins. He didn't doubt there had been an attempt, just as he didn't think the timing of the break-in and stall-market attack was coincidence. But Boo Bear and the jewels were gone. The people in Toland who were involved with Elayne's death had to know that. He didn't think Captain Felix Scaffoldon was directly involved in Elayne's murder, but he'd bet the captain was keeping someone in the information loop.

Which meant there was still a piece missing. Someone was still searching for something and thought it had reached Lakeside. Could some of the jewels have been hidden in something besides Boo Bear?

Monty stood absolutely still, letting that thought coil around him.

Something in a story he'd been reading to Lizzy before he'd been transferred to Lakeside. Pages of a book had been cut to form a secret compartment. She'd been excited when he'd read that, had wanted to turn one of her own books into a hiding place for secrets. He'd intended to look for a used book so that she wouldn't ruin one of her new books. But she hadn't brought any books with her, just . . .

"The diary," Monty whispered. He set the whiskey glass down and rushed over to the dresser, pawing through the drawers. Why bring a diary if Lizzy had lost the key? Unless the diary wasn't being used as a diary but was, in fact, another hiding place, and Lizzy had never been the person who had the key.

He checked the closet, checked the suitcases, checked under the bed and behind the few bits of furniture in the apartment. He checked under the mattress, shook out all the bath towels and extra linen. When he was done, he searched it all again.

Then he sat on the narrow bed and thought for a long time.

Tess had returned everything except the locked diary.

CHAPTER 51

Earthday, Maius 27

It was early morning when Tess walked into one of the Courtyard school's classrooms to wait for Nyx. No one would be there to interrupt them or ask questions. Equally important, the school had been built in the interior of the Courtyard, so humans didn't have even a glimpse of it from the surrounding city streets. Most humans didn't know it existed.

Yesterday's attempted break-in didn't make sense. Trying to snatch Boo Bear in order to reclaim the jewels that had been hidden inside him would have made sense. The Sanguinati made it a point to learn about things that had value in the human parts of the world, and Nyx had told her that the jewels that had been concealed in Boo Bear were worth a lot of money.

But Boo Bear had been handed over to the Toland police, and the bear had been stitched up by the Wolfgard bodywalker so that no one would suspect that anyone had poked around inside the bear's body. Thieves shouldn't be looking for sparklies among Montgomery's possessions. Not anymore.

No, this wasn't about jewels. This was about secrets hidden inside a pink book.

Nyx flowed into the room as her typical blended form of smoke and human. "I brought the book."

"Now we just need . . . ," Tess began. She stopped and turned toward the door. Her hair began to coil in anticipation of dealing with the noisy intruder. Then she blinked in surprise as the Courtyard's dominant enforcer entered the room.

Blair Wolfgard usually moved quietly because it was his nature, but he wasn't making an effort to approach with any stealth as he walked in and shook a small toolbox.

"Tools aren't that easy to acquire right now, so I'm not handing them over unless I know what you intend to do with them," he growled.

"You don't have to hand over anything," Tess said. "You just have to open the lock on this book. That's why I told you to bring your tiny tools."

Nyx tipped her head. "That sounded nasty, but I'm not sure why."

The Wolf showed his teeth and held out his hand. "Give me that thing."

Nyx handed him the pink book with gold stars on the cover.

Blair fingered the catch. "Where's the key?"

"Don't know," Tess replied. "That's why you're here with your tiny tools. We need to know what's in that book."

"Why?"

"Because Meg saw a pink book with gold stars that is connected to a secret. And because someone is still searching for something that the Lizzy brought with her."

"You care if anyone knows we opened it?" Blair asked.

"No."

He selected a tool and broke the lock.

Good thing we aren't interested in locking it again, Tess thought when Blair handed her the somewhat mangled book, picked up his toolbox, and left.

Opening the book, Tess studied the writing. "I can't picture an adult using a pink book with gold stars, but this writing doesn't look like a child's."

"No, it doesn't," Nyx agreed. "But female, based on the human handwriting I've seen."

"Time to find out what it says." Tess settled a hip on the teacher's desk and started to read.

Meg dreamed she was a luscious cake and someone kept licking her frosting.

She jerked awake when Vlad said, "You'd better stop that before she catches you."

Pushing herself upright on the sofa in Simon's living room, she stared at Simon and Nathan, who were giving her an "I don't know what he's talking about" look.

The last time Wolves had given her that "too innocent to be believed" look was when she discovered empty containers stacked in a cupboard in her sorting room—containers that had been full of Wolf cookies when she'd gone to lunch that day.

"You two have had enough frosting," she muttered.

"How are you feeling, Meg?" Vlad asked.

Placing her feet carefully to avoid stepping on toes or tails, Meg stood up and took stock. Stiff, sore, hungry. And she really needed to pee—and probably wasn't the only one. "I'm okay. I need to use the toilet. Would you open the door so Simon and Nathan can go outside? When Jane looked at them last evening, she said it would be better if they didn't shift at all for another day."

"Sure. You need help going up the stairs?"

"No, I can do it."

As she went up the stairs—one stair at a time since the bandaged knee didn't bend well—she heard Simon and Nathan struggling to get to their feet.

Jane Wolfgard would be here to check on the Wolves and Henry. She would ask the Wolf bodywalker to suggest some quiet activities that would keep Wolves occupied while they recovered. And Dr. Lorenzo should be arriving soon to check on her. She really hoped she could convince him that the Others knew he'd taken good care of her and it was all right to remove the bandages and let her take a shower. It was, after all, just a cut.

Even the Controller, who had valued her skin for profit, hadn't made this much of a fuss over her well-being. Then again, the *terra indigene* valued *her* more than they valued her skin.

You have no reason to feel guilty, Meg told herself. But she did feel guilty, and she dreaded the scolding that was bound to come now that things were quieter.

She would wait until Dr. Lorenzo and Jane had made their visits. And then, once Simon and Nathan were settled with a dish of food and some water, she would walk over to the other side of the Green Complex and visit Henry.

"Well," Tess said a while later. "This explains why the HFL movement is still after the Lizzy. But I don't think it's sufficient proof that humans will do anything about it. They could say Elayne Borden made it up to cause trouble."

"Would they have killed her if she'd made up what she wrote in the book?" Nyx asked.

"Truth or lie, it would have caused trouble," Tess replied. "There are a lot of accusations here by a woman who wasn't as important as she'd believed." She might have felt a stir of pity for Elayne Borden if the woman's judgment and actions hadn't brought the trouble to Lakeside through the presence of the Lizzy. "Humans will say she wrote these things out of spite, or jealousy that the man who was living with her and making promises to her was also mating with other women. They'll say she's trying to discredit the HFL movement as a way to get back at him."

Nyx thought about that for a moment. "Whether humans believe it or not doesn't matter. It is human confirmation of what the *terra indigene* already know. We need to show this book to Vlad and Grandfather Erebus."

"Simon is the leader of this Courtyard. He should be told first," Tess said, wondering if there was a potential power struggle between the Sanguinati and the Wolves. There had been some tension between the two groups because of Meg.

"He is wounded and needs rest. Vlad and Grandfather are not injured. Besides, this problem began in Toland, and the Sanguinati control the Courtyard there." Nyx paused. "In fact, the Sanguinati control the Courtyards in every human city that is a major port on the eastern coast. Urban settings suit our way of hunting, so we're the best form of *terra indigene* to watch those places."

Tess couldn't argue about Simon needing rest. She hadn't realized the Sanguinati controlled so many of the Courtyards in Thaisia, although what Nyx said about them fitting into urban settings made sense. They had that much in common with Harvesters, who were also drawn to the glut of prey packed into cities.

If the Sanguinati were usually selected to control the Courtyards in port cities, why was Simon the leader in Lakeside, the major human port on Lake Etu? Why choose a Wolf when there was such a strong gathering of vampires here, not to mention the presence of Erebus? Had they yielded to a leader from a different gard by choice, or had they been *asked* to yield?

"We'll show this to Vlad and Grandfather Erebus," Nyx said again.

"All right. But we should show it to Henry and Elliot too. And we should wait until Simon has a chance to see it before we make any decisions. Whatever we do with this information will affect Lakeside and our Courtyard."

"In that case, Blair, as the dominant enforcer, should be included as well."

"Agreed."

She and Nyx settled into a thoughtful silence as they considered all the choices. Just like so many decisions they had made recently, whatever the Others in Lakeside did now would ripple through the whole of Thaisia. That made Tess wonder if it was this book or Simon Wolfgard who had been the real target yesterday.

Henry sat in the summer room beneath his apartment, sanding a wooden paw. The right side of his face hurt, and the furrow left by the bullet that struck him would leave a scar he would carry as human and Grizzly. He wasn't concerned about that. Some scars were a part of life, while others . . .

Catching Meg's scent, he raised his head and watched her approach his apartment. Then, when she realized he was in a summer room like the one she shared with Simon, he waited while she looked at him through the screen door.

"You can come in," he finally said.

She opened the door and limped to the table he used for all kinds of work.

"What are you making?" she asked as she studied the pieces on the table.

"A replacement for Boo Bear."

She reached for the head, then hesitated and looked at him for permission. When he nodded, she picked it up and explored the wooden bear head with her fingers.

"The carving is done. I'll finish sanding the pieces this morning and give them to the seamstress to attach to the cloth body she made." He put down the sandpaper and paw, sat back, and waited. She looked unhappy, and he was partly responsible for that because some scars were a part of life, while others . . .

Meg set the bear head on the table. "I didn't make a cut on purpose. I fell on the stairs."

"I know," he rumbled gently. "I also know if you hadn't fallen, if you hadn't bled and spoken prophecy, we would have known something was going to happen at the efficiency apartments because you sensed that much without cutting, but we wouldn't have known about the attack at the stall market. We wouldn't have had any warning about that, wouldn't have had time to call for help—and more of us would have died."

"Are you mad at me?"

Henry shook his head, a small motion since the movement made his face hurt. "No, Meg, I'm not angry. This isn't simple, and it's . . . hard . . . for us. I am grateful that you gave us warning, and I am sad that you have another scar."

"I'm not sad about this scar," she said softly, waving a hand toward her knee. "I *am* sad that you'll have a scar."

He smiled carefully. "I'm not sad about this scar. I got it saving Simon's life . . . just as you got your scar because you were taking care of us."

"It feels different, this scar."

"It's a sign of a caring heart. It should feel different."

She looked at the head and paws of the bear he had carved for the Lizzy. "We take care of each other, don't we?"

"Yes, we do."

A howl rose from the other side of the Green Complex.

Meg sighed. "I thought Simon would sleep longer. I'd better go before he does something foolish."

Henry watched her walk back to Simon's apartment. There were two grown Wolves staying there right now. He found it interesting that Meg had known it was Simon calling to find her.

Simon hobbled after Meg. Trees and bushes prevented line of sight between the human streets and the complexes where the Others lived, but the buildings had been located close enough to make use of the utilities the humans had to provide for the Courtyard and yet as far back from human sight as possible. Not an easy compromise, and yet the *terra indigene* had made it work. Had no alternative but to make it work, because someone had to keep watch and report behavior that would indicate the humans had become too much of a danger to Thaisia and all the creatures who lived there.

Despite his sister, Daphne, being shot and killed a couple of years ago, being able to hear the cars driving by hadn't made him feel edgy. But he felt vulnerable now. He couldn't rush forward to challenge an enemy or run fast enough to get out of the way if the enemy was too strong to face alone. Right now, he couldn't protect his pack, couldn't protect Meg.

He caught up to her when she reached the kitchen garden. It was, maybe, two stones' throws from the Green complex, but he panted with the effort to walk even that far.

At least Meg seemed to be feeling better. Dr. Lorenzo had put a smaller bandage on her knee, mostly to keep it clean—and to discourage anyone from licking the healing cut.

He hadn't licked the cut last night after Meg fell asleep on the sofa. Neither had Nathan. But licking her hand and foot, which had dangled off the sofa right in front of Wolf noses, had soothed them both enough that they could sleep for a couple of hours before their injuries made them hurt again. Didn't seem like a bad thing to do, and if she'd been awake, he was sure Meg would have agreed to let them have a couple of licks for medicinal purposes, but maybe he should have asked permission first. After all, Meg was Meg, not a bottle of medicine.

"Look, Simon. The seeds we planted are sprouting!"

Little green things. Not edible yet. Wouldn't be edible for weeks and weeks. He wanted some water.

Simon looked at the pump nearby. The pump and the well had been there before the city had put in pipes for its utilities, and the Others still used that water, along with water gathered in rain barrels, for the food they planted.

<Meg? Water?>

<Meg will pump water for us?> Nathan asked, joining him.

She couldn't hear *terra indigene* speech and he couldn't shift to ask.

"*Arroo?*" Simon hobbled to the pump, followed by Nathan. "*Arroo?*"

Meg looked at the pump and then at the garden. She limped to the pump. "You think the plants need water?"

He didn't know about the plants, but the Wolves would sure like some.

Nathan whined, then licked the pump's spout.

"Oh, *you* want water." Meg studied the pump for so long the Wolves sat down to wait.

"I wasn't paying attention to the water when we planted the seed part of the garden, but I think I can do this," she finally said.

Well, yes, she could work the pump, and water did come out. It wasn't a trickle that could be lapped, and the bucket that should have been under the spout to catch the water wasn't there. Eventually they got their drink, mostly from licking the water that was dripping off each other.

"Sorry," Meg said. "There must be a trick to it."

Simon stood there, unable to shake off the water because the movement would make his shoulders and forelegs hurt.

Someone coughed lightly.

He tried to pivot and almost lost his balance.

<It's Vlad,> Nathan said.

Vlad let out a gusty sigh that sounded more like a laugh. "I leave the three of you alone for just a little while, and look what trouble you get into."

<Didn't get into trouble,> Simon growled. <Just got wet.>

"The bucket gets blown around, so it's kept in the toolshed," Vlad told Meg, pointing to the small structure.

"I wasn't coming out to *do* anything except look at the garden," she said. "But Simon and Nathan wanted a drink." She looked at the Wolves. "You're very wet."

"They'll dry," Vlad said.

<See how much sympathy *you* get when Meg dumps water on you,> Simon grumbled.

<Meeting has been called,> Vlad said, no longer sounding amused. <There's something you need to see before we decide what to do.>

<I can't shift today.>

<No humans are invited to this meeting, so you don't need to look human.>

<Meg shouldn't be out here alone.> A Hawk passed over Simon, a reminder that there were *terra indigene* keeping watch.

<She won't be alone. And we won't be far. We're meeting in my apartment.>

"Vlad?" Meg said, looking from the vampire to the Wolves.

"Business meeting. Simon is needed," Vlad said easily.

"But he should rest today," she protested.

"I know, but this can't wait."

She wanted to protect him, and that pleased Simon in all kinds of ways because he wanted to protect her too. But a leader couldn't always be protected, so he started back toward the Green Complex and Vlad's apartment.

Vlad talked to Meg for another minute, then caught up to him.

<Nathan will stay with her,> Vlad said.

<He can't protect her against intruders.>

<No, he can't, but he can sound the alarm if needed. And several of the ponies just showed up, including Tornado and Twister. No one will get near Meg while they're grazing around the complex.>

Telling himself to be satisfied with that, Simon walked into Vlad's apartment. When he saw who else was in the room, he knew this wasn't just about yesterday's attacks but something more . . . and worse.

Meg opened the door to the summer room beneath her apartment and waited for Nathan to go in. She hoped all the cuts on his face and forelegs would heal without scarring. It was upsetting enough to think of Henry, as man or Grizzly, with one scar along his right cheek. She didn't want Nathan to look in the mirror every day and be reminded of human betrayal.

What did the Others think about her scars? Did the old scars matter to any of them except the few who understood what the number of scars meant to her lifespan? What about humans? Was it difficult for them to look at her scars? She didn't have any on her face, but the shorts and short-sleeve tops that were practical to wear in the summer revealed some of the scars on her arms and legs.

None of the humans who were her friends had said anything. Not to her anyway. What about the deliverymen? By wearing summer clothes, was she advertising that she was a *cassandra sangue*? With the plight of the girls who had been released and abandoned, and the mounting number of deaths caused by their inability to cope with the outside world, more people would understand the significance of evenly spaced scars. Wouldn't they?

Although, now that she thought about it, the blood prophets weren't being mentioned on the news or in the newspapers anymore. Now the news was about the foods that would be added to next month's ration books and the shortages that were being predicted—and the accusations that the Others were to blame for the decrease in available food and the increase in prices. That didn't have much effect on her. Except for pizza, she bought all her food from the Market Square stores, which were supplied by *terra indigene* farms, but Merri Lee and Ruth had said a couple of times that they were glad they were allowed to shop in the Market Square and even more relieved that they would receive a share of the food grown in the Courtyard.

"*Arroo?*" Nathan queried softly.

How long had she been standing there, holding the door open?

"Busy brain," she said, entering the room. Picking up the book she'd left on the table, she chose the new lounge chair that faced the Green Complex's courtyard. Merri Lee and Michael Debany had given her two lounge chairs as a housewarming present. Ruth Stuart and Karl Kowalski had given her a small round table and two chairs that provided her with a place to eat or work on a project.

Someone, probably Vlad or Tess, had done a little rearranging in order to move the Wolf beds into the summer room.

After a confirming sniff to determine which bed was his, Nathan lay down, put his head on his paws, and dozed off.

Meg didn't know where her human friends were today. In mourning, certainly. Were they at the MacDonalds' house, helping Lawrence's parents and Theral do whatever was done at a time like this?

She had seen videos, and sometimes live demonstrations, of girls being abused or even killed, but she didn't have many training images of men being killed. Instead, there were images that, put together with another image, would mean a kind of death. A wrecked car and a sympathy card. A gun and a cremation urn. Not that the Controller or Walking Names had told the girls what those combinations of images meant, but eventually she and Jean had figured it out.

Did the blood prophets who were floundering see that kind of combination of images as they made their final, fatal cut?

Meg shook her head as if that would dislodge the thoughts. When she realized she was rubbing her arms to relieve that pins-and-needles feeling, she also realized Nathan was awake and watching her.

"It's all right. The prickling is going away," she told him, which was true.

"Arroo."

Despite being hurt, he was still on guard. In her own way, so was she.

Meg opened her book and tried to read. But she couldn't settle into the story because she kept thinking of Henry carving a new bear for Lizzy. Here in the Courtyard, they looked after one another.

Lawrence MacDonald's friends were looking after his family, but what about Jenni and Starr? Was there some way she could take care of them?

She polished coins until they shone. A small token, a gesture of sympathy for the loss of a sister. And . . .

A big paw pushed against her thigh with considerable force.

Meg gasped. Nathan stood next to her chair, looking like he was about to howl his head off.

"I'm fine," she said, although how could she be fine if she'd just had a vision without cutting? That had happened only once, before the attack on the Courtyard earlier that year, when she'd been making deliveries during the day and suddenly thought she was driving at night.

"Rroo!" Decisive disagreement.

"I'm fine," Meg insisted. "I was *thinking*." She raised her hand to give him a reassuring pat and keep him quiet, then remembered not to touch his face. "I was thinking."

"*Arroo?*" Not convinced yet that she was fine, but listening.

"This is different, and I'm not sure how to explain it."

Nathan sat next to the lounge chair and waited.

"I was thinking about Jenni and Starr and if there was anything I could do for them. And then I saw something I could do. I thought it was a vision because I have visions. But it wasn't really a vision. It was my mind supplying an answer to the question by showing me doing something nice for them." Excited, she swung her legs over the side of the chair, which put her nose to nose with Nathan. "It wasn't blood-prophet thinking, it was regular-girl thinking!"

He sniffed her face and apparently decided there was no cause for alarm.

"Could you tell Julia Hawkgard that I'd like to see her?"

Nathan cocked his head. When she didn't say anything else, he went back to his bed and lay down. A minute later, Julia showed up.

"Is something wrong?" Julia asked.

"No," Meg assured her. "I just need a few things from the Market Square, and my knee . . ." She gestured to the bandaged knee. There was nothing that wrong with her knee. All she needed to do was avoid bending it so far that she would split the healing cut. She could have walked or driven her BOW, but Nathan would have come with her no matter what she said, and he needed to rest.

"Oh. Sure," Julia said. "What do you need?"

Meg told her what she wanted. While she waited for Julia to return, she wondered what the Others thought about her request. Maybe Julia thought it was something peculiar to humans. Or maybe the Hawk had understood the reason for the request. Either way, Julia returned swiftly with all the items.

While Simon was at his meeting and Nathan snoozed, Meg sat at the table in the summer room and polished two rolls of dimes until every coin shone.

Simon wasn't sure if Blair and Elliot shifted to Wolf because it was Earthday and they customarily were in this form on the day that was free of contact with humans, or if they didn't want him to feel uncomfortable about being the only one who wasn't in human form for this meeting.

Either way, once he chose a spot in Vlad's living room and lay down, Blair and Elliot settled on either side of him. Vlad, Nyx, and Erebus Sanguinati sat on chairs that faced the Wolves. That left Henry and Tess sitting at opposite ends of the room.

"There aren't many entries in the book that are of interest to us, so I'll just read those bits out loud," Tess said.

"Diary," Vlad said. "That kind of book is called a diary. Where did you get it?"

"I took it from Lieutenant Montgomery's apartment. It was in a drawer with the Lizzy's clothes, so it's likely that this came with her—and after Nyx and I read it, we realized this was the reason someone is still after the girl."

"The Lizzy is young," Erebus said. "What could one so young write down that would have so many hunters on her trail?"

"The Lizzy didn't write anything," Tess replied. "Elayne Borden, on the other hand . . ."

<Read it,> Simon said, eyeing the diary as he would an angry rattlesnake.

Tess read the entries. When she finished, Simon waited to hear what the rest of them would say, but no one spoke . . . unless he counted Blair growling.

"This confirms what the *terra indigene* already figured out, but now humans in government should be told why their people won't have enough food, why some possessions will be difficult to buy," Henry finally said.

"You think the humans in government don't already know?" Vlad sounded skeptical. "It's the rest of the humans who need to know that, as far as the HFL movement is concerned, the humans who have first claim on food live in Cel-Romano, and the humans in Thaisia will get the scraps, if there are any. Hunger will push them into trying to take more land from the rest of Namid's creatures."

<I agree with revealing this to human governments,> Elliot said. <But how do we do that? How many copies of that diary can be made?>

"Most of what was written is personal," Tess said. "I doubt it would be of interest to any human except Lieutenant Montgomery."

"What is important to the *terra indigene* can be distilled into a couple of paragraphs that will confirm to *our* leaders which humans are responsible for the shortages of food and materials," Vlad said. "That's all human governments need to know too."

<We should make two copies of the whole thing,> Elliot said. <Keep one copy for ourselves and give the other copy to the Toland Courtyard since they'll have to deal with the part of the trouble that's in their city.>

<It's not our place to howl this information to humans everywhere in Thaisia,> Simon said. <That choice must be made by the *terra indigene* taking care of each region of our land. We make decisions for Lakeside.>

"We've been making decisions for a lot more than Lakeside lately," Henry countered. "At the very least, the whole Northeast Region will abide by our decisions."

<Well, if we're making decisions for those who aren't . . .> Simon stopped. Was Montgomery not quite their own, or was he part of the human pack now? <I think the original diary should be given to Lieutenant Montgomery. That Elayne died so that the Lizzy could escape the bad humans and bring the words to him.>

Silence as they all thought about this.

"Two copies of this diary will be sufficient," Erebus said with a nod toward Elliot. "One for Lakeside and one for Toland. Vlad, when this meeting is finished, you will call Stavros. Tell him there are things he needs to know that cannot be discussed over the telephone."

Vlad nodded. "I'll call him and ask him to catch the next available train."

<I still think we should tell more humans,> Elliot said.

<It doesn't matter now how many humans know,> Simon said. <They lied to each other and tried to blame us in order to cause trouble. They deliberately did things so that their people will be hungry in the coming year in order to create more conflicts. Because of that, it's the *terra indigene* in the wild country who will decide what happens next.>

No one spoke as they considered the implications. Humans had little understanding about the *terra indigene* they could see. They had no understanding at all about the earth natives who lived in the wild country.

"Train. Train," Tess said. "When she spoke the last prophecy, Meg said that word twice. The Controller and his . . . *people* . . . spent years training her, so everything she says in prophecy has meaning."

"Stavros will be coming by train," Vlad said.

"And so will someone else. For good or ill, I think we should expect a second visitor."

Simon grunted with the effort to get to his feet. <Enough. I'll be able to shift tomorrow. Then I'll see how the human form feels and what limitations it may have.>

"I'll go over to the Three Ps now and make the copies of the diary," Tess said.

Since there was nothing more he needed to do at this meeting, Simon hobbled to the door, then had to wait for someone to open it. He wanted to walk a little and rest a lot. He wanted to curl up with Meg and get petted while she watched a movie.

He wanted to be strong and well enough to protect, just in case the second visitor who was coming to Lakeside turned out to be an enemy.

Jenni Crowgard returned to her apartment in the Green Complex early that evening. The Crowgard had spent the day together, mourning the loss of Crystal, not dissimilar to the way the humans had gathered to mourn the loss of Lawrence MacDonald.

Will the Crows open Sparkles and Junk tomorrow? Meg wondered. *Or will they abandon their shop in the Market Square?*

Feeling awkward, she knocked on Jenni's door . . . and tried not to stare when the Crow answered.

Jenni's black hair, usually shiny and well groomed, hung dull and unkempt around a face drawn by grief.

"I have something for you and Starr." Meg held out a small decorative box, one of the items Julia Hawkgard had picked up for her.

Jenni took the box and stared at it for a full minute before lifting the lid. She poured a few dimes into one hand. "Shiny," she whispered. "Coins aren't always so shiny. Crystal liked shiny coins. She kept them in a bowl on the counter."

"I know. That's why I polished these. I thought you could add these to the bowl in her honor." Meg stopped. "I don't know how to help, and I want to help."

"You helped. You warned Simon, but we didn't listen when he said we had to leave. There was so much shiny, so many treasures to look at and touch, we didn't want to listen. He had to wait, had to argue with us, and that gave the humans time to attack."

"Those men had planned to attack the *terra indigene*. It wasn't your fault, Jenni."

The Crow poured the dimes back into the box. "Doesn't change things. Crystal is dead. MacDonald is dead. And we have learned, again, that humans can't be trusted."

The anger in Jenni's eyes chilled Meg. "Jenni . . ."

"Our Meg can be trusted. Our Meg would not betray us."

"No, I wouldn't. Neither would Merri Lee or Ruth or the other humans who work here."

Jenni shrugged. Meg thought that was a very bad indication of how angry the *terra indigene* were about this latest clash between themselves and humans.

"Merri Lee and Ruth wouldn't betray the Crows or any of the *terra indigene*," Meg insisted. "Neither would Debany or Kowalski. They *wouldn't*."

Jenni stared at Meg. Then, finally, "Crystal being killed in that place. It wasn't their fault either."

Meg nodded, relieved to hear that much of a concession.

Jenni hesitated, then stepped back to close the door. "Thank you for the shinies."

"You're welcome."

Rubbing her arms, Meg returned to Simon's apartment—and wished she could believe that nothing was going to happen.

CHAPTER 52

Earthday, Maius 27

The girl waited for Jackson or Grace to fetch the dishes from her evening meal. Earlier in the day, she had opened the shutters that covered her window, wanting more light. A screen covered the window, and white paper was tacked outside the screen, preventing her from seeing anything. But she had heard them talking, growling. Upset.

Something bad had happened. Simon, the other Wolf she had drawn in that picture she'd made for Jackson, had been hurt. And because the bad had happened, something else would happen.

The girl looked at the drawing she'd made that day. Storm clouds and lightning. Cars full of people driving away from the storm. But on the other edge of the paper, something waited for the cars and the people—something she couldn't picture in her mind, something her hand refused to draw because it wasn't meant to be seen. It simply *was*.

And it, unseen and terrible, waited for the people in the cars.

Hearing a sound outside her door, the girl shoved the drawing under her bed before Jackson walked in carrying a mailing envelope. He placed the envelope at the foot of the bed.

"Meg, the Trailblazer, said we should take pictures for you to look at."

New images? She was ready to look at new images.

"Thank you." She must have said the right thing because he nodded and picked up the dishes she'd left on the desk.

She waited a minute. Then she carefully lifted the envelope's flap and removed the photographs.

Her breath caught as she looked at each one, drinking in the images.

"Not in order," she muttered as she rearranged the photos. "Need to be like . . . this."

A place. All the photos were different images of a wonderful place. But . . . where? Her old keepers used to identify images. How else could she tell someone what she saw when she was cut?

Nothing written on the backs of the photos, so she turned the envelope over. Carefully printed on the front was one word: Sweetwater.

The girl spent the rest of the evening listening to the Wolves howl as she studied the photographs.

CHAPTER 53

Moonsday, Maius 28

Monty didn't want to be included in the meeting with Mayor Franklin Rogers and Police Commissioner Kurt Wallace. He'd lost a good man, and the rest of his team were recovering from lesser injuries and the shock of the attack. And for some reason, his daughter was still a target of an unknown aggressor. But Captain Burke wanted him there since he dealt with the Courtyard and could offer an informed opinion.

Well, fine. He'd offer an informed opinion to His Honor. If there was going to be any criticism about actions at the stall market that led to human casualties, his men deserved to have him stand for them. Especially Lawrence MacDonald, who could no longer speak for himself.

Nodding to Captain Zajac, who had also been called to this meeting, Monty took a position to Captain Burke's left. Mayor Rogers sat behind his desk, a position of power. None of the police, including the commissioner, were invited to sit.

"Dreadful business," Mayor Rogers said. "Can't minimize the damage the Others did to human property, or the number of injured and dead that resulted from their attack."

"Counterattack," Zajac said at the same time Burke said, "Self-defense."

"If you read my report, you know that men connected to the Humans First and Last movement started the incident—and fired the shots that killed a police officer and one of the *terra indigene*," Zajac said. "Other HFL members attacked the Courtyard's bus, tipping it over and attacking the Wolf inside."

"They shouldn't have been there in the first place," Commissioner Wallace said sharply. "They should stay inside the Courtyard. Isn't that why businesses are required to make deliveries? So the majority of our population doesn't have to deal with those creatures? And, gods below, is there really an entity made of fire?"

There is much more, and worse, than a fire Elemental in the Courtyard, Monty thought, angry that all the effort he and his men had put into creating a dialogue with the Others could be destroyed by fools. Having a police commissioner pretend he didn't know about the Elementals after the storm that pounded the city back in Febros was beyond foolish; it was a level of denial that could get them all killed.

Zajac hesitated before answering. "It appears to be the case. And it's unlikely that it was a fluke gust of wind that tore the roof off the building or piled up heavy debris against the other set of doors, preventing anyone from getting out that way."

"Then the Others should be held accountable, should be required to pay for damages to the building as well as pay for all the cars that were burned," Rogers said.

"Pay for damages?" Monty repeated. "I guess the pledge you made when you replaced the previous mayor, who died because of his involvement in the HFL movement and his subsequent role in the deaths of several *terra indigene*, was nothing but political hyperbole."

"Now, see here . . . ," Rogers shouted.

"You pledged to work with the Courtyard to avoid future conflicts, and now you're trying to start a fight?"

"That's enough, Lieutenant," Burke said. His voice sounded mild, but his eyes sparked with a warning.

"You have anything to say about this, Burke?" Commissioner Wallace demanded.

Burke stared at Wallace. Then he looked at the mayor. "Three words. Jerzy. Talulah Falls."

Rogers and Wallace stiffened.

"You may want to check how many years are left on the land lease for this city before you suggest to *terra indigene* leaders that they keep their residents inside the Courtyard's fence," Burke said. "You may want to check how many years are left on the road and railway right-of-ways. If the Others don't renew the land lease, they can evict everyone in this city, the same as they did in Jerzy. Or they can make sure we can't leave."

"Are you suggesting that they'll block all the routes out of the city?" Rogers said.

"They closed us in with a snowstorm and glaciers blocking every road leading out of the city. I imagine they can be equally efficient even in warmer seasons," Burke said.

"That may be, but we have to consider people's reactions if we give the impression that the loss of human life is insignificant," Wallace said. "The way the Others retaliated . . ."

"The *terra indigene* defended themselves against an attack," Monty said. "They defended themselves and their human companions, one of whom was a wounded police officer, from the aggressive actions of humans who were, for the most part, not merchants but men who were there that day for the express purpose of starting a fight and killing or seriously injuring the Others. The *terra indigene*'s actions were their typical response to being attacked."

Before Rogers or Wallace could respond, Burke added, "The Others have not yet retaliated for the attack or for the HFL's attempt to kill Simon Wolfgard." After a moment of stiff silence from everyone else in the room, he continued. "Let's stop pretending this was a spur-of-the-moment action by some hotheads who didn't want a few Crows to buy some trinkets. The HFL wanted to stir things up, wanted to get people stirred up and angry at the Others so that no one looks too closely at what *they're* doing."

"You've made your dislike of the HFL movement quite clear," Rogers snapped.

"I certainly hope so, because the blood of the next human who dies in a conflict with the Others is on *your* hands," Burke snapped back.

"That's enough!" Wallace said, stepping forward. "You're out of line, Captain!"

Burke took a step back. "Say that after we find out what the HFL is going to cost this city." After giving Captain Zajac a sharp nod, he walked out of the mayor's office.

Monty rushed after him but didn't try to speak until they were in the car. "You've just made enemies of the mayor and police commissioner."

"The only thing *they* can kill is my career. I'll choose that over the alternative any day." Burke rubbed his hands over his face and blew out a breath. "Let it go, Lieutenant. For now, let it go."

Seeing no choice, Monty let it go. But Lizzy and the Denby children were playing in the Courtyard because someone still wanted something that had come to Lakeside with Lizzy. Until that outside threat, that *human* threat, was eliminated, he had to trust that Simon Wolfgard and the rest of the Others in the Courtyard would hold to their rule of not hurting the young—even if the young belonged to a species they considered an enemy.

Meg kept her eyes on the road, her hands on the steering wheel, and refused to say anything when Simon sighed—again.

"Meg, with the way you're driving, we can reach the Market Square faster by walking."

"I'm being careful. There's nothing wrong with being careful. You're still healing and don't need to be jostled."

"Dr. Lorenzo is waiting for us."

"He can examine Nathan first."

Okay, maybe she *was* going a bit too slow. Maybe the BOW couldn't go any slower and still be in motion. But she hadn't known it would be so upsetting to see a friend hurt. And he *was* hurt, even if he wanted to shrug it off. Which he couldn't do because his shoulders were still too bruised and sore from the beating he'd received during the fight. He couldn't raise his arms to hold the steering wheel, which was the reason she was driving them to the Market Square.

"Nathan needs to stay in human form for a full day to let that shape heal, so Skippy will be watch Wolf today," Simon said. "But Nathan will be nearby. And Henry will be working in his studio. He'll hear you if you need help. And Jake Crowgard will keep watch. So will Marie Hawkgard. And Nyx."

As she tried to decipher the message, she pressed on the BOW's power pedal, bringing it up to a typical speed.

"Why all the guards?" she finally asked. Simon hadn't indicated that anything unusual was happening today, and she hadn't had any pins-and-needles feelings either.

Simon looked out the passenger window. "Not guards, exactly. Just more *terra indigene* keeping watch."

"Why?" Crows were always keeping watch. And a Hawk or two always soared over the business area of the Courtyard. And Nyx had been spending more time at Howling Good Reads lately, so that wasn't unusual either. So why make a point of telling her who would be around when they were often around, especially when Skippy was the watch Wolf?

"The humans started that fight in the stall market, but now the monkeys on the radio and TV are yelling about how the surviving humans who were involved in the fight are in jail and we aren't. So we can't trust anyone who comes into the Liaison's Office. Not for a while."

Maybe never again? Meg wondered. Having a few humans spoil things for everyone could make an exciting story, but she didn't like it much when her friends suffered for it. "Those people have no right to be angry with you. You just defended yourself." Her hands tightened on the steering wheel. She stomped on the power pedal, and the BOW shot forward.

"Meg? Could you slow down?"

"You were the one in a hurry."

"Not that much of a hurry." Simon braced a hand against the door.

She lifted her foot—and heard him breathe.

"Is it . . . ?" He stopped. Sniffed delicately.

"Is it what?" she growled, knowing *exactly* why he'd sniffed.

"Nothing."

They were running out of road, so she slowed down a little more. "You were going to ask if it was that time of the month, weren't you?"

"I did not say those words." Then he added in a mutter, "Already learned *that* lesson."

She pulled into one of the wide parking spaces that were used by the earth native delivery trucks that brought in supplies from the *terra indigene* settlements and took back human-made products.

Meg turned off the BOW but made no move to get out, even when Simon opened his door. He looked at her, then settled back in his seat and closed the door.

"Do you think people will stop coming after Lizzy? Stop looking for whatever they think she has?"

"Yes, they will, because we found it."

She felt light-headed. It took a moment for her to identify the feeling of happiness mixed with relief. "You found it?"

"Something you told Tess helped her find the book that had secrets about the HFL movement. That's why humans were chasing the Lizzy. They wanted to get the book back before someone read the secrets."

Just because the Others found the book didn't mean Lizzy would be safe. "But no one knows you found it."

"The *terra indigene* already knew the secrets, Meg. We found out a few days ago. Now some humans will know too."

"Will they believe you?"

A long pause. "It doesn't matter if they believe the words or not."

"No, I guess it doesn't matter. People will stop coming after Lizzy, and that will be enough." She opened her door. "Come on. I need to get to work. Let's get our doctor visits over and done."

They walked the short distance to the medical office. Theral was at the reception desk. She looked pale, and her eyes were puffy, but she gave them a small smile. "Thanks for sending the flowers. My aunt and uncle . . . It meant a lot to them that you sent flowers picked in the Courtyard. And it means a lot that you're going to let them have Lawrence's share of the produce from the garden this year."

The examination room door opened. Nathan stepped out, looked at them, and said, "You're next."

But Meg stopped at the examination room door, despite seeing Dr. Lorenzo waiting for them. She studied Simon. "Sharing food is important. You did that for Lawrence's family?"

"We wanted them to know Officer MacDonald was . . . valued."

Friends were valued. Family—pack—was valued. And the loss of a member wasn't forgotten.

Meg walked into the examination room and let Dr. Lorenzo check her knee and make his notes. Happy that she no longer needed a bandage of any kind, she waited while Lorenzo poked and prodded Simon, wincing in sympathy when the Wolf tried to stifle a whine.

Simon was hurting plenty, but Dr. Lorenzo didn't think there was any permanent damage. Simon just needed time to heal. They all needed time to heal.

Feeling the prickling along one side of her back, she hoped they would have that time.

———

"Arooeeooeeoo! Arooeeooeeoo!"

Tess hurried out of the back door of A Little Bite with the coffee and bag of food she'd put together for Meg and Sam. And Skippy, who was the designated watch Wolf today.

"Meg isn't there yet, Skippy," Tess said as she walked toward the juvenile Wolf sitting by the back door of the Liaison's Office.

He turned his head, stared at Tess for a full count of five, then continued his yodeling *arroo*.

Sometimes his antics amused her. But there was nothing amusing about today, not with what Simon had to tell Lieutenant Montgomery. And now Vlad was holding the phone because someone wanted to talk to Simon—and she'd been asked to deliver the message and distract Meg and the youngsters.

Come on, Simon. How long does it take for a human doctor to figure out you're sore and bruised and you won't be chasing down a deer anytime soon?

Her hair started coiling and turned green. They had known a decision would be made in response to the trouble humans had caused with their lies, but receiving a decision through a phone call? That could not be good.

"Arooee—"

"I get to stay with Meg *for the whole day*."

Sam's excited voice, coming from the direction of the Market Square, interrupted the yodel. Skippy turned his head, focused, and rushed toward Sam, Meg, and Simon as they came abreast of the garages.

Simon said, "Not the whole . . . Skippy, no!" He stepped in front of Meg to prevent the youngster from knocking her down in his haste to greet her and get a cookie and get brushed and get whatever else Skippy got when he was supposed to be guarding Meg.

True to his skippy brain, the youngster tried to go between Simon's legs and ended up trapped when Simon tightened his knees.

"Skippy!" Sam grabbed the Wolf by the scruff. "Don't pester Meg!"

What's that human saying about a pot calling the kettle black? Tess thought.

Sam might be younger than Skippy, but he was more dominant. Maybe because, mentally, they were more on a par than the other Wolves, Skippy responded better to Sam than he did to the adults.

"Figured you wouldn't get much breakfast this morning, so I brought some," Tess said to Meg. Then she looked at Simon. <Someone wants to talk to you. Vlad is holding the phone.>

<Tell him to take a message, and I'll call—>

<*Now*, Simon. It's urgent.>

He watched her hair as it coiled and changed colors. Then he touched Meg's arm, a simple gesture that was somehow intimate.

"I have to take a phone call."

"All right." Meg watched him run to the back door of HGR. Then she looked at Sam. "You and Skippy wait for me by the office door." Finally she looked at Tess. "There's trouble."

No point denying it. "Yes."

"How bad?"

"We won't know until Simon is done with that phone call."

Meg hesitated. "Did I see this? When I fell and you listened, did I . . ."

"No."

"Are you sure?"

"Believe me, Meg. If you had said anything, even a hint that *this* phone call would come, I'd have told someone." Everyone. She had seen the look on Vlad's face when he realized what was on the other end of the phone line. Harvesters were an old form of *terra indigene* that had adapted their masking shape many times to be the most effective hunters. Wolves were also an old form of *terra indigene*. So were the Sanguinati.

But some forms of earth native were much, much older. And there were good reasons why they should be left undisturbed.

"Here." Tess held out the sack of food. "Mostly human food, but a couple of cookies for Skippy."

"The sandwiches and pastries are better than the ones you had before," Meg said, taking the sack.

"So far, Nadine's Bakery and Café has delivered what it promised."

"That's good."

"Come on, Meg!" Sam called.

"*Arooeeooeeoo!*"

Meg looked toward HGR's second-floor window, then hurried to open the office and get the noisy youngsters inside.

When they were gone, Tess saw the gate to Henry's yard open. The Grizzly tipped his head toward HGR's back door, but he didn't wait for her. She ran to the door. As she turned to close it, she noticed the black smoke rushing toward her. Three of the Sanguinati, followed by Blair and Elliot, also in a hurry.

She held the door for them, then followed them up to the bookstore's office to find how just how bad it was going to be.

Simon raced up the stairs to HGR's office. Just as well he was in human form; his forelegs wouldn't have supported an attempt to mount the stairs at that speed.

Vlad said nothing; just held out the phone. But Simon noticed the tremble in the vampire's hand.

"This is Simon Wolfgard."

It was not a voice meant to shape human words. It was not a voice that should have been heard over any device created by humans.

Simon sank into the chair. "Yes, I'll listen." And he did. For several minutes, he listened and said nothing. Then, "Yes, I understand." And he did.

By the time he hung up, the office was full of the individuals who would carry some of this weight along with him: Erebus, Vlad, Nyx, and Stavros; Blair and Elliot; Henry and Tess. But at the end of what was said, one individual had been singled out, and she wasn't in the room.

The sweet blood has changed things. You have changed because of her. We are intrigued by the humans who have gathered around your Courtyard, so we will give you some time to decide how much human the terra indigene *will keep.*

How much time was *some* time? And what, exactly, was he deciding to keep—the products humans made that the *terra indigene* found useful, or the pieces that, taken in total, made up the essential nature of humans? Was he supposed to decide if it was possible to have a human form of *terra indigene*? A century from now, would there be a Human and a human, like there was a Wolf and a wolf? What if there weren't enough *terra indigene* who were willing to become *that* human?

How much time was *some* time?

"So," Henry finally said. "The Elders have declared a breach of trust?"

"Yes." The consequences were going to roll through Thaisia like a terrible storm.

"Have they decided on extinction?"

Simon shivered. "Not yet."

Silence as the rest of them absorbed the words.

"What are you going to tell Montgomery?" Vlad asked.

"The truth."

CHAPTER 54

Moonsday, Maius 28

As Monty reached the doorway of Captain Burke's office, he heard an unfamiliar voice say, "Thanks for seeing me, especially at a difficult time. My condolences on the loss of one of your men."

Giving the visitor his typical fierce-friendly smile, Burke wagged a finger at Monty—a silent command to come in. "Appreciate the sentiment. As for seeing you, well, you caught a train and came to talk to us. The least we can do is listen to what you have to say. Lieutenant Montgomery, this is Greg O'Sullivan, an agent in the governor's newly formed Investigative Task Force. O'Sullivan, this is Crispin James Montgomery."

"It's a pleasure to meet you," O'Sullivan said, extending a hand toward Monty.

Monty shook the offered hand while he assessed the man. O'Sullivan looked to be in his early thirties. He had green eyes, dark hair that was cut short and starting to thin at the top. The lean build could be the luck of heritage or a deliberate result of diet and exercise. However, the skin on O'Sullivan's face was so tightly stretched over bone and muscle it lent the man a kind of burning intensity and made Monty think of a warrior who chose an austere life in order to be constantly ready for the next battle.

Am I the next battle? Something about the way O'Sullivan looked at him gave Monty the feeling the man already knew too much about him.

Monty and O'Sullivan sat in the visitors' chairs. Burke sat behind his desk—and waited.

Looking at the two men, Monty wondered if Burke was seeing a version of his younger self. O'Sullivan certainly came across as having the same kind of fierceness under a veneer of manners.

"It's your meeting," Burke finally said.

"Is this room secure?" O'Sullivan countered.

"Nothing you say here will go any further without your consent."

O'Sullivan sat back in the chair and crossed his legs at the ankles. "There is a file on you in the governor's office."

"Every police officer has a file," Burke replied easily. "For that matter, every government employee has a file. Standard procedure."

"Yes, it is. Until you joined the force in Lakeside and began rising through the ranks, your file . . . Well, no one's file is that clean, so when Governor Hannigan called a few of your former commanding officers, they filled in a little of what wasn't on the page."

"And why would the governor be interested in a patrol captain in Lakeside?"

O'Sullivan smiled. "He was trying to decide if he should recruit you for the ITF."

"Why?"

O'Sullivan's smile faded. "Because you were assigned to small human villages near or within the boundaries of the wild country in your early years on the force. Because you had direct experience with the *terra indigene* at least once during those years, and that experience has informed the choices you've made ever since when it comes to dealing with the Others. Because two of your former commanders hinted that you saw something or know something too dangerous to put in a report or pass along to anyone else, and whatever happened in those early years makes you a dangerous man because you actually know what's at stake when humans tangle with the Others. Because you're someone Governor Hannigan wants as an ally."

"You're here to offer me a job?"

"No. After careful review, the governor decided you're ideally situated right where you are."

"How kind of him to think so."

"I'm not here to start trouble, Captain Burke. I'm here because I need help." He looked at Monty. "From both of you."

Burke leaned forward and put his folded hands on his desk. "I like to know who I'm working with. Don't you, Lieutenant?"

"Yes, sir," Monty replied. "I do. Especially when that person seems to know a great deal about me."

O'Sullivan nodded. "Fair enough. Before I joined the ITF, I was on the police force in Hubbney. Being the governor's brainchild, the ITF's office is located a block away from Governor Hannigan's office as well as the police station I used to work at. Which means, happily for me and the other handful of agents who currently make up the ITF force, we can count on assistance and backup from the police there. That's something I hope I can say about Lakeside too."

O'Sullivan paused, as if considering what he needed to say. "Patrick Hannigan married my mother's younger sister, so he's my uncle by marriage. He's pro-human but not a supporter of the Humans First and Last movement. Considering how many of the movers and shakers in Toland *do* support the HFL and are lavishing attention on the motivational speaker from Cel-Romano, that's not a politically savvy position to take, since only humans vote to elect human government officials. But after what happened to his predecessor—and seeing the Midwest Region receive that warning shake last month—Hannigan wants to be more active about keeping trouble from starting in the Northeast."

"Prudent decision," Burke said.

"Uncle Patrick says he takes after his grandmother, who was referred to as 'a canny one.' She had a way of sensing the truth about a person."

An Intuit? Monty thought.

"Does the governor's canny sense give him reason to think the police in Lakeside aren't doing enough to keep the peace?" Burke asked.

"Just the opposite," O'Sullivan replied. "Lakeside is strategically important because it's a human port on one of the Great Lakes, and it's one end of that whole water route. That means a lot of goods produced in Thaisia flow into the warehouses and then are loaded on trucks and trains that deliver those goods throughout the Northeast and Southeast. We can't afford to lose control of this city. Toland is strategically important because it's a port that serves coastal merchant ships and oceangoing vessels that take goods and people everywhere in the world. Goods and people go in and out of both cities." He leaned forward. "And right now, the governor is concerned about the survival of both cities. Lakeside has had some rough patches these past few months, but you haven't been slammed with the kind of response other human places have experienced when people crossed the *terra indigene*. And that is why I'm here. You actually have a dialogue with the Others. Not only can you ask questions; you can get answers. One of the things I'm investigating is a string of thefts in Toland's elite neighborhoods, and the accusation that the Crowgard might be involved."

"Thefts?" Monty felt chilled and didn't dare look at Burke. "Why do you think the Crowgard would be involved?"

"They like shiny." O'Sullivan thought for a moment. "The burglars took some silver, some cash, but mostly jewelry. Flashy pieces with stones worth a fortune. A couple of days ago an accusation was made by one of the victims. She claimed to have seen a Crow wearing her brooch."

"How did this woman see a Crow?" Monty asked.

"She's a society matron, so no one in Toland asked that question," O'Sullivan replied. "Toland's police commissioner suggested that I talk to the Others rather than doubt the word of a woman of good family."

"What happened?" Burke asked.

"Nothing. Couldn't even get in the door, so I left my card and asked someone to call me. And someone did later that day. He didn't identify himself, but he informed me that the Crows had found a couple of pieces of discarded jewelry. The items had been tossed over the fence into the Courtyard. Finders keepers. He was certain that Crows had not flown up to a window ledge on a high-rise apartment building, gotten in through an open window, helped themselves to the contents of a woman's jewelry box, and then flown away, which had been suggested by another investigator."

"What, exactly, do you want to know?" Monty asked.

"I have some suspicions about what might be going on, but I'd like to know what the Others know about these burglaries." O'Sullivan reached for a briefcase that had been resting against a leg of his chair. "I can show you . . ."

"Hold off on that," Burke said. He looked at Monty. "Didn't Kowalski mention that a Sanguinati visitor arrived this morning?"

"Yes, sir." Feeling uneasy, Monty eyed O'Sullivan. "Stavros Sanguinati."

O'Sullivan stiffened. "The vampire lawyer from the Toland Courtyard? *That* Stavros Sanguinati?"

Monty nodded. "He's visited before. I think he's close to some of the Sanguinati who live in the Courtyard here, especially . . ." Out of the corner of his eye, he caught the tiny movement of Burke's head. "You've heard of Stavros?"

O'Sullivan looked at Monty, then at Burke. "Hubbney is only an hour's train ride from Toland. Everyone on the force there has heard rumors that Stavros is the Toland Courtyard's main problem solver, and if *he* solves the problem, the police won't find a body floating in the river."

Of course not, Monty thought. *After the Sanguinati drink all the "problem's" blood, they'll give the meat to the Wolves in that Courtyard.*

"Can you arrange a meeting?" O'Sullivan asked.

"Sounds like we have to," Burke replied. "And sooner rather than later. Lieutenant, call Simon Wolfgard. Tell him we have an urgent matter to discuss and would like to talk to him . . . and Stavros Sanguinati."

Monty hesitated. "This might not be the best time to discuss the Crowgard or accuse any of them of stealing." To O'Sullivan he added, "One of the Lakeside Crows was also killed in the attack that killed Officer MacDonald."

"I'm not here to make accusations." O'Sullivan lifted the briefcase. "I'm here to ask questions and hopefully get a few answers."

"About stolen jewelry," Burke said.

O'Sullivan nodded. "And if they have any information about an object that could be opened with a small gold key that was found on a woman who had been murdered at the Toland train station early this month."

Oh, gods, Monty thought. *The missing diary.*

Burke studied O'Sullivan, then looked at Monty. "Make the call."

Monty left Burke's office, went to his own desk, and reached for his phone. Then he hesitated.

He'd wished more than once that Lizzy had left Boo Bear on the train, that the bear and jewels had just disappeared. But Elayne would still be dead and Lizzy would still be in danger because Boo Bear wasn't the only thing someone needed to reacquire. Maybe now, with the help of O'Sullivan, he could piece enough information together to finally have some answers. Maybe.

Blowing out a breath, Monty picked up the receiver and made the call.

Simon hung up the phone and turned to Vlad and Tess, whose hair—green with red streaks—was twisting into tight coils.

"Another problem?" Vlad asked.

"Lieutenant Montgomery would like us to talk to an investigator who is visiting Lakeside."

"Not that Scaffoldon?"

"No," Simon said. "A different human from something called the Investigative Task Force. See if Stavros has heard of it. Montgomery also asked if we'd seen the book that opens with a gold key."

"When are they coming?" Tess asked.

"They're on their way." He glanced at Vlad, then focused on Tess. No black threads in her hair, which was good, but all the green was swiftly being replaced with red.

She said, "Then it's time to return the book and show Montgomery and the other humans the truth."

CHAPTER 55

Moonsday, Maius 28

"**A**rroo!"

Meg jolted, dropped the stack of mail, and rushed to the front counter. "What is it? What's wrong?"

Sam grinned at her. "Nothing. I just wanted you to know the police are here."

Her heart banged in her chest. It banged a little harder when Skippy, catching on that something was happening, rushed to the glass door and looked as if he'd crash through it.

"You could have said the police are here," she grumbled. "You *are* in human form. And don't be standing on the shelf like that."

"But I can't see if I don't stand on it."

"There's nothing more to see." She gave his shirt a tug. "Come help me with the mail. The ponies will be here in a minute."

"I didn't see Karl or Michael in the car," Sam said, following her into the sorting room. "How come they weren't in the car?"

"I don't know. Maybe they're in another car today since Lieutenant Montgomery and Captain Burke have a meeting with Simon." Why had Simon called to tell her about the meeting? So she would know where to find him? Was the phone call a substitute for a Wolf howl to say, *I am here*? Did Karl and Michael make similar calls to Ruth and Merri Lee? She would ask when she met the other girls for the Quiet Mind class.

"They had another man in the car. Is he a bad guy?" Sam asked.

"No, he's a guest."

"*Arooeeooeeoo! Arooeeooeeoo!*"

Skippy would keep that up until he forgot why he was howling. Or until he was distracted.

Out of desperation, Meg dug into the sack Tess had given her and came up with a chocolate chip cookie for Sam and a cow-shaped cookie for Skippy. "Go. Eat. Be quiet and let me finish sorting the mail."

Sam dashed into the front room, opened the go-through, and plopped on the Wolf bed. Skippy rushed to join the boy and get his share of the cookies.

Peace. Well, a crunchy silence. Meg finished sorting the last stack of mail, then pulled the new box of sugar lumps out of her carry sack. Hearing the clomp of pony hooves, she opened the sorting room's delivery doors—and watched the ponies hustle past her and surround the three men who had been about to enter the consulate.

Snow swirled around the men's legs as dense fog covered the delivery area.

This wasn't playful showing off. This was a tipping point.

"Hey, Meg!" Sam called. "Come see! It's all foggy outside."

The ponies had never shown interest in an expected visitor before, let alone displayed intimidating behavior. Not knowing what else to do, she went with what had worked before. When in doubt, insist on good manners.

"Avalanche! Fog! Stop showing off and come over here to get your stacks of mail." She could barely see them. Since the men weren't screaming or shouting for help, she had to figure Quicksand hadn't done anything—yet.

A movement at the edge of her vision. Air riding Tornado.

"Air? Is something wrong?"

The Elemental looked at her. "Many things. But not here."

The snow fell faster and the fog got thicker. No sign of Air and Tornado now, but Meg had the feeling they weren't that far away. And it was obvious Air wasn't going to call off the ponies.

Meg raised her voice. "I guess nobody wants a sugar lump today."

Snow instantly stopped falling. Fog began to dissipate as the ponies, including Tornado, hustled to the delivery door and got in line, with Thunder in his usual lead position.

"Whew," Meg said. "I was worried that I was going to have to eat all that sugar by myself." Smiling, she raised a hand in greeting to Lieutenant Montgomery. After a moment's hesitation, he returned the greeting before he followed Captain Burke and the stranger into the consulate.

Meg filled the baskets with mail, handed out sugar lumps as the special Moonsday treat, and refused to think about anything else until she was in the bathroom washing her hands.

Many things were wrong. But not here.

Maybe that was why, despite the ponies' behavior, she hadn't felt even the lightest prickling beneath her skin.

The stranger's voice and movements hid it well, but he smelled nervous. And wet.

All the humans smelled wet.

Peering through the blinds that covered the conference room's windows, Simon looked at the mound of melting snow, then at the three men.

<Jake?> he called to the Crow perched on the wall that separated Henry's yard from the delivery area.

<Avalanche snowed on the humans. Now the ponies are delivering mail for our Meg.>

Feeling a warning swirl of air around his ankles, Simon decided not to ask why the Elementals' ponies had focused on the humans. He moved back to the table as Captain Burke introduced Agent Greg O'Sullivan of the ITF. Simon, in turn, introduced the other *terra indigene* who were participating in the meeting: Vlad and Stavros, Blair and Elliot, Henry, and Tess.

O'Sullivan had asked to meet with Stavros, but now that he was in the same room, the man seemed reluctant to get close to the Toland Courtyard's problem solver. Of course, Stavros had come to the meeting wearing his black-on-black shirt and the suit that had a sheen when the light struck the material in the right way. Like the multicolored sheen of oil on water—or the sheen of a Crow's wing.

Taking his seat, Simon glanced at the humans. Burke set a folder on the table. O'Sullivan did the same. As Tess placed *two* folders in front of Simon, he saw the humans eyeing them, no doubt wondering what *he* had brought to this meeting.

"I appreciate you talking to me, especially during this difficult time," O'Sullivan said.

"We all have information to share, messages to convey," Simon replied.

Burke stiffened slightly. Montgomery looked alarmed. Would the lieutenant be less worried once he understood that the Lizzy would be safe now? Maybe. Then again, the message *was* intended to alarm the humans.

"Let's begin." Stavros smiled at O'Sullivan. "I recognize your voice. You were asking about jewelry. Since you couldn't do it in Toland, have you come to Lakeside in order to accuse the Crowgard of stealing? Or are you now including the Sanguinati in those spurious accusations? After all, we, too, are capable of entering an apartment window set high above the ground, and unlike the Crows, all we need is a crack in order to enter."

<Were the humans in Toland that stupid? Did they really accuse the Sanguinati?> Simon asked Vlad.

<They did. Stavros is furious enough to tear out throats.>

O'Sullivan shook his head vehemently. "No, sir. No. I think the Crowgard and the Sanguinati are being blamed for these thefts in order to cover up an insurance scam." He focused on Stavros. "The Crowgard had no reason to lie about where they found the settings. I don't know much about the Crows, but it seems to me that if they were going to take something because the look of it appealed to them, they wouldn't deface it and remove the gemstones. Why remove the sparkly bits?"

"A valid point," Stavros conceded.

Opening the folder, O'Sullivan set several photos on the table. "These are photos of the stolen jewelry, taken by the insurance companies that wrote the policies for the pieces. These two pieces were allegedly seen being worn by the Crowgard in the Toland Courtyard. And this ring . . ." He took another photo out of the folder. "This ring was a one-of-a-kind commissioned piece with half a dozen diamonds. It was valued at six figures."

Stavros studied the photo and shook his head. "It doesn't matter how much it cost. It's ugly."

"We could make something just as good out of silver wire and chips of glass," Vlad said.

That caught O'Sullivan's attention, Simon thought. He pointed at the photo. "That ring was inside Boo Bear."

O'Sullivan blinked. "A *bear* ate the actual ring?"

"Careful," Burke breathed, staring hard at O'Sullivan.

Simon wasn't sure if O'Sullivan heard Burke, but all the *terra indigene* did.

Burke opened his folder and set three photos right above O'Sullivan's set. Two photos were of the loose stones. The other photo was the ring. "Lieutenant Montgomery's daughter Elizabeth arrived in Lakeside with a small suitcase and a stuffed bear that was her favorite toy. After an incident with a couple of young Wolves, we discovered a bag of jewels hidden inside the bear. That ring was also in the bag. The bear, and the bag of jewels, was handed over to Captain Scaffoldon as evidence in a homicide. Didn't anyone in the Toland police force mention this to you?"

O'Sullivan frowned. Then he looked at Montgomery. "The woman who was killed at the train station."

"Elayne Borden was Lizzy's mother," Montgomery said. "The gods know, Elayne was many things, but she wasn't a thief."

"No," Simon said gently. "She wasn't a thief. She didn't steal anything, because nothing was stolen."

"That's what I've been thinking," O'Sullivan said. "My theory is that members of the HFL were giving the jewelry to the movement but reporting the items as stolen to receive money from the insurance companies. The gems rather than the settings had the monetary value, so they were removed to be sold elsewhere or, more likely, used as currency for the purchase of supplies that would be shipped from Thaisia to Cel-Romano, which is where the HFL movement originated. The ITF believes that everyone involved in the so-called thefts belongs to the movement. That's the only way this would work, from the companies selling the food and other supplies to the ships carrying the cargo, and everyone in between. But while Toland's elite might be infatuated with the HFL movement, I'm guessing the companies providing the supplies and transportation are in it for the profit. When the jewels that were supposed to be the payment disappeared, so did the profit and the incentive to sell to the HFL."

"HFL members could donate the insurance money and pay for the supplies that way," Burke said.

"A few of them have. But more of the members aren't dedicated enough to feel a real pinch in their wallets." O'Sullivan smiled grimly. "At first it's kind of luscious and glamorous—a secret group within a very public movement. Secret handshakes and meetings late at night—or held during a public event under the noses of the followers who aren't privy to the plans."

"It sounds like a movie," Stavros said. "Does the hero get to mate with many beautiful women?"

"Probably. Nicholas Scratch was oddly unavailable when I tried to talk to him, so I couldn't ask about his sexual exploits."

Montgomery winced. Simon noticed it. He was sure Burke had too.

"Suddenly the HFL's great scheme to ship supplies to Cel-Romano falls apart." O'Sullivan stared at Burke. "Did Felix Scaffoldon know you had found the jewels?"

Burke gave O'Sullivan his fierce-friendly smile but finally said, "He did accuse me of swapping the gemstones for fakes, but that's a defamatory accusation. I handed over the bear, as he requested. I had nothing to do with whatever he found inside."

"Since this supply scheme of the HFL's depended so much on everyone making a profit, isn't it odd to hide the fortune inside a child's toy?" Stavros asked. "It assumes the toy will not be damaged or lost. It also could put the child in danger."

"*Did* put the child in danger," Vlad said. "Hiding the jewels that way is either arrogant or stupid."

O'Sullivan looked at all of them. "Or habit? Maybe the person who hid the jewels in the bear used to hide things in toys when he or she was a child. Does that fit anyone connected with the thefts?"

"I can think of one person," Montgomery said very softly.

"Lieutenant?" Burke asked.

Montgomery shook his head.

"Which still begs the question," O'Sullivan said. "Where are the real gems?"

Vlad smiled, showing a fang. "Consider them lost for good."

O'Sullivan blinked. "Gods," he breathed. Then he said nothing else.

"You're quite clever for a human," Stavros said as he studied O'Sullivan. "I hope you will continue to be clever in the days ahead." He sat back. "Based on that hope, I will talk to you as Vladimir and Simon talk to Lieutenant Montgomery and Captain Burke."

"That's a generous offer," O'Sullivan finally said after a heavy silence. "Why make it now?"

Henry stirred, his first movement since the meeting began. "Because of what is coming."

Simon glanced at Henry. <Let's show them why first.>

Tess set the pink diary in front of Montgomery, who sucked in a breath. Simon pushed one folder toward Burke and the other toward O'Sullivan.

Gently, because Montgomery had been gentle with the *terra indigene*'s grief, Simon said, "This is what the humans were looking for when they searched your apartment, when they broke into the efficiency apartments here. This is why your mate died . . . and why humans hunted the Lizzy even after that Scaffoldon took Boo Bear back to Toland."

He sat back and let them read.

After a few minutes, Montgomery closed the diary and said, "Gods, Elayne. You died for this? For *this*?"

Burke and O'Sullivan closed the folders. Both men looked sad and . . . embarrassed.

"Your reaction is not what we expected," Stavros said.

"This is rubbish," O'Sullivan said. "I'm sorry for what it cost you and your daughter, Lieutenant, but this is rubbish." He looked at Stavros. "You're a lawyer. You know what is said here about the HFL is only the word of a woman who would be labeled hysterical, jealous, and vindictive. There's no proof that the shortages people will be facing in Thaisia are the result of a farming association selling its crops to Cel-Romano under the table to get around the limit of goods that can be exported. Or that a steel company was doing the same. And without the real jewels, we can speculate about the insurance scam, but there's no proof that Leo Borden or Nicholas Scratch knew the jewels were in Elayne Borden's residence, let alone that one of them put the jewels into a child's toy as a hiding place."

"You have formulated a theory about all of those things," Stavros countered. "You told us right here in this room."

"I have a theory, but no proof."

Montgomery shook his head slowly. "Someone must have thought Elayne knew more than she did. Or thought she had actual proof. I could see her making such a claim in a moment of anger, and then realizing afterward that she had put herself and Lizzy in real danger."

"I agree with your assessment, Agent O'Sullivan," Stavros said. "This writing would have no value in a human court of law."

"But this isn't about human law," Simon said quietly. He had let the humans talk about things that no longer mattered because they thought those things were still important. Now it was time to deliver the message.

"We wondered why the human pack was so concerned about having enough food this year when nothing on *terra indigene* or Intuit farms indicated a reason for such concern. So we asked, and the question traveled throughout Thaisia. We have the answer. *All* the *terra indigene* have the answer. This?" He gestured to the folders and diary. "This is for you. These words, written by a human, confirm the betrayal of humans by humans." He leaned forward. "You may not know the name of the farming association that sold food to Cel-Romano and then lied about why there wouldn't be enough to feed the humans in Thaisia. But we know. You may not know the owners of the railroad line that shipped the food to the port at Toland, but we know. We know the names of the ships that traveled on the Great Lakes with cargo that shouldn't have left Thaisia if there was truly a shortage of materials. We know humans betrayed their own kind and tried to blame us. All the *terra indigene* know these things."

O'Sullivan quietly cleared his throat. "Governor Hannigan should know about this."

"He will. All of Thaisia will know by tomorrow. That's why you and Stavros should leave tonight." Simon took a deep breath and let it out slowly. He'd never had to deliver a sanction of this magnitude. "The *terra indigene* who live in the Court-yards make decisions about the cities we watch. But we don't make decisions about the rest of Thaisia. The earth natives who live in and guard the wild country make those decisions. Because the humans' act of betraying their own kind has turned into a threat to us, those earth natives have declared a breach of trust."

Burke paled but said nothing.

"This is the most serious offense humans can make against the *terra indigene*. Any, and every, agreement made with the humans living in Thaisia can be re-scinded because of a breach of trust."

"Mr. Wolfgard," Montgomery began.

Simon shook his head. "It's already done, Lieutenant. The breach of trust was declared before the news reached this far east. I am just the messenger."

"What is going to happen now?" Burke asked.

"Human-owned ships traveling on the Great Lakes cannot carry any cargo that humans said was in short supply. The Five Sisters will retaliate against any ship that tries to defy that decree."

"Five Sisters?"

"Superior, Tala, Honon, Etu, and Tahki."

Burke frowned. "Those are the names of the Great Lakes."

Simon nodded.

"Are you saying the *lakes* are Elementals?"

"No, but an Elemental controls each lake, and she takes its name as her own."

"They'll sink the ships?"

"Yes. However, ships from human settlements that belong to the *terra indigene* or *terra indigene* ships *can* travel on the Great Lakes and sell food to other parts of Thaisia. But no food grown in Thaisia will leave Thaisia until there is no longer a shortage."

Burke, O'Sullivan, and Montgomery looked stunned.

"There are other human places besides Cel-Romano that buy food from Thaisia," Burke said. "Will those agreements be honored?"

"I don't know," Simon replied. "It will depend on what the *terra indigene* say about the place. By tomorrow, all the governors will know why there was a breach of trust and the consequences of human actions. By tomorrow, the right-of-way through the wild country will be restricted, and *no one* who belongs to the Humans First and Last movement will be allowed to leave the land that is still leased to humans. In other words, they can continue to live in the cities where they are currently located, but they can't leave. Not by car, train, or ship. The moment they step outside the boundaries of a city, they will be hunted down."

Montgomery stirred. "How can they tell if a person belongs to the HFL movement? And if someone from the HFL *does* try to board a bus or train, how many other people might be hurt?"

"Possibly many. Possibly all. If a human is suspected of being an enemy and is outside the boundaries of a human-controlled city or town, that human will die." Before Montgomery could protest, Simon told him the one thing that wouldn't be told to any other humans outside of that room. "Lieutenant, the *terra indigene* in the wild country are very angry. You're no longer just a troublesome species; now you've shown you're a real threat to earth natives and to the world."

"Keeping humans penned in cities isn't the solution," Montgomery said.

"No," Simon snapped. "Extinction is the solution."

Stunned silence.

He took a moment to regain control. "Do you know why those earth natives are waiting to make that decision, Lieutenant? Because we changed things. Because Officer MacDonald died trying to save a Crow. Because you have helped us. Because this Courtyard, unlike any other, has a human pack. Because Steve Ferryman and the residents of Great Island want more of a partnership with the *terra indigene*." He looked at Burke. "This Courtyard. Your police officers. The humans in Ferryman's Landing. We are all that's preventing the extinction of humans in Thaisia. Do you understand?"

"Yes," Burke said. "I understand."

"There has to be something the rest of us can do." O'Sullivan's voice shook. "Governor Hannigan is willing to work with the *terra indigene* to build a prosperous life for everyone."

"I think we should create some kind of identification for humans like Agent O'Sullivan who need to travel in order to help maintain the peace," Stavros said. "I will devise something."

"Identification can be forged," Vlad said.

"The ITF only has six agents at the moment," O'Sullivan said. "If you know who we are, then you'll know if anyone else is trying to travel using forged documents."

"Then it can be done."

"We have much to think about and things to discuss with our own people," Burke said. "Unless there is something else you need to convey, I think we should leave now." He stood but made no other move. "Thank you for your honesty."

Simon also stood. "From now on, human survival in Thaisia is going to depend on honesty."

Burke left the room, followed by O'Sullivan and Montgomery. Before Montgomery left the room, Stavros said, "Lieutenant? Your Lizzy will be safe now."

Montgomery didn't respond. Simon wasn't sure he even heard—or understood what it meant that Stavros had said those words.

CHAPTER 56

Moonsday, Maius 28

"**S**weetwater," the girl said as soon as Jackson entered the room with her next meal.

He set the plate and the glass of milk on the desk before turning to give her his attention. "What about it?"

She could barely sit still with wanting to know, but now that he was here, did she dare ask? "You've seen it."

"Yes. It's outside."

"I know it's outside. *Everything* is outside. But you've seen this place. You took pictures of it." Something about the place pulled at her, settled her, lifted her. She wanted, *needed*, confirmation that this wasn't a made-up place, that the photographs weren't some kind of trick, because she could live in that place. Truly live beyond the four walls of a room. He said she could ask for anything she wanted, but she wasn't sure she could ask for that much.

She felt her courage wilting under his stare.

He moved until he stood by the bed and could see the photos that she'd put in order so that the land flowed properly. Then he crouched so she didn't have to look up at him.

"Sweet blood," he said gently. "We live in the *terra indigene* settlement at Sweetwater. This"—he touched one photograph, then raised his other hand and pointed at her covered window—"is outside."

She trembled.

"Do you want to see it?" Jackson asked.

She nodded.

He stood, walked to the door, and opened it. "Come on."

She hesitated in the bedroom doorway, then rushed to follow him, barely noticing the big room that might have been the main living area if it had had any furniture.

Another door. Sunlight beyond an open, roofed area. Porch. Steps. And then . . .

She stood in one of the photographs. Grass and trees and the mountains rising as a natural barrier. The glint of sunlight on water. She wanted to touch it all, smell it all.

"That's far enough," Jackson said.

She turned to look at him, feeling crushed. Then she noticed the distance between them. Not that far, not really, but he still stood on the bottom step and she didn't remember moving away from him. "But . . ." A weak protest.

"A pup doesn't stray far from the den on her first outing. There's a lot to learn, so she explores a little more each day." When she didn't move, he added, "Come back now."

She obeyed because she didn't know what else to do.

"Sit there." He pointed to the top step.

She sat—and Jackson sat beside her.

He allowed her to sit on the step in the sunlight for a little while. He didn't say much. He couldn't tell her the names of the different trees. Wolves didn't care about such things, but the Intuit village down the road had a bookstore and might have books that named such things if she wanted to learn about them.

She wanted to learn.

When he'd decided she'd had enough sun for her first day out of the den, he didn't make her go back to her room. She sat on the porch, and he brought her the meal she'd forgotten about. She watched how the little bit of the world that she could see stayed the same and yet kept changing, just as she had to change position on the porch to remain in the shade.

Jackson stayed with her the whole time, fending off the young Wolves who wanted to give her a thorough sniff and might accidentally scrape her skin with a nail as they jostled one another.

Finally tired of looking, seeing, *feeling*, she agreed to go back to her room—

especially when she saw Jackson remove the white paper that had kept her from seeing out the window.

"You can see more tomorrow," he said when she hesitated in the bedroom doorway.

"Hope," she said, hearing a truth in the word.

He cocked his head. "What?"

She gave him a brilliant smile. "My name is Hope."

Elayne Borden's Diary

"What's a man like him doing with someone like her?"
"I don't know what he sees in her."

Sometimes I hear those words as Nicholas and I walk past the audience who have come to hear him speak, me on his arm, trying not to show too much how thrilled I am to be the one he's chosen.

I felt so ashamed after Monty left. To everyone who mattered, I was the lover of the cop who had killed a human in order to save a Wolf. How could I live with that? And Lizzy, with the other children slapping her and calling her hurtful names for something that wasn't her fault.

Then Nicholas came into my life—a man from a wealthy, distinguished family in Cel-Romano. He dazzled me just by wanting me. He said he knew from the moment he met me that I was different from any other woman he'd ever met, and that coming to Toland and meeting me was fate.

I was with him when he made his speeches promoting the Humans First and Last movement. I was with him when he attended banquets hosted by the crème of Toland's society. He took me to parties that even Mother couldn't wangle an invitation to attend—which impressed her greatly.

Mother no longer snubs me in public, no longer gives the impression when I visit her that I am as much of an embarrassment as something smelly that's smeared on the bottom of her shoe. Now that Nicholas is living with me, she's even encouraged my brother, Leo, to watch Lizzy on the evenings when Nicholas and I have an event.

I am vindicated. I have shed the disgrace of my middle-class police officer lover, shed the doubts that I would be welcomed again in the level of society my family enjoys. Being Nicholas's lover puts me several rungs up the social ladder, and now it is Mother who has to ride my coattails to attend the poshest parties.

Nicholas talks about taking me and Lizzy to Cel-Romano to

stay at his family's estate. He wants them to meet me, wants them to get to know me. And Lizzy too. He always includes Lizzy in our plans.

He is the best thing that has ever happened to me.

He came back from a meeting reeking of that skanky slut who had been hanging on him after his last speaking engagement. And what did he say when I accused him of sleeping with her? "Don't be so provincial, Elayne. A man of my background is entitled to diversions outside the comforts of home."

Is that what I am? A comfort? Someone to screw if a diversion isn't available?

Did he give her that ugly ring made of white gold and diamonds that she was flashing around? Is that why she was giving me sly looks, because Nicholas hadn't given me anything with sparkle? Gods, he doesn't even offer to help pay for the food he eats—and the man has expensive tastes. Nothing but the best for Nicholas.

But Mother smiles at me. She smiles and smiles, so pleased to see me with a man like Nicholas Scratch. But her eyes don't smile. They never have; not like they smile when she looks at Leo.

She doesn't like me. She tries to hide it, and for so many years, I believed the reason she didn't like me was because there was something lacking in me. I thought if I could just be what she wanted, do what she wanted, she would approve of me the same way she approves of Leo. But she won't because she doesn't like me, and she doesn't love me. I'm not sure she ever did.

Sometimes I think her chest is made of ice, and she has to stay emotionally cold in order to hide the smell of a rotting heart.

"What's a man like him doing with someone like her?"
"I don't know what he sees in her."
When did I begin to ask myself those same questions?

I heard Nicholas talking on the phone. I didn't hear the other side of the conversation, but what he said was enough.

Thaisia will experience food shortages—grains, flour, I don't what else. Why? Because a farming association is selling their harvest to Nicholas, who is shipping it to Cel-Romano, because food equals victory, whatever that means. But here, some families won't be able to afford a loaf of bread, assuming there is any to buy.

How can there not be something as basic as bread?

Humans first and last. I think I've figured out which humans will come first.

I always wanted my mother's love and approval. I never got either one, but she made sure she kept me under her thumb enough that I kept trying to get them. The only time I acted for myself, the only choice she hadn't managed to control, was when I fell in love with Monty and we moved in together. My mother didn't speak to me for several months as a punishment. Those were the happiest months of my life.

Gods! I found a bag of jewels inside Boo Bear. Lizzy had mentioned playing hospital and Boo Bear needing an operation, but Leo had shrugged it off, and I'd had too much to drink after a quarrel with Nicholas—who had sent me home early because, he said, I was causing a scene. But the way that skanky bitch was looking at me as he escorted me out, I knew he was planning to sleep with her tonight.

Then there's Lizzy using up all the adhesive bandages on that damn bear . . .

Jewels. I wanted to believe they were glass, something Lizzy had picked up somewhere. I wanted to believe she'd hidden them inside Boo Bear after Leo told her a story about how he used to hide things in his toys when we were kids so that Mother wouldn't find what he wanted to keep secret.

But that ugly white gold and diamond ring is in the bag.

And I remembered that Leo would hide things in my toys,

especially things that would get him into real trouble if anyone knew he had them.

Has he done the same thing to Lizzy?

Leo and Nicholas. Are they stealing during the benefits people were holding for the HFL movement? Are they working together, or is Nicholas unaware that Leo is using him?

Is Leo using Nicholas? Or is Nicholas using all of us?

I tossed Nicholas Scratch out on his sorry ass. I packed his bags and had them sitting outside the apartment door. He's too aware of his reputation to indulge in a shouting match through the door. That's probably why Leo showed up a little while later "to talk some sense into me."

Leo was sweating, and he was trying to look around without being obvious about it.

Three guesses why he really wanted to see Lizzy.

Mother called. I shouldn't have answered, not when I was so angry and scared. She started in on me, with her cold criticism, and I lashed out, screaming that I knew everything about the underhanded deals and I was going to tell the whole fucking world that Nicholas Scratch was a liar and a thief and I could prove it.

Then I hung up and realized what I'd done. She would tell Leo. Of course she would. And Leo would have to make the problem go away in order to stay in Nicholas's trusted circle.

And he would need to make the problem go away in order to get his hands on Lizzy and retrieve the jewels he's hidden in Boo Bear.

I won't let that happen because he'll hand her over to Mother. Let Mother raise Lizzy? Never.

Can't trust the police. I've seen too many of them at Nicholas's speeches and events. Can't trust anyone. Except Monty. Have to get to Monty. He'll know what to do.

CHAPTER 57

Moonsday, Maius 28

With Lizzy safely asleep in the efficiency apartment's single bed, Monty sat on the closed toilet and read the entries Elayne had made in the pink diary with gold stars. Had the look of the diary been a cunning choice on her part or an unconscious return to the girl she had been?

O'Sullivan was right: the entries were a rant, a cry of unhappiness with a couple of bits of information that would have been dismissed. Nothing worth dying for.

If that farming association hadn't made a grab for more profit by jacking up prices and claiming a shortage of crops too soon, no one would have known until there really was a shortage. Maybe that hadn't been their idea. Maybe that had been the decision of the HFL, who wanted to stir up trouble and generate more followers for their cause. What better way to stir things up than to tell people they were going to go hungry because *animals* controlled the land?

On the way back to the station, Captain Burke had speculated that the *terra indigene* wouldn't block the transport for foodstuffs completely from one region of Thaisia to another, but he suspected there would be strict limits from now on about the size of the truck that could be used to transport food, strict limits about the quantity that could be shipped by any train. And shipping anything by water . . . There were already reports of ships adrift on one of the Great Lakes, minus crew and cargo.

And the ships trying to cross the oceans? Vlad Sanguinati had walked them to their car after the meeting and had said, too casually, "The Sharkgard and Orcasgard will be watching from now on, and they will report any ships that have committed a breach of trust." When O'Sullivan had asked who they would report to, Vlad had smiled. "Think of the Atlantik as Lake Etu's big sister."

An Elemental who could command the power of an ocean? Monty shuddered at the thought of it—and felt a dreadful curiosity about what she might look like.

Setting the diary on the bathroom floor, he unfolded the single sheet of paper that he'd found between two pages that had been partially glued together.

Monty,

> *It's too late for a lot of things, at least between you and me. I've had some time to think, and I understand some things now.*

> *My mother never loved me. She loved the potential I represented, what social doors my achievements might open for her. I was some kind of scorecard in a way that Leo never was. I just never saw it clearly until now.*

> *I don't remember my father, don't remember a time when he lived with us. I don't even know where he lives, but I think Mother goes to visit him occasionally—her naughty secret. I don't remember his voice, and thinking about how you read to Lizzy every night, I realized she will never say that. Your voice, your presence in her life . . . I took that away from her, telling myself it wasn't important.*

> *I'm trying to be careful, trying to move quickly without seeming to do anything unusual. But now that I've kicked Nicholas out of the apartment, Leo has been checking up on me. And after I pulled the suitcases out of the storage bin, Lizzy has been beyond excited, even though I haven't told her anything except we're going to visit you and it has to be a secret from everyone, including her grandma and Uncle Leo. But I think Leo suspects I'm planning to run. So we have to run tomorrow.*

> *I have a lot of regrets about the choices I've made in my life. But, Monty, my biggest regret is that I didn't move to Lakeside with you when you asked me to.*

> *Elayne*

Monty folded the paper and tucked it in his shirt pocket as tears ran down his face.

Elayne had been an accommodation for Leo and Celia Borden, a stalking horse that had provided a reason for why someone like Leo Borden would be rubbing shoulders with a man like Nicholas Scratch.

It wasn't his case, wasn't his jurisdiction. There was no proof beyond the entry in the diary that Leo had a reason to go after Elayne and knife her in the train station. There was no proof that he put a bag of jewels in Lizzy's bear.

Nicholas Scratch didn't know how much Elayne really knew about the shipments to Cel-Romano or the jewels that were supposed to be the payment for those goods, so anything that might inconvenience the HFL movement had to be destroyed or retrieved. But Scratch hadn't counted on the reaction of the *terra indigene*. Since the man hadn't cared about Lizzy, why would the Others? A big miscalculation on his part.

Monty scrubbed his face with his hands.

He'd never be able to prove that Leo had killed Elayne, and he didn't think Felix Scaffoldon was going to try very hard to solve the case, not when Nicholas Scratch was going to be doing plenty of damage control once the HFL's involvement in the food shortages was revealed. He didn't doubt Scratch would spin it to at least neutralize the damage to the HFL. But having a member accused of murder? No.

Monty picked up the diary and got to his feet, feeling the weight of the world on his shoulders. Then he went into the living area and looked at Lizzy, fast asleep and hugging her new friend.

Henry Beargard had carved the wood for the head, paws, and feet, which were sewn to the jeans and plaid shirt that the Courtyard's seamstress had made. A stern-faced bear. A warrior rather than a cuddly friend. As much a weapon as a toy.

Lizzy had named it Grr Bear, a name Monty thought quite appropriate.

A few hours ago, Simon Wolfgard had told him—told all of them at that meeting—that the *terra indigene* were considering the extinction of the humans living in Thaisia. Yet those same beings had made a special toy for his little girl, understanding what she had lost.

Do you know what happened to the dinosaurs? The Others is what happened to the dinosaurs.

A joke Captain Burke had told him his first day on the job in Lakeside. Except it wasn't a joke. Burke had known that, at least to some degree.

And now so did he.

Captain Burke,

Leo Borden was found in the water near the Toland docks yesterday. His throat had been cut. Inside a secret pocket in his jacket, investigators found two emeralds and a white gold and diamond ring of distinct design that match items recently stolen. Police speculate that a falling-out among thieves might have led to Borden's death. ITF tried to question Celia Borden about her son's associates. However, neighbors said she left home two days ago and has not been seen since.

—Agent Greg O'Sullivan, ITF

P.S. Felix Scaffoldon didn't show up for work today and no one has heard from him.

CHAPTER 58

Windsday, Maius 30

"This morning's top story... Government officials throughout Thaisia claim they had no knowledge or involvement in the deal to sell grains and other foods to the Cel-Romano Alliance of Nations while claiming shortages at home in order to drive up prices. The farming association that was fingered by an anonymous source is denying any wrongdoing, but officials say there will be an investigation and this particular association, owned by a group of businessmen, will be under careful scrutiny from now on. Meanwhile, independent farmers and other farming groups who are not currently under investigation say that, barring natural disasters, they anticipate the usual yield from their crops this year.

"In other news, on the orders of Northeast Region Governor Patrick Hannigan, a task force of humans and terra indigene removed all of the alleged 'blood prophets' from halfway houses and other institutions in Toland. Citing health and safety concerns, the girls were taken to undisclosed facilities elsewhere in the Northeast. A spokesman for Governor Hannigan said some of the facilities could be facing charges of pandering and abuse.

"This just in. The captain of a ship from Brittania reported seeing a cargo ship sucked down by a whirlpool that appeared and disappeared without warning. The Brittanian ship looked for passengers and crew but found no survivors. The captain did say an unprecedented number of sharks were in the area. He also noted that, after leaving the area, his ship was followed by orcas until they were well away from the Fingerbone Islands, which the other ship was approaching when it went down."

Meg tried to distract herself from the pins-and-needles feeling that roamed under her skin since their little caravan had left the Courtyard. She should have made a controlled cut yesterday, but Simon had asked her to wait, saying he needed a day to make arrangements.

But he wouldn't tell her what kind of arrangements, only that they would take a little trip before she made the cut.

A moving image, like a movie. She absorbed the experience of riding in the backseat of a car. Merri Lee was in the backseat with her; Simon was in front with Michael Debany, who was driving. The hum of the tires on the road. Trees and grass and flowers growing wild. And the river! She wanted to stand on the bank and just watch the Talulah River.

She jumped, startled, when a hand closed over hers.

"You're trembling," Merri Lee whispered. "You okay?"

Meg nodded, then noticed Simon watching her. A whisper was as good as a shout to Wolf ears—even when those ears were human-shaped.

"I'm fine," Meg whispered back. But she looked at Simon when she said it, then waited until he turned his attention to the front of the car before continuing. "The river is . . ." She shook her head, reluctant to admit just how much the river pulled at her.

"Closer to Talulah Falls, where there are rapids, it's a powerful experience. And the Falls themselves. I saw them once." Merri Lee smiled. "Hard to describe."

Meg nodded.

They turned off the main road, passing a large, unappealing building before they drove up to the dwellings. House, garage, garage, house. That kind of dwelling had a name, but she wasn't interested in searching through her training images to recall it, not when Karl and Ruth drove up, followed by the Courtyard's minivan. Blair got out from the driver's side, Henry from the passenger seat. Nathan and Tess got out from the side door.

"Simon?" Meg said as another group of cars drove up and parked nearby.

"That's Steve Ferryman," Simon said. "He's bringing some of his people for this."

"For what?"

"Look around, Meg. Before anyone says anything, just look around, get an image of this place." Simon pointed at Merri Lee. "You stay with her."

He walked away, gesturing for Michael and Karl to follow him.

Ruth joined her and Merri Lee. "Did you know there was a development here? It looks . . ."

"I don't think we're supposed to offer opinions yet," Merri Lee said. "Meg needs quiet time to absorb."

Ruth nodded.

It felt a little odd to stand there quietly with girls who weren't *cassandra sangue*, absorbing images. She wondered what they saw.

She looked over her shoulder and watched Simon talking to Steve Ferryman and the people he'd brought from Great Island. She noticed Nathan carrying a basket over to a blanket that Tess had set over weedy grass.

The pins-and-needles feeling that had been roaming under her skin during the drive settled in one spot on her back.

Time to cut, she thought. As she looked at the houses and saw the columns of black smoke shift into Sanguinati, she thought she understood why Simon had brought her here.

"This is Emily Faire," Steve Ferryman said. "She recently received her degree as a nurse practitioner. After you called and told me what you wanted to do, I asked her to join us. Thought it would be a good idea to have a trained medic on hand."

"I'm pleased to meet you, Mr. Wolfgard," Emily said. "Is it okay if I go over and introduce myself?"

Simon nodded. He waited until she was out of earshot before turning back to Steve. "You had a feeling?"

"No, not that kind of feeling," Steve replied. "But Dr. Lorenzo is on that task force regarding the *cassandra sangue*. He may not be able to have regular office hours, so you should consider having someone else working in the Courtyard's medical office. Emily is interested."

"Not many humans to look after."

"I thought she could split her time between the Courtyard and this community. And she doesn't have to treat humans exclusively."

"We have our own bodywalkers."

"Yes, you do. But it wouldn't hurt for the *terra indigene* to become familiar with human healing. To learn simple things, like how one of our healers takes a person's temperature, or uses a stethoscope to listen to heart and lungs, or measures blood pressure."

He couldn't see the harm in any of those things, especially now that he needed to consider how much human the *terra indigene* wanted to keep. "I'll think about it."

<Simon?> Nathan called. <Meg is getting itchy.>

"It's time," he told Steve. "Go on up. We'll be there in a minute." He fixed his gaze on Michael Debany, then walked away, expecting the human to follow.

"Problem?" Michael asked.

"Merri Lee is your mate. Why was she holding Meg's hand?" He hadn't known he'd felt angry, or even threatened, until he heard himself snarl the words.

Michael blinked, swayed a bit, but didn't actually take a step back. "It's a girl thing. Friendship. Comfort. Nonverbal communication."

Simon narrowed his eyes. "You're not female, and you hold Merri Lee's hand. That's friendship?"

Michael smiled. "That's friendship. But with me and Merri, it's also romance."

Romance. Something to think about. But right now, there was something else he needed to know.

Hurrying to join the rest of the *terra indigene* and humans assembled, Simon focused on Meg.

"I wanted you to see this place as it is now," he said. "And then I'd like you to tell us what you see as its future. We need to know what we can do here. Can you tell us, Meg?"

"It would be like what we did the last time you made a controlled cut," Merri Lee said. "You had focused on the Courtyard that time."

Meg nodded. Then she twisted her arm to reach a spot on her back. "I can't make the cut."

"I can," Emily Faire said. "And I brought a first-aid kit with me."

Meg pulled the razor out of her pocket. After a moment's hesitation, she handed it to Emily before sitting on the blanket, her legs loosely crossed to avoid pulling the skin on the knee that was still tender. After another hesitation, she pulled off her top. The bra adequately covered her breasts, but the thin straps didn't hide much of her back.

Simon heard Emily Faire suck in a breath. So did Steve Ferryman. Merri Lee and Ruthie paled as they looked at the scars already on Meg's back.

A thousand cuts. Someone had figured out that was all a *cassandra sangue* had before the cut that would kill her.

He refused to count Meg's scars.

After Meg explained how to make the cut, and Emily located the exact spot where the skin prickled with prophecy, and Merri Lee indicated she was ready with her notebook and pen, Simon went down on one knee and looked into Meg's eyes.

"What do you see here in the coming months? What can we build here? Speak, prophet, and we will listen."

Meg kept her eyes on his as Emily made the cut.

So hard to be so close to Meg, to smell the fresh blood flowing from the wound and know how good it would taste, how good it would make him feel after he licked it up. But he stayed.

Connection. Communication. Friendship.

He saw the change come into her eyes before he smelled the lust of euphoria that filled her when she began to speak prophecy.

But this time, it was different. Meg looked around at the houses, at the land.

"What do you see, Meg?" Simon whispered.

She smiled. "Jackson is here. He's throwing a ball for some of the younger Wolves. And there's a gold cat shifting to human. Roy. I remember him. And a smaller cat. Pretty. Short tail and pointy ears. And people working in gardens and painting houses. A woman is feeding some chickens. Horses and carts. Cows and goats and sheep. Big shaggy animals." She frowned, clearly searching her memory. "Bison."

Bison? Simon thought. *Here?*

"Windmill," Meg said. "Bus full of books. Lights in the windows. Wolves howling. Owl in the moonlight. The sound of a guitar. Laughter." She sighed.

"That's it," Merri Lee said quietly.

Simon stepped away to distance himself from the bloody cloths Emily Faire was placing into a plastic container. Henry and Steve Ferryman joined him.

"Sounds like we don't want to depend on the highest forms of technology for everything," Steve said. "A windmill is Simple Life, but it would provide a mill for making flour and cornmeal at the very least."

"Library bus," Henry said. "Ming Beargard told me the other day that your village is sending a library bus to the places where the gards live on the island."

"We've included those residents ever since we turned a bus into a rolling library," Steve said. "But Ming and Flash Foxgard and a few other *terra indigene* were the only ones who entered the bus to make a selection. Now more *terra indigene* approach when the bus stops."

"They can't pass for human," Simon said, understanding why they wouldn't have approached before.

"No, they can't pass," Steve agreed. "For generations, the Intuits have shared the island and the work of providing food for everyone, but there was a barrier and most of the Others kept their distance. Something changed in Lakeside, and that changed things for us too."

They all knew what had changed in Lakeside.

"If Meg can tolerate a little more *new*, I'll treat you all to a meal at Bursting Burgers," Steve said.

Simon caught her scent and turned as Meg approached. "I'll see how she feels."

Steve and Henry moved away to talk to the rest of their group.

"Did you get the answer?" she asked. "Is it . . . bad?"

Simon smiled. "Actually, it's good. You saw the community we're hoping to build here. Intuits living in some of the houses; *terra indigene* living in others. Farmers growing the food. Humans and Others working together."

"That is good." Meg's stomach growled.

He laughed. "That sounds Wolfish."

"I'm hungry." She pressed a hand to her stomach. "*Really* hungry."

The euphoria was supposed to make her mellow. She didn't look mellow. She looked like she was considering the best place to sink her teeth into *him*. He didn't like the way that made him feel because he had the uneasy thought that bunnies felt the same way just before a Wolf pounced.

"Steve Ferryman invited us all to go to Bursting Burgers in Ferryman's Landing. Lots of food there. Beef."

"A burger sounds good."

"Then let's go."

As they walked toward the group waiting for them by the cars, Simon's hand brushed against Meg's. He hesitated for a step or two; then he took her hand, ready to release her if she growled an objection. But after a startled look, she smiled and curled her fingers around his.

He had opened some stores to human customers for years; he had hired humans to work in those stores and in the Market Square. But nothing had really changed between humans and Others until Meg stumbled into the Courtyard, half-frozen and on the run from the man who had owned her. Her efforts to fit in and build a life were stories that drifted on the wind—or on a Crow's wings—into the wild country. Either way, the earth natives who touched human cities only when they came to destroy were sufficiently intrigued by what he and Meg were doing to keep their distance a while longer. Maybe they would stay intrigued long enough to give the *terra indigene* who had learned the human form time to prepare if the earth natives who were Namid's teeth and claws decided extinction of humans was the best way to protect the world.

For now, he and Meg were going to have the adventure of seeing a new place and having a new experience. Together.

He wasn't human. Would never be human. And Meg didn't expect him to be. But feeling her hand in his, Simon thought maybe he could learn to be human enough.